I0818270

·FEYLIN LORE·

REFLECTIONS

P.A. WIKOFF

Edited by Crystal Wikoff. Copyediting by Cheryl Wikoff.

Beta readers: Lila, Marc, Levon, and Tehlor.

Visit the author's sites at:
twitter.com/pawikoff
facebook.com/pawikoff

Also check out:
levonjihanian.com
mirandameeks.com

ISBN: 0-9990058-0-4
ISBN-13: 978-0-9990058-0-4

THE BEST THINGS IN LIFE ARE TRANSPARENT, NEVER LEAVING YOU TO GUESS THEIR MOTIVES, BEAUTIFUL AND PURE, LIKE A CRYSTAL.

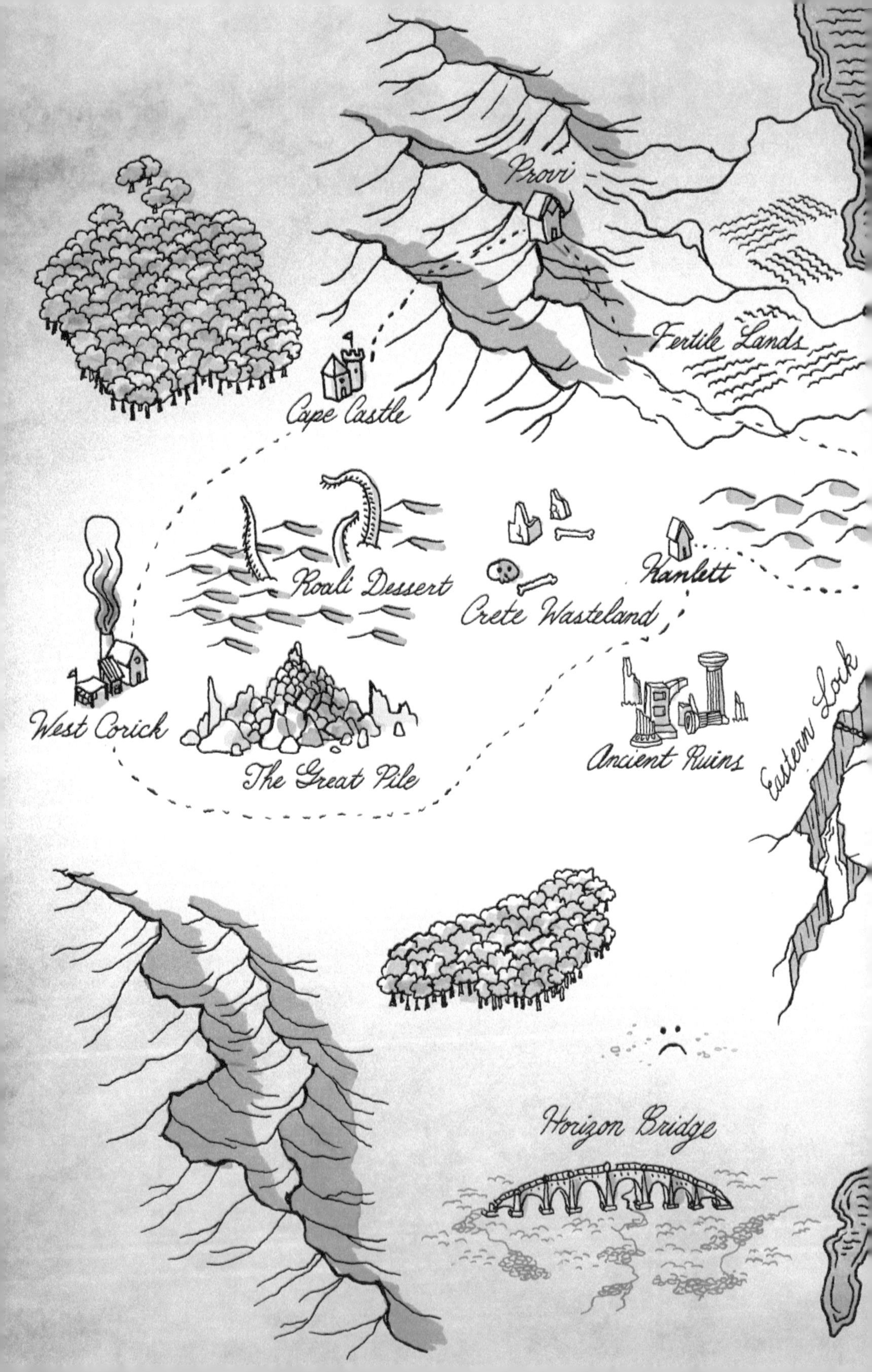
Provi
Fertile Lands
Cape Castle
Roali Dessert
Crete Wasteland
Kanlett
West Corick
The Great Pile
Ancient Ruins
Eastern Lock
Horizon Bridge

Fawn Outpost
T'shara
Steelward
N

Moments

Prologue

In the distance, I hear the cry of a familiar voice calling out, pleading for clemency. I feel the cold, cracked marble pressed against my cheek. The air smells stagnant and faintly of warm candle wax. The echo of voices sends a chill through my bones, which prompts me to snap into action.

In an instant, I open my eyes, unaware of my surroundings as I start to focus. I muster all my power just to pry my body off the ground. The combined effort of my aching muscles is barely up for the task. My head is spinning as I begin to piece everything together.

Was I unconscious?

I size myself up. I can't help but notice that my white, silk robes are torn and damp with the warmth of blood.

Am I injured? I wonder, reluctant to pat myself down, due to the appearance of my garb. My finger glides through the shredded fabric near my chest. I feel the frayed cloth tickle my finger. I'm surprised to find the skin under my garment completely intact, though it seems likely that the blood stain originated there.

After a full assessment of my physical status, I appear to be unharmed, except that my memory is suffering. It is disconcerting when you look at an object and know its name and how it came to be but don't share the same knowledge about your own past and identity.

Who am I? How have I come to be here?

I hope to regain my memories soon.

With each movement my bones and joints ache. They ache as if they are moving for the first time in years. Most of the pain is a sharpness and stiffness emanating from my left arm.

I must have been lying on it for some time.

I glance forward, observing my surroundings. I speculate that it's an ancient temple as it appears to be wearing away, time the most likely cause. The grand hallway shows ample history by its disheveled state.

I stand admiring the marble floor; certainly it was spectacular within its time. I can only catch a glimpse of the once beautifully crafted stonework through recent footsteps, footsteps that managed to wipe away the thick layer of dust which blankets every surface.

The echoes get louder as I stagger toward two human-like shadows at the end of the hall. I can't help but be drawn in, like a fish caught on a line. My feet uncontrollably land exactly inside the same footprints of another, as if it were kismet. With each step my fingers twitch with anticipation. In the shadow of a pillar, there seems to be a fresh hunk of meat, maybe a ravaged rat or a piece of a cat. In either case, it's raw and not appetizing in the slightest. I am not able to determine its origin, nor am I persuaded, my curiosity is preoccupied.

Up ahead, I spy a fallen beauty. Without breaking my stride, I indulge in her sweetness. Her girlish figure and golden shimmering hair give her the aura of a goddess. Her eyes are closed and she seems so peaceful, like a harmonious song you hear in repetition; you're drawn to it and how it makes you feel. I am certain she is unconscious or possibly sleeping, and not in fact slain, due to the rise and fall of her chest. A tiny, well-crafted dagger is tucked in her right hand. She holds it tightly, as if in a death clutch. I'm overwhelmed with sympathy for the young maiden.

Did I suffer the same fate?

While I attempt to reach for her, fear is holding back my shaky hand. Instead, I give way to my urge to reach the two voices up ahead in time—but in time for what is unbeknownst to me. As I approach, I begin to make out their words. I focus on each syllable, trying to make sense of them.

"With your last breath and last thought, I accept your Vigor and fate as my own," a voice bellows.

This phrase sounds familiar but triggers no significance. My stride changes to a double step. It feels as if my ears are conversing with my feet, without letting my mind in on the conversation.

There is an immense amount of light pouring out of the room, more than an infinite number of candles could ever produce. Standing, almost blocking the entryway, is a dark figure with a hooded shroud. I stand there, dumbfounded, as I witness him slowly lower his hand upon a gruff man who is lying on the floor, almost lifeless.

The victim has a somewhat scholarly look about him. His breath is labored, and I get the sense that he is using all he has left to merely keep himself alive.

I know him, but how? I wonder, trying to overcome the ringing discord that envelops me internally.

The dark figure is now aware of my advance and turns to face me directly. I feel his gaze boring directly into my soul, followed by a cool sensation, as my body begins to tingle.

Suddenly it is all clear. My memories flood inside me like an avalanche. I remember everything, without time to absorb any of it—my former self, this temple, the woman lying on the ground, the dark evil that is about to do the unimaginable…

Without time to even recount their names or process a single memory, my body begins to activate my true power. Instincts are in command, and my consciousness is just along for the ride. At first I clench my fists and spread out my arms, flexing every muscle in my body, creating the perfect implement for what will soon follow. Then I use my mind, emotion, faith, even my body to generate feylin energy, which I need for my next attack.

I am energy itself.

With each extremity, I can feel power flowing out of me like a river. This ritual is familiar to me, but this time is different because there is no time to think, only time to act.

"Interesting little trick. It seems as though even *you* cannot defy your own destiny," Kamen says.

Rafee, the man on the ground, lets out a big sigh of relief as Kamen releases his hold upon him. With each second, I feel my thought process evolving. Kamen then whips his hand my way. With his piercing finger, I feel a disturbance, but don't allow myself to be distracted.

I attempt the third and final step in harnessing my true potential when I realize that I have already lost. I'm unable to open my metaphysical eye. My sight into the other world—the Feylin world—is blocked. But why?

Without opening my mental eye, there is no hope of triumph. Alas, I have failed again. Cheating death only worked once, a trick that is not going to repeat itself.

Out of desperation, I lunge at Kamen with a closed fist. A foolish attempt, I know, but I'm not giving up without a fight. As I lunge, I feel my arm freeze in place as Kamen points a second finger toward my striking limb.

"You never should have come back. Now I *can* finish my role in this odyssey. You really had me worried there for a second, my boy," Kamen says with confidence.

I pause for a brief moment, attempting to speak, but my lips won't let me. A stealth finger is the cause. He knows he has won and will not let me leave this world without gloating just a little bit.

"What have you done?" Rafee asks, under his breath.

Despite my arm not operating, I make one final attempt to kill my enemy. With any luck, there is a chance that we will both perish.

I advance at him. My heart is pure, intentions resurrected. I'm almost in range when Kamen draws a fourth finger, which causes my right leg to become completely powerless, and I fall flat on the floor.

"Ha, you almost got me there," he says with a slightly gleeful undertone.

My blinkless eyes unveil the tragic mistake that caused my ruin. Of course, how could I forget one of the most basic rules to being a feylin? You cannot be in this realm and the Feylin realm simultaneously. Kamen knows this and had already won at the outset. I have admiration for his tactics.

With only my one hand and leg still under my control, my attempt to stand is arduous but still successful.

"This is what you've always wanted and it is my pleasure to give it to you. Too bad you were too foolish to fulfill it yourself," Kamen says in an almost sympathetic manner.

I bow my head, accepting my fate. Then I feel the presence of another. I feel her energy surrounding me. My heart is jump-started with faith as if my prayers have been answered.

An explosive sound echoes through the hall. Kamen and I turn our gazes toward the woman who was previously on the ground. She is now awake, in full fighting stance, and is even more captivating than before.

To my surprise, I feel something familiar in the palm of my hand. I look down to find the goddess's dagger where it wasn't just moments before. I feel the texture of the hilt, and its balance is perfect.

With this sudden change of events, a new plan unfolds.

There is only one way to regain my power, and she handed me the solution.

With all my might, I strike the dagger into my right blinkless eye. I give it a bit of a twist, but take great precaution not to go too deep. The pain enrages me to an almost blood-drunk state, and I flop to the floor without bracing my own fall. The agony is counterbalanced by the energy I feel as the dawning of my third eye, my mental eye, commences.

"You cannot win this. I have foreseen my victory!"

"I already have," I murmur. I feel him move his Focus—his feylin power—to my remaining eye.

My hands cannot stop shaking. I jerk my head back, causing blood to spray in the air like a fountain. I use my last one-eyed glance to look at my savior. She is partially shielding her eyes and wincing from my grotesque display. After a beat, I roll my head, positioning the blade next to my remaining eye. We look at each other one last time. Her eyes are rich with emotion, though she struggles to hide it. A poetic image to remember always. I drive the blade into my other eye socket, ending my sight forever.

Her sorrow erupts and burns my ears as she loses her composure.

All is black. The pain is nearly unbearable. I feel both sadness and anger, which fuels my feylin energy—energy I use to enter the Feylin dimension. The blade slowly slides its way out of my socket and creates a high-pitched sound as it collides with the hard, marble surface.

My mental eye is open. Having sight into the other realm, almost makes me forget my recent misfortune. My soul is whole and my hope renewed.

I'm touched by the familiar blur of this parallel dimension. Time is perceived more slowly. I can see the secrets to the laws of nature, the architect's design. I see gravity, air, distance and time;

everything is connected. All that is hidden to the natural eye is visible to me in the Feylin realm. Physical objects keep their initial shape, but the detail and depth are replaced by their essence, or life force—their Vigor. Non-living objects have a dull shade, whereas living things have a glow about them. The ones who have tapped into their feylin power have quite an active Vigor, with colors swirling, and located in the center of their head is a beaming gold eye that's only visible here.

I feel the room's emotion and see Kamen's Vigor as a silhouette glowing three distinct shades, mixing and blending with each other. Emanating from three of his fingertips are colorless control strings that he is using to manipulate my body in the normal realm. It's these strings a feylin uses to bend the world with their power. One is attached to my lame leg, the other to my lame arm. The third one was attached to my eye, but is now flailing around like a headless snake.

On the floor, I see Rafee's Vigor which seems dull and lacks movement. His silhouette gently shakes, indicating constrained laughter. He fought hard and his body is almost completely drained. His projected thoughts are greetings to his afterlife companions.

Two of my own control strings emerge from my chest, out of my Vigor. They quickly attach around Kamen's control strings, which are still attached to my limbs, and I hold them tight. I activate my Focus which sends a surge of energy along my strings' path—Kamen jolts from the shock wave.

I take control of his two strings and bend them away from me. Now I have regained control over my extremities. Fists flying and feet stamping, I rush at Kamen. I can feel his anger, and my face mimics his emotion. I need to buy some time, as I search his Vigor for the key to end this madness.

I see projectiles soaring past my head, aiding my assault. I push him back with each punch. Redirecting his control string I attach it upon his left leg, rendering it useless. This causes him to stumble over himself, allowing me to connect with a punch to the chest.

It feels good to hurt, to hurt him. He is stronger than me and much more powerful, but I am unwavering in my advances. I can see the conflict in his soul, hindering him from making rash decisions. His kindness and hatred are battling for control.

Catching him off guard, I raise my fist heroically, forcing energy into my next attack. Using his power to freeze his head in place, I wrap two of his control strings around it tightly. I'm not going to miss, not this time, not ever again. A feeling of relief is projecting from his Vigor.

"I will only come back stronger," Kamen threatens.

"For as long as it takes, I will end your existence until existence itself has ended," I say, horrified at the very thought.

Then I find what I'm looking for. I locate a different power, or feylin Focus, inside him and activate it, looking for another solution. This Focus brings the sight of the normal world, complete with crisp detail and colors. His ability allows me to see past each layer, peeling them back like an onion. I can see the forest outside and an eagle soaring…but she has another more permanent outcome. I feel her emotion guiding me there.

I dart a look at her, and I see inside her. I see her beating heart taunting me with a new solution. I cannot utter her name, for fear that doing so would cause me to waver in my decision.

"It had to be you. It was always you," she spoke softly as she ripped the necklace off her body and let it slip through her fingers. She wanted me to witness her without vanity, as she really was… perfect.

With my attention fixated on the woman's Vigor, I send our combined strings sailing toward her with great speed. She opens her arms, awaiting impact.

"No, this is not the plan. It was supposed to be me," Rafee yells out.

Ignoring his request, I know exactly what I have to do and what she wants. I take the four strings, placing them into her Vigor. Calling upon Kamen's native Focus, I locate her beating heart. I bend his second string to wrap around the organ. It has a wonderful rhythm flowing through it.

With a light squeeze, I use his other Focus to cause her heart to stop beating. I know I have to hold it steady for a full six minutes. I feel its struggle as it tries valiantly to pump her blood but cannot. I feel a multitude of conflicting emotions. Her shape collapses to its knees, gripping its chest, hoping to dull the pain of the cardiac arrest.

On his own accord, Kamen attaches his last control string on her Vigor and it changes to a bluish hue. Time seems to be at a standstill, each second an eternity. This is, single-handedly, the most difficult challenge I've had to face.

Slowly her control strings slither out of her and delicately dance around Kamen like a ballad. I feel the connection between us three, and I start to see images of her early life. I see her childhood memories—running so happily, with a dandelion in her hand. Chasing the wind, she looks over her shoulder at the past as if she were saying goodbye.

She was beautiful, even then. So innocent, so eager to explore the unknown. Her eyes were big and pure, taking in the world and painting it in her mind. She saw the good in the simplest of things, but that was then. I hope she still sees the good in me, even while I extinguish that spark which sets her apart.

Each of her memories play back in double speed. I slow my mind down so that I can really take them in. I value her too much to just let it pass me by. Each image makes me feel more remorse for what is happening, though I know that my feeling on this matter can't change what is destined to happen.

I see the funeral of her mother. It was the first time she felt alone, tears streaked on her dirt-dusted face. This was how she found her bravery—through sorrow and solitude. She was mature now and hardened. I see her face shimmer as it is illuminated by the moonlight, a spotlight from the gods. Her lips curve upward, showing veiled joy. The smell of the night, the call of the birds, that was the moment I fell for her completely.

Then I notice a figure which I'm quite accustomed to—I am looking at myself through her mind—and the impact catches my breath. I finally see the echos of everything I've ever wanted her to say to me.

Chapter One
Connection

"In the midst of everything…"

Talia!" I heard myself being beckoned from inside a crowd. I ignored it with a sigh. The streets were busy for West Corick on this warm and sticky afternoon. Once a handful of desolate streets, now a seedy bazaar filled with dirty perspiration. Nothing like warm weather to bring the rats to the surface.

Today, I long for simple serenity.

I had been leaning on my fist for what felt like no time at all, yet my cheek was numb. I was addicted to searching inside my fantasies for something…mostly what I could not fulfill for myself.

I like myself more in my dreams.

My senses were taken in by the busy energy of the crowd amongst the oddly built structures. The sea of people, the blurred movement. It was hypnotic; my mind wandered.

I was fixated on the enormous, mountainous wreckage that touched the clouds. No one knew the cause of the catastrophic event that happened a mere two hundred years prior. The anniversary was coming up, and everyone loved a good speculation story.

The monument was once the great city of Corick, and its destruction stood as a memento convincing even the faithless not to tempt fate again.

Merchants in West Corick could be classified as rogues, with their shady sale tactics. Often outsiders and passer-throughers might find that some of their belongings had been plundered, only later to discover new merchandise hiding in their coat pocket. This was referred to as a "gullible transaction," and perfectly in accordance with the local laws.

Times were tough and everyone knew it—one couldn't simply browse in West Corick without being considered disrespectful. If you admired something, you bought it, case closed.

Even friends swindled each other without getting cross. This behavior made me keep to myself, as everything being sold here was salvaged junk. And payment? More salvaged junk.

I could imagine just how grand Corick had been. I envisioned myself there. The smell of the oil from the machines and sounds of the advanced transit systems, it was truly the heart of the old civilization. I let my mind go.

I feel so free, and…happy.

Outside of my subconscious, I waited for some sort of change. To feel excited about anything would be revolutionary. I had this cadaver of a city to serve out my sentence—a sabbatical that was forced upon me after my most recent "episode." A failure I was reminded of every time I happened upon my reflection. Since that day, I'd given up on vanity altogether.

I had exhausted my break. *I wasn't even supposed to be working today,* I reminded myself, justifying my negligence.

My ego was scarred after being demoted to a position a monkey could do. *Oh, I remember that little guy. He literally worked for fruit.*

Admittedly, I too took full advantage of the "browsing law." I would first draw them in with a soft wave and whistle. Then the real work would begin—my gift, or Focus.

I would take a visible item out of their hands or off their clothing, right in front of their eyes. Commonly it was a small button or parchment. Then, I would hold up the item that had mysteriously appeared in my possession. I would finish my routine with my dancing finger and a smile.

Mostly curiosity got the better of them, and they'd approach me with high hopes of learning my "magic trick," or at the very least to reacquire their belongings.

The truth was much more frightening, and never revealed. It was manipulation at its finest, and without my "trick," I would be just as ordinary as the rest of the lot, destined to die of boredom. My pride was wrapped up in my ability like a blanket. People of my ilk referred to it as our "Focus," and mine was my passion. I painstakingly tried to perfect it, mostly with little gain. There were many inexplicable things in the world, but at the bottom of each one was a feylin with a Focus. Each one unique, such as mine was to me. As it was, my ability was the sole reason I had employment—overqualified and lying low, that was my predicament.

I interacted with the males and left the females to my partner, "The Parker." That was the term used when we made our acquaintance just a year prior, and the nickname stuck—not my preference.

The Parker didn't have a Focus or "trick." What he did have were his sculpted, lean muscles. He never missed an opportunity to show off his physical progress. It was his personality that he really should have spent more time perfecting.

One of The Parker's sales tactics was that he always stuffed his pockets with fine jewelry. His theory was that women have a heightened sense he called "treasure hunting," which helped him keep their interest longer. I found this sentiment annoying, but learned to accept it—as I did with a lot of things that managed to creep their way out of his sexist maw.

I understood that the jewels in his pocket were mainly a tool to instill self-confidence, but with a body like his, I wouldn't think he would need any. Or maybe his body was the result of those same insecurities. However, his percentages were slightly higher than mine, and he pointed out this fact one hundred percent of the time.

The Parker always took an interest in his prospects and often made "house calls," despite knowing full well that philandering around was flat-out punishable. I had seen the lashings and other cruel punishments first-hand. I used to think of it as quite usual, but I had changed in many ways during my time here.

This was exactly why we made a wonderful team—he didn't bust me on my long breaks and I didn't question his after-hours escapades.

I snapped out of my daze.

There was The Parker heavily putting the moves on another, "prospect."

This wasn't anything out of the ordinary for him, but he was doing it right in front of her mate, who had his eyes locked on The Parker intensely. Normally he was not so brazen—he'd always been a lover, and me the fighter. The haggard woman was quite smitten with The Parker's charm, as expected. Her arm wrapped around him like a dog to a bone.

I decided to do some *extra* work. My responsibilities were only to draw them in and look pretty while one of our testers did their part. At this particular juncture, the humdrums were all engaged with the fruits of our efforts.

I pulled back my dark hair, leapt off my perch and let out all of the stagnating air in my lungs. While heading over, I was getting into character. My mandatory work attire was uncomfortable and not at all practical, although it served a purpose to, "draw attention."

The so-called boyfriend had interesting features and appeared young, around my age. He wore a poorly crafted jerkin. I assumed he had made it himself. This brought a smile to my face for some reason.

As I got closer, I noticed that he seemed more bored than jealous.

Based on his facial expressions alone, I gathered he was, "not buying anything The Parker was selling." In fact, similar words blurted out of his mouth before I interrupted with my fake, plastered smile and cleavage.

"Ah, Tal', there you are. Can you do me a service and escort this fine gentleman to a local eatery? Thanks," The Parker commanded without even shooting me a glance.

My persona changed quickly.

Sidekick duty? I thought he needed me to save him again from a jealous boyfriend or over-protective brother. That would have been exciting.

I did an about-face on the balls of my feet, and prepared to leave.

"Talia? Don't forget your food slip."

Catching on to his bribery, I conceded, "This way," and took the slip out of his hand without making eye contact. The mate followed me like a lost animal, scared in unfamiliar territory.

"Is she going to be okay? I mean, is he proper?" the man questioned.

I shrugged his question off.

"Why are you walking so fast? Hello? Maybe I should go back for her," he continued.

This broke my stride, and I turned. The man was grinning widely. "Parker is a perfect gentleman who…"

"I'm trying to crack that hard exterior you got going on," he chuckled, with a wave of his hand near my face, causing me to flinch slightly.

Is he serious?

"We've been friends since forever. She is scrappy," he continued, while making clenched fists and jabs.

"I'm sure," I said, mildly sarcastic.

"What happened to that smile I saw earlier?"

"That's a work tool."

"Are you not working anymore?"

"Well, I'm not in the business of babysitting, so…no."

"I'm hardly a baby. I only cry when I hurt myself, which is a lot, really. I don't *have* to cry, but I like to," he joked, while gauging my reaction, which was non-responsive.

"You like to…talk…don't you?" I mocked him by mimicking his mouth with my hand.

He slowly nodded, ironically without using his words.

Well, our numbers are atrocious today.

"Come this way, sir. I have a wonderful opportunity for you to recognize your true potential," I muttered, getting back into character with the return of my fake expression.

"Oh no, I'm not going to be a test subject for you to poke and prod. Not on a first date, anyhow," he mocked as he pressed on in another direction.

"This isn't a date."

"I know my potential and it is non-existent," he argued, dragging his feet.

I paused, glanced back at The Parker and the woman. They were busy laughing and carrying on and looked fitting from this distance.

"I'm Hark, and who might this amazing specimen be?" he cooed.

My face instantly felt flush and warm. I turned around to accept his invitation of an introduction, I gleaned that he wanted to start over. "Well, I'm Talia, but I wouldn't say amaz…" I paused as he knelt down to pet a furry little scamp. I was so embarrassed when I realized he was talking to the mutt, that I almost didn't warn him of the dangers he was about to face. "That's a pongo dog, and if you're unaware of what that exactly means, I recommend that you kick that pesky thing out of here right quick."

"Pongo? Is that your name, guy, Pon…go…?" he admired in an annoying baby-voice while he stroked the beast.

I reiterated, slower this time, "A pongo dog, as in, 'If you pet me, you will have to adopt me, my groomer, nutritionist, veterinarian, personal trainer and spiritual adviser.'"

Hark pulled his hand back as if he had touched something hot.

"You mean they really do that?" he whispered incredulously. "All the time. They're a pedigreed breed that requires close attention."

Hark stood up and quickly dusted himself off, appalled at the notion.

"Were you adopting this pet, sir?" a scratchy voice spoke from behind.

We both paused.

"Say nothing," I mouthed silently before turning back around.

After taking a deep breath, I turned to face the stocky West Corickian male who smelled worse than he looked.

"Psssttt, get out of here, you parasite. This is *my* lead!" I challenged.

"No! I believe he purchased the pet, miss. Would you so kindly disengage," the man demanded protectively.

Quite excited at the thought of a fight, I balanced my legs and took a fighting stance. I knew I could take this guy.

"First, don't *dare* call me miss. I'm not one to be patronized by the likes of you. Second, he is conducting some preliminary tests for me and definitely not petting your smelly mutt. Isn't that right?" I asked Hark, with a convincing nod.

Hark looked at me for answers, then caught a glimpse of the pongo dog's silky soft fur on his hand. He attempted to be discreet about moving his hands behind his jerkin.

"Mutt? Smelly? I am outraged! This is one of the finest pongos in all of Westcor'," he contested, looking at Hark.

"We will have to take your word for it. I know the implications of looking at that scoundrel, and to tell the truth, I care not to," I interrupted, trying to bring the focus back to me.

"Mister, wouldn't you agree that this pongo is the fairest you've ever touched?" he asked, hoping to catch him in a lie.

Once the man took his eyes off me to face Hark, I gave my best "lie-your-pants-off" face.

"He was softer than a cloud," Hark couldn't help but admit.

"So you *did* adopt him with your consenting touch."

"Well, I…uh…the funny thing is…" Hark fumbled.

I talked over him, hoping to veil his inability to maintain composure. "Look, I have a full day's worth of routine analyses to run here, and I'm sure you are well aware of the local law regarding prospect poaching? I'm quite ready to remind you with these, if you need clarification," I clenched my fists.

"Well, which is it? Were you petting my *cloud-soft* pongo, or were you taking *her* tests?" the man demanded.

Hark's body tensed up while he undoubtedly tried to figure out which con was going to have a worse outcome.

"We better go, if we want to finish all these '*tests*' you have in store for me," he said reluctantly.

I happily waved off the West Corickian scammer. The grouchy man snatched up his pet and walked off, scoping out the crowd for another victim.

"Don't ever lie again, you're awful at it," I noted.

"Does this mean I really have to do your…"

"We can always get you some food. Wasn't that the plan?"

"I wasn't hungry. Just an excuse to meet you," he confessed.

What did he mean by that?

"Can you at least explain what I've gotten myself into exactly?" Hark asked.

"We represent a group called The Lustarians. We're looking for prospects with exceptional abilities, ones that may aid us in trying to establish a workable government to create some order out of this chaos," as I pointed out the dregs surrounding us.

"Lus-st-arias? I've heard of that. Aren't you guys sort of exclusive?"

"Extremely."

"So, you represent them? Or are you a member?"

"Both actually. What have you heard?"

"Just that Lustaria is a city that only grants access to its own members. At night it is said that strange sounds echo throughout the halls. Fairly creepy."

I led him to an empty room equipped for the task we had ahead of us. Hark paused a moment before entering, entrenched in thought.

"Don't fret, this won't take long."

"You promise?"

"Nah, I'm horrible at keeping them. Are you coming?" I asked, ignoring his unusual behavior.

"Yeah, I guess," he said, looking around as if something might jump out at him.

Hark edged in and knelt down across from me with a table in between us.

I set up the mercury-infused shield meant to block my own emotion from his. I laid out seven colorful rocks on the table and organized them neatly.

He made eyes at me, as if he were memorizing my features. It made me feel uneasy, so I fidgeted with the rocks as a distraction.

"We are here looking for someone. Well, maybe 'someones.' And these infused rocks help with that search," I explained, starting the process.

"Am I this someone, or someones?"

"Maybe you are. Do you happen to have multiple personalities?"

"What do you think? I don't think so. Me neither. Then we agree!" he conversed with himself. "Only many of the same personalities here." He brought me into the conversation.

"That's fine. I apologize for going off script. It's one of those days."

"Please don't go on script. I couldn't stand that smile any longer," he quipped, which generated a genuine grin from me.

Why am I falling for these antics?

"See, that's much better," he said.

"Don't get used to it, it's a rarity," I cautioned.

I picked up the red stone and placed it in front of him. His fingers caressed its smooth surface.

"Think of something that makes you angry," I instructed, studying the stone.

"I don't like to disappoint people, but that doesn't really make me angry, more sad," he said, while bracing the back of his head with his hands, forcing his elbows to jut out.

Nothing…

"I suppose I don't get angered very easily. Am I doing it wrong?"

"Actually, there is more to it, but the short answer is 'yes.'" I decided to switch to another emotional stone.

"That was a rhetorical question, and it couldn't hurt to lie to me, just a little."

"That was a lie. You're doing it exactly right."

"Wow, you're really good at it, lying that is," he leaned forward in his chair, inspecting my every move.

I don't like how he is looking at me. It's distracting.

"It could be worse. I mean, you could be a pet owner." That comment showed a slight reaction on the blue stone, causing it to glow. "Good. See, that wasn't that hard," I said.

"Am I normal, then?"

"No. Oh, you mean on the test? Yes, very much so."

After testing him on each of the emotion stones, I pulled out the mana crystal to test the positivity or negativity of his persona. It was a rare charm that most norms didn't even know existed.

As I placed the mana crystal on the table, it flew out of my hand and launched right at him.

Oh, shoot!

My instincts manifested. I knocked the mercury-infused shield off the table. I had to enter the Feylin realm.

I imagined what would happen if the crystal damaged his face permanently. A massive influx of emotional energy gave me more than I needed. I closed my eyes while opening my mental, "third eye" with the energy.

In this parallel dimension, I witnessed the secrets to life, it was the Maker's workbench. Time felt slower here; nevertheless, I had to act quickly. I used my Focus to grab the crystal's energy, I felt how powerful and drawn to him it was.

I then activated my soul, or Vigor, causing the location of the crystal to be permutated into the Feylin realm. It nearly missed colliding with his face. Wind from the force blew his hair upward.

While lingering inside the Feylin world, I noticed something special about his Vigor. The swirling colors, ripe with energy and innocence—it was beautiful.

I returned to the sighted world with the mana crystal in hand and secured it back in my pouch.

"Whaaat was that? How did you…" he said as he launched to his feet.

"That happens every now and then," I lied.

Why was it so drawn to him? Why am I?

"It was a little scary for a second there," he admitted, while kneeling back down.

You haven't seen anything yet.

I spent several hours putting him through the grinder. We have all sorts of analysis—physical ones like speed, sight, strength and reaction time. Mental ones like memory, problem solving and logical thinking, along with the ability to see through lies. Finally, we did the spiritual analysis like faith, psychics, luck and loyalty. During our time spent together, I felt close to him, and I wanted to be closer, but I hid my emotions with sarcasm and bitterness.

Nearing the end of testing, I looked down at my clipboard and asked him one last question, which was not a standard one. "Are you emotionally involved with someone, which might inhibit your abilities, if you were found dead in a ditch or something?"

Why did I ask that?

"No. No one like that. Well, just my friend from before. But at this point, I don't think she would care that much because, if you recall, she left me here to rot hours ago."

"Great you pass, err…passed. I mean the exam…well, analysis."

He leaned in with a smile, "I didn't know this was that type of test."

"What do you mean, the question is here…right here, want to see it?" I stammered, hoping he wasn't going to call me out.

"No…not the question. I mean that type of *passing* test."

"Oh. It isn't, but…you did," I said in the most uninterested tone I could muster, while staring intently at my clipboard, scared to look up.

This is different.

When I was nervous, I faltered, and I almost never faltered.

"I had a great time, Talia," he said, reluctantly.

I couldn't admit it out loud, but I did too. Instead of letting down my armor, I stood there dumbfounded until the whispers in my mind evaporated like mist.

"So, we will have your results tabulated within a couple of days. Now just give me the information on where to contact you and you can be on your way," I said, almost too fast for audible understanding.

The truth was that I wanted to see him again, needed to in fact. I never was one to get controlled by anyone, let alone my own emotions, but this was different. I felt exactly like the crystal. I wanted to rush into him and share myself with him, but unlike the mindless artifact, I refrained.

I quickly motioned him to the door. "Thank you for being part of my day. Your interest is important to us. We will be sure to have a representative contact you in seven to ten days and inform you of the results. If your skill-set is of any interest to us and our cause, we will require your immediate assistance. So please account for this possibility."

Hark tried to speak, but I quickly showed him out with an encouraging gesture.

It was late and all of our regular analysts were long gone. As for The Parker, he had been in the corner, eagerly awaiting our completion.

Hark did fairly well on most accounts, despite that I was certain he was trying to score low in order to get out of this fiasco early. We are quite aware of this tactic and adjust accordingly. His memory was impeccable, which was the exact sort of thing we were looking for, yet I left that important finding off the exam. I didn't know why I was protecting him, or if he needed my protection.

There was one other field in which he tested very high. So high in fact, it made me add it up three times.

I found a chair next to The Parker, leaned back, trying to search within myself.

This is your new life. A chance to start over. Anything is possible.

"Was it worth it?" The Parker questioned.

"Let's get out of here. I'm not feeling like myself today," I said, abruptly jumping out of my chair.

"That's obvious. Do you want to talk about it?"

"Do I ever?"

"What about that time you thought a prospect was your twin sister? You were really chatty then."

"Well, that was…"

"Or that other time you felt connected with that cat, and were convinced it could read your mind?"

"Okay, okay. I get your point. Can we leave now? I'm exhausted."

"Are you sure? I got enough of these that I could go all night."

"C'mon," I said, tossing The Parker his belongings without warning. He flinched, of course, not being very dexterous.

I walked over to where Hark had been sitting. Reluctantly, I touched the spot gently with my fingers and felt his warmth. Like a ghost, I was haunted by something that wasn't there. I knew then that I would never be the same.

Chapter Two
Bicentennial

"...as imagery shows truth through the past..."

Weeks went by like raging wildfire. The traffic in West Corick slowed down as the season came to a close. Within a month or so, rain and dust would intermingle to develop a mud layer that would inevitably cover every surface. This was the worst of all times to be a resident. Better to be safe inside the confines of the city than the desolate landscape, plagued with meat-eating birds. Their appetites were always in full bloom when the floods came.

The Parker approached me while looking over our productivity for the month.

"Whatever happened to that fellow you can't stop thinking about?" he asked offhand.

"Which one?" I tried to play it off like I didn't know who he was talking about.

"You mean there's more than one?" He looked up suddenly, like a ground squirrel out of a hole.

I could hear it in his voice, I could see it in his face—he was up to no good.

"You know who, Talia. Your ice face is no match for my insight," he taunted with fluttering fingers.

The Parker's outgoing nature enabled him to read people well, and at the moment he was reading me like a signpost—even though I tried to give him nothing.

"What about his friend? You seemed smitten with her," I deflected.

"She's dumber than a frog's tail, and I've been seeing her twice weekly. But you knew that already, didn't you, little miss?"

"I can't possibly keep track of all your women," I spat, feeling rather chagrined.

"Really? Yet here we are."

"Idiot," I said as I walked past The Parker, nudging him with my shoulder.

"Settle down. I only mention it because he was asking about you."

"Oh, really?" I forgot about my ice face, and let a slight grin escape.

"Well, more about his exam results," The Parker said, waving them defiantly in my direction.

"Oh," I grumbled.

"Talia, oh Talia, do you like another human being?" he nagged at me like an older brother.

"Well, I don't like *you* right now," I retorted.

"Hmm, he did exceptionally well overall—much higher than average. It's unlike you to miss a lead. Maybe I'll drop by tomorrow if you're not going to," he exaggerated, pushing my buttons just enough.

"Oh, it was bound to happen sometime," I said. I cleaned some debris out from under my nail, as if to seem bored with the entire subject.

I should have destroyed his results when I had a chance.

"Well, I'm going to meet up with Urna for dinner tonight. We can ambush him there," he said.

"Urna? You mean she's smart enough to know her own name?"

"Yes, but who knows if she can spell it." He winked, half smiling.

"If it'll get you off my case, sure. Why not?"

"Here," he said, handing me Hark's results, along with a hand-drawn map. "Just show up around sunset. What do you got to lose? It isn't like you have any friends or family to meet up with for the festivities."

Right, it's the two hundredth anniversary of our annihilation.

I snatched the parchment from his grasp. The Parker had a way of influencing me. Probably because he could see though my excuses.

Before nightfall, I went to the location The Parker had drawn on his map. I was nervous and annoyed at the same time. It's hard to convince someone to believe in something you *used* to believe in, yet I still wanted Hark to join us, for selfish reasons.

These past couple weeks I had battled with my anxiety of never seeing him again. I felt like an addict, and that was the very reason I conveniently forgot to bring him his results.

What would happen if I saw him again? Would it get worse? I was willing to take that chance by informing him that he didn't make the cut. One final visit and I would stop seeing him altogether. That would end all of these feelings and allow my life to continue as it always had—without distraction.

Standing there like an object rather than a person, I stared at the cracked door of the Inn decorated with real live plants. After a beat, I wondered where The Parker was, and started to feel like it was a setup.

On instinct, I reached at my hip where my weapon wasn't. I'd been without it ever since my demotion.

Just control yourself and this won't end badly for anyone.

With that notion fluttering around like a mosquito, I prepared to knock.

I was startled by Hark standing at the open door, flinching at the sight of my fist swinging toward his face. I hadn't even heard the door open.

"Yup," I said in a desperate attempt to make this moment seem normal.

"'Yup' what, exactly?" Hark said.

I met his glance. I longed to feel his thoughts. He looked much handsomer than I recalled as my eyes lingered, mouth frozen.

Stop it, you have work to do. "Uh, congratulations, *they're* interested in accepting you." I cringed as the words left my mouth, knowing that I had just sabotaged my own plan to keep him away. I needed him around, just for a little while longer.

"Maybe we should take a walk. We don't want to miss the celebration." Hark bowed respectfully.

"That would be less…awkward."

While we walked deeper inside the city, I forced my hands behind my back to stop them from fidgeting. I felt like a magnet, drawing in closer.

"What are your goals for your future?" I asked, trying to keep the conversation professional.

"You know, being raised solely by women, my priorities are a little out of kilter."

"You said women? Like more than one?"

"Yeah, I grew up with the Tharl."

"Really? Aren't they gender exclusive. Wait, is this one of your jokes?" I asked.

"No joke. I was raised by some of the strongest Valkyrēnēs, and they put me to work. Cooking, cleaning, mending armor, you name it, I've done it. Except fighting, or anything adventurous."

"Is that why you left, to find adventure?"

"I guess, but instead I found you," he said with a grin.

Hark jumped hearing the sharp sound of a party favor going off.

"Is it always this chaotic?" he asked.

"You wanted adventure. I never understood why they celebrate the destruction of an entire era. It's morbid."

"But fun?"

"Yeah," I said. I thought about all the past years I had dreaded this event, and this one was by far the best.

"I know I'm only passing through, but what's the appeal of West Corick? Besides us, of course."

Hark almost stumbled over a couple of youngsters who quickly ran between us.

"Without the grand pile and the salvage, no one would congregate on this dust bowl."

"Is that what initially brought you here? Being one of those scrappers?" he asked.

"No, I got demoted," I explained while admiring a majestic dancer covered in bells.

"May I ask why you got in trouble?"

"No."

Music and excitement surrounded us like rainfall.

"Well, what did you do for fun before you found yourself here?" he said, almost yelling to project through the noise.

"I don't do anything that I used to enjoy, not anymore." *I miss the warmth as blood speckled on my skin, the pain of it all…*

"That's sad," he nodded, requesting my hand in a consolatory dance.

I turned him down with a wince. I was not that person, not now anyway. "Quite the opposite, really." For "not a date," this was beginning to feel a lot like one.

"Wow, Talia, you're a real mystery, aren't you?"

"What about you? Surely you don't make your way by poorly crafting jerkins?" I said, pointing out his attire.

"It's that obvious?" he said sizing up his appearance.

"Maybe you should measure twice."

All throughout the city, merchants and locals were handing out special flares. They were salvage pieces, doused with some chemical that made them change colors as they burned. We each picked one out and placed it in one of the many metallurgical braziers scattered around.

"Lately I've been trying to get by as a tracker. I've always had this keen sense of being able to recognize footprints. But even that hasn't been what you call 'lucrative.' It's always a struggle, you know?"

"Wouldn't you rather make your own tracks leading your life forward than following someone else's adventure?"

"I…I used to think that, but not anymore." His voice softened. For the first time, he was not hiding himself within his humor.

"I might be inclined to believe in you."

"You shouldn't."

I could see my own reflection in his glassy eyes as they shifted from left to right. I didn't like how I looked at him, but I couldn't help it.

The brazier ignited into an artistic shower of colors which mixed together perfectly.

"What's that?" I asked as he fiddled with a strange box.

"Just something I found in the desert. It's some sort of symphony." He started to crank a small lever on the bottom. The hand-crafted top opened up showing a wonderful scene of two figures dancing.

"I could report you. It's got mechanical parts, you know? I saw a man get his arm lobbed off for hiding an old timepiece. The worst part was that it was broken to begin with," I warned, slicing my hand across my shoulder.

"But I'm sure he didn't pass your test," Hark boasted, tugging on his jerkin.

"Dead can't work," I quipped.

"I thought you said he just had his arm severed. Who said anything about dying?"

"Oh, did I leave out the part where he bled out? Maybe that was an important part of the story."

Before Hark could have an opportunity to be amused by me, a shrouded individual snatched the music box out of his hands and concealed it inside his garment. I tried to intercept him, but fell short while he instantly camouflaged himself in the crowd.

"You'll hang for this," I proclaimed intently, changing the mood.

"Maybe he just wants to sell it?"

"Then *he'll* hang for this."

I motioned for us to split up around the herd of people who were shoulder to shoulder. Hark went to the right side, manhandling people, trying to locate the thief. Taking a different approach, I sought after the closest authority. I figured this was the thief's most probable action.

There.

Having gone our separate ways, I dodged and weaved until I had a clear view of the authority or "peace enforcers" as they were known. Their judgment was simple—punish hard, and punish often.

Hark looked as if he was discouraged by his inability to find the culprit. Each second caused my heart to race faster. I knew the implications if he got caught with the object.

I just can't let that happen.

I found the rogue ratting us out in exchange for a small reward, where I expected him to be. He held the box up to the peace enforcer, then proceeded to point in Hark's direction.

It was time to turn to my training. I entered the Feylin realm. Twisting and weaving, my control string flowed through the crowd of unsuspecting norms like a ribbon in the wind. The string followed my thoughts almost before I had a chance to think them. It was en route to intercept the music box before it was too late.

It took all the feylin energy I had generated. I used my Focus to transport the object to the Feylin realm, making it appear as if it had vanished from the peace enforcer's hands. My control string pulled back to my Vigor like a rubber band releasing tension. Finishing my ability, I secured the object back in the normal realm into my palm.

Any other feylin would have seen my actions, and the mystique would have been lost. Although to a norm, it was simply magic.

An argument erupted between them. The peace enforcer drew his sword as he screamed about the missing contraband.

He got what's coming to him.

I shuffled my way back to Hark who was almost out of breath, and seemed distressed.

"Got it. Let's go," I said, surreptitiously handing him the stolen artifact.

"But how?"

Hark looked ahead and witnessed the brutality unfolding as the peace enforcer punished the thief by striking him repeatedly with his shield.

"What will happen?"

"A proper punishment," I replied.

"We have to go back for him."

Hark turned around, showing his compassion, even for those who had done him wrong.

Without any forethought, I went back into the Feylin realm and reclaimed the music box from Hark's hands in the same way that I had from the thief.

"How did you do that? Is that how you got it from him. Just stole it back? How does that make us any different?"

"There might be a worse punishment in store for us." I urged him to follow my lead, but he refused.

"I can't be responsible for this," he stated, already making his way to the display.

"You didn't force him to rob you," I yelled at the back of his head.

"I know. I just can't."

He was already halfway there when I realized that I couldn't stop Hark any more than he could stop the enforcer from distributing his retribution. I shrouded my face with a scarf I lifted off a merchant the old fashioned way.

He is just going to get us in more trouble.

I overtook Hark's stride and control over the situation, as I do. I rushed into the mess head-on. The enforcer noticed me with just enough time to raise his shield to block my assault.

Even then, as I compromised my lifeline, I had Hark on the front of my mind as I performed for his audience alone, like a child trying to gain approval from their parents. I didn't even know if he was impressed by this type of thing.

Still moving my body in the normal world, I shot out my control string and attempted to transport the shield into the Feylin realm, but it was no use. It was just out of my size limitations.

I have to do this the hard way.

Moments before he received yet another blow from the shield, I grabbed the scruff of the thief who was already bleeding. I whipped him around and used his weight to counterbalance and launch myself into the assailant.

As I slammed into the iron great-shield, I felt more than a few bones dislocate, popping like corn. In another time, I used to enjoy pain, even looked forward to it. It didn't have the same effect anymore. Now it hurt, bad.

I hope this is worth it.

The peace enforcer staggered as he started to lose his footing, and I followed up my attack by sweeping his legs. He tumbled upon himself in his heavy armor. Like an overturned turtle, he was lost on his back.

"Get out of here you piece of garbage," I screamed at the thief who didn't move from the spot where I saved him.

The thief was confused until Hark crossed his path of vision and a fear emerged quickly, giving his legs a reason to move.

While slamming the peace enforcer's shield into his helm, I could hear his head rattling around inside the loosely fitting head-piece. I continued to bash him over and over again, hoping to knock him out. Finally, my efforts paid off and his body slumped to the ground.

"How did you do that?" Hark asked.

I pointed to my ear, "It wasn't a perfect fit."

Hark no longer questioned my lead as we darted through town, trying not to look suspicious. His guilt was on his face, and nerves kept him checking over his shoulder.

"Stop that," I snapped.

"I've just never done anything like that before."

"You didn't do anything," I said, adjusting my hurt shoulder.

This evening wasn't turning out how I had expected, and even worse than I had hoped.

Arriving at the forge, I noticed it was much quieter here. We had already missed the massive melting that kicked off the festival.

Twenty-four hours a day, for the last two hundred years, this forge had been obliterating technology and gadgets from our lands. Corick was the last city of old, and in the process of being erased from history forever. The heat from the forge alone kept the city warm during harsh winters.

"It has to be done," I asserted, holding out the box.

This was the proper way to dispose of old-life artifacts without getting in trouble with the peace enforcers. I knew from experience.

"How did you do all that…stuff back there?"

"It wasn't that hard. I just crashed into him."

"I couldn't have done that. I was planning on having a polite conversation. What a joke that would have been."

"Look, I've seen a lot of bad things. That object will only welcome some of the worst. Do you trust me?"

He looked at me for longer than I felt comfortable. I had broken his naive outlook with the weight of my actions; they were hard for him to hold.

"I trust in your eyes. They give away what you can't hide."

All my anger and pain instantly vanished, as I lost my breath from the surprise of his candor.

"What are they telling you now?"

He approached and gently took the box out of my hand, nearly missing my finger. My fingers twitched, wanting to intercept his hand with my own.

"That you're one of the good ones," he admitted kindly.

He saw me.

Staring at the glowing forge, a silent moment turned into a minute, turned into an hour. We were mesmerized by the forge as we watched the past melt down into something new. My thoughts and emotions did the same, until he broke the silence.

"What did you get out of joining the Lustarians?"

"I had no choice. They took care of me—gave me purpose." For once, I was speaking honestly, from the heart without motive or duty.

"That sounds quite nice actually. I spent most of my time growing up with Urna and yet I don't feel close to her at all. Does that make any sense?"

Our bodies inched closer to each other while still looking forward, pretending to ignore the attraction.

"Like you share memories and experiences together, yet you feel no more than strangers?" I proposed.

"Exactly. I always thought there was more and maybe taking a chance would suit me well."

He looked down at the music box and wound it up one last time. The song was unfamiliar—sweet and endearing.

"How much does it pay?" Hark inquired, rubbing his fingers together.

"Enough scrap to make you want to work someplace else."

"You're not painting a pretty picture here," he said with a snicker.

The music box's harmony slowed down, until the last note lingered.

"Although they give amenities—food, supplies and shelter," I spouted.

He then made an unusual expression. It was like a frown and a smile cohabiting on one face. I couldn't help but let out a fair amount of laughter.

Accepting defeat, he nodded his head as he heaved it into the forge. I could tell the box held sentimental value to him in some way.

"You didn't find it in the desert did you?"

"It was an heirloom," he lamented.

Another precious artifact, lost forever.

"When and where do I start?" he asked, accepting our lifestyle as his own.

"Are you serious? Or are you just trying to get me to smile again?"

"Neither have to be mutually exclusive."

"I mean…why?" I pressed the issue.

"You seem pretty great, and maybe a little could rub off onto me," he admired.

"Well...I..." I tried to figure out an appropriate response, though I was not used to complements and shifted back and forth.

"Thanks for saving me," Hark finally acknowledged.

You, too. Being with him made me feel human again, but in a way I never knew. Judging by his reaction, I was not alone.

He brushed my arm gently, bridging the gap that I'd been yearning to overcome. Each hair that connected with him stood on its end reaching for more.

AHHHHHHHHHHHHHHH, a deafening scream engulfed me from inside. I put my quivering hand over my mouth to make sure it wasn't coming out of me as well. I had trouble breathing, and my eyes welled up. Still, I didn't want our connection to end, even under these harsh conditions. I experienced a multitude of emotions simultaneously—fear, pain, happiness, desire, sadness, and betrayal.

He took his hand away, noticing my anguish, and the shrill sound vanished.

I thought I had blocked her out for good.

It was a small gesture for him, but a huge moment for me. I had never wanted to get close to anyone again, and now I never wanted it to end, even with the dissonance.

"Is something wrong?" he asked, as he noticed my discomfort.

"Sorry, I...just can't be here right now. I hope you understand." I had to open my eyes wide to halt any moisture from escaping.

"Did I do something?"

"No, uh, I just—have to leave, but it was nice. Really niiice," I spoke while biting my lip. The words almost didn't come out completely.

"Are you sure you're alright?" he asked with arms outstretched. For a moment, I imagined myself pressed inside them.

"Someone will send for you. Sorry," I sputtered, flinching at his offer.

"Can I see you again?" Hark looked down at a wild flower he had stowed away.

When did he get that?

It had delicate, circular petals and looked lovely.

"Not likely," I said, making my retreat.

I paused and spun around, taking his image in one last time, as he smelled the blossom longingly. I knew I had hurt him, and this was just the beginning.

Chapter Three
Gaining Favor

"...never could any second be more relevant than that which is now."

Months had passed, and recruitment was incredibly slow due to some crime activities that had resulted in several tourists' deaths. We got word to hold off on our operations and return to Cape Castle immediately. I felt in good spirits somehow, looking forward to the future—the unknown.

The Parker tossed over a parcel wrapped in faded parchment and tied with twine.

"Don't remind me," I said, tearing it open.

There it was, the flashy, gold-with-silver-trim Lustarian uniform, complete with matching pants, shirt, cape and gloves. My body shivered. I'd been in the field so long that I'd almost completely forgotten about the attire.

I would rather be objectified.

In my peripheral vision, I caught The Parker trying to fit into his uniform. I couldn't control my laughter which was followed by some shameful pointing as I watched the disaster. Poor Parker had grown at least a full size of muscle since he wore it last.

I was certain that mine was going to fit me like an old gauntlet. It surely felt like one. It was almost as bright as the sun, and just as hot.

After my uproarious laughter had subsided, I quickly got dressed. The Parker tried to make some adjustments to his uniform with a knife.

"I was in a fight, right?" The Parker attempted to corroborate what he had done to his uniform—sleeves cut off, slash marks everywhere—it was ruined.

"No one's gonna believe that was an accident. You don't have a scratch on you."

"Okay, fight me. Let's make it look *real* authentic." His voice got low and guttural.

"If I start to punch you now, I don't think I could stop myself."

The smug expression left his face.

Giving up on his wardrobe, we loaded our raptor-drawn land skiff. Two raptorial birds were bound to leather straps, eager to soar. The winds were strong and going our way, as fate had decided.

We both marveled at some Elemental zealots as they ran to the open landscape with their lightning rods held high.

"Every storm, fire, flood, or freeze, leave it to these dullards to lead the charge," I scoffed.

"Do you really think they found a shortcut to Celestial Eden with those things?" The Parker speculated.

"The only thing they found is a shortcut to death," I said, shaking my head. "But not short enough."

The saddest part was that they actually looked happy.

"Let's move. I don't want to get caught in it," I said, looking at the rolling clouds.

With a whip of the straps, our raptors took flight, dragging the skiff through the western outskirts.

The Parker was an impatient man, and opted to take the shorter, more dangerous route through the arid sands of Roali. Knowing it was barren of trees, roads or food, I met his decision with a shrug and leaned back to catch a couple of winks.

Hours went by, but I couldn't settle down. I felt impatient with knots in my stomach. Like a never ending loop, I kept recalling the day Hark was taken away from me to begin his training. Each time I reflected upon it, it hurt more. Still, I kept punishing myself.

Having hid in a trinket shop, I had suffered from afar. I thought about buying him a stone flower, to make amends for rejecting his sentiment before. Unlike the delicate bloom he had picked, this one wouldn't ever dry out.

As Hark and the other recruits started to embark on their journey, my emotions overwhelmed my better judgment. My feet pounded in time with my heart as I rushed to him to wish him well, and to leave my image in his eyes.

Unfortunately, I was stopped by the salesman, forgetting the stone flower was still in my palm. "You must pay for that," he announced loudly, making a spectacle out of me.

"Here, take it. I have to go," I said, handing it back and pushing the clerk out of the way.

It was too late. They had already left.

I had entered the other realm just to follow him with my control string—to feel close to him as he slipped through my fingers.

I closed my eyes and listened to the skiff slide through the pink sand. I hoped that seeing him again would erase my regret.

Shortly after crossing the Roali border, we were stopped by a guardian mounted atop his worm-like tentacle which poked out of the sand. Spear in hand, the guardian tried to wrestle the reins away from my companion. I knew the fables but had never met the challenge of adventuring this path before. What I did know was that we were in trouble for trespassing in their lands.

Not wanting to be the subject of my own "mysteriously vanished in Roali" story, I lit a torch and quickly entered the Feylin realm. Fear radiated off of The Parker. I sent out my control string. Like a painter with his brush, I relocated the torch upon the beast's back.

As the flame started to sear its rubbery flesh, the tentacle whipped and flailed around violently.

The distraction caused the rider to crash on the soft sand.

The Parker was cowering, protecting his valuable features.

"Stop goofing off and get back over here!" I yelled.

The Parker peeked out from under his arms and noticed the coast was clear.

Off in the distance, I saw more tentacle riders descending upon our position.

Unfortunately, his hesitation was his downfall. A third tentacle rider burst out of the sand underneath his feet, causing him to stumble and almost fall into the pit it created as it displaced sand. His only option was to grab hold of the beast as it ominously loomed over him.

Mounted midway down, the rider was equipped with strange accoutrements, tubes coming out of his mouth and disappearing into a pack by his side. He was held on by a harness strap that wrapped around the appendage. The tentacle crested over and started to dive back under the sand.

"Let go," I commanded The Parker. Like always, he was making things worse.

The Parker reluctantly released his grip and flailed to the ground.

I readied my next move in the Feylin realm and attached my string to the small tube in the rider's mouth. I was almost certain that this was his breathing apparatus. At the exact moment he entered the sand, I tried to activate my Focus to remove the tube from his face, but I was unable. Something was blocking me.

Are you kidding me?

One final attempt, and still nothing. This had only happened once before, and I had a pretty good idea why.

I had run out of time. He was fully submerged underground.

One of our raptors was already freed from its strap and circling above.

In the distance, another tentacle rider emerged from the sand and faced us—waiting for us to make the next move. We were officially outnumbered, three to one. I knew The Parker was useless in any fight. It was up to me, as always.

"Feel that?" The Parker nodded.

I felt the rumbling of sand that started to swirl next to us. I got down low, predicted the moment perfectly, pounced and grabbed ahold of the rider. Without the rider's control, the tentacle started jerking around almost knocking both of us off.

I repetitively punched the rider in his face region. His head was protected by a helmet made of shell. It hurt against my fist, but I pressed on through the pain. He did everything he could just to hang on. My fist slowed. I felt something—guilt.

First my Focus defies me, now my body.

My knowledge of our blood-thirsty raptors sprouted an idea while noticing a jagged piece of the shell that had been cracked from my assault. Applying pressure, I sliced open my arm on its razor-like edge. I knew I had to turn off my mind and act without thinking. I waited for the right moment…

Now.

Throwing a punch, intentionally missing the rider, my blood splattered all over him. I quickly covered my arm while sliding down the tentacle, putting as much distance between us as possible.

The horrifying sound of the bloodthirsty raptor ripping the rider apart like an insect tore through the air. Without the full mobility of my arms, I wasn't able to slide the whole way down. I fell off a mere ten feet from the ground.

To my surprise, I was caught by The Parker. He easily carried my small frame.

"They're not just for show after all," I joked, showing my appreciation for his strength.

"I know how much the ladies love a good hero story."

We ran back to our skiff and forced the remaining raptor to carry the full load. We were no match for the tentacles. Even so, I was not going to give up.

"For the record, you got us into this mess in the first place."

The two remaining tentacles descended into the sand. I tried to determine their probable strategy for our demise. After a beat, my calculation was complete. We had no chance.

"Jump!" I said as I tumbled off the skiff.

"Are you crazy?" The Parker was reluctant but followed suit.

A flash later, a tentacle burst through the bottom of the skiff. The rider was quick to skewer the raptor with his spear.

"How did you know?" The Parker observed in amazement.

"It was the best option. It's what I would have done," I explained, shielding my face from falling debris.

Soon we were surrounded by four tentacles with riders.

Why can't I kill them? I want to kill them.

"We seek safe passage," The Parker yelled out. It was a little late for his poor attempt at diplomacy.

The riders used hushed tones as they spoke to each other in a guttural dialect that we didn't understand. The ground started to rumble and shake. The dirt and sand shifted. This wasn't a good sign. It felt like the world was turning upside down.

"Why do these worms hate us?" The Parker asked, trying to keep his balance.

"They're not worms. They're much worse," I said, using my eyes to point out the mountain-sized object that emerged from down below. The dirt and debris fell off, revealing man-made structures attached to the very top of the monstrosity.

"Is that thing alive?" The Parker asked.

Each grain of sand that fell off the thing uncovered another grotesque feature I wish I hadn't witnessed.

"I think that is their God," I shouted over the rumble of the earth. The Parker's eyes widened as he realized the truth in my words. The creature's bloodshot eyes pierced open. It was nearly unearthed. Now I could see that the tentacles were attached to the colossus's sides.

"Hangover," I said quietly to The Parker.

"What?"

"Hang…over," I repeated, referring to an incident where I had to save The Parker from a bar tab he had accumulated the night prior. Despite nursing a crippling hangover, I forced him to serve as bait. It was the only way I was able to split up their numbers.

"Oh, man. Fine."

I entered the other realm as The Parker ran off yelling, "I'm not going to die an ugly death."

I sent a control string to trail The Parker and pushed my body to dash at the nearest tentacle.

His diversion was met by flying spears. Lucky for me they were staggered in distance.

I wrapped my string around the first spear that was clearly en route to skewer The Parker. With the use of my Focus, I transported it the to Feylin realm, then to my hand. I leapt into the air and stabbed the spear deep into the nearest tentacle. Thick liquid spewed out as I punctured its wrinkly tissue.

Switching to the next spear that was getting close to connecting with The Parker's leg, I used my Focus again, and that one was now in my hand. I pulled myself up on the first spear and stabbed the second one higher on the tentacle, enabling me to climb the beast.

It thrashed around in discomfort.

The third spear was pursuing me, while the fourth was at The Parker. They were learning.

I had to act quickly. First, I transported the one heading my way, even though my control string was closer to The Parker. I dropped the spear. There was no time to continue my climb.

My next string raced through the Feylin realm beautifully, with purpose.

The Parker braced for impact.

My body was thrown from the tentacle, although I didn't let that misfortune deter me. If I lost any of my concentration, I would miss my mark, and we would both be dead.

The spear started to tear through his uniform and slowly entered his skin. As it began to press against his ribs, I activated my Focus and prevented him from getting skewered.

Still flying through the air, I managed to get close enough to stab another tentacle with the spear, still wet with The Parker's blood.

This rider commanded his tentacle to slam the ground, tossing me off. I fell close enough to The Parker that it was easy enough to help him up. We bolted.

It seemed as if every time we injured one of them, two more took their place. We were now being chased by six tentacle riders. Off in the distance there was a tree—that was our main objective.

Spears flew past our heads and sand splashed at our backs, but we didn't slow our surefooted sprint.

We reached the tree and placed our backs to its protective bark, catching our breath. I inhaled deeply and it burned my lungs. The Parker peeked over his shoulder and almost got a kiss in the face from a hurled spear.

"Why aren't…they…smashing us?" he asked, still winded.

"This old tree—its roots are preventing them from burrowing."

"Oh...lucky day."

"Luck is only a poorly calculated equation. Speaking of bad decisions... At least your alibi for your uniform will check out *now.*"

A rider flew in the air and grabbed onto a branch, after being whipped from his mount.

I quietly pointed to the rider climbing down to us, jabbing his spear. Using the branches as cover, I found an opening in his attack. I jumped off the trunk, grabbed the weapon and pulled him to our level.

The Parker grappled with him. We used the rider's body as a meat shield, slowly making our escape. I felt the rocky landscape under my feet as we departed Roali.

Apparently, they valued their own and didn't attack us. That was unexpected, coming from a bunch of raiders.

We rewarded their virtue by releasing our prisoner, once out of their range. The rider ran to the fold without looking back.

While relieved to make it out of Roali alive, I wasn't looking forward to anymore adventure today. Never again would I allow The Parker to be in charge of any decisions.

"What do we do now?" The Parker questioned, touching his wound.

"It's a long walk. We better not do any more sightseeing."

As we trudged on, every step annoyed my blisters that The Parker was undoubtedly responsible for. He too had discomfort of his own, and wouldn't stop complaining about it.

After a tiresome journey throughout the night, we approached the large, flashy building—Cape Castle—only a few hours behind schedule.

The Castle rested in the center of the Lustaria city-district. The walls were a partial translucent material called plastica. This substance was recovered from our fore-fathers' wreckage.

It was well guarded and highly illuminated. I remembered the feeling of awe I had felt the first time I set eyes on this impressive compound. It might have been the turning point when I was a young recruit. The way the light shimmered through the domicile was spectacular—it was like an orchestra of lights. It had been a long time since I had admired this place for the piece of art it was.

The guard finally waved us through after recognizing The Parker. He gave me a haunted gaze, as if seeing a ghost. I touched my cold cheeks to make sure I was still full of life.

The Parker and I parted ways, silently nodding our pleasantries. Out of habit, I strolled to my old room. I was interrupted by believables rushing past in the opposite direction. "Believables" was a derogatory word I had picked up while mingling with the common folk of West Corick. The word specifically targeted people who were aligned to a group or faction. I used the word mostly out of habit, forgetting that I too was subject to its meaning.

"What's all the hubbub about?" I asked a hurried believable as I gripped his arm.

"There's a mandatory gathering in the auditorium. You should come with us right away," he replied eagerly.

I wondered if I was exempt from such an event.

"Uh, I know where it is."

"If we hurry, we can get a great view."

"I'm aware of what he looks like," I said, rolling my eyes.

After feeling rather guilty for keeping this believable from what appeared to be the greatest moment of his life thus far, I urged him to continue without me.

"I'm right behind you, kid. Save me a spot."

After the last of them rushed out of the hall, I decided to attend the meeting. The invisible hand of duty guided me there.

All of the one hundred some-odd believables were eagerly awaiting their conference. Maybe it was my exposure to the outside world, or maybe it was the long journey. Either way, I had practically zero interest in this gathering. I wasn't in the same head-space that I once had been.

As I sauntered into the well decorated auditorium, I was certain the décor had changed since my last attendance. Never had I seen such extravagance—fine linen, painted arched ceilings and imported colors. The room held dozens of benches made of logs split in half.

Nearly every seat was occupied. I contemplated standing when I spied the young man I had met moments before, fanatically trying to gain my attention by flapping his hand like some sort of one-winged bird. He had actually saved a seat for me.

I guess they stopped teaching sarcasm here.

I accepted his invitation with a grimace, which he mistook for a smile.

"Hurry, you almost missed the best part," the young man said.

"You mean it's over, then?"

"No, the grand entrance," he said quite mysteriously.

"This is going to be a really long night," I mumbled and plopped down next to him.

"Oh, I really hope so. By the way, people call me Ri'," he said.

"I'm sure they do."

"Of course they do. It's my name."

I hoped that I had never been that pathetic. I was about to say something cruel to the boy when I was interrupted by the roaring cheers. The chancellor walked out onto the creaky wooden platform. No one showed more excitement than my companion Ri'.

I had to admit to myself, the chancellor's great presence did change my attitude from being "tired and borderline hostile" to "almost too tired to care" which was an improvement to say the least.

The chancellor was a short, older gentleman with white and gray hair. If there was a war going on between them, I would guess that the gray was winning. His exalted demeanor added a lot to his charisma. His long golden robes had beautiful calligraphy stitched on the back. I doubted even the chancellor himself could read the ancient text.

"He always comes groomed to perfection," I said as I slowly joined in the applause.

The chancellor's arrogance was evident as he soaked up the admiration before beseeching people's silence.

"Greetings, fellow feylins, and feylins-to-be," he started his grand speech.

That was the only sentence I heard before my conscious mind decided to drift away into a daydream. All the while, my body would clap and make sounds of jubilee when it was called for. I felt like a baby elephant holding on to the tail of appropriate gestures as I followed suit, unknowing what exactly I was going along with.

In my dormancy, I had a wonderful vision of a polar bear bounding in the grasslands. I felt its soft fur up against my face as we played together. It was much more affectionate than one would expect from such a large beast. It felt so real, and if the crowd hadn't abruptly cheered, I would have loved to have stayed there forever.

The other drones were thriving on his every word of inspiration and faith.

While I scoped out the audience, I couldn't help but think that I didn't recognize anyone from the time of my training. Well, except for the chancellor, of course. He had saved my life once, and I owed him a smidgen of respect.

My heart lurched when I noticed Hark in the crowd. Time had deceived me into believing I had missed him less. It was then I realized that I hadn't come here for duty at all—I came for him. Something came over me making me want to crawl over everyone just to be closer to him.

Hark's grin was stretched from ear to ear, and he too was hanging on every word. He really fit in. A brown cuff dangled from his wrist signifying his progress. He was almost a full-fledged feylin.

That couldn't be right. It had taken me almost a year to get past the tyro stage. It had only been a few months.

At the end of the speech, everyone seemed energized and ready for action. But ready for what, I was unsure. I had successfully missed any information of substance from the event.

Never taking my eyes off Hark, I fought to reach him through the wall of people blocking my desire.

I finally arrived at Hark who was speaking with a young woman I'd never seen before. She seemed plain by all standards. She wasn't unattractive by all means, just...normal. Safe. Her curly hair bounced as she laughed. I was growing impatient.

"I mean, I got here way before you, and I'm not even close to becoming a feylin. You're a savant—a real natural," the woman praised Hark.

"Just because *you're* below average doesn't mean he's some kind of prodigy," I finally interrupted.

The woman didn't waste any time shooting me a really dirty look—the type you spend hours looking at your reflection to master. She had it down perfectly.

"Talia, there you are. Long time," Hark said.

My mouth opened, but before my greeting could escape, the woman counter-interrupted.

"Talia? As in, *the Talia* the chancellor was just talking about?" the young woman quickly changed her tone, like a chameleon changing its skin.

I nodded without granting her a look. I tried to start my conversation with Hark for a second time.

"You heard, Hark. She's dangerous, real dangerous," the girl protested, positioning herself between us, as if she could protect him against me or anything, for that matter.

On any other occasion I would have thrived on this much fear, but right now it was getting a little annoying.

"Rumors, I'm sure. Or are they?" I teased.

Hark was quick to congratulate me on the upcoming mission. After a couple minutes of conversing, I realized that not only did the chancellor mention me in his speech, it appeared this whole event was centered on my arrival and the events to follow.

This was possibly the worst meeting to check out of.

"Are you nervous about your mission, Talia?" Hark questioned.

"Gosh, I know I would be nervous," the girl interjected.

From off in the distance, I caught the chancellor starting to make his way as the sea of followers parted, creating a path to intercept me.

"Hmm, it looks like this *dangerous mistress* has work to do," I said, leaping at the opportunity to exit this awkward conversation.

"Good seeing you," Hark chimed in as I walked away.

I had been cheated out of my moment with Hark. It felt like getting poison for a present. There was no way I was ever going to get a word in edgewise with that atrocious girl around. Another time would have to suffice.

I was in no mood for reprimands, but after observing the look of daggers on the chancellor's face, I knew I was done for.

During my career, it seemed the more I went against the rules, the more decorated I would get—except when I went against the chancellor's direct orders. That move was the primary reason I ended up in West Corick in the first place. A move I didn't wish to reenact.

As a cadet, I had witnessed many members get excommunicated for speaking out of line, which I had done myself on many occasions without repercussions.

A group of believables stood between us. After a slight raise of the chancellor's eyebrow, the group dispersed rather quickly. Some might think that was part of his feylin ability, but I knew better. Rather, it was good old-fashioned fear at its best.

"Chancellor," I greeted, once we were face-to-face.

The chancellor extended his hand to grip my arm, and I shook it with delight.

"How is my beacon of hope—my angel of destruction?" he said with admiration.

"I am honored by your gracious speech," I said, hoping not to let on to my ignorance.

"The ancients' shapes have guided you to find us Hark. His indoctrination has proved almost perfect in every way. Far more obedient than my former favorite subject..." He stopped himself cold, as his face was noticeably scrunching up like a prune.

I had to change the subject off my insubordination. He obviously hadn't forgotten the incident any more than I had.

"Bygones, your greatness. I'm elated to be in your confidence again."

"Ah, that is why I've brought you back. What do you have to say for yourself?"

"Oh, here I am. Ready to serve."

Surely he had grand plans for me, and if he discovered I had been daydreaming during his speech, everything could be compromised.

"That is why you're the perfect candidate," he said, chuckling under his breath. "Always looking up, even while a martyr."

"A what?" I blurted out, almost blowing my own cover.

"Just know that death without success is not acceptable."

I've prepared for death my whole life.

"Understood. I would love a fully detailed briefing first thing, if you are so willing," I requested with a bow. This was my plan for getting all the information without letting on how blind I was to the scenario.

"Get some sleep," he said with a nod.

Making my way to my quarters, the shuffling of my feet was almost hypnotic. I went straight to the hard, bristly plant which was the customary cot of the Lustarians. Within a moment, I was ou…

Chapter Four
Mission for Fools

"The present is all you can grasp. Don't think, because it's gone."

In the morning, I felt unusually important. What wonders a full-night's sleep can do. I prepped my uniform and brushed my hair. Every strand had to be in place for my mission.

Who am I kidding? I want to see him.

I was pleased to do something other than recruitment, but also concerned about the nature of the chancellor's request. He had to think I was back to my old ways, before my demotion—even if I wasn't.

After my preparations were complete, I was met by Ri', the young man who had sat with me at the meeting. He escorted me without uttering a word—quite the opposite of the night before. The poor boy must have been under strict orders not to speak. So, of course, I intentionally asked him as many questions as I could muster. It gave me great pleasure to watch him squirm as he tried to answer them, using only a simple shake or nod of his head.

We arrived at the war room. I strolled in after messing up my escort's nicely groomed hair. Even that didn't seem to get a reaction out of him.

The musty room was filled with treasures from the old world. Etched on the back wall was our holy symbol, the Chakraan. It was a half circle, with intricate lines and ancient writing on the top. Inside, was a silhouette of a man with an arrow flowing through him. Setting eyes on it gave me goosebumps.

All the other walls were covered by conceptual paintings depicting a past technological system. Each one had a righteous feel, inspired by the ideology of our faith. I knew the chancellor had hand-picked these for that very reason. One in particular caught my liking. It was a beautifully painted scene of a figure wearing similar attire to the chancellor. The man stood, valiantly raising his sword-like weapon in the air, with a dominating foot crushing some unfamiliar contraption.

How much is fiction and how much is our forgotten past?

"Ah, admiring the glory days, are we?" the chancellor greeted from a side passage.

"If that's what they were," I said, forgetting to get into character. I had to think disgusting thoughts—a rotting corpse with soft festering skin. That hardened my face.

He knows nothing.

"What, you cannot imagine a world depicted in such a light?" the chancellor pressed. "The Lord Seven purged the wretched."

"The past feels like a dream."

"Oh, they existed all right, my dear. I've seen them with these very eyes. One of those mechanical menaces was slated to be melted down in a forge, when I was just a squire. It still had some fight, and took my uncle down with it," he said, clenching his fist.

"I wasn't aware. Forgive me."

"We are far past sorrow. He fought with honor, and we must remember his sacrifice, as we will yours."

The chancellor always spoke with an inspiring air that could really make a person want to take on anything.

"What makes you believe it's my time?"

"Our faith is pure. Don't stray from the cause."

"I'm yours, completely," I lied. I'd been pushed to action many times under the guise of my destiny. Never had it been fulfilled. I was beginning to lose hope.

"Enough time wasting. Let us make haste with the preparations. As you are aware, our last attempt to infiltrate the Telandric failed with severe repercussions," he said.

I was assuming this was mentioned in his speech, so I simply nodded.

"We lost a lot of good feylins, but it was their fate to fail to shed the light upon *your* more promising destiny. The Telandric have been stockpiling massive amounts of shar-prisms from the crater. We believe it's integral to their plan to wipe us out once and for all."

"What's our path?"

"I'll look to the Lord's virtues for the answer."

The chancellor brought out a vial of blood-flame, a mixture commonly used in Lustarian rituals. He coated the fine bristles of a small wooden brush with the concoction, and whipped his hand back and forth until he created a symmetrical design of triangles and circles. The blood-flame stagnated in space as he painted the air.

He handed me a sparking device as I stepped into the center of his design. Squeezing the trigger caused two stones to crash into each other. A spark shot out, igniting the blood-flame scattered around me. The blue flames followed the exact order in which the chancellor had painted them. Reaching the end of the cycle, a divine flash of light erupted, showing an image which he hadn't painted—a scorpion.

"Sacrifice seems to align with your feylin energy. You weakened their privilege, but that wasn't enough. You must finish what has already been started. Put an end to this war, and carry us to the top again. The burden is yours to bear," he said.

The blood-flame ritual started to fizzle to the ground as the fuel dissipated, leaving a trail of smoke in its wake.

"I don't know what to say. I'm honored," I said. He trusted in me, but I doubted myself.

"This is your second coming, and I have come to terms with your last…incident. You were immature then, not exactly ripe. But now, it's time to harvest," he preached, fidgeting his fingers with excitement.

"It's possible for me to succeed without dying," I said.

"No. It is thinking like that which got us in this mess in the first place. You owe a debt to the Lord Seven," he said, gritting his teeth. "If you had just disposed of The Craftman like you were told, this wouldn't be an issue." The chancellor took a moment before relaxing his jaw.

"My past misdeeds won't be repeated," I assured him.

"The missing piece. It's so clear to me now. Last time, you came back alive, rich with failure. This time, however, you will finish what you started. Only in resurrection will you return, cleansed from your past, renewed and reformed. The words—have faith in them, and in yourself." He reached to the sky with arms outstretched.

"You want me to render the prisms useless?" I reluctantly asked.

"Precisely."

That was where my life played its role in this opera, to destroy their surplus of prisms, which requires the death of a feylin. I was expendable to him now, and he was ready to expend.

"I *will* earn back your approval," I promised as tears that were not my own welled in my eyes.

"Pathetic waste of liquid. What I want you to shed for me is red and powerful, not weak and clear."

"With all my being, I fight for you, sire."

"As long as you breathe, they have hope. Hope turns into courage and courage will turn into an assault upon this very castle. I knew once you brought Hark to me that you indeed have a destiny—something much more important than I'd hoped for."

"He's my replacement?" I asked.

"Yes, but he cannot replace what isn't yet destroyed," he said.

The guilt started to press on my shoulders while he continued to lecture me on fate and failure. I couldn't subject Hark to this life. Despair grew from deep inside me, where it had been rooted long ago. My time was almost up. I had to do something meaningful before it was too late.

"I need Hark to come with me on this mission."

"You are in no position to make demands."

"I'm merely surmising based on the link between us you have already stated. Surely it wasn't coincidence that Hark came to us now?" I said, knowing the chancellor would take offense to the notion that anything happens by chance.

He stroked his beard and paused for a moment.

"I will have to make sure this *is* your true path," he said, with a wave of his hand.

Without warning, two bulky men came marching in. The dull echo of their heavy boots filled the room. Their muscular arms interlocked with mine, lifting me off the ground.

I met them with little resistance as they directed me against the back wall, beneath the holy Chakraan.

My doubt caused my palms to sweat, but I knew there was no way to get out of this.

Out of his robe, the chancellor, pulled a finely crafted dagger.

"If you don't survive this, Hark stays," the chancellor said, carving out a piece of his oak table—making sure the blade met his slicing standards. His eyebrows divulged his pleasure.

Squinting with one eye, he took aim at me. After a deep breath, he pulled back with all of his strength, chanting and moaning. In all the years that I'd known the chancellor, he had never pulled a punch. If you did him wrong, you paid the price, and this wouldn't be any different.

His eyes closed. I followed him into the Feylin realm, or "The Lord's realm," as he referred to it.

I studied the chancellor's Vigor, flowing with power, as it increased exponentially.

Well aware that he wasn't just going to hit me with his physical strength, I prepared for his feylin strength, which was far greater.

Control strings emerged out from the chancellor's arm and started to spiral around, gaining momentum with each rotation.

In the normal realm, a soft breeze blew against my face. The temperature of the room grew colder. It felt as if I were a bird soaring through the air. However, I was still being held against the wall by the two brutes, who were now struggling to hold their ground as the wind increased.

The chancellor triggered tiny manipulation points to appear in the space in between us.

The two men lost their grip, fell back, and were plastered against the wall. The wind stream was too much for them. I channeled all my energy into breathing, which was becoming harder to do.

The building started to rattle and shake. The small space of the war room created a whirlwind, causing all the paintings and items to take flight, crashing into each other while airborne. Giving in to fate, I closed my third eye and returned to the normal world. The moisture in my eyes was blown away; I started to lose sight in my left eye.

You're stronger than you know.

I thought about Hark, and I suddenly felt at peace—as if my world could end right now but everything would be okay.

"Demons, if you shall challenge me, feel my wrath," he cried out with conviction. His words stuttered from the resounding airflow. My eyes felt as if they were about to pop out of the back of my head when he hurled the dagger at me. Its speed increased as the air current picked it up like a leaf. In less than the blink of an eye, the dagger reached my head, but I didn't flinch. I sat, looking down at death, as it soared.

To my surprise, the dagger stopped midair, about an inch from my face. I saw my own reflection glinting off the blade as it rattled from the airstream. I saw the horror in my own eyes. It just stood there, held firm by some unknown force. This was a curious turn of events. I was not one to give in to fate, as it is not practical, but this had proven to be most exhilarating.

The chancellor broke off his attack, amazed by the outcome. The wind subsided and the dagger dropped out of the air. I reached out and caught it mid-fall. It fit my hand perfectly, and I felt one with it.

The two men next to me fell to the ground, dead from asphyxiation.

"A small sacrifice for a very successful trial. You may keep that for protection, as it has protected you here," the chancellor praised.

I'd never seen him so impenitent before. I felt remorse for all my past endeavors. Surely he should have some compassion for the two men that lay beside me.

"It was forged to penetrate non-believers, and you have proven yourself well, my dear," the chancellor said, bracing himself upon his desk, also winded from the events.

How could that be? I have lost my way. I really have.

"I do everything in my power to strengthen my faith. Every week, I test it," he said, pulling back the sleeve from his arm. Every inch of his forearm had small scars on it, like a cracked piece of glass.

"Chancellor, please don't," I begged as he reached for the blade and pressed it against his arm, drawing a single drop of blood.

"It's okay, I've come to enjoy the pain. I used to be exempt from the dagger's sting…until you fell and took my faith with you." He returned the hilt to my hand.

"This means, I passed…" I said.

"So be it. Take Hark. You must teach him to hate; teach him to love to hate, as you once did. He cares about you. He must see you taken away from him. Only then will you be forgiven by me, the Lord Seven and by yourself," he said, handing me some parchment with instructions inscribed on it.

Death would be much less painful.

"Reveal their secretive plans. Destroy their prisms, while persecuting yourself. Spare no lives—no exceptions, no survivors, no more chances," he said, giving his final word.

Flesen, the chancellor's favorite sycophant, and total dirt-bag almost crashed into me on my way out of the war room. He hissed at the sight of me.

I looked back to see Flesen using his Focus. All the shattered belongings began to repair themselves, as if time were reversing. The chancellor patted down his brow. Then the door closed itself, blocking my view. It was the first time I had seen uncertainty in the old man, and it scared me.

Ri' was looking through me with an air of horror upon his face.

I tossed the chancellor's order at him. He floundered to catch it as it feathered to the ground.

"Take this to Hark," I said, straightening out my uniform.

"What is a Hark?" Ri' asked, forgetting his code of silence but catching himself by covering his mouth.

"Just figure it out. I'm going to prepare," I said, and distanced myself from him.

During the next couple of hours, I pushed my emotions down. Was I ready to die for this cause? My death was all I had been waiting for, but now that it was in sight, I wasn't so sure. I mustn't think of such things. There was no choice. I knew what I had to do, and everything was how it had to be. To serve a greater purpose, nothing in this world was worth more than that.

Inside the foyer, I awaited Hark's arrival. I thought about him incessantly, and maybe it wasn't at all rational, but I was determined to tell him.

I've been thinking of you, and it hurts more when I don't.

Maybe a couple days of bliss might be worth a lifetime of servitude.

"Talia, hey." I recognized his voice as he made his approach. Tingles tickled my spine.

"I've been thinking—" I said.

"Me, too. I read the chancellor's orders, and I can't let you go though with this mission. It's too dangerous," Hark interrupted.

What if I get him killed?

I couldn't believe that it was the first time I had pondered such an outcome. Now that I'd seen him face to face, I felt my priorities shifting. I couldn't let the chancellor turn him into me anymore than I could let him go down along side me. I'd just have to keep him close until I could figure it out.

"We have no choice in the matter. I *have* to go, and you *have* to come with me," I said sternly.

"None of this sounds right…not for me, nor you," he said.

I had no time to reason with him. If I didn't go they would send someone else, someone less experienced. The plan was already in motion and he was privy to the sensitive orders. There was no turning back now.

"Just do as I instruct you to," I exclaimed.

Hark's face turned red. "I won't let you down, miss." I knew by his tone that he wasn't pleased with the decision.

He helped me gather the essentials and we headed to the stables.

Noticing the cut from my journey back, he reached for my arm. "What happened to you?" His voice softened.

"Leave it alone," I snapped, fearing his touch would cause another painful connection.

"Who are you, anyway? When we first met, you were a simple recruiter, and now you're some holy freedom fighter saving humanity?" he queried.

"I was demoted. You knew that."

"This is not you."

"I just do what I'm told."

"Are you jealous of me or something?" he asked, dropping the gear he was carrying.

"Jealous? Of what? Of course not."

"Just when I feel like I belong, you come here with your death wish and just want to bring me along like it's a fun-filled outing. There are plenty of fully trained feylins—ones that can protect you."

"None that I trust." *I don't even trust myself anymore.*

"I don't want to be any part of this. It's lunacy. And, why are *you* going along with it?" Hark said, looking down, trying to hide his emotion.

"I have a purpose. It's better to die for something than live for nothing."

"You can change your mind. I'll just tell the chancellor…" Hark said, kicking the bags he dropped.

"My death was promised long before I even existed."

"Well, you can do it alone." He turned away.

"Hark?"

"What?" he said, not even bothering to face me.

"No one wants to die alone…even me," I admitted, thinking about my last moments and how I hoped he would be there to share them with me.

Hark faced me, and took a step closer. "You won't be alone," he said.

Out of the shadows, in walked the same young woman that Hark was talking to the day I arrived. I wiped my face with my shoulder, wondering how long she had been lying in wait.

"Oh, great. Now what?" I thought out loud.

Perky and overexcited, she rushed to stand next to Hark.

"Are we ready?" she asked, tossing her bag in our pile.

"You're not coming," I asserted.

The woman was quick to ignore me and started loading *our* equipment double-time.

"Hark already showed me the orders, and it would be a security risk to not take me along," she threatened.

"What do you think she could possibly add to this excursion?" I glared at Hark who looked away sheepishly.

"I can read lips," Daleta answered.

"That doesn't help us at all."

"She goes, or I don't." Hark drew a line, and I was in no mood to call his bluff.

"You, come here," I demanded of the woman.

She complied with my order this time.

I drew close to her ear so Hark couldn't eavesdrop.

"I'm quite a vicious person. I know you know this. I don't know how, but you do. It's your job to save Hark from me. If it comes to it, you have to end my existence. Do you hear me?"

"I already had that in mind. That's why I'm here," she whispered, dropping the act.

"Then we're in accord." We shared a silent nod.

"What's this all about?" Hark inquired.

"Welcome to the team, girly." I forced a smile to assure him that everything was fine.

She resumed her task of loading the gear.

"Her name is Daleta, and we're coming out of this alive, okay? All of us," Hark said, optimistically.

Having her on mission with us forced me to feel somewhat responsible for my behavior toward her. We were on the same team now, whether I liked it or not.

"I have never lost at a game of survival…don't ruin my streak, Daleta," I welcomed her in my own way.

I brushed the matted fur of my murk. It slightly resembled a camel, but with the stocky features of a hornless rhinoceros. Murks made a great option for long travel, due to their massive size and strength.

We continued to work in silence, with extreme tension between us. Hark's determination to keep us alive was apparent by the excessive amounts of supplies he loaded on our caravan.

Once our crates were secured to our individual murks, we were prepared to go forward with our adventure, or sudden doom.

We traveled well into the night. Our murk transports swayed through the miles and miles of man-made rocks called "crete." For as far as the moonlight showed, they were jutting out of the ground in patterns everywhere.

"Are those grave markers?" Hark asked, observing the landscape.

"They might as well be. It's believed that they were foundations for old buildings, houses and such."

"But there are so many," Daleta chimed in.

"What really boggles my mind is *where* did all the structures go?" I added.

Hark and Daleta both looked up, hoping to see some kind of clue.

We rode for hours, taking turns leading. This allowed the remaining two some rest. Murks' backs were more comfortable than most beds I'd been accustomed to.

Struggling to sleep, I followed the sound of a far-off night bird seeking companionship. I found solace in its song. My attention moved to Hark who was currently leading us. The moonlight reflected off his brow as his body bounced with the stamping of his mount.

Every moment I looked at Hark, I felt more despondent. I had to close my eyes and try to rest up before I lost all my strength.

The room was dark, covered in black dust. It was everywhere, even on the ancient spider webs. I pushed through, coughing up soot. I held my candle up to a pedestal. There it was, as I knew it would be. An ancient bottle, corked and lost to the world. Wiping off the dust layer, I uncovered the markings. A sound echoed off the stone walls and continued to get louder.

Tap, tap, tap.

It was coming from inside the bottle. A tiny ball bearing was moving on its own and banging against the glass. I pulled out the cork, and the smell of death burned my face.

The bottle slipped out of my hands and shattered on the ground.

What have I done?

In the dust, small metal particles swirled around like a cyclone behind me. Then I heard his voice.

"Nothing lasts forever."

I turned around to face a man I didn't recognize, but he absolutely recognized me. He pierced my soul with his hatred as fear ran through me. He beckoned me to come closer, and my body moved towards him. I didn't want it to, but it did. He started to choke me…and I let him.

I woke up gasping and holding my own neck.

"Bad dream?" Hark halted our caravan.

"I'm just a little nervous," I said, rubbing my eyes.

Hark looked at me in disbelief. "I'm sure you're just tired. Your confidence will align with your path," he reassured me, continuing our journey.

"Now you're starting to sound like them."

"May I ask you a silly question? And, please don't be offended."

"I'm thick-skinned."

"I was making great advancements in my training, and this *is* a major setback. Why pick me?" he asked, glancing at Daleta, who was fast asleep.

"You're getting close to becoming a feylin and, well, you should be aware of what you lose when you become one," I warned.

"You gain abilities, you don't lose them," he retorted.

"But at what cost? Do you know what's worse than dying?

"Are you saying becoming a feylin is worse than dying? Are you insane?" he said, turning to the night's sky.

"Not becoming one, remaining one."

"You recruited me, and now you're trying to inhibit my progress? Why?"

I slowly moved my hands through my hair, collecting my thoughts before answering. "You're just going too fast. I was worried," I said, changing my demeanor. "There are ramifications if you're not mentally and emotionally ready for the trials."

"I've never heard of such a thing," he said.

"Life is a mystery, and the fun is in the details, not learning its secrets."

"How many feylin factions are there?"

"Just three. Lustarian, Telandric and Kailur. There used to be four but…"

"What happened?"

"They went extinct, a long time ago. That's all I know."

The silence that overtook the conversation felt like an eternity.

"What's your mundane skill?" he asked, finally putting an end to the quiet.

"Math. Percentages, to be more exact," I answered.

"Don't you want to know what mine is?"

"I know what it is. I did your testing, remember?" I said with a smirk.

"You could learn that from those dreadful tests?"

I responded by shrugging my shoulders.

"Then…what is it?" he challenged as we drifted closer together.

I noticed that I had trouble breathing when he was that close to me. I pulled back, giving myself space.

"You can remember everything," I said, looking up at the stars.

His expression faded into amazement.

"How did you…" he stammered.

"I bet you could remember every one of these stars, if your heart so desired."

"That seems like a waste."

"I'd rather choose to forget," I mumbled with a sigh.

"There are things I wish I could forget," Hark said, his tone dimmed.

"It's more than that. You'll remember this exact conversation, word for word."

"Will I?"

"Every detail."

"So, you're saying I'll remember how this moonlight accentuates the tiniest hairs on your face, creating a beautiful glow?" he said, caught in the moment.

My chin quivered. "Yes, forever," I barely got the words out.

I met his gaze as he looked deeply into me—far past my exterior, past the part of myself I hid from others, and bore into what I hid even from myself. All sound and thought faded away like the wind. I could feel his heart beating from across the distance, calling out like a siren's song. We were the only two beings holding on to this fraction of time, while the rest of the world moved on.

It's all I ever wanted…to be worth remembering.

"Good," Hark's voice cracked as if they were the first words of the morning. His single word broke our connection. All the sounds from outside flooded in as the moment washed away.

"I might forget it tomorrow," I looked away as I forced the words out.

"I won't…I promise."

My vision blurred.

The conversation fizzled as we shared this pleasantly awkward moment. I was fixated on his breath entering and exiting his body, and I felt as though he was also listening to mine.

"No, you take off *your* hat," Daleta mumbled, half sleeping.

Our eyes widened in anticipation for her next words. Then she lay back down and returned to her slumber.

We shared a pleasing smile and embraced the stillness of the night.

The morning light was a spectacular sight. All three of us were awake and ready for action. By the time the sun crested over the mountain ridge, we were near the outskirts of the city of Kanlett, our destination.

I crouched down and started to go over our last-minute preparations after Hark and Daleta tied up our mounts.

"All you need to do is pretend you're together…emotionally," I explained. It made both Hark and Daleta blush.

"So, why do you want us to sniff this vapor again?" Daleta asked, inspecting the blue vial in her hand.

"It's used to increase your mental ability, right, Talia?" Hark chimed in.

"Correct. It was developed for people with mental deficiencies, but it only lasts a couple moments. So, use it wisely. Take a whiff every now and again, but don't make it too obvious," I recommended.

"Right," they both said in unison.

"What are *you* going to do?" Daleta asked.

"My job," I said, stashing my dagger inside my belt.

"Which is what again?"

"Destroy their prisms," I said. "I will be monitoring you from over the ridge, and as soon as you do *your* job distracting them, I can go in."

Daleta stood up, pulled her curly hair back and tied it with some twine. As they approached the Telandric City, I couldn't take my eyes off their interlocked hands.

I wish it were that easy.

I watched eagerly as they flirted and appraised some beast skins at a shop across from the guard post. Even I believed them.

I waited for them to be approached. I knew the art of recruitment, and this was a solid plan to distract the staff so that I could enter the city undetected.

Suddenly, I realized that I was too mixed up in my own agenda. I forgot to warn them to be clear with their thoughts. The Telandric are infamous for their ability to read minds.

Is it too late?

One of the Telandrics was already coming their way. I had to get there fast. I frantically raced over the peak of the hill, thinking about a family emergency—something...anything to get them away long enough so that I could tell them this key piece of information. I started my descent down the hill. I was so blinded by my concern for Hark's well-being that I didn't notice the club until it hit me squarely in the forehead. A numbness swept through me as I fell backwards, tumbling over myself. In that instant, all went black.

Chapter Five
The Dance of Despair

"The experiences shared have molded our dreams…"

My "third eye" was open, while my actual eyes were shut tight like a clam, wincing in pain. I was awake, though my body was not. There was another Vigor hovering over me—a feylin—I was sure of it.

His Vigor paced back and forth impatiently. Never had I been so careless.

My attacker's feylin "eye" briefly opened in this realm, peeking at my condition.

"Ah, there you are, my sweet," his deep voice resounded.

"What are you waiting for?" There was no sound in the Feylin realm, so I simply projected the concept.

"So, you're not dead. What great news. Would have been very disappointing. I like to play with my victims before devouring them, piece by piece."

"What are you doing to me? Why can't I move? Enough with your mind tricks."

"Mind tricks? Ha. Don't insult me. It was my strength that knocked you unconscious. It's ya' frail head that's the problem here. I haven't even started to kill you yet."

I could hear the sound of him cracking his knuckles.

"What's the hang-up, then?" I projected.

"First, I will absorb your information, then your soul, and finally I get to do you a great honor by eating your flesh, RAWR."

I started to feel my fingers get that tingling feeling—like when you sleep on your arm.

The figure's Vigor moved in closer. I felt pain from my scalp as he started to drag me back over the hill.

"I wouldn't want your friends to interrupt our little date, sweetheart," he chuckled.

One hundred feet away lay a small, sharp rock. I figured I had a good chance of catching him off guard—if I had calculated his arrogance correctly.

Like a flash, I extended my control string out from my Vigor, through my hand. It reached the stone, though not as swift as I'm used to, then engulfed it like a hungry snake.

I waited for my opening. I knew that the further he dragged me away, the softer the sound would be when it exited the normal dimension and entered this one.

His feet staggered and started to slow. My back was caught on a large rock. Instead of lifting me over it, he kept tugging as if his fishing hook was trapped in a reef.

Ignoring the pain, I knew it was time.

He pulled my body harder, tearing off my skin on the rock's sharp edge.

With a crackle, the sharp rock was in my hand.

I opened my eyes and saw my dark-haired, goliath-looking foe staring off into the distance, where the sound originated. I swiftly threw the stone, aiming for his eye socket. Unfortunately, my arm didn't have all its feeling back. The projectile clashed with his shoulder, making a decent-sized slash.

Shaken, he released his grip on my hair.

I wedged my foot against the rock that had just torn my flesh, stepping in my own blood, and wobbling like a new-born calf.

"Grrraawww, impressive shot! You won't catch me off guard again, lady."

"Are you ready for more? Because I'm ready to hurt you," I said, hoping he wasn't going to call my bluff.

"Is that a promise?" He lit up, then descended upon me fast.

"It is."

I felt my strength return, and used all my might to push my body at him. A head-on attack was the last thing he would expect.

We collided in the air and fell to the ground, rolling back to standing positions, as if it had been choreographed.

"While I would love you to destroy me completely, I don't think you have the stones," he said with a chuckle as he snatched up his club from the ground.

My head remembered the blow, and it pulsated at the very sight. I couldn't help but feel violated as he licked my blood off of it.

I tried to act tough, but he was right; I *was* no match for his brute strength.

He came at me like a bull—his club raised, ready to smash.

Without thinking, I went back to my third sight and shot my control string around his weapon.

His massive arm fell down upon me like a guillotine, when…" crackle."

Within a second, I felt its jagged hilt in my hand, its weight pulling on my arm.

Disarming him didn't stop his hand. It crashed into my left ear, which caused me to writhe on the ground once again.

Everything was shaking too much for me to make anything out. I was disoriented and started to feel cold. I took a couple swings at him with his own club, poorly calculated and easy for him to dodge.

"Not even your Focus can save you from my strength. Just give up now—'tis pointless to struggle. Here I thought I'd found a formidable opponent," he chided.

I had to take a moment to think, to uncloud my mind. The real issue was Hark and Daleta over the hill. I needed to keep him talking.

"Why, nar hap coll…" Those weren't the words I wanted to come out.

"Ha! Were you trying to speak? Pathetic. You're not even worth my laughter, yet I can't help myself."

I started to lose vision in my left eye.

Listen to my voice. I will guide you back, a voice that was not my own beckoned inside me. I followed every syllable. *You never give up. Not on yourself, or your mission.*

My vision returned, allowing me to connect the club squarely with his shoulder. I recoiled and lost my grip on the weapon.

"You faith feys lack resilience," he observed, proudly.

It was then that I realized he wasn't Telandric at all; he was a Kailur. Suddenly it all made sense. The Kailur worked hard, mostly on their body strength, and believed it was the only way to attain true power. Judging by his assault on me, I was starting to believe them.

I reached for his club again. This time, his foot caught my arm mere inches from it.

"Not so fast, beautiful. You touched my 'Bella' once already, and that's once too many," he said as he wielded her again.

I spied a shimmering light. It was the reflection of my blade being stored in his belt. I must have been out for some time before he started dragging me.

I used my control string to take my weapon from his belt and place it inside my hand, which was still trapped under his weight. I scrambled to turn the dagger so I was holding it by the blade and not the handle.

He readied a mighty swing, aiming to kill.

"Silly girl, you should have put that dagger in the hand I wasn't about to crush," he boasted, thinking himself clever.

At the exact moment he tightened his grip around "Bella," I manipulated my control string around both of our weapons and used my Focus to switch their places. This caused him to grab onto the blade with all of his might. Blood started to squirt out from between his fingers.

He screamed.

I returned to my normal sight, just in time to see his suffering.

He had gripped so hard that the blade was stuck in his bone, and he was unable to unclench his hand. He used his other hand to pry open his own fingers, but still struggled.

This gave me the opportunity to rush off as quickly as I could. Glancing back, I noticed him pulling the blade out by its hilt with his disgusting mouth.

"You're not going to breathe much longer, darling," he bellowed. I could feel his rage and power getting stronger.

I managed to get back over the hill.

"Hark!" I yelled out, right before my foe kicked me in the stomach with his jagged boot. The force caused me to tumble down the hill and over myself like a rag doll. After I stopped rolling, I caught a glimpse of Hark talking to some Telandric. He had not heard my warning.

I ripped off a piece of fabric from my clothes and used my own blood to write one simple word, "run."

I quickly diverted my attention to the Feylin realm, ignoring my assailant, and pushed my control string as fast as I could toward Hark's hand.

"Where's your destiny now?" the maniac yelled as he leaped off the hill and landed on my ribs, causing more than one to snap like a twig. My control string fell limp and my eyes jolted open.

I forced myself not to look at him; I was fixated on Hark. I called out again, but no words came out.

Forget him, save yourself. You, too, are worth saving, said the voice inside me.

The pain was so immense that I had to command myself to not die. Tears were leaking out of my eyes faster than the blood was leaking out of my head. My attacker held me up by my skull to perform his coup de grace.

No, he is it. He is everything, I argued with myself.

Then I shall save us both.

"Is your faith going to stop me right now?" he asked as he licked his lips. His laughter started as a low rumble and began to boom like thunder. Without warning, he thrust my dagger as hard as he could toward my skull.

The blade stopped one inch from my temple. The wind and force from his attack caused my head to reel. He continued to press with great frustration—this time using his other hand on the back of my head, trying to pull it onto the dagger.

"Evil witch," he grunted, and swiftly let go of my skull, causing my body to flop to the ground like a fish.

He fell to his knees, gripped both hands around the dagger's hilt and proceeded to try and push it inside my neck. Again, he pushed and pushed, but the blade would not enter my body. His rage was turning his entire body bright red. He quickly let go of the weapon and fell backwards.

"No force can match my strength and power," he said, trembling.

The blade floated above my neck like a hummingbird.

"How are you doing this?" he demanded.

When I didn't answer, he slapped my face repetitively, asking the same question over and over again.

I was thinking about my odds of survival, which were at zero percent. I had to use my last moments to warn Hark. I harnessed all of my energy to make my control string reach his hand, but before I could activate my Focus and transport the note, my control string started to retract against my will.

"HOW ARE YOU DOING THIS?" he repeated.

My feylin string wrapped around the blade and it vanished. I lost complete control of everything.

Do the math.

I complied—as if I had a choice in the matter. I made my face feel the wind, feel the curvature of the planet.

Once the calculations were complete, I marked a destination high above my attacker, within the clouds. My control string shot up in the air faster than light, and with a clench of my fists, it was gone.

"Your…name?" I barely got the words out.

He looked back and forth, wondering where the blade had gone.

"Hordox, The Bloodshed," he said with great disdain.

Just then, he looked directly up and noticed my blade descending on him, from the heavens, with great speed.

He closed his eyes, and for the first time I saw his feylin power. His body turned metallic and transformed into thousands of tiny balls, just as the dagger descended upon him.

The weapon hit directly into the pile and caused them to disperse from the impact. Each ball moved independently and rolled off like a wave, into the distance.

I couldn't believe he had inflicted such damage upon me without tapping his ability. I managed to follow a single ball bearing and used my Focus to teleport it to my hand. It vibrated fiercely.

The herd of ball bearings halted and faced me intently. It was as if they were a hive, each one an equal part of him.

I placed the bearing to my lips and gave it a trembling kiss.

"Come and get it," I taunted as I quickly swallowed it down and tried to pick up my broken body.

I felt it inside me, rattling to get out.

Each metal ball came at me faster than the next. I used my Focus over and over—first transporting them to my hand, then off in the distance—saving myself from getting pelted to death by the metallic orbs. This was both mentally and physically exhausting. I had always had the upper hand in a fight because I was more than willing to die, maybe today I would get my wish.

I wavered in my defense, and one ball got through, hitting me in the shoulder. My body couldn't keep up with my mind's commands. I was unable to fend off the assault and shielded myself as the onslaught of bearings hit me rapidly. My arrogance had gotten the best of me. I should have let him flee when I had the chance. Running out of everything, I fell to the ground.

Suddenly a large shadow cast overhead. The bearings quickly scattered violently in all directions. Blocking the light above was a human-like figure. I tried to stand, then everything faded away…

~

I dreamed of surgery and sedation. Glimpses of people's faces blended with the cascading time.

When I awoke, I had no idea how much time had passed. The air smelled clean.

As I tried to move my limbs, it became quite apparent that I was tied or bound to something. I opened my eyes and took in the strangeness of the colors refracting. I couldn't tell how high the ceiling was, or if there even was one. My eyes had forgotten how to focus.

Gliding my nails against my palm, I felt how much they had grown, though the ends still shattered from the previous assault. Based on their length, I had spent several months unconscious.

My attention quickly turned to the straps on my arms as I frantically tried to remove myself from the bed.

A slender male with a strange mechanism over one of his eyes barged in. He was obviously one of the medical personnel. He had heard the entire ruckus and had come running in, surgical instruments in hand.

This was going to hurt, I was certain. Desperate to make a weapon, I wedged my thumb under the nail of my index finger and pushed with all my might.

Slowly, the nail detached from the cuticle, tearing the flesh. It was torture. My silent mouth reflected the feeling.

"Wait, I mean to help yo…" the man started to say, but he was too late.

I was fixated on his mouth's movements—anticipating his next word. When he started to say, "you," that was the moment I had been waiting for.

My third, "mental" eye opened and I looked into the realm. Shooting my control string into the back of his mouth, I transferred my bloody nail there. He started to choke and grabbed at his throat.

When I reverted back to my normal sight, everything looked as if I were underwater.

Short on time, I continued to wrestle with the straps, causing the bed to fall off its frame. My muscles relaxed and finally allowed my body to slip out. I caught my breath before I rose to my feet.

During my escape out the door, I heard the man cough up my nail and then struggle to breathe.

I darted out to the hallway, knocking over almost every table and flowerpot in my path.

Instincts readied for battle, I confronted a figure at the end of the corridor. My cloudy vision had deceived me—it was merely a statue. I studied the stonework; it seemed familiar somehow. My stomach twisted as I recognized it. The chiseled art-piece was of the former Prophetess of Kanlett, hundreds of fresh flowers draped at her feet.

She was loved, even in death.

Enraged, I entered into the center keep. I heard several footsteps running swiftly towards me in unison.

Quickly, I ducked behind a large urn located next to a water well.

Their footfall faded as the two men entered the room I had just fled. I caught a glimpse of my own refection and was shocked to see the face looking back at me. I had avoided looking at myself for so long—since before my demotion—that I looked like a stranger. All I had known was that I was different, and that was a bad thing.

I started to unwrap the bandages on my arms, legs and torso, noticing that my wounds had healed.

Here we go again, I thought to myself as I observed my new scars.

Since removing the bandages, I was not appropriately dressed and borderline naked. The cool air blowing against my bare skin caused goosebumps, and all my little hairs stood on edge. Besides the undergarment I had on, I decided to leave the bandages that were covering my chest area, for both warmth and modesty. This added a new equation to my escape plan. I couldn't exactly blend in.

They must not have known I was from Lustaria, or I wouldn't still be alive.

I peeked out of a doorway and could see the whole compound was afoot. Men and women alike were armed with torches, not a single weapon in sight.

In and out of the shadows cast from the torch light, I evaded. I knew I couldn't keep this up forever.

Climbing inside a large supply crate, I pressed myself against the inner wall and peered out of a crack.

After a while, a figure approached the crate slowly. I hid in the corner, making myself as small as possible, keeping my system calm.

Be still. Breathe shallow. Heart slow, I ordered myself.

Above my head, the torchlight illuminated the crate. The arm holding the torch appeared small and slender.

I grabbed hold of the intruding limb, and managed to flip the individual over the edge, into the crate.

Quickly, I snatched up the torch that had fallen on the floor during my attack, while simultaneously resting my knee on top of the figure's neck, using my weight to conserve my strength. To my shock, it was a face that I recognized. I was taken aback and released my hold from her neck.

"Daleta, I'm so glad you're in one piece," I whispered with genuine excitement, an emotion I never thought I'd associate with her.

"Who are you?" she asked.

I pulled the torch closer to my face to reveal my features.

"Wait, Talia?" she uttered in disbelief.

"Yes, I've come for you and Hark" I explained with a sigh of relief.

"Intruder!" She launched up.

I was not expecting this response. I advanced on her.

She kicked out her foot, attempting to shoo me away.

I caught it. With a twist of my arm, she fell, and I grappled her. She landed on her shoulder which popped out of place.

I blew out the torch and held the hot embers to Daleta's face. Her eyes widened with fear.

"There's about five minutes before the temperature of this torch goes down. Which leaves me with two options. One, we talk this out and you make me believe that you're not going to try something like that again. Or two, I disfigure your face while you scream for help," I said with great intensity.

Scared out of her wits, she started nodding. I raised my index finger to cover my lips as three men approached the crate.

"It was coming from here," one man said to the others.

"Maybe by that old crate," the other man said.

Frantic, I opened my third sight. I searched for something, anything. There was a wind chime just outside the door. It would do. My control string pulled it into the Feylin realm. The loud noise from it breaking the dimension barrier got their attention. They quickly rushed over and called for more backup.

"Why are you turning on me?" I interrogated Daleta.

"You set us up. You never intended on helping us," she retorted.

"I did no such thing. I was accosted."

"You have a lot to answer for. Why have you come back?"

"We have a job to do. What happened to you guys?" I asked.

"They spotted us right away, and you left us to deal with the consequences," she said.

"Look at me. It hasn't been a picnic at all." I pointed out my bandages.

"I don't believe you. It makes perfect sense—taking only inexperienced people with you to take the fall when you high-tail it out of here."

"That was never my intention."

"Really? So, it *was* your true intention to die on this suicide mission?"

"Yes."

"No way. No one would do that."

"This one would, and I still plan to."

"And to think, all that stuff about saving Hark…"

"You got it all wrong. Just listen to me for a minute. I was assaulted by a feylin and left for dead. I've been recovering here the whole time," I explained.

I lifted up my shirt to reveal a long scar about ten inches in length on my back.

"Oh, my. Okay, but we need to be careful. There's talk of an anomaly about," she hesitated. I could hear the fear in her voice.

I knew that they were probably referring to me, but I didn't want to undo the little bit of trust I had just gained.

She winced in pain from her shoulder as I finally released my hold on her.

"This may hurt." I grabbed her shoulder and popped it back into place. She squeaked in discomfort.

"Where's Hark?" I asked, concerned.

Her eyes raced back and forth.

"Daleta," I said while putting her face inside my cold hands, "Where?"

"See that structure over there?" She pointed through a crack in the crate.

I nodded.

"That's where my quarters are. Wait a couple hours. Once everyone is asleep, meet me on the 5th floor, room 17," she said.

I agreed, knowing it was my only real option.

"Take this." She removed her jacket and handed it to me. I quickly put it on and felt her warmth still inside.

"Thank you."

She took off into the darkness.

I meditated for the next couple hours. Exercising your mind was essential for being on top of the feylin game.

I heard singing in my mind, but it wasn't my own. I know this because I've never sung a day in my life. Maybe that's how I would have sounded if I tried.

My eyes abruptly opened.

It's time.

I climbed out of the crate carefully to avoid any patrols that might have been strolling the hallways. The structure Daleta indicated was very minimalistic and barren of all decorations. I crept up the stairs on all fours like a cat, keeping my head low, trying not to make a sound on the old oak steps.

When I reached her floor, I stepped out cautiously. The hallways seemed very quiet. Her door was closed. When I placed my hand on the handle and started to turn the knob, I suddenly felt suspicious.

What are the odds it's a trap?

I decided to take a peek, to see if there were any feylins hiding inside. I slowly closed my eyes. As I opened my sight in the Feylin realm, I only saw one Vigor in the room—it was Daleta.

Feeling confident that it was safe to enter, I finished turning the knob and quickly tucked into the dimly lit room.

Daleta was startled and appeared on edge.

"Good, you made it safely," she said.

The room was small and other than two sets of bunkbeds, quite sparse.

"Let's find Hark and get out of here," I said abruptly.

"I'm right here," a familiar voice spoke.

"Hark?" I spun around. I scanned the area but didn't see anyone.

"The Lord Seven's virtues are not what the chancellor has stated," Daleta said.

"What are you saying?" I demanded.

"His lies have forsaken us—all of us," Daleta preached in a monotone voice. "We know the truth about him, and about you."

I knew I never should have trusted her.

"Lies, all lies. You must trust in yourself," I said. "It's all a deception. Listen to me, they have ways of getting in your head."

"You already admitted to me that you were a vicious person. They merely showed me the extent of your brutality."

"Who did?"

A haze lifted from the room. Three figures appeared out of nowhere. They were there the whole time, but masked somehow. I must have been under someone's Focus.

One was wearing medical garb, another was short and seemed somewhat reserved, and the third one was Hark.

"Hark, we can take them. Just fight it," I pleaded softly.

"Your mission failed, Talia. You cannot hurt anyone else—not anymore." Hark's voice lacked warmth.

This can't be happening, not again.

"Are you serious? Please remember me, like you promised you would," I cried, inching backwards.

"You need to join us and atone for all your misdeeds," Hark insisted.

"Just remember…please," I said, choking on my own words.

"I don't know what you are talking about," Hark said, sharing Daleta's vacant stare.

"We saw the truth for the first time," my two old companions said in unison.

"Can you even hear yourselves right now?"

I need him badly. Now more than ever.

"Greetings, Talia, I'm Syntox. I helped nurse you back to health." The man in medical garb stepped forward.

I remembered several bits and pieces of their mental assault upon me. It wasn't as *nurturing* as he made it out to be.

"We mean no harm. We aim to help you," Syntox said.

"If you mean me no harm, then I shall take my leave."

Attempting to call his bluff, I edged toward the door. I gently placed my hand the knob, not letting Hark leave my sight.

The door opened halfway before my arm ceased to let me open it any further.

"You will be free to leave once you return what is rightfully ours," Syntox said ominously.

I felt my arm closing the door against my will.

They knew.

"You will repent for what you've done. When you do, we will be waiting for you on the other side with open arms," Daleta said.

Continuing to use a feylin power, the two men escorted me out of the room—my legs moving on their own, like a marionette.

"You'll be happier this way," Hark said.

I knew you were going to break my heart someday.

I tried to enter the Feylin realm, but I was blocked. I protested and scratched at the doorway. The feylin doing this wasn't powerful enough to render me completely paralyzed.

We reached the lower barracks, and soon my cell. The doors slammed behind me.

After Syntox left, I regained the ability to move my limbs. Over and over, I tried to open my third sight, but was stopped by some force. Outside my cell door, I noticed the second man was still there guarding me. This must be his doing.

Being weak and powerless wasn't my favorite feeling. I screamed until I lost my voice. The guard was unfazed.

I fell on the dusty ground, mentally and physically exhausted.

Without Hark distracting me, none of this would have happened…all the suffering, hardship and misfortune.

Still, I wouldn't have had it any other way.

Chapter Six
Escape or Rescue

"...and cohere our thoughts into a noble idea."

The feylin guard was motionless. I knew statues that moved more than he did. His fingers cradled a glass orb that rested on his lap.

I decided to follow some of my early feylin training—testing my limits and his as well.

"Pictures are heavy. Words are light and easy to manipulate. Now, think of all the words that signify pain or sadness," I recalled the chancellor's teachings.

Betrayal. Broken. Deserted. Alone.

"Now replace those words with the exact opposites," he had instructed.

Rescued. Whole. Home. Hark...Hark?

I caught myself by surprise. Though once I thought it, I knew it was true. It did feel like home when I thought of Hark.

"Now harness that feeling and hold it close to your heart. It is all you have right now," I remembered him saying.

This exercise was used to create shifts within your emotional state by drawing from deep within the subconscious.

Hark.

A calm washed over me. I was not scared, nor was I in pain any longer.

At daybreak, I was approached by twelve guards as they formed a double file line. Each one took a step to the side, making way for the grand entrance like a blooming flower. My first visitor was the Telandric leader himself, Bondal, and his entourage. Every one of them gave off an aura of self-importance, whereas I was an exhibit to be stared at.

Bondal's clothes were disheveled, his eyes had bags beneath them, and even his hair was unkempt. This was not the great leader I had remembered.

"You hardly look menacing," Bondal said, pacing back and forth outside my cage like a hungry lion.

He seemed to have an ax to grind with me, and not the usual retribution that had been going on between our two factions.

"Hello, Lord, to what do I owe the pleasure?" I greeted, showing false respect, hoping to glean some insight as to his position.

"To think something so frail-looking destroyed everything we worked so hard for," Bondal sneered.

I knew exactly what he was referring to, and there was *no* chance for bygones on this one. My identity had been compromised.

"What can I do for you?" I asked, changing my tone.

"A fitting name—The Plague. Isn't that what they call you? A disease to infect and destroy everything…and everyone. Only now, I'm here to act as the cure," he spat.

He was pushing me around, and whenever that happened, I pushed back harder. I felt the heat raging from behind my eyes.

"She cried," I taunted, addressing his bone of contention head on.

His face snarled and his neck bulged as he lost control.

"Aaaahhhh..." Bondal screamed until his voice cracked, his words inaudible, his body shaking.

Staring him down, I got as close to the barrier as possible, showing I was not intimidated by him.

"Cut out her tongue! Right now," Bondal commanded, forcing his own nasty muscle to crawl out of his mouth like a worm.

"Your breath is just about as foul as your personality," I said, feeling my veins pulse with blood.

Two guards approached the bars to my cell, pulling out their short swords.

"If I may interject, my Lord. She is harboring quite a valuable asset. We need her intact until her own...uh...execution," the medical officer said.

With an unceremonious wave of his hand, Bondal called off my mutilation.

"Very well Syntox. Begin the preparations to extract her essence," he ordered.

Faster than they'd come in, they made their retreat.

The next couple days were quiet. I was only given water and flavorless cake.

I yearned for something to change as the days drifted into each other. Being disconnected from the outside world puts you in a subservient state. It was hard to not be broken within my own thoughts. I was starting to feel like I deserved their punishments.

I used my time exercising—trying to get my body back into shape. I played through every possible outcome so that I wouldn't be surprised when the moment to act presented itself. My body memorized the movements needed, like a dancer preparing for the stage. Counting the repetitions kept my mind active and stopped it from wandering.

On the eighth day Syntox returned. He seemed to be quite methodic with his process. Surely, I wasn't the only one they held prisoner, but I knew what they wanted from me…and they wanted it desperately.

"Good morning, Talia," Syntox greeted pleasantly.

"Could you skip the niceties and get to it? I'm a little busy." *12, 13, 14.*

"Very well. The last time you engaged with our society, fourteen of our people ended up brutally killed. I know you remember that day.

"It was thirteen." *23, 24, 25.*

"Fourteen lives were lost and I will not let you belittle their memory. It's all they are now. I want to hear you say the words, 'It was fourteen.'"

"Now you made me lose my count," I said as I switched to stretching.

"You cannot make light of this. You are a murderer; admit it."

"So is life."

Syntox took a moment to try another angle. "Do you believe in people living harmoniously?" he asked.

"Sure, who doesn't?"

"Do you believe that plotting an attack on our system is a peaceful act?"

"No, the intention is quite the opposite," I admitted.

"So, how can you align yourself with the Lustarians and still say you believe in peace and harmony?"

"I said I *believe* in peace. I didn't say we should have it with your faction."

"For peace to exist, you need to stop fighting the truth and allow healing to happen," he said.

"I'm not a white flag bearer. I'm a problem solver," I said.

"You're an implement of destruction," he countered.

"I would love to end this war, but you give me no other choice."

"I'm offering you peace right now, and you openly refuse it!"

"Peace cannot coexist with greed," I said.

"Our purpose is to keep our own safe. That is survival, not selfishness."

"In the name of peace, you create war," I protested.

"This is going absolutely nowhere. Maybe tomorrow you might want to speak truthfully," he said.

"I've no reason to lie, it just wastes time," I lied.

He brushed the back wall, keeping as far away from me as possible. Fear was my only ally. I had to keep it stoked, like a fire. They had to believe I was my former self. If they'd known the truth about my weakness, I would have already been exploited and destroyed.

"Then will you admit before me that you murdered our beloved Prophetess in cold blood?"

"Is she dead?"

"You know very well she is. You watched her die."

"Did I?"

"I'm done here. Maybe Bondal is right about your worth after all," Syntox said, his eyes getting heavy.

He truly loved the Prophetess. Just bringing up Capri caused both Syntox and Bondal to lose control of their emotions. She was their weakness, and ironically, mine too.

The next day when Syntox returned, I decided to ignore his questioning, despite my boredom. It was a game of wills, and I didn't want to play anymore.

I just kept doing equations in my mind. It was another old training method, using my mundane ability to keep myself sharp and generate feylin energy, even if I was unable to use it.

"Why did you kill her? Why did you come back?" he kept repeating the same questions over and over again.

Each time it was harder and harder to ignore him. I could feel his frustration, even though his voice and facial expression showed no sign of it. I noticed the pause in between each question was getting slightly shorter. Maybe he wanted me to notice to distract me. Intentional or not, it was working.

I knew I had to speed up my calculations to get to the point where I couldn't even hear him speak. To accomplish this, I had to come up with the answer at the exact same time I presented myself with the problem.

As my feylin energy built, the sound of his voice turned into a slight hum without any audible qualities. He was pushed out, and my wall was up.

"Here…I…am…" Clear as day, I heard a voice that was not Syntox's. This new voice caught me off guard and broke me out of my trance.

To my surprise, Syntox had already left the prison. I was alone.

Where did that come from?

The guard was still in the same old position, however now he was tensing his neck muscles.

I glanced over to the cell next to me and noticed a wiry figure. His mouth moved, but no sound came out. I squinted my eyes in disbelief, then the figure vanished.

Was it real, or had I imagined it in the absence of my sanity? After this new turn of events, I decided to rest up and ready my mind to try and recreate it tomorrow. It was the only way to be sure.

The next morning, I woke up earlier than usual. Everything was the same, although it felt different because now I had a purpose. Ever since the figure appeared I thought of nothing else, and reaching him again was my top priority.

This time I knew I had to play it safe. I started out by doing simple problems and slowly got to more complicated ones. It didn't take long before I was solving problems and creating them at the same exact time. Thinking two simultaneous thoughts was very taxing, but it was easier without the distraction of Syntox's questions.

Time was no longer present and all I knew were equations, like some ancient machine. I had to push my mind to the limit. It's what I'd been training for.

Three equations solved simultaneously.

"Welcome…back," the same voice from before echoed inside my head.

The world around me started to change slightly. A bed and articles of clothing started to appear in the cell next to me.

"Hello?" I managed to get a word out, in between problems. For the first time since my incarceration, I was hopeful.

Soon the figure I saw yesterday appeared again in the same spot. This time, I could see him clearly.

He greeted me with a nod.

My excitement made me solve the problems faster.

"This is not real," his voice haunted.

"What isn't?"

"Tomorrow, before he questions you, recreate this but faster."

That concept perplexed me and snapped me out of my trance. In a flash, everything disappeared—the bed, the figure, everything—I lost it.

My face was soaked in sweat, and I was breathing heavily, as if I had just run for miles. Everything seemed to be the same as I had left it, except for one major thing. The guard's eyes were open, and he was standing.

Instead of hypothesizing and trying to analyze what had just happened, I decided to rest my mind and body.

Tomorrow seemed to come faster than any other day. I awoke barely in time for my daily interrogation. I was late. The previous day had taken everything I had and I barely recovered. How was I supposed to repeat it again, and faster, no less? I tried to clear my mind, but my curiosity overtook it.

I noticed the guard was back, complacently sitting.

Syntox approached, chair in hand. He studied a parchment note. There was a canvas pack next to him, which was new.

"How are we today, Talia?" Syntox started.

"What's in the pack?" I asked.

"You're observant, I'll give you that. Today is the day we have decided to squeeze all that is ours out of you, like an orange. Since you're not cooperating, you've lost all usefulness to us."

I had never heard of such a thing, but I didn't doubt it either.

"I know how to bring her back," I said, attempting to stall.

"Who back…and from what, exactly?" he said, opening the pack.

"Capri."

Hearing her name caused Syntox to nearly fall off the chair he was sitting on.

"You have my attention, but be warned that I've no patience for your lies," he said, shoving an instrument that looked like a metal saw back inside his pack.

"I can access her memories."

"That's not possible! The assimilated feylin is always dormant," Syntox said.

I knew the truth of his words, but something was different about our bond.

Please, if you want us to get out of here, give me something, and fast.

Syntox was intrigued.

Putting my hope in an impossible hunch was dangerous, but it was all I had. I gently closed my eyes to start my trance. I began my equations, charging up my feylin energy. With each one, the gap between the question and answer got closer and closer. Soon the answers were near instant but not yet simultaneous.

"Give me something soon," Syntox demanded, reaching for his pack.

My bluff was wearing off faster than I had anticipated. I started to lose vision in my left eye, and I heard my voice saying words beyond my control.

"Syn, your brother saved you from an avalanche when you were a youth. You never forgave yourself for his death that day. You sat outside holding his crossbow, hoping he would reclaim it. You stayed until your tears froze on your cheeks."

As the words came out of me, I saw images of Capri in my mind. Her beautiful, golden hair glistened in the sun as she comforted a young Syntox, who was sitting in a snowbank.

I wasn't sure if I was going crazy or if she was really inside me, but it was as clear as glass, and Syntox knew it too.

"Capri…" he whispered, falling to his knees. He hid his sorrow in his hands, peeking out through frightened fingertips.

This was my chance. I pushed as hard as I could to overextend my mind past his weeping. I could only do two problems simultaneously. I felt bad for him, which forced me to regress.

"All will be okay, as it always has. One cannot change the past; we must change ourselves," her voice sang through me. It was melodic and beautiful.

Her encouragement empowered me, and like second nature, I was solving four problems at the same time.

A drop of blood started to drip from my eye.

I alone am in control. I am powerful. No, more than that, I am unstoppable.

I saw the figure in the other cell. This time he seemed to be meditating as well.

"How are you doing this, Kay?" Syntox demanded.

I noticed the bars of the cell start to fade in and out. Kay, I learned, was the name of the figure in the other cell.

"I AM…MIND!" Kay started yelling.

He continued to chant this over and over. Each time, it was getting clearer and easier to understand.

Syntox looked scared and backed up against the wall.

Soon I heard the phrase in its entirety, "I AM FREE OF YOUR MIND!"

At that moment, I realized all the bars were gone.

There was a loud crash from the front of the room. The guard fell to the ground, on top of his orb. I had made him over-exhaust his Focus until his body had caved. On his forehead, there was blood flowing out from an invisible incision. He was still alive, but barely.

Kay leaped out of his cage, like a bounding animal thirsty for blood. He pounced directly onto Syntox, causing them both to tumble to the floor. Kay was overpowered by the talented Syntox, who was using his Focus to freeze Kay's pounding fists before they connected. They both leered at me as I advanced.

"Learn from Capri. Look inside yourself, she is there," Syntox pleaded.

I entered the Feylin realm—my third sight no longer being blocked by the guard. Both their Vigors were on top of each other, struggling for dominance. Syntox had a control string emanating from his finger onto Kay's arm, rendering it powerless. Seeing this showed me how his ability really worked and how he had previously walked me to my cell. Only in the Feylin realm could you see the secrets of the universe, and only a feylin's control string could exploit those secrets.

Kay's third eye opened wide. He was a feylin too, but something was different—his Vigor was black.

"What are you waiting for?" Kay asked.

My mind was too exhausted to run the odds of who was a better candidate to bet on.

Part of me wanted to help Syntox, and I walked over to do just that. Then a thought entered my mind that I just couldn't ignore.

He wants to take me from you. Is that what you want?

Suddenly my leg answered for me. It whipped in the direction of Syntox's face.

He turned his control string on my foot, halting my attack. "You're making a huge mistake," Syntox warned.

"It's mine to make," I said as I reached out and grabbed hold of the very finger that was directing his control string. I snapped it in two places, falling to the ground as his control string lost its connection with my foot.

My distraction proved successful and Kay managed to overtake Syntox.

"I see inside your weeping heart," Kay told Syntox, while he punched his chest with all of his might, causing Syntox's ribs to cave in.

Syntox started convulsing. He wheezed from his punctured lungs.

Kay repeated this assault over and over until Syntox's control string fell limp on the floor. Kay held the dying feylin tight in his arms and placed his own control strings inside Syntox's Vigor.

Their energies were linked as one. The unique shape and color of Syntox's Vigor traveled along Kay's control string and entered his black silhouette. The colors swirled around Kay, like the wind.

"With your last breath and last thought, I accept your Vigor and fate as my own," Kay recited.

I couldn't bear to watch the inconceivable. I knew this ritual—I had been part of it once, when every part of me had changed. Kay was absorbing Syntox's energy, his destiny, his very essence.

Syntox's lifeless corpse was now dull in color. His body began to meld into Kay's until there was nothing left but his clothes, hair and nails.

I knew now that Kay had just gained Order…and Syntox's power. He even started to resemble him slightly.

It made me sick to my stomach.

"Power isn't given, it's taken," Kay said as he walked over to the guard, preparing to absorb his Focus too.

"No, we have to leave." I couldn't bear to watch that ritual again, the process was far too familiar and terrifying.

"I'm too weak, anyway," Kay said as he stumbled.

His voice seemed gentler than before. I could sense that Syntox was inside, changing him slightly. His body was having trouble adjusting to his new-found Focus. Each of his limbs was randomly seizing up. Maybe Syntox was fighting back, even in death.

I lifted Kay's frail arm over my shoulder, helping him walk up the many stone steps.

"I can walk. I can walk," Kay groaned, once we reached the top of the stairs.

I scouted for a good place to hide and take a breath.

"That tree over there," he said.

The complex had so many buildings, I couldn't distinguish one over another. I took his suggestion and made a break for the tree. The sun pierced my eyes as they tried to readjust to the outside world.

"There's a passage here," he explained, moving a false root, uncovering a crawl space.

My bones ached at the very thought of leaving this place. *I can't leave Hark. But he turned on me…he let me down. Did he even have a choice? Wouldn't he just do it again, if given the chance?* Hark was one of them now. It would only end tragically if I interfered. There was just one way to save him, to save everyone. I knew what I had to do.

"I can't go, not yet," I explained.

"Suit yourself." He didn't waste any time chatting, and climbed inside the hole.

After he had disappeared into the darkness, I went my own way.

Locating their treasure hoard wasn't difficult at all. It was the tallest point in the center of the city, decorated with gems and runes. Getting there however was quite a different story, what with all the Telandric about.

The Telandric-prized treasure room was within my grasp, only now I was completely out of cover. Inspecting a small group of Telandric nearby, I walked out of the shadows and approached them with purpose, my head held high.

Puzzled, they looked at each other for answers.

"You three, report to Bondal immediately. Move!" I said, causing them to disburse without questioning my authority.

I was now at the entrance of my destination and soon my mission would come to a close. As I passed underneath the arched doorway, I felt my feet become heavy as if they were filled with iron.

Inside were many cages of hybrid beasts and strange tissue floating in bright liquids. They really liked to mess with the laws of nature. Their curiosity was an appetite that forever craved nourishment.

The Telandric never invested in armed guards. When your whole group is made up of mind readers and high-level cognitives, you never have to worry too much about intruders. They sense them coming a mile away.

However, I knew how to shut down my mind—how to say one thing but think something entirely different. This method had always thrown off the persona tracers. There was something else, although it was too painful to think of. It kept me safe from their influence, for the most part.

My mission was simple, figure out their ploy and destroy their surplus of prisms. Unfortunately, I knew there was only one way to accomplish that—the death of a feylin.

Inside the grand gallery, there were more shar-prisms than I had thought even existed. The chancellor wasn't exaggerating.

Each prism was clear, void of power. I felt them pulling at me in the Feylin realm, a phenomenon that I had never witnessed first-hand.

In the center of the room, displayed on a podium was the largest shar-cluster I'd ever seen. It was uncut and jagged. I glided some fabric from my robe on its edges, and it cleanly sliced through it.

While admiring its rarity, I caught my reflection through the light of the prism, and it still startled me. We were prettier than I had been. Her soft features complemented my sharpness.

I thought of the first moment I saw Hark. I didn't know it then, but he gave me my smile back, giving me a reason to feel joy. Redness came over me. I felt sorrow welling up in my eyes.

It's not his fault…it's mine. He had no choice. Everyone had pegged me right; I could never amount to more than this. I'm nothing, not even a memory. I should have never tried to become something great.

"I'm sorry. I never meant to hurt you."

It was time to complete the task the chancellor had commissioned me with. I had to take the life that I was given, to bring order back to the unrest.

Thank you for giving me a second chance to make things right, I thought as I wrenched my head back hard to gain maximum damage.

One hit would be enough. I had to prove myself to myself, or to any Gods that may be watching. My body would be absorbed and nothing left—nothing to be mourned or remembered. I wasn't doing this because of destiny or orders; I had to do it for Hark. He held my happiness hostage, guarded by a wall of pain. This was the only way to free him and myself.

"I live to die," I said, imagining Hark's face one last time.

Hoping for an instant death, I plunged my head forward. There was a loud crackle. My neck strained, missing the cluster.

Bewildered, I opened my eyes. The cluster had vanished. Quickly, I spun around and noticed it ten feet behind me.

Heel to toe, I approached the cluster. This time I pushed him out of my thoughts and held the cluster within my hands one more time.

Stop, I heard her voice inside me, angelic and pure.

"You did this?" I said, realizing she had somehow used my Focus without my knowledge.

I want to…live, she said inside my head.

I knew she was sincere, because I felt it too. The Lord Seven had predicted my destiny, written deep within my skin. Ever since that day, I had been going through the motions until this very moment. My sacrifice was a privilege, one which bore much sorrow.

That isn't your path, not anymore.

No, this was how it had to be. I never took advice from others and today was no different, even if she was a part of me. "It has already been decided," I said.

You cannot ignore my purpose and serve only yourself. If you believe everything has a reason, then why have we come together simply to fall apart now?

Gently I placed my hand on the prism cluster, its sharpness slowly entered my skin like a knife in butter.

Does this feel like the moment you've been pining over?

My mind erupted with a sudden change of heart. She was right, it felt foreign to die here alone—not at all how I had imagined it. My fate must have intertwined with hers during our amalgamation. Woven from the threads of time, into what exactly? That was what I needed to find out.

Your existence is paramount to this world, not just a weapon to use up and discard.

I suddenly realized the persona tracers would have heard her too. I had to leave, and fast.

"Maybe I should live for myself for once."

I exited the prism room, hiding in the shadows the sunlight cast. I had to reach Hark, but where was he?

Feeling almost intoxicated, I staggered as a mental shock wave rippled through the compound. Their telepathic alarm had been tripped. My moment of surprise was long gone. Every single person in Kanlett was afoot and on high alert. This included many feylins that could turn your greatest fears into reality.

Moving on instincts alone, I could hear them as they surrounded me. I tried to enter the Feylin realm, but struggled.

They were onto me, and there was no place to go.

"I can't leave him."

You have to.

"I won't."

Sometimes to move forward you must take a step back.

Dizzy and disoriented, I had to go against my nature and retreat. I needed time to gather myself and abandon my purpose, just for a little while longer.

The sensation I had felt in the prison remanifested itself.

Not again. I cannot go back there.

Entering inside the Feylin realm, I followed the feeling, moving closer to it. There, he was, the guard who had the power to block the Feylin realm, but not if I was already in it.

Using the shapes and colors of the other realm as my guide, I blindly got a jump on him in the normal realm, grappling him from behind. His Focus had created a sphere around his Vigor, distorting reality and access to the Feylin realm. Like in the prison, everything outside his effect was hidden from the outside world. He shrouded my existence, and was my only way out of here.

"If your Focus runs out, then so will your life," I whispered into his ear.

He nodded profusely.

With my hostage in hand, I managed to reach the secret passage in the tree unnoticed.

Cutting off the air supply to the guard, he struggled in my arms as he perspired heavily. Once he fell unconscious, I was again able to return to my normal sight.

"Dream of another life," I said.

Backed into a corner, I had no other option. Fight another day, or die trying to save tomorrow. Forcing myself to make the rational choice, I crawled through the narrow hole until I reached the light at the other end. I arrived at a slender ledge on the outer wall of the city.

It wasn't long before I spotted Kay off in the distance. It felt as if my legs were going to give out on me as I ran to reach him.

Kay was staggering back and forth like an intoxicated peasant. "Back so soon?" he greeted.

I let him lean on me until he got his footing.

The sound of roaring water masked our escape. It was almost peaceful. We scrambled along the jagged cliff until we reached a rickety old rope bridge.

"If we want to live, we need to cross this," Kay said.

"On the contrary," I added as I sized up the condition of the old death trap.

"I traveled this path before and I'm still alive. Mind you, that was over five years ago."

"After you."

"Fine, just step exactly where I do," he instructed.

I memorized his every movement as he made his way across. The bridge was comprised of old woven rope, no wooden slats, no guardrails. On our side the rope was tied to a tree—on the other side, to a medium-size rock. I wished that rock was bigger.

I followed every step as if my life depended on it, because it did. We shifted our weight so that we both wouldn't end up on the same side at the same time.

As we reached the halfway point, I was about to mention how this wasn't as bad as it looked, when I heard a voice behind us.

"Talia, come back!" I would recognize how he spoke my name anywhere. There was Hark, standing at the cliff edge. He was pressing *my* dagger against the rope.

"I really don't want to do it," Hark said.

I opened my mouth to speak, but before I could get the first syllable out…

"Then don't, you fool!" Kay interrupted.

Without taking a moment to think, Hark slashed through the rope.

"No!" I cried out as we both grabbed ahold of the other side. It stretched and struggled to hold our weight.

The cut rope dangled down to the jagged rock and unforgiving stream below.

Kay started to go into the Feylin world.

"Let me," I whispered, my heart pounding like a drum.

"I'm only going to ask you one more time. Talia, come back," Hark demanded.

"I know you have it in you to cut that rope, but I know for a fact that you won't," I said, trying to catch my balance.

He raised the knife high above his head.

"And let me tell you why," I said, inching my way toward him, hand over hand.

He distanced the blade from the rope, widening his eyes.

"I know you, Hark, and right now I would bet that I know you better than you know yourself."

As I spoke, I felt Kay slowly making his way to the other side, showing little faith in my negotiations.

"No matter what they did to your mind, I know something they don't."

I could see the doubt on his face. For the first time, he looked at me as everyone else did—like a monster.

"Stay your distance," he said, placing both his hands on the hilt.

I didn't want to leave without him, and I wouldn't let him throw me away, not that easily.

"I've been instructed to stop you at all costs, and I will. Don't make me," he said, his hand rattling against the dagger's hilt.

"What they don't know is that I lied. I lied about your test. I told you—everyone—that you tested poorly on the critical thinking. But in fact, you not only tested high, but the highest I've ever seen. I knew you were special, and I had to protect you—even from yourself," I confessed, reaching the ledge.

His hand trembled as he mulled over what I had said. "Why?"

"I did it because I care about you," *...more than you can imagine,* I finished my sentence inside my mind. I had to break what they had done to him.

"I don't trust you...not anymore," Hark admitted.

The sting of his words left an aching in my chest. As I approached, I could see his thoughts on his face. He wanted to stab me. Oh, how he wanted to.

"You don't have to trust me, just trust in yourself."

My hand gently touched his and caused it to stop shaking. As our skin touched, I felt a hot burning sensation—as if I had stuck my hand in a flame.

His irregular breath started to calm.

"Is this what you want? Or what they want?" I said.

His eyes fluttered as they felt my breath. He was searching within himself for the answer.

"Don't make me hurt y..."

I placed my other hand on his heart, which was racing. He flinched at my touch. Just some thin fabric stood as a barrier between my hand and his chest. His heat seeped through the tiny holes.

"You can do whatever you want. No one is forcing you," I asserted. I focused on the softness of his hand, trying to ignore the pain that was getting worse as each second clicked away.

His inner turmoil was escaping outward.

"You can't…go. Why did you want to?" he stammered, fighting each word as it escaped into the air.

"Whatever you decide, I stand by you," I said, fighting the searing pain in my hand.

And with that, I felt him swing the dagger down again. I closed my eyes, embracing my fate, giving my life to him, to harm or hold. My hand gripped his arm tighter. I could hear the blade cutting through the air. All I could focus on was that I was holding him.

The blade connected with something, but it wasn't me, and it wasn't the rope.

"Hurry, go now." Hark's voice strained.

I opened my eyes to see that he had stabbed his own leg. I stepped back, breaking the agony of our connection. He was letting me go. His injury a defense against his allegiance to me.

He isn't lost to them completely. The dagger doesn't lie.

"Is it true?" Hark asked.

"What?"

"Did you kill the Prophetess? Did you kill Capri?"

"It's not a simple 'yes' or 'no.'"

"No more vague answers to shield yourself. Not anymore."

"Capri is gone because of me. That's the truth."

"What about the rest? All the other stuff they said about you?"

"I have a lot to be ashamed of, but I was different back then. They have been making your mind much more suggestive. You must fight it," I said.

"Why are you still here? You have your out," he said, crouching down, gripping his wound.

"Just leave with me. Your place isn't here, it never was." I heard the sounds of stomping feet approaching fast.

"I can't. I need them."

I need you. "Start over with me—please?" The fear of rejection trembled in my words.

His eye winced as he looked into mine. In that moment, he really saw me.

"Just take my hand."

He reacquainted our touch and I pulled him into me. The pain increased more with every second. My tolerance was my only protection. I squeezed his hand slightly as my eyes reddened. Energy flowed through us like a tornado. This was more than simple attraction. It was a power bigger than I could even fathom.

Just then a slew of Telandric men came bounding into sight. I entered the Feylin realm. Everything was disoriented and hard to follow. It was difficult, but I managed to use my Focus to remove the dagger from his leg and return it to my hand.

I cut the rope with a swift slash and we both jumped off the cliff, never taking our eyes off each other.

Never let me go. Never again.

The rope got taut, thrashing our bodies closer together. He cradled my body with his as we soared toward the other side of the chasm. My happiness counterbalanced the agony caused by our contact.

We spoke to each other through only our eyes. He was scared that he had made a mistake, but I reassured him that mistakes were there to make.

As much as I wanted to die in his arms, I had to break our connection—the cliff wall was approaching fast.

In the Feylin realm, I searched within myself. Where had she hidden it? I went through my emotions and pushed aside the ones that were native. Like a treasure, it was locked away, buried deep in the place I feared more than anywhere else…my happiness.

I saw a face of the past—the person I'd completely destroyed. Never had I been able to forgive myself for what I had done. His pain was mine to bear. His life, mine to mourn. His image was trapped inside, guarding the gift I sought.

I'm so sorry.

Imbedded deeply, I found her power—the ability to push objects and space.

Aiming at the fast-approaching cliff, I used both of our control strings like a spiraling stream of power to create a steady force against it. Rocks shattered and fell into the ravine. We collided against the cliff at a safe speed. I loosened my grip on the rope, and I held on to him tightly as he ascended, finally reaching safe ground.

As I began to pull away, he brought me in closer.

"You don't always have to carry the burden yourself. Let me help you." Guilt marred his features.

Never had anyone wanted to fight for me. I wanted to open myself up to him and live some fairy tale life, but that was not me…that was weakness.

"Let's get out of here," I said, swallowing my nerves.

Chapter Seven
A New Vision

"It is possible that you were once a simpleton, or even a monster."

Hand in hand, we ran out of range of the Telandric desperately trying to kill us. The burning pain from our touch was insufferable, but I tightened my grasp.

I wanted to be like Hark—to feel remorse for my actions, to feel something for that matter. Losing him scared me, because I ached inside when he was away, yet it physically hurt every time we touched. I had no solution, but I would gladly accept the pain over feeling nothing.

Were we too out of breath to speak. When you're running for your life you sometimes forget about the possibility of running yourself to death.

Hark suddenly stopped and gripped his head in pain.

Once I was able to, I spoke, "That's normal. You're just experiencing withdrawal."

"From what?"

"The Telandric are quite clever with their techniques. They feed your neurons mental energy, and you will believe almost anything to keep the supply flowing. That pain you're feeling is called 'the thirst.'"

Turning to my own discomfort, I noticed my palm was singed where our hands had met. Discreetly, I hid my wound from him and began etching something into the rock I was resting on.

"Why are you unaffected?" Hark peered at me with only one eye open.

"I closed off that part of my mind long ago."

"Look, I'm sorry about turning you in. They had a way of getting inside my head, and it just made perfect sense when they said it…"

"I know. It's what they do, what they've always done. There's no need for apologies," I interrupted.

In the distance, we heard a whistle call. Someone was trying to catch our attention. I scanned the clearing.

"There. Come." I indicated a cluster of trees nearby.

Hark was limping at this point, his absolute agony was hard to watch.

We spotted Kay taking cover, looking just as tired as both of us.

"What's the plan, Kay?" I asked.

"Why is he here?" He nodded at Hark.

"The plan?" I reiterated.

"I have none, really."

"Then I guess I'm in charge. Let's go," I said, pushing forward.

We continued to move farther away from the Telandric district, along the rolling hills that scattered the landscape. Up, over and down, our continuous motion was almost nauseating. The tall grasses scratched at our ankles.

"He's slowing us down. Ditch him," Kay said, after observing Hark's stride.

"How about we ditch you here for holding us up with your chatter?"

"Fair enough. Why not just get rid us both and serve yourself, as you always have?"

"What are you getting at?" I asked, my eyes narrowed.

How was it that he knew anything about me, and as a prisoner, no less?

"Talia, can we really trust him?" Hark whispered.

"How many lives have you taken—Talia, is it now? Kay asked, trying my patience.

"Why? Do you have a death wish?" I asked.

"I don't know, are you granting wishes?"

"Not today, not for you."

"We didn't just escape a fight, to fight each other," Hark reasoned.

All this walking was causing Hark's leg wound to open up significantly.

"He is leaving a trail right to us, you know?" Kay argued.

"Well what's he supposed to do about it?" I interrupted Hark, whose mouth was open and ready to respond.

"Who stabs themselves, really?" Kay said, shaking his head.

"I was trying to help you guys escape. They wouldn't have believed me unless I was wounded."

Kay rolled his eyes shut. His nose twitched, and just like that, the bleeding slowed and started to clot. Unbeknownst to Hark, his limp all but vanished. I gave Kay a look of gratitude, knowing he had just used his Focus. Our journey continued at a faster pace.

After some time passed, we reached a small village consisting of maybe ten structures. The place looked deserted and overgrown.

"Let's see what we can find around here," I said to Kay, while helping Hark sit down on a rubble wall.

The first door I kicked in was filled with fresh vegetables and wine. I grabbed as many supplies as I could hold, shoving them into an old bag with straps.

Kay came in with a box of hand-crafted garments. I rummaged through his find and procured an exquisite dress that was just my size. It lay softly against my skin and made me feel feminine.

"This stuff is too new," I concluded, picking up a small pack.

"My thoughts exactly," Kay agreed.

"Where are you really heading?"

"Like I already said, I don't know."

"You really have no plan at all, do you?"

"All I know is my prison cell. I have no place out here, or anywhere, for that matter. I don't know what I like, what I don't like, what I want to do, or don't want to do. Except I know I don't want to go back. That's it."

"That works for me," I said. "What did you do to end up in there?"

"I've always been there."

Kay removed his shirt, upgrading to a leather armor he had scavenged. He revealed something I never thought I'd see—the most perfect shar-prism lodged directly into his chest. It looked alive, rife with energy. Why was it lodge inside him like that, jutting out like a stalagmite? And why wasn't he dead because of it?

"Is that what I think it is?" I reached for it, but quickly stopped myself.

"Do you think it's a prism? Because then my answer is 'yes.'"

"Why is it stuck there like that?"

"I am what they call a pseudo-homunculus," Kay explained without emotion.

My expression dropped. I'd seen and heard many tales, but never of artificial life, not like this. I looked inquisitively at him. He looked just as real as Hark or myself. It was almost too much to fathom.

"Are you being serious?" I asked.

"Completely. I'm a living prism, not human at all."

"Not human?" I realized that this just so happened to be the big secret plan the Lustarians were looking for. All the signs were pointing to that conclusion. If he was made, he must have been made to be some kind of weapon, or killing machine...or worse. The Telandric never meddle without gaining something in return. My mission wasn't a complete failure, not yet, anyhow.

"What's *your* plan?" Kay asked, buttoning his shirt.

"Take you back to Cape Castle."

"As a prisoner?"

"A gift."

"Will I have freedom?"

"You will have your mind, which is a better offer than the Telandric would give you."

"I accept. What about the guy? Is he also a prisoner—I mean, gift?"

"I don't know what he is yet, but I am going to find out," I said. *He is special, even Kay feels it.*

I couldn't help but wonder about Kay taking Syntox's life. Did he gain Order like normal feylins? If so, did his Focus get stronger during the process? Was he more powerful than I was? So many questions were on the tip of my tongue.

"One last thing, Kay. Do you ever feel him, like...his innermost thoughts?" I asked.

"You mean Syntox? Never. Why do you ask?"

"No reason. Let's go." I wasn't sure if it was his abnormality or mine, but we were far from similar.

Taking our loot back to Hark, we found he had company—and not the welcoming kind. He was surrounded by two men and a woman armed with peculiar weaponry.

The woman was missing a hand, and had attached a curved sword in its absence. She was missing more teeth than she had.

One of the men was missing a leg, but had attached a crossbow to it. As he walked, the loaded bolt clicked.

The other man was missing one arm, one eye and one leg. He sat in a three-wheeled contraption armed with many spikes. His missing arm had a metal, spiked ball-and-chain attached.

They were a gruesome lot to look at.

"Ah, here are our honored guests now," the man in the chair announced, mumbling his words together.

Meeting strangers in the untamed wilds was never a good idea. I dropped my goods and quickly reached for my dagger. On instincts alone, I threw it directly into the chaired-man's remaining eye.

He screamed in pain as I blinded him.

I started to dash at them when the woman placed her blade upon Hark's neck.

"That's gonna cost you both your eyes now," the man slurred, as if he had forgotten about the dagger sticking out of his face.

At a loss for options, I sent my control string over to the girl's blade and tried to transport it to myself. Unfortunately, it was attached to her, and I couldn't move it without transporting her whole body. My feylin level, or Order, wasn't high enough for that.

"Let him go and you get to live," I demanded.

"Look at us. We survive; we don't *live,*" the crossbow-legged man interjected, now pointing it directly at me.

"If you kill him, you all die. It's that simple," I reasoned, returning my dagger to my hand with the help of my Focus.

"Your feylin voodoo doesn't scare me. Any way you slice it, we're gonna take a slice out of this one. Maybe you end our suffering, maybe not. Or maybe you offer up one of yours, and the other two get to walk? Maybe even you offer yourself up? That's our deal," the man in the chair counter offered.

"Move," Kay ordered.

Complying, I leaped to the side as the bolt from the crossbow took flight, on track to hit me square in the chest. I was not fast enough to avoid it altogether. As it flew to intercept with me, I switched to the Feylin realm and used the push Focus to send it off course.

In the Feylin realm, I saw that Kay had his control string attached to the woman's arm-blade, rendering it frozen in place.

"Get up," Kay commanded Hark.

Hark scrambled away, ignoring his limp altogether.

The bolt was no ordinary projectile. It curved its way back around for another pass at me. I pushed it off course, nearly getting hit by it a second time.

The man in the chair activated something. His chair started to rumble and smoke, launching him forward haphazardly. He crashed into a structure, and it collapsed. His chair was clearly illegal, but these people didn't seem like your typical, law-abiding citizens.

This was my opportunity to charge at the girl, who was still powerless, struggling with her immobilized arm. I knocked her to the ground and proceeded to remove her sword-arm—this time from the elbow. She hissed and snarled, but with my knee on her neck, I continued to drive my dagger deeper until I hit bone. This wasn't my first amputation, nor was it hers.

The one-legged man was busy repositioning his companion's chair in our direction.

I used my other hand to snap the joint, making the rest of my work easy. Removing what was left of her arm from her body, I positioned the blade against her neck.

Looking into her hideous bloodshot eyes, I wanted so much to rid the world of her filth. Such a scavenger, such a waste of space.

I...I...just can't.

Her arm-blade fell out of my grasp. I kept pressing on her neck with my knee.

Then I saw the loose crossbow bolt had a new target. I was much too far to push it away. It was about to hit Hark in the head.

I positioned my control string alongside his forehead and intercepted the bolt, transporting it to the nearest tree.

My rage increased. I wanted to unleash it upon her, snapping her neck in two, but I refrained. I couldn't bring myself to do it. I felt the woman go unconscious under my pressure.

The one-legged man started to load his crossbow leg with another bolt, while the chaired-man took another pass—this time aimed at Kay. I used my Focus to disarm the bolt from the crossbow chamber, right before he had the chance to fire it loose. Then I ran to intercept the chair.

Kay used his Focus on me, stopping my legs from working.

"Get out of here, you idiots," Kay yelled at us right before the chair skewered him through the chest. He threw up blood all over himself.

The blinded cripple let out a foul laugh.

No one could survive such a hit, I was certain. I ran toward Hark without taking my eyes off Kay.

The savages descended upon Kay, claiming his limbs as they ripped through his body like a pack of hungry wolves. His bloodied face stared blankly at us.

I saw the horror in Hark's eyes as he turned away.

We ran until we collapsed. It was hard to bring air into my lungs. I picked up a rock and started to carve into it with my dagger, until Hark caught his breath.

"Let's go," I said, tossing the rock into the woods.

"Where? You act like nothing just happened back there."

"He was heroic. Who knew? We must admire his sacrifice."

"No, I mean causing pain is so easy for you, isn't it? Killing and death, don't they mean anything to you?"

"What do you want me to say? I didn't like seeing him die."

"It's not just about that. It's all those other unfortunate people. What you did to her arm? Were you enjoying that?"

"They were harvesting body parts. I've no sympathy for their kind."

"Well I do. Who are you, Talia? Are you that sweet girl who recruited me back in West Corick or this murdering Plague that everyone is warning me about? Give me an answer, one or the other," he pressed.

His words cut deep. Life wasn't that simple nor was coming up with an answer. I knew a "yes" or "no" wouldn't suffice. I had to force myself to do something out of character…I had to open myself up to him.

"Okay, I will, but you have to calm down."

"Deal," he conceded, taking several deep breaths.

Hark reached for me and I found myself reaching back, accepting his gesture of defeat. I quickly pulled my hand away before making contact.

Confusion distorted his face.

"See that flock of birds? They are called bloones. They only survive in groups. If you catch one and separate it from the flock, within twenty-four hours it will perish," I said, squinting from the sun as it pierced my eyes.

Hark looked at the flock circling around and feasting on insects.

"It used to be a hobby of mine, catching birds," I confessed.

"You know from experience, then? Did it die?"

"Yes. They all did."

"Poor bloones."

"Not bloones, all birds."

"I don't follow," he admitted, taking a step away from me.

"When I first learned of my feylin ability to transport objects, I could only use it on stationary things. Eventually, birds caught my attention—soaring around, owning the sky. They saw me as much as I saw them. Even in the Feylin realm, they would dodge my advances, almost taunting. Finally, I caught a sparrow. After I chased it for a long time, it fell from the sky. Using my Focus, I tried to save it from the fall. When it appeared in my hand, it was dead. I wasn't sure if it had been the chase or my Focus that caused its death, but I enjoyed the outcome just the same. I continued to hunt these birds, day after day, night after night. And I got quite good at catching them, even big ones…especially big ones. Like the sparrow, they all appeared dead in my arms. I was obsessed with finding out why."

"How many?"

"Many. More than you could imagine. The sad thing is, I miss it—feeling their life escape my grasp. Like that bloone over there." I closed my eyes and entered the Feylin realm. Without even thinking about it, my control string was in chasing it, closing in on the bloone. It tried to flee, but it was no match for me. I felt the rush, as I once had. It was exhilarating.

"Talia, don't!" Hark begged, his hand on my shoulder.

Even his painful touch couldn't stop me now. My string was wrapped around its life force and…

"Stop!" Hark yelled, with tears in his eyes, as the bloone vanished from the skies and appeared in my hands.

"You're truly sick," Hark accused.

I'm going to ruin him.

I presented him with the feathered gift in my clutches.

He refused and turned his face to hide his utter disappointment.

I released my grip and the bloone flew back to its flock, unharmed.

"Is this some kind of joke?" Hark asked, his teeth chattering.

"Hundreds of birds have died in this manner, but ever since our souls merged, they always come back alive within my hands. I don't even know why."

"Your souls didn't just magically merge, you butchered Capri, taking her power for yourself. Just like you butchered those birds." Hatred replaced the sadness in his eyes.

"She changed me."

"She did this? Capri?" He wiped a tear from his face with his shoulder.

"I want them to die, but she won't let them."

"How could you want them to die?"

"I'm trying to explain the truth, like you asked me to." *It isn't working. I can't fix this.*

"You cannot explain away how you murder for sport. That's just cruel, any way you spin it."

"I'm trying to be honest with you." *I lost the words to make him understand.*

"Try to not be a murderer!"

"I need you to tell me it's alright." *I'm pushing him away.*

"I can't."

"It's who I was. I haven't hurt anyone since that day."

"You mean since she won't let you? Don't you care about their well-being at all?"

"I care about you." *I'm losing him.*

"This isn't about me. Did you want to hurt those people, like the birds?" Hark asked, his voice shaking.

"That question is a trap. I had no choice."

"There's always a choice. You may not like it, but it's there, and you must live with the consequences of those choices."

"I pay for what I've done every single day. Don't think that I don't. You want to be like me? You want to feel what I've felt, see what these eyes have?" I screamed, releasing my temper.

Hark jolted back by my response. "Then why did you do it—hurt all those people?"

"Because I chose to," I said, my voice becoming scratchy.

"Why would you ever choose to?"

"For reasons bigger than myself, regardless of how I felt."

"Real courage isn't in overpowering your opponent, it's in restraint," Hark said, calming his words.

"Sometimes you have to make hard choices and even if you find a way to forget about them, the past never does. It has a sick way of making you remember."

"I'm not saying you didn't have your reasons, or that you don't harbor regrets. I wish you had made different choices, or at least, I wish I didn't have to know about them."

"No one can merely wish away the past. Life isn't some dream you wake up from when it turns into a nightmare. One false move and people die, or worse. That's real regret. And yes, I have some —tons actually—and I don't 'harbor' them, as you put it. I cherish them so that their memory will eat away at me, making damn sure I don't follow in my own footsteps the next time, and the time after that."

"I've lived just as long as you and never killed anyone," Hark said.

Save me. I cannot change who I am, but you can make him understand. I beg you. End my pain or I might end us both.

I stepped toward the cliff longingly. A single rock slipped off the edge and danced to its end, shattering against a larger rock.

"Are you listening to me?" Hark asked.

Then something new happened. I lost a moment of time, and all control of my body. Feeling weightless, I gave into gravity as I fell.

Too much went into keeping you alive. Stop trying to ruin it.

Hark managed to catch me from slipping off the cliff face, forgetting his anger for the moment.

The air felt quiet with opportunity. Looking upon Hark's face for the first time, I knew she was no longer in control. Things were going to happen my way for a change.

"Yes, she did want to kill them, but I stopped her as I always do," I said, with a softer voice, still in his arms.

"What just happened? Your eyes are different…they're blue," Hark said.

"I have awakened. I'm in control now," I said.

"What?!"

"Talia is not with us at the moment."

"Then that must make you…"

"Yes, Capri. I've been in here all along…waiting."

"I thought you died. They said she killed you. How is this possible? I was told that the victor always takes control over the fallen feylin," he said, amazement replacing his anger for the moment.

"Strange things happen when feylins destroy each other. We both lost our former selves when the merge occurred. Like the bloones, we need to stick together, for now anyhow."

"Two of you?"

"I know this is a lot to take in. I'm not sure what went wrong with our assimilation. She just…took over. We are a little at odds right now…I don't know why exactly," I lied. I couldn't bear to tell him the truth, that I had let her take control because I was too weak.

"You look the same, but also different. As much as I don't want to, I do believe you," Hark said, helping me to my feet.

"Our plans have shifted. We need to seek an audience with my father," I said, changing direction. If I'd learned anything from Talia, it's that the only way to become fearless is to face your fears.

I was back, and now things were about to get interesting.

Chapter Eight
Meeting Myself

"Seeing the unspoken, I revel in emotion."

We walked for hours in silence, like strangers. Each time I caught Hark staring at me, I met him with a bashful smile. It happened so often that my mouth was getting tired.

The area was overgrown with wildflowers, foxtails and tall grasses, even more than the last time I had visited. It smelled almost as wonderful as it looked.

"This is it," I exclaimed.

"What is 'it' exactly?" Hark asked, watching me trail off the path.

"Talia. This very spot is where we met." My dress flowed in the wind.

"It looks so different, so…ruined." I tried to stand a collapsed statue back on its end, to no avail.

"Well, it *is* a ruin," Hark said with a shrug.

"No, it's a graveyard."

"How was she…like…before?" he asked, his eyes showing how scared he was of my answer.

"Powerful, intense, inspiring, even beautiful, underneath all those scars," I said, spinning around. "…and ruthless."

Hark looked puzzled by my affection toward her. "I wish I knew you both before. I can't seem to figure out what aspect of your personality is one or the other."

"Even I have that problem sometimes. I remember that day from both our perspectives," I said.

"What happened? If you don't mind me asking."

"I still don't know why she came for me. Nevertheless, she did come. She wore a crimson, flowing dress. I remember thinking how impractical it was. Now I know that color was carefully chosen because it wouldn't stain." I circled a building that had been reduced to rubble.

Hark made himself comfortable on a pile of stone.

"We were tipped off on the Lustarian's plan to assassinate me. Nothing was left to chance. I was well guarded by thirteen soldiers ready to counter the ambush and assassinate my assassin. It was assuredly overkill, fourteen against one, I remember thinking. Yet I was wrong, very wrong," I said, dragging my palms delicately along the overgrown grass, feeling it tickle my skin.

Hark winced. I was unsure if he wanted me to continue.

"Awaiting her arrival, I wore my polar bear hide for its protective blessing." I touched my shoulder, remembering its warmth.

"Talia arrived much earlier than expected, and I was so terrified. She was known as The Plague back then, because everyone she fought met their inevitable end. I didn't want to suffer a fate like that. She didn't kill for glory or financial gain, it was for sport. Or at least, that's what we all thought back then. At first, I thought my eyes had deceived me—a flash here, some movement there.

"That's where I sat, on the outlook, ready to absorb the hatred and put an end to her reign." I pointed at the top of the steep hill on the outskirts of the ruins.

"From that vantage point, I observed her make quick work of three of my non-feylin guards before they even knew what was happening. My breath couldn't keep up with my reactions. Two were stabbed in vital organs and left to bleed out their last moments. The third died instantly from a slash to the neck. Her dressed flowed with each refined movement. She disappeared out of sight again, like smoke."

Hark looked around at the site differently, like he was looking at a cemetery.

"Was I really worth protecting? I wanted to warn the remaining brave soldiers. However, I was instructed not to give away my position. Left to wait and pace back and forth, while my three feylin guards used their Focuses to prepare," I said, shivering.

"Vilus, the siren mage tried to comfort me while seven seasoned guards surrounded Talia. They all advanced at the same time to overwhelm her. I was very nervous. Some of them were my friends, but I even felt for the ones that weren't.

"Talia was fast, too fast. She dodged their spear and sword attacks flawlessly. Approaching two of the men, she used her focus to transport their weapons out of their hands and into her own. She swiftly stabbed the unarmed men, hitting her marks with pinpoint precision.

"To be killed by your own weapon is an unfavorable way to finish your life. And not an honorable story to be told to your kin," I said, my frown growing deeper.

"Her defense wasn't impenetrable, though. One of the men managed to stab her arm with a spear tip. I forced myself to watch as she grotesquely decapitated the guilty guard who caused her to lose her rhythm in the fight. Out of respect, I kept myself engaged, to remember his sacrifice," I bowed my head.

"They're here to weaken and draw her out, I reminded myself, but it didn't dampen the pain." I inadvertently clenched my fists, reluctant to tell this part of the story.

"I braced myself on a stone wall. My heart sank, my legs weak. Only five guards remained. She threw her dagger squarely, finding a weak spot in the chest plate of one guard's metal armor," I said, gripping my own ribs, indicating the very spot. He was a friend, butchered right in front of me, and I knew from her memory that he was less than an insect to her.

Hark was speechless.

"This enraged another guard who began to charge at her. She teleported a sword in front of him, and it entered his skull as he ran straight into it. The gurgling sound he made gave me chills. It revisits my dreams sometimes." I covered my mouth.

"Two more descended upon Talia. She spun around, hitting both with a slashing motion. They were struggling merely to keep her at bay.

"I couldn't stand by any longer. I went against my instructions and reached into my quiver. One of my feylin guards placed his hand on me, imploring me to stop. I started to brush him away, but I realized he was right," I said, showing how my defeated hand slowly retracted from my quiver.

"I hadn't known what to expect, but this was not how it was supposed to happen.

"Feeling helpless, I commanded them to do something, anything," I paused for a moment, running my fingers through my hair, trying not to weep in front of Hark.

"What happened next..." Hark finally spoke, his eyes blinkless.

"My friend and protector, the feylin Quaal, with his sharprism twinkling brightly, went out to face The Plague...on my command alone."

"What is the purpose of those prism necklaces? Every feylin in Kanlett had one," Hark asked.

"It is the Telandric way of protecting their Focus upon death. The prisms absorb your power and deny the victorious feylin the ability to gain Order. I had one, but mine was intended for The Plague. Everyone favored me as the victor of this fight. I was the only one doubtful."

"Interesting."

"Quaal approached cautiously to aid the remaining infantry. As he approached, Talia managed to find a weakness in their routine and hacked off one of their hands."

"I can't believe she was so vile," Hark said.

"Is this upsetting you? I'm sorry. I can stop," I said.

"No, I'm the one who's sorry. I need to hear this. Go on," Hark admitted.

"Where was I? Right…Quaal entered the Feylin realm. He used his control string to draw colorless objects, each detail materializing as he perceived it. This was his Focus, to bring his art to life. Quaal was an exquisite artist with brilliant vision. He drew a spike gauntlet where the guard was missing his hand. This action energized the guard, and he fought through the pain with his replacement limb.

"The Plague…I mean, Talia was caught off guard, and the gauntlet connected with her chest.

"She teleported the remaining weapons from the guards, but Quaal replaced them with larger versions from his imaginative armory. She stumbled a bit, while the three guards pushed her back."

I felt a rush of anxiety from her, a ripple of her past emotions. She had feared she would never reach me.

"One guard charged at her with an enormous spear Quaal had made. It looked light for its size."

Hark wiped the moisture off his brow.

"Talia rolled left, and the spear stabbed into this tree," I said, pointing out the scar and caressing it gently.

Hark was quick to follow in my footsteps as I trampled the wild growth.

"Talia pulled out the spear, snapped it in half with her knee and was able to throw the short tip at another guard. It was a perfect throw, which he was not ready for," I said, blocking my face, imitating the guard's reaction.

"Luckily, Quaal was ready for it, and the short-tip projectile was blocked by a plank that he materialized to intercept it."

She was fueled by fear, and finished off the weakest of the lot first. I wish I had had the talent and courage to face her alone, but alas, I was a coward.

"Talia grabbed an adjacent guard under the chin. Then, faster than I'd ever seen, she attached her control string to the spike in the plank, bringing it to her grasp. The spike passed through the guard's neck before the plank even hit the ground." I mournfully touched my neck, and winced as I recounted the experience.

"Talia set the stage and never took her eyes off Quaal as a warning. She didn't blink as the guard's blood spilled down her arm, dripping off her elbow. Like nothing had happened, she ran at the two remaining guards."

We took a moment to take in the view, to pay some respect to those that had given their lives for mine. The air smelled pure and crisp, like it had that day.

"One started to flee. I felt for him. I understood his fear. Never did I judge him, not even now. In fact, I rooted for him. I hoped he could make it, escape this nightmare forever.

"Talia was on his heels, like a dog chasing a rabbit. Quaal tried to stop her by creating obstructions in her path, but they barely slowed her down. Her reflexes were faster than his Focus could keep up with. She reached down without missing a beat, and retrieved her dagger from the chest of the dead guard. She took aim and threw it with all her might. Quaal used his Focus to create a wooden box to intercept the dagger.

"She anticipated this, and transported her dagger to the other brave guard, who was standing his ground. It still had some momentum from her throw, and partially stuck in his back, causing him to fall to the ground.

"Talia made an example of the fleeing guard. She pounced on his body and began striking him over and over and over again. She just wouldn't stop. Quaal begged her to stop. I did too, under my breath. Not until there was nothing left did she ease up."

Tear drops drizzled on my bare feet while I relived the horror. Hark couldn't look at me as he tried to hold it together. "How is she so evil?" Hark asked.

"Reputation and fear played a large roll in her success. I've never seen such brutality. She was far worse than I possibly could have known. My siren mage protector started to sing a song of tragedy to increase our feylin power. It was beautiful and soothing—a great farewell," I said, turning to a low hum, remembering her sentiment.

"Quaal started to retreat to his main objective—protecting me. He created a barrier, giving himself space to meet up with us on the peak. Once he got there, he was quick to create as many arrows as possible.

"Norrow, my third feylin guard, linked his Vigor with mine, and we readied our synergistic assault. While we were linked, our thoughts were in sync. My left hand was taking aim, while my right hand pulled back as if I were holding an invisible bow, though I didn't need any such weapon for my attack. I used my push Focus to launch the arrows faster than any bow could muster.

"Talia was hiding in the shadows. She wiped the blood from her eyes, clearing her vision. She dashed, making her way to the walls for protection.

"Quaal linked his Vigor to ours like we had practiced countless times before; it was seamless. I took aim, while ammunition materialized in my hand. Norrow ignited the arrow with his own feylin Focus. He was so precise on timing the detonation, that it exploded almost upon impact. Each arrow narrowly missed her, due to the quickness of her step." My fingers danced like soaring arrows.

"Luck was in her favor, but it couldn't last forever. Soon Talia was caught in a blast which tore down the stone tower. As it was falling, she managed to climb it faster than any staircase could have carried her." My bones remembered her pain.

"The whole north side was destroyed." I pointed at the huge pile of rubble off in the distance.

"We brought down the last standing tower with seven arrows. This ancient place survived for thousands of years, and within a few moments it was erased from existence.

"Talia came in strong and straight for us. We were now so close that I could see her chest heaving up and down as she breathed through her mouth. For the first time, we shared a look. It was then that she showed me how to hate—when I saw how she felt about me. It was only too brief as the onslaught continued."

Even now I feel that her opinion for me hasn't changed much. Maybe seeing this event from my eyes will help her see things differently.

"Now she wasn't running, but dodging at the last possible moment. This caused Norrow's explosions to go off too late, as she weaved in and out between the arrows. He adjusted his timing, but then she retreated, and my arrows exploded too early. I felt Norrow's frustration and Quaal's disappointment. Norrow started adding random timing to the arrows so that she couldn't anticipate our next move. The explosions were so bright, it must have looked like a celebration to distant spectators.

"Even in randomness, she found a pattern. Talia entered the Feylin realm and found her opportunity. She clutched an exploding arrow with her hand. She dashed as close to us as she could, then transported the arrow right next to Norrow's head." My words slowed as the melancholy crept in.

"I saw his eyes before they went inside out and covered me in liquid. He felt he had failed me. He saw the anguish on my face. I wish I could have given him a smile before he disappeared from my life forever. His body and Vigor subsumed into the prism. Even the pieces of him that had covered me were no longer there. Just his clothes, hair and nails remained in this world to remember him by.

"Quaal made himself a sword fit for a king. He charged in after her, breaking our link."

It was clear that Hark wanted to speak, but no words came out.

"We couldn't let her bridge the gap. I was on a limited supply of ammunition now. I had to make each arrow count. Aiming true, each shot forced her back into cover. Quaal met her with slow, powerful attacks. If only he could hit her with one strike, it would cut her down for good," I said, simulating his attacks, holding an imaginary weapon.

"While attacking, he used his Focus to make small pieces of armor for himself. First a helm, then half a breastplate. Each time she found an opening in his technique, I shot an arrow forcing her back. Soon his body was completely covered in his dull, makeshift artistry.

"Her dagger couldn't penetrate his craftwork. She got down low and used his body as protection from my projectiles. Without a target, I had to stop. I felt so powerless," I said.

"That's a horrible feeling," Hark sympathized.

"Quaal assured me he was protected and wanted me to continue shooting.

"Against my gut feeling, I started to fire arrow after arrow. One ricocheted off his helm, grazing her skin. It was working. She couldn't anticipate where they would land.

"An arrow stuck through her dress and pinned her down. This allowed Quaal to perform his final attack. He raised his sword, his muscles flexed, as he brought it down upon her, putting an end to the madness," I said.

Hark held his face in anticipation.

"As his sword descended, Talia entered the Feylin realm and just like that, it was over. Held firmly in her hand, was the gorget Quaal had made himself," I said, grasping a rock as a prop.

"Quaal's mighty sword slipped out of his weak fingers and crashed on the ground next to Talia. One of my arrows was lodged in the back of his neck," I said, biting my lip.

"Oh no," Hark gasped, covering his mouth with his hand.

"I lost control over my legs and steadied myself on a weapon rack. Spears, swords and other armaments scattered everywhere as I tried not to faint." My body started to shake.

"I'm sorry, I just…" I said.

"It's okay. I'm here for you," Hark comforted me, touching my shoulder. It felt nice and soothing.

"I had never taken a life. Dizzy and disoriented, I lost my footing. How did I fail at every turn in this battle?" I asked, looking at Hark as he became blurry, my misery setting in.

"It wasn't your fault," Hark said.

"Of course it was. All my companions' deaths were tearing at my soul…and still do.

"I looked over at Quaal, who had already merged with his shar-prism. I couldn't even give him a fitting farewell.

"She kicked his prism aside like a piece of garbage," I said, throwing down the rock from my hand. "She was close enough to see my face, and mocked my pain with a smile, as she freed her dress from my arrow. Bravery expanded and overtook the cowardice that resided deep within me," I said, clearing my voice.

"Fires were born from the explosions. The flames reached great heights, blanketing the whole battlefield with dense smoke. Wasting no time, she came at me. The smoke caressed her every movement, like oil in water.

"I reached into my quiver and pulled out my first arrow. I took aim, closed my eyes and went into the Feylin realm. The arrow launched from my fingertips.

"Before it reached her, Talia teleported it into her hand and snapped it like a twig. The next shot came faster. She barely dodged it, losing her balance," I said, staggering—my movements a clone of the past.

"We both paused and stared at each other for what felt like an eternity. My eyes were frightened, and hers were ravenous. I unloaded my arsenal of arrows. She leaped, rolled and dodged them…only one grazed her," I said, touching my cheek gently.

"My quiver was empty. I rushed to the table to resupply. She was nearly upon me now. The calming voice of my siren mage gave me goosebumps, and a surge of power energized me. Rapidly, I fired fifteen arrows at her without letting up.

"She used her Focus to move each one to another location, not even flinching."

"I took my last arrow and used all my power to create a single missile. It moved so fast that it broke the sound barrier. It was disintegrated in flight. Only the arrow's tip remained."

"Did you get her?" Hark said, his mouth agape.

"No, Talia used her Focus to catch it. It bore through her hand, instead of her head. I saw her rage build as she peered at the hole I had made," I said, borrowing her expression.

"I can't believe it," Hark said breathlessly.

"I rushed to a pile of the last twenty some-odd arrows, and picked them all up at once. Instead of launching one at a time, I decided to fire the whole lot. My companion's song increased my power beyond its normal limits. Knowing that Talia couldn't teleport something with such mass, I let the cluster loose. The feathers hummed as they flew—spreading apart, creating a zone of arrows so large that there was no escape."

Hark tightened his fist in anticipation.

"Talia used her Focus to grab several arrows as she rolled into the eye of the shot. Once she stood up, there were only two arrows sticking out of her—one in her leg and one in her shoulder. Anyone else would have died from such an attack, yet it only reduced her to a limp," I said in awe of her strength.

I climbed to the top of the peak, retreading her path step by step.

"She teleported one arrow out of her clutching hand, but to where?" I said, looking back and forth.

"I quickly turned to the Feylin realm to observe her control string. I followed it upward and saw the arrow falling from the sky like a meteor. I stumbled back and it stabbed my foot, pinning me to the ground. I felt the hard wood of it lodge inside my flesh. Even the smallest of movements caused the pain to intensify.

"The pain was so immense—I had never felt anything like it. I was panicking. I couldn't breathe. All I could do was brace for my imminent death. I wished I had never existed. What a waste of a destiny. Her ability had surpassed even her own reputation. Everyone's sacrifice was in vain without victory…and currently that was not an option." I blew out all the air in my lungs.

"She fired off the remaining arrows from her hand in the same manner. Vilus draped her body over mine. She was my angel.

"I cried out, feeling more internal agony than I would have from my own death. All the arrows stabbed through her protective body. Blood rained on me, her face emotionless. She died instantly. Like the two fallen feylins before her, Vilus's sacrifice disappeared into her shar-prism. Every drop of blood that drenched me vanished. I wanted a souvenir of her bravery, but there was no evidence of her heroism—only a purple prism and six clean arrows," I said, letting dirt fall uninhibitedly from my hands.

"I pleaded with her that I wanted no more sacrifices. No more deaths.

"Talia promised just one more death as she hobbled closer to me.

"I gently pressed the precious prism down in the earth with a silent prayer of gratitude."

Hark's eyes turned glassy.

"To push myself up, I used my Focus against the ground. Rising up, my foot slid off the arrow." I touched the spot where a scar should have been.

"Talia used her Focus to transport the arrow that was lodged in her leg, into her hand. She lunged at me with it. My only defense was to use my full Focus to push against her, knocking the arrow out of her hand while she fell to the ground. She slammed down squarely on the remaining arrow that was sticking out of her shoulder. It snapped from the impact. I knew that didn't feel at all pleasant."

I looked at Hark and his face was stark white. He must have forgotten to breathe.

"But that didn't stop her. She came at me hard with her fists clenched, and again I pushed against her. She was so resilient and relentless.

"Talia's eyes started to twitch. I knew it was beginning.

"She figured out my arrows were laced with something. It was only a matter of time before the poison wore her out completely.

"There would be no victor tonight," I said, alluding to the fact that I too had been struck by my own poison arrow.

"Her eyes welled up. I saw her pain, sorrow…emotions I never thought I would see in a monster such as her. She was having trouble standing, and I had to stop my good nature from helping her up. She had such passion. I pulled out my shar-prism, hands shaking."

"I don't want to hear any more," Hark interrupted, holding up his trembling hand.

I felt ashamed for talking about such a gruesome time.

"I mean I do, but I…I just need a moment," Hark said.

I looked down at my own shadow, putting my hands to my hips. Even the darkness I cast didn't feel like my own.

"Everything comes out okay in the end, right? I mean, here you are…" Hark asked, looking for comfort.

"Nothing from that day is okay. But life gives reasons to forgive, or at least forget," I admitted.

"I just wish I could have done something. It's hard to just listen without being able to do anything," Hark said.

"This took place years before we even met. There is nothing you or anyone could have done. And if it didn't happen, you and Talia would have never met, and I wouldn't be here talking to you today," I explained.

"Are you talking about fate?"

"Every moment in our lives affects the next, good or bad. We cannot stop the river. So, we must embrace it and just float along with it."

"Okay, I'm ready," he stated, standing up strong.

"Never giving up, Talia Overloaded her Focus beyond mine. Her body couldn't withstand it for very long. Each second was stealing time off her life. She got a second wind, and sprang to action with a closed fist. She was determined to take me down. Her sadness turned back into hatred.

"The only course of action I had was to use my Focus to create a wall of air pushing against her. Making a stand, she inched closer and closer with her head down, tucked in the crook of her arm." While I explained, the wind kicked up, adding to my story as if it were listening.

"I began to step backwards, not quite matching her speed. As I moved, rocks and other objects that got in my Focus-stream flew at her…some hitting her, some not. My power was peaking.

"There was a red ribbon of blood blowing behind her from her open wounds. She was inches from reaching me. She pulled back, ready to push through my defense and end what she had started.

"It was that very moment where my power gave way. She had so much counter-force, that when my wall ended, she flew past me. Turning around, I saw Talia skewered on a sword."

Hark gasped.

"It must have fallen off the weapon rack when I crashed into it before. It was unanticipated fortune," I gulped. Remorse flooded my heart.

"She dropped to the ground and rolled facing me, the sword sticking out of her chest.

"Talia told me to collect…my…prize, barely getting the words out.

"Placing my hands over the sword's hilt, I closed my eyes, knowing that I just had to move it around some to end her suffering. She was already broken beyond repair. I could feel her breath, moving the sword up and down. She was so brave, such a work of art.

"Her death was a real gift. She wanted me to take it. I just couldn't." My weakness was pouring out.

"Every one of my protectors had volunteered for this mission, and they each met their end because of it. I had been responsible for their deaths, and I wasn't even strong enough to make their sacrifice valid. She had killed everyone and everything, and I couldn't end her," I confessed. I couldn't bear that judgment. To live with that guilt—I would have rather died.

"She told me how many stronger than I had failed in this task, while slipping away." I knew she felt like I had stolen her death out from under her and hadn't earned it for myself.

"She activated her Focus one more time to execute one final attack—her swan song."

"Unbelievable." Hark shook his head.

"I started to crawl backward, not knowing what to do next. I too felt the effects of my poison, as the shar-prism slipped from my clutch.

"I met her in the Feylin realm, her control string reaching for me as I scrambled," I said.

She had beaten me on all fronts, and I had to stop running from my inevitable demise. I had wanted her to end all the pain, release me from this twisted world.

"Then suddenly her control string changed course. Talia used the last of her strength to pull out the sword. She turned her control string toward the now gaping hole in her chest. Wrapping it around her faintly beating heart, she transported it to her hand, although it didn't reach her hand. Instead, she died instantly," I said, looking at the ground.

"Why would she do such a thing?" Hark asked.

"At that moment, we felt the same emotion—envy. I admired her strength and she admired my love.

"I couldn't let her end the way my fellow feylins did—alone. I quickly grabbed the empty prism as her Vigor was flowing toward it.

"Never had I seen anyone so determined in my life. She was everything I was not," I said softly. She cared far more about her own death than I cared about anything in this world.

"I threw the shar-prism, pushing it out of reach, and I embraced her. I accepted her into my soul, hoping my weakness would be diluted by her strength. As I spoke a single word, 'panacea,' we became one. I held her empty dress in my hands as ash fell from the sky like snow. Both our lives ended that day.

"You were the one who killed her?" Hark asked, astonished.

"She killed herself." *Even in your own mind, the moment is never the same when you recall it.*

"I thought this was her body and you were the dormant one."

"Everyone just assumed that. I allowed her to take control over the vessel."

"I don't get it. Why then…Uff," Hark said as he stumbled over a rock, upsetting it.

The glint of a shar-prism twinkled from the earth. I dropped to the ground and brushed away the dirt to reveal the accidental treasure. Frantically digging, I ignored the rocks and debris under my nails. Finally, I gently removed it from its grave, where it had sat for years. I held it delicately, like the precious treasure it was, and placed it against my cheek with both hands, feeling its energy. I recognized its force.

"Greetings, Norrow, my darling friend," I whispered. I moved the prism to my chest and looked up at Hark, who was towering above me. Hope filled my eyes as I held on to a piece of my past, like a child holding a toy.

"Even now, somewhere around here, in the Feylin realm, her heart beats. It will remain there until the end of days," I said.

"Wait, it's…"

"Yes, still beating."

Chapter Nine
Nothing Remains

"I cannot know your future…"

We walked on, using the old roads as our guide. Like a forgotten fossil, the path was covered by soil and debris.

"I'm hungry. Let's see what we can find," I said, searching the wooded area for anything to satiate my rumbling stomach. I looked under rocks and fallen branches. When I had just about given up, Hark handed me edible bark that he had foraged. It was tough, like over-cooked meat, but I ate it all the same.

"You're quite resourceful. It's much appreciated," I said, my mouth full of the stuff.

"Growing up with the Thral, I learned quite a few useless skills."

"It's not a useless skill. You just used it, and thus it becomes just a skill."

"To the Thral, fighting is the only useful skill."

"How did you end up with them?"

"My mother was one. She left me there when she died." He drew a breath as he spoke.

"I'm so sorry."

"She left me before I knew her, but I feel like I know her. Is that weird?" Hark closed his eyes. "Like, sometimes I can smell her, and it soothes me."

"It's not weird, it's sweet."

"How are we going to rescue Daleta? That's our next move, right?" he inquired.

"Oh, she's a spy. She'll be just fine," I said, struggling with my last bite.

"What are you talking about? She stuck out her neck for both of us. Well, Talia and me…you know what I mean."

"She has been feeding information to the Telandric for…well, always."

"That's some pretty important information to be withholding from me. Why didn't you say anything before?"

"I didn't know before."

"But you said…"

I quickly cut him off by raising my hand.

"*I* remember Daleta quite clearly, but Talia never met her and, therefore, has no history to remember her by."

"She's spying *on* us, or *for* us? I'm confused."

"That's a good question, actually. Where does your allegiance lie—Telandric or Lustarian?" I looked at him inquisitively, tipping my head slightly.

"Teland…I mean Lusta…is this some kind of test?" Hark asked, rubbing his face.

"Everything in life is a test of some kind, it just depends on who's grading it."

"So, who are you loyal to, Tal…I mean Capri?"

"We may seem different, but our goals are very much the same. My loyalty is to myself, and to my purpose."

"Which is what, exactly?" Hark asked abruptly.

"What it's always been—to save existence," I said, and continued on course, leaving Hark to mull over my words for a moment before he followed in my shadow's wake.

Before long, we reached the eastern lock. Blocking our path was a spectacular gorge so deep that lava flowed freely at the bottom.

A roaring river poured into it from the opposite side, creating a waterfall cascading into the depths. I marveled at the rumbling sound of steam being birthed as water met magma. The thick plumes blocked our view of the other side. A mammoth chain left over from the old world stretched across its sides and disappeared in the white haze. Each link was bigger than a grown man.

"Wow, so this is The Great Lock?" Hark asked.

"The only thing keeping the easterners apart is this wondrous spot," I said, reaching my palm out. I could feel the heat from here.

"How do we get across? Climb the chain?"

"That steam will burn your flesh right off your bones, but people still try sometimes. No one ever makes it, though."

"So, what do we do, then?" Hark asked, looking around for a clue.

"We wait."

I closed my eyes and started to hum a tune, but I was distracted by his presence. My mind wouldn't clear. I kept imagining myself with him, holding each other tight, smiling and sharing the day together. I knew they were solely her thoughts and not mine, though they felt so real.

"What are we waiting for?" Hark asked, getting more restless as time went on.

I tried to not let him disrupt the trance that I was not having. He smelled almost sweet, and images of us dancing flooded my mind. Just as he leaned in close, I was abruptly snapped back to reality. *Click, click, click.* The sound echoed in the chasm and shook the landscape.

"Let's go," I said, bouncing to my feet, my eyes adjusting to the light.

The sound of metal on metal got louder and faster, as the gigantic chain started to move in our direction.

"I don't get it," Hark admitted as we made our way toward the chain.

A dam fell in place, blocking the stream. Once the steam cleared, we could easily see a platform attached to the chain, moving our way.

"Do you have any scrap?" I asked patting myself down, even though I knew I had none.

"Nope, I wasn't exactly planning on leaving when we did."

"These things are not exactly free," I said, scrunching my nose while I thinking over our options.

We approached the docking station and spotted five men turning a wheel, which was connected to a gear. The gear linked into a huge cog, that in turn rolled the chain.

"I guess we need to sneak on," Hark said.

"Maybe not." I hesitantly walked up to the foreman, who was keeping rhythm for the five men doing the grunt work.

"Excuse me, sir. How much is safe passage?" I asked with a smile.

"40 scrap,"the dirt-riddled foreman said, between chants.

"But, sir, we have all our scrap on the other side. Can't something be done?"

"40 scrap," he repeated.

"How about this dagger? It's worth much more than 40."

"40 scrap," he scoffed.

The platform had nearly reached us with a couple of livestock and their owners ready to disembark.

"You see, I need to meet with my father, and he will pay you 80 scrap once we arrive."

"Collateral," the man insisted.

"This dagger has mystical powers. Does that change things?" I mustered up the cutest smile I could make in a moment's notice.

"Do I look like a blacksmith to you? How about him?" He pointed at Hark.

"We can find another way…" Hark chimed in.

"Deal," I interrupted.

Hark's mouth was still wide open as the foreman escorted me onto the platform.

I couldn't look at Hark. I hated letting down others, and if I saw an ounce of disappointment on his face, I knew I would change my mind.

"Capri?" Hark said, shocked by my decision.

I felt Talia's anger grow inside me. She didn't want to be apart from him. The irony was, that I never would have made such a callous decision if I hadn't learned from her.

I will come back for him, don't worry.

The chain started to move, pushing the platform out of reach of Hark. He took action and ran off the edge, leaping for the platform.

"Don't…you dare!" I yelled as he soared in the air, arms outstretched like a bird.

Hark descended. He would miss his mark, and was certainly going to meet his demise in the lava below.

I had to do something, he needed me to. I tapped into my feylin Focus and pushed the air under him, yielding enough lift to gain the few inches he was short.

His hands caught the edge, his nails digging into the wooden plank. Hark pulled himself to safety.

His expression of shock mirrored my own.

"I couldn't let you leave me," he panted.

The foreman stopped the chain and the floodgates opened, releasing water out of the dam. "No free rides," he bellowed.

"Run!" Hark said.

We both jumped off the platform and ran along the huge, rusted chain. Water started to drop into the gorge. The explosive sound of the steam billowed below. I was quite fond of my skin.

Don't get cooked! Don't get cooked!

The steam was approaching slowly, but not slow enough.

"We're not going to make it!" Hark yelled.

The chain started to melt the bottoms of Hark's shoes, making it hard for him to move.

My feet moved swiftly, trying to limit my contact with the ever-increasing heat from the chain.

I used my Focus to create a wind tunnel protecting us from the scorching mist. The tunnel was preventing me from breathing, and my feet still burned underneath. Hark gained speed and made it to the other side, but I couldn't keep up.

"Come on, you can make it." Hark turned to me eagerly.

His encouragement gave me hope, but it was not enough; my chest was tight. Looking to the sky, I broke off my attack and breathed in deeply. The searing vapor was rising fast. I tried to move, but I was frozen with fear. My eyes fixated on the cloud that would soon end me. I knew my next breath would burn my lungs on the inside. The moment you accept your own demise is the only moment you really feel alive.

A heavy cloak wrapped around me. Hark was using it to shield our bodies from the steam. Cheek to cheek, I felt his heart beating throughout his body and breathed in his smell.

The mist surrounded us now, the heat singeing our clothes. I returned to the Feylin realm, creating a wind tunnel yet again. Hark scooped me up and carried me to safety on the other side.

"You came back for me," I said quietly.

"I couldn't bear to see you go. You've gone through too much to end like this."

"So you're not angry with me?"

"Far from it."

He freed us from his cloak, and I felt her hunger inside me as she pined for his lips. I pushed it aside, waiting for him to make the next move.

"Thank you," he said, dropping his half-melted cloak on the ground.

"For what?"

"Helping me get rid of that tattered old thing."

I giggled softly, bringing myself to the support of my own legs. As we ran deep into the woods, I looked back at the lock.

This is where earth is made, and life begins.

~

The dew of the morning jolted me out of my tranquil slumber. I didn't want to wake, but feeling his body against mine made me happy I had. Touching him was like a stolen moment from within fantasies, and it was fleeting. It was nice feeling close to someone for a change.

No, no, no. What am I doing? This is exactly what she wants. This is bigger than her, bigger than us.

I came to my senses. Realizing those were Talia's feelings, I quickly shook them off.

The last thing I remembered from the previous night was asking Hark for his protection while I slept. I didn't like being out here, vulnerable to the unknown.

We had made our camp under the roots of a fallen tree. Bats hung upside down above us, undisturbed by our presence.

Carefully, I picked Hark's limp arm off my waist. It felt wonderful to be able to touch him without debilitating pain.

Hark started to stir as I released myself from his protective hold. His arm searched for me in my absence.

How innocent and kind he was, even in his sleep. I tried to imagine the dreams he was having—full of bright colors and jovial punchlines.

My breakfast was already laid out for me. Berries and other edibles were perfectly placed on some lush leaves. He was very thoughtful, and I saw what she saw in him.

My life was never intended for such simplistic pleasures. I had so much more expected of me. I couldn't relax. I had to find my purpose in the grand scheme, though it was tempting.

Sneaking away, I needed time to reflect. I cringed as the morning light pressed against my face like a weight.

What are we doing?

The dangers of the wild were too serious to ignore. Aligning with a faction was paramount to long-term survival. We were marked. None of the larger groups would have us without repercussions. Our past affiliates didn't act kindly toward deserters.

After escaping with Kay, the Telandric would induce a long-term mind warp leaving nothing left for individual thought. Whereas the Lustarians would require years of recanting for my failure in destroying the prisms with my life.

Still, my father had to be the best option. I just didn't know if he would want to see me after the last time we'd spoken.

In the distance, I heard the sound of chewing. Approaching surreptitiously, I spied a stocky man having his breakfast of cooked rabbit.

Noticing his Lustarian uniform, I opened my mind to her thoughts.

Baron, Talia projected, remembering him from her days with the Lustarians. **They must be looking for us.**

We could never return to the chancellor empty-handed, and it had been a long time without sending word. I had to warn Hark, and we had to leave. Before I could retreat, there was something else that caught my attention—another figure off in the distance, stalking Baron. This was no man…not anymore. It was a reaper.

Reapers were hairless, nailless, nameless monsters. We never knew where they came from, or who they were. They sought only to gain Order and power from slaughtering feylins, from any faction. Most times when a feylin had gone missing, they had fallen prey to these demons.

Where was his partner? Lustarians always traveled in pairs to avoid ambushes.

The reaper crawled on all fours, like a cat with his eye on his prize—Baron, who was a sitting duck. He pulled out his jagged, black sword as he positioned himself on a boulder above.

Baron was still chewing, food falling out of his mouth.

The reaper launched at his target, blade drawn.

Never would I sentence a reaper death to even my worst enemy, which Baron may have been at this very moment. I had to do something, and fast.

I went into the Feylin realm and used my push ability to create a shock wave that moved all the branches in its path aside until it reached the reaper, slamming him against the boulder.

This got both of their attention. It was bad. I froze, unable to figure out my next move. Two enemies glared at me menacingly. They both wanted to claim my head for their own.

Someone's hand grabbed my arm tightly. It was Hark. I noticed his wound had reopened and blood drenched his leg.

"What happened? Are you okay?" I asked.

"They're after us," he said, almost out of breath.

"Who is?"

Out of the clearing behind him bounded six Telandric. Half looked as though they were feylins. One had a floating weapon by his side, and he was not scared to use it. In fact, I got the impression that he was itching to. I put my restless arms up, not giving him the luxury.

"Where's the other one?" one Telandric barked.

"Gone," I claimed, guessing he was referring to Kay.

The guards positioned themselves around me and narrowed the gap between us.

"Where?" another one asked. Tension rose, as they gripped their weapons.

I recognized the Telandric twins, Nalo and Norum, as they slowly approached. These two had identical faces, but their bodies were different sizes. It was almost like they were physical opposites. Nalo was more lower-body strength, and Norum was bulky upper-body strength. This did make it much easier to tell them apart. They were ill tempered children when I last saw them, and now they were charged with my retrieval.

"Na, Nor, there's no need for violence. We need to hurry, I spotted a rea..."

They both raised their opposing hands in my direction, cutting me off. I could feel a Focus scanning my mind. A ringing drowned all other sound from my ears. I felt violated.

"'Conceived in smoke, born from ash'...it's her!" one of the twins declared, and the ringing faded, along with their power over me.

"In the ageless hour, when hope is hopeless, hair of the sun, pure of spirit shall soothe the endless rage of oblivion," I continued the sacred prophecy, which had been recited to me before I even knew the meaning of the words.

"...with only the love in her heart," they repeated from memory.

I had never thought I'd hear those words again, not from another, not from myself. It felt as if I was reading my own eulogy.

"She's been reborn. We must rejoice!" one shouted from the back of the lot, and the remaining repeated.

The final feylin met me with a bow and started to generate feylin energy. Time and space blended together inside a swirling vortex. A portal of some sort opened, and I could see the blurred image of Kanlett on the other side.

I couldn't go back. Last time I was there, they wanted to purge Talia from me. If I was to fulfill what the words commanded, I needed her strength now more than ever. I was better off living life than waiting for it to live me.

"Only enough room for me to take one, my lady," the feylin who created the portal instructed.

An old feeling washed over me, the sense of being revered and loved, and doing nothing except existing to earn such admiration. I was no better than the statue they constructed in my honor. It was time for me to earn their praises, on my own. I would never go back to Kanlett; it was no longer my home. Lord Bondal was no longer my leader, and it was clear that under his leadership I would never get to complete my role. I had to make my own way. They were right about one thing—I had been reborn.

Hark staggered his body in front of mine, facing the portal, like a human shield.

"You need help," I whispered, my words tickling his ear. This was no place to die.

"Let me protect you. And, Capri?"

"Yeah?" I hesitated, reaching out to hold him from behind.

"I like you better this way."

My hands returned to my side. It took a moment for his words to sink in and burrow under my skin. I couldn't hold back the dam any longer. I was fortunate that he wasn't able to see my face. I felt her sadness as my own. I knew I shouldn't feel guilty. She's the one who put me up to this task, to keep him close. Still, I felt horrible…like a no-good, lousy fake.

"Stand down, Hark. This isn't your path," the twins said in unison.

"Can't we control our own destinies?" Hark asked.

"All feylins are connected. It's fact, not fate," the feylin with the floating weapon said.

"Well, you seem a lot more concerned with Capri's 'fact' than she wants you to be," Hark countered.

"She's coming with us. That's the only fact you need be bothered with."

"I'm not letting you take her."

His blood wasn't letting up. He needed treatment soon.

Suddenly, the reaper soared out of the brush and sliced one of the non-feylins directly in half.

"Forgive me," I said under my breath. I felt bad for what I had to do, though I couldn't ponder the consequences.

I used the diversion to shove Hark with both my arms and my feylin Focus directly into the feylin who created the portal.

"Wait!" Hark said as they both disappeared, along with the portal.

Talia's soul burned me from the inside out. Her control string reached for him. I pulled it back like a lasso, trying to discipline her actions. I lost vision in my right eye—feeling her gazing at his empty footprints in the ground, where he had stood just moments ago.

I will make it all better, I promise.

They would take care of Hark. He had lost way too much blood; he would never be able to make it back alive. If anyone was going to die for my prophecy, it would be me.

Baron joined in the fray. It was a free-for-all. Swords clashed against armor and flesh. Feylin powers were erupting without concern. The non-lins were merely fodder, and going down fast.

Curling up in a ball and hiding behind a boulder was my only defense, shielding myself from harm's way. Blood misted through the air, as everyone tried to kill each other. I closed my eyes to block out all visions of violence.

"I want to build a world without fear," I whispered as I rocked back and forth. Holding on to the memories of all the lives that had been lost because of me.

Too many horrors would result from this fight. Baron, the Lustarian who was probably sent to execute me, could be probed by the Telandric mind scramblers, or devoured by the reaper. Neither of these options seemed like something I wanted to be a witness to. I had to flee before the victor came to claim me.

Trying to scale down the steep grade, I tripped over myself and slid down the hill. I heard a rustling behind me getting louder. Something was pursuing me. I moved faster, looking for a spot to hide.

"Stop," a voice announced from behind me.

I was frightened to face my future. Was it Baron? He definitely wouldn't be the worst outcome—the reaper was, hands down. The best option would have to be the Telandric, at least they wouldn't torture me.

Turning around, I matched the voice to the face. I suspected by his Lustarian attire that it was Baron's partner. He was dragging a large cage, covered in moss, with a huge ringlet on top. He unclasped the lock, and the door swung open with a clang. His scornful face didn't flinch. His only movement was a steady finger indicating for me to get inside. This was my end. He had proved to be faster than me. There was nowhere I could run. I knew he aimed to take me back to Cape Castle. The chancellor would see through me for sure, and he would finish what Talia had started.

I imagined myself overpowering the solider with physical prowess, like Talia would. My hands clenched. *What if he's someone's father or friend? He could be truly evil, but how can I know for sure?* Then the truth set in—I wasn't a fighter, I was a poltroon. I relaxed my fists. I couldn't lay a finger on him. Ashamed, I crawled inside and brought my knees to my chin. The metal door slammed shut behind me.

He blew on a sharp sounding whistle, and out of the sky swooped a large, winged beast. Its talons gripped the metal ring on top of my portable cell.

Before I knew it, we were hundreds of feet in the air. My failure streaked off my face and vanished in the wind. The endless blue sky stretched as far as my gaze could reach. Shivers ran down my spine, from either the cold or the beauty, I was uncertain. I pulled on the unwavering gate. *Stupid, stupid, stupid. I should have at least tried something.* I was a prisoner of my own doing, my own cowardice. I opened my mind.

The beast started to descend under a huge bridge left from our ancestry. I recognized the Horizon Bridge, named after its huge arc.

This is your moment.

"I'm scared."

You have to stand on your own.

"I don't know what to do. Help me."

The moment we passed directly under it, I went into the Feylin realm and Talia positioned her control string above one of the beast's wings, and mine in front of me. The next step was resting on my shoulders.

Everything is in place. You know what to do.

Using my push Focus to create a force of wind, then combining it with Talia's Focus to transport that wind above the beast's wing caused it to soar upward from the lift, spinning out of control.

The hideous creature screeched as it slammed head-first into the underbelly of the bridge. The cage also smashed against the hard steel. I ricocheted around inside as it broke into pieces. I felt in pieces too as I dropped out of the sky like a stone.

The dry, cracked ground was approaching fast as the world was spinning around me.

Fight.

I can't.

Images of murder bombarded my mind, one after another, after another. They wouldn't stop. Men, women, the elderly, these were her victims. They all had the same sadness stored in their eyes. It was that same look that stopped me from killing Talia, and it was that same look that had burdened her every time.

Make it stop.

Make me.

I activated both our control strings to increase the effect, combined them with my push Focus, aimed them at the ground, and let out all her rage as she visualized someone's flesh ripping off their face from my attack. It propelled me like a bird, saving us from the impact of the dry seabed below. My mind was clear, and the view was breathtaking.

I was finally free, but not from myself.

Chapter Ten
Alone at Last

"...yet I can cleanse myself from it..."

In my roseate journey, I found myself holding my fingers up to the sun, watching the light flicker between them. For some time, I had been wondering if I should pursue my father to the East, or head West to reunite with Hark in Kanlett. I embraced the sun's warmth as it was setting and decided to go East, as I knew the burning orb would return there sooner.

You have to go back for him, Talia's projection echoed in my head. Her melancholy was like an itch I couldn't get to. I felt her feelings, and when he was gone she felt like she'd lost everything.

Although, I found something new—my voice. "Not today," I said to the wind.

I was no longer going to listen to anyone other than myself, even if she was part of me now. I had no idea how many days or minutes I had left, and I had to live them all as if they were fleeting, because they were.

The long grass brushed my calves as I walked barefoot. I had never ventured outside alone before. I had always been accompanied by bodyguards, teachers, family or guides. I had never really figured things out for myself. Advisers would give me the best course of action for the situation, and I would follow their guidance. Currently, I had no plan of action, no scheduled mealtimes, no directions.

I felt a chill as the sun finally hid itself. The winds tried to tempt me to fly with them. Curiosity of the unknown got the better of me. Every rock, tree, and grain of sand was an untouched experience waiting to be discovered. This drove me to move at a slower pace. Not like someone needing to get somewhere, not someone fleeing from a reaper, or hiding from two groups rich with feylins. My stride was my own, and it was the first time I did something self-serving. It felt strangely natural. All I had to do was…nothing.

It was soon the dead of night. The scarce trees became more abundant as I got closer to the forest's mouth. Seeing less of the stars and crescent moon brought on a loneliness I hadn't expected. To remedy my mood, I distracted myself with a song, which I hummed over and over again. The unseen creatures in the forest grew quiet as I passed nosily. My humming turned to singing, which got louder and louder. Soon I found myself skipping around, belting out the tune. No logic could explain my euphoria. Maybe I was reacting to the lack of sleep, but I would have gladly traded all the nights of sleep to feel this way forever. It continued until fatigue set in.

I pressed my head against the cold earth and spoke directly into it, giving my praises. "Thank you for a wonderful day. I'm sorry I've enjoyed it so much. Please forgive or punish me for being so selfish."

I hope tomorrow is the same.

Saying goodnight to the day, I rested my tired eyes from every splendor they had observed.

An elderly woman met me inside a mushroom-filled cave. I couldn't contain my anxiety any longer, tapping my nails together frantically.

"When we spoke before, you told me there was a way to infiltrate them undetected," I said, cutting to the chase.

"You've changed your mind, then. What about what will be lost? It can never be regained, you know." The woman spoke eerily and slowly.

"That's no longer a concern," I said, tossing a fairly large sack of scrap at her feet.

"So I see." The woman strapped me to a table and bound my hands, legs and neck. She met me in the Feylin realm and surrounded my Vigor with her purple control string. Like a knife, her string carved at my soul, causing more emotional pain than I had ever felt.

I wanted it to stop; I begged her to. The price had been paid, and she would finish what was started. I screamed until my voice was lost.

She removed a piece of my Vigor attached to an emotion…to an idea that had been lost. It didn't take long before she was finished. I was drained and felt like a shell of a person, a husk.

"Be warned, your body may become confused if you ever experience such feelings again," she foretold. The woman erupted into thunderous laughter that consumed the cave, echoing over itself until fading into a deep hum.

I awoke panicked. I wiped the moisture off my face, feeling better knowing it was only a nightmare.

The morning light unveiled the scene where I had laid my head to rest. It was an ancient, overgrown garden. Past civilizations had used this area as farmland, but as humanity had neared extinction, no one was around to tend to the crops or feed the animals. The hourglass of time had weathered their homes, and the animals had moved on, but the crops thrived, free from their cages.

Time, what a beautiful mistress…so giving, yet so unforgiving.

I watched the sun grow as it illuminated everything with its watchful eye. "Good morning. You've done well," I congratulated it on its return.

I brushed the leaves off my dress. Who knew what insects and other critters had crawled all over me during my slumber. I felt stiff but amazingly rested. It was a lucky spot to awaken in, because my stomach was grumbling. I harvested the garden and had a delightful picnic of lettuce, wild onions and carrot tops.

On this bright, new day, I walked around until I happened upon a vast sea of vivid rocks. Each one was smooth and wore a unique design. They were so exquisite. Never had I seen anything so magical. Every stone was like a painting telling a different story. I spent half the day searching through the mass array of sizes and colors. I wanted to find the perfect keepsake—one that spoke directly to my heart, that would remind me of yesterday and the many yesterdays to come.

How fortunate was I to have found such a wondrous treasure in the uncharted wilds? I couldn't fathom how no one else had discovered such a huge gift out in the open like this. There were entire knolls made completely of these rocks. It was like a rainbow had exploded.

Digging deep within the rock-scape, I pulled out a crimson jewel, finally making my choice. Almost forgetting to check the other side (hours of searching had taught me that each of these special rocks had a completely different design on the opposing side), I flipped it over and saw an image of an eye looking back at me.

"Ahhh!" I dropped the stone, frightened.

That looked almost real.

"Maybe this isn't the one after all." I hesitated before reclaiming my rock, thinking of never turning it over again.

Reaching to throw it back into the endless sea of stones, curiosity got the better of me. Again, I turned it in my hand and studied it—closely this time. It wasn't a picture of an eye; it *was* an eye.

Disoriented, I let it slip through my fingers.

Everything became clear. The beauty I had seen just a moment ago suddenly became a nightmare. They were not just random designs, they were petrified people, all their pieces strewn all around me. Tripping over myself, I suddenly realized that they were touching me...everywhere. I was in too deep. Miles of rocks lay between me and the forest. Scrambling to my feet, I started to see other shapes within the rocks—hair, mouths, skin. It was sickening. This was no treasure, it was a tomb.

Running with my sorrow trailing behind, I slipped on a loose pile. A small avalanche tried to cover my legs. Swatting them away like insects, I noticed other things within their patterns, like signs, lights and even trees.

It wasn't *only* people who had turned to pebbles, it was a whole city. The huge expanse of the sea of stones showed how massive it must have been. Just another casualty from the old world.

Climbing on top of a pile, I found a large pebble that appeared to have once been a bench. It seemed safe for me to rest on, even in its afterlife. Folding my arms and legs into myself, I wanted to make certain that no other stones were touching me.

What did they do to deserve this? What did the world? Would the people of the future see our time in the same way, as a faded mystery?

Vicious thoughts poisoned my mind. They were scary, dreadful things that were beyond my own imagination, keeping me too terrified to close my eyes. I wasn't sure if they were from her, or my own dread manifested.

Thank you. I'm sorry. Please punish or forgive, I kept repeating to try and drown out my madness.

Hours had slipped away until the scent of smoke pierced my nostrils, though the clear sky gave no clues to its origin. I followed the smell, keeping my face upward, until I felt no more smooth rocks under my toes. It was getting stronger, though still without a trace.

Mustering the courage to bring my eyes to ground level, I soon found the answer, and it was frightening. It was a crimsonbeetle—a large, cat-sized insect that can set its shell ablaze for protection. These bugs were dangerous because if they felt that you posed a threat, they might ignite the whole forest.

Crimsonbeetles were carnivorous, and though I couldn't identify the exact species of the charred meat it feasted on, it sure smelled good.

I crept backwards, hoping it didn't want any dessert.

A huge column of fire burst out of its backside, about five feet in the air, as it made the most horrific sound.

I took off like a bat out of a cave. Finding a small pond, I dove in for protection. Dirt clouded the water around me as it lifted off of my skin. How ridiculous, it wasn't even pursuing me.

The pond was rich with fish, however. Since I was already wet, I tried to catch one using my hands. They were much too smart for that tactic. Finding a sharp stick didn't help me any. I attempted to use my Focus to push the stick quickly into the water like a harpoon, but my timing was off. My hesitation came from my remorse.

"I didn't want fish anyway," I tried to console myself.

On shore, the birds were also looking for a morsel—things like worms, seeds and fruit.

"Fruit! I love fruit."

I climbed a skinny tree trunk. My flailing feet caused the bark to flake off like day-old bread. It was much harder than I had anticipated. All the hungry birds fled the tree as the branches shook from my weight. After only climbing about eight feet, I gave up. Luckily, I found a golden fruit that must have fallen during my failure. It smelled sweet and sour, as my nostrils first sampled its flavor. When my teeth sank into it, I realized that it was far better than eating it peeled and sliced into artistic shapes, as I was accustomed.

"From now on, I shall only eat fruit from the ground," I joked to myself, ignoring proper etiquette as juice dribbled down my chin.

A green and white bird was also enticed by the sweet nectar. Never having had a chance to interact with any wild animals while being held up in Kanlett or Provi, I cautiously approached the feathered friend, who was occasionally snapping its beak with a "chuckoo." Such soft-looking feathers that would ruffle each time it inched closer to me. I extended my hand, gently offering it the last piece of my treat.

It reached its neck out and quickly pecked, missing the fruit and landing directly on my hand. The sting sent my arm reeling. The bird, now on edge, made itself appear twice its size—almost the same as my own. It hopped at me, lunging its beak.

I stepped out of the way, and it matched my movement with a long leap. Just then, I realized it was never interested in the fruit but rather the owner of it.

Using my Focus, I pushed it back. Unfortunately, my Focus merely lifted it, hovering it in place.

With heavy flapping, the menacing bird soared closer, pushing me backwards until my spine was met by stone. It was a dead end.

This had been its plan all along. Dried bones lay at my feet. I didn't want to be added to the collection.

It continued to snap at me, this time drawing some blood, pinching off a small taste of me. With each appetizer, its hunger incited a more vicious attack than the last.

My heart pounded slow but hard. All I could do was envision all the birds Talia had disposed of. Somehow they didn't fear me like they feared her.

Her Focus.

I closed my eyes and searched within myself. I felt my soul cross over to hers. Only then did I locate her transportation ability, as if it were waiting for me. The only problem was that I had no understanding of how to use it. In the Feylin realm, I moved her control string and chased the bird. It kept hopping out of the way, knowing what I was up to. I just couldn't catch it long enough to call upon her power. I hoped that threatening the thing would be enough to drive it away. Somehow, it knew I was not out for blood the same way it was out for mine.

I had to use her power and anticipate its movement. While activating her Focus, her thoughts became my own. She was judging me, and I was weak and pathetic.

With a loud crackle, I felt something in my grasp. I felt her power. Unfortunately, I only had a fist full of feathers.

I was ready to give up, when I felt her moving the control strings, adding my own to the mix. It was majestic to watch them move independently, meeting our enemy before it even got to its destination. Both strings wrapped around the creature. It was easy for her, as she taunted my lack of skill.

Now! she projected.

I called upon her transportation Focus, seeing the bird disappear from this world and appear in the feylin one. I ended the transport, bringing the beast to its new location within my arms. We had done it. I felt unstoppable. I opened my hands, hoping it was enough to scare the foe away.

It fell to the ground, lifeless.

I hesitantly gave it a quick shove. I knew for certain it was dead. The feeling of empowerment faded fast as my guilt festered. This was the second time I'd ever killed anything. Both times Talia had been responsible.

"It was him or me, him or me," I pleaded with myself, trying to find redemption.

Leaving a bloody trail behind, I hobbled across the grassy plateau. Tucked among some wildflowers, I spotted a huge fur pile wrapped around itself.

Upon hearing my approach, it uncurled and let out a huge yawn. Straight away, the creature slowly approached me. It had fur like a wolf, but tusks like a boar.

Looking soft, I wanted to pet it, but I remembered the incident with the bird and refrained. I knew I was trespassing, interrupting its slumber. Desperately rummaging deep inside my pack, I found the hilt of Talia's dagger and held it up with a shaking hand.

Before I could get my wits about me, the beast pounced on me, biting deep into my shoulder. Somehow my dagger didn't connect with any part of the thing.

This is a sad way to go, as lunch, I thought to myself.

Fight, you fool! I heard her ringing in my head.

I struggled with the beast, but my muscles wouldn't yield me the strength I needed to overwhelm it. All I could do was try to avoid another bite.

Talia was summoning me in the other realm. I was reluctant to look, but I had no other option.

Time slowed down as I entered the Feylin realm. I saw my body's essence still wrestling with the hungry beast.

Talia's memories were wound up inside a sphere, images wrapping around as they repeated. Opening myself to them, I witnessed a piece of her life. In a flash, the experience was revealed.

There was a young Talia, dirty and disheveled; she was maybe ten years old. Close behind burst a slob of a man, who appeared like a giant from her perspective. He swung at her, holding nothing back. She kept on counting—one, two, three...one, two, three...over and over again, while managing to avoid his hits, one after another.

Why would someone so big be willing to hurt someone so small?

She baited him into chasing her up to a rock, still counting. Suddenly she stopped and he connected with her body, along with the rock behind her. He swung so hard that the impact shattered the bones in his wrist.

I realized that she was timing his attacks and let him hit her on purpose, using his own strength against him. One of her eyes was closed and bulging from the impact, but her open eye had enough hatred to fuel one hundred eyes.

She unleashed the pain that she had received, tenfold, as she straddled him. Talia felt nothing—not sadness, not happiness—not for him, not for herself.

I couldn't watch any longer. I returned to my match with the beast. Like Talia, I started to count and search for a pattern.

One, two, three, four. One, two, three, four. That's it.

I found what I was looking for—what she wanted me to find. I counted again, and this time on "four," I plunged the dagger into the creature's sharp mouth. It bit down on the blade, hissed and jumped off my scratched body, tearing my dress. I stood up ready for more.

It was then that I saw something unbelievable, its body started to shine as the beast entered the Feylin realm. This was a beast of legend, armed with its own Feylin ability. Never had I seen such a thing.

Joining it in the Feylin realm, I watched it use its animal Focus to enlarge its tusks to twice their size. Its neck had trouble supporting such an arsenal.

It came for me, hard.

I sidestepped, using my push Focus to give me a boost. The beast missed and crashed into a low shrub. I lost my grip on the dagger, leaving it just out of my reach.

My instincts told me to retreat, but the beast switched its Focus to enlarge my foot, stopping me dead in my tracks. The pressure pounded as it bulged, feeling as though it would burst.

Again the beast pounced.

"No!" I covered my head.

I entered the Feylin realm and used Talia's control string to wrap around her dagger. It was drawn to it, like an old friend. I felt the beast's claws dig into both sides of my head. Remembering how she had felt as a child, I transported the hilt of the dagger to my teeth. The beast's head was almost completely around mine when the dagger appeared and stabbed the roof of its mouth. I quickly called upon my Focus to push the dagger deeper into the creature's skull until it exploded out the other end, and I lost it to the sky.

I opened my eyes, looking out through the hole I had created and pushed the heavy corpse off me.

That's when it happened—the beast's Vigor started to reach for me.

Clawing at the ground, I tried to flee. Its body had already dematerialized. I had never thought a beast could obtain such power, nor did I conceive of the danger in killing one. I didn't want to gain Order, I couldn't, not again.

The beast's Vigor pulled itself into me. Having no choice, I absorbed it all until there was nothing left. Its power coursing through my veins, it was part of my soul now. I felt different, changed—nothing like I had when I merged with Talia. This was new, and I didn't like it one bit.

My shoulder was tender. In just a short time, it had started to fester and ooze. The damp leaves I dressed it with were not helping with the infection. I gathered some dirt to try and dry the wound.

You're going to make it worse.

"I'm trying my best. What are you doing?" I reasoned with myself. I felt her sharing another moment from her past in the Feylin realm, but I chose to ignore it.

Stop being so arrogant and learn something for a change.

"Insults are not going to get you anywhere with me."

My body was moist with sweat. The pain in my stomach made me hunch as I buckled over. Laying myself down to rest, I started to close my eyes. "It's okay. You're okay."

No, we're not. That bird was poisonous.

"I...don't...die, until...I, alone, will it..." I gave up on giving up. I fought through the excruciating pain, looking for a solution.

I found a rock and used my second wind to chip away at it until a point was formed. Using the make-shift tool, I dug at each of the small incisions the bird had made, opening the wounds further. I squeezed each one, bloodletting the poison out. With each drop that left my body, I felt only slightly better. I knew I had to rid myself of as much as I could, without losing it all.

My eyes were ready to give in to the pain and anguish I was feeling. How I wanted to cry.

No more, never again will I let the world break me. I shed for no one, as of this moment," I vowed, wiping my eyes.

I looked outward, taking a moment to enjoy my surroundings. Flowers blew in the breeze, their dulcet fragrance conditioning the air.

I squeezed the last cut the poisonous bird had made, and nothing came out. Longing to return to the earth, I knew that it was time. I made it to the sole tree perched on the landscape. As I collapsed under the oak's great canopy, I closed my eyes—leaving my being in the hands of the Gods, if they were present. Time blended together, as insanity overtook reality.

~

As the sun broke through the night, the day beckoned me to live. I had no idea how many hours or days I'd been out. My face twitched when I felt a drop of liquid hit my cheek. The drips increased exponentially from nature's alarm.

"I am alive!" I outstretched my arms, embracing the rainfall. "Thanks, old boy." I kissed the bark of my protector and scooped up some dry dirt from where I had rested.

I walked to the edge of the cliff overlooking the ocean below. The rain had cleared, and it was captivating.

"We must save it from ourselves." I held the dirt tight within my grasp. I felt its energy beating with my pulse.

"When I too return to the earth, I only hope someone will find my beauty worth saving." Letting the dirt slip through my fingers, I offered it a new adventure.

"Thank you for gracing me with life. I'm sorry for needing your help. Please forgive or punish me, for I might need again. Tomorrow I will echo these words until I have none left to say, and only then will you know I'm free."

I observed my wounds, and they were all scabbed over. Then my stomach made a thunderous eruption, screaming from starvation.

Without thinking, I found myself eating flowers and bugs in the wet meadow. The taste was masked by my desire to survive.

Drudging through the muddy landscape was slippery at best and horrifyingly dangerous at worst. My body was weighed down by caked-on soil.

I managed to walk through the day without anything eventful happening. It was quiet, and I liked it that way.

Unable to find any source of food, I climbed a large spiky tree and rested upon a sturdy crook. I felt safe, even though I knew I wasn't.

Every time I closed my eyes, I was haunted with wicked thoughts that kept me awake. The hours wasted away as I got more and more frightened of my surroundings, and of myself. I was getting closer to my past, to what I had left behind.

I began singing a song that the siren mage used to sing to me to keep me calm. It was soothing. Its melody drowned out the horror within myself. Finally I dosed off, having survived one more day.

~

Climbing down the tree's spikes, I found the ground again. I wiped the morning dew off my face, which just smeared the cracked mud from the prior day.

I got the sense that I was being followed. I decided to give it somewhat of a chase. As I started to dart over fallen trees and duck under low-hanging branches, the sound magnified as it tried to keep up. It was metal of some kind. I abruptly skidded to a stop, turning my body to face my challenger. The forest was dead quiet, except for a small tapping sound. I could tell it was close. I searched around as it continued. Standing perfectly still, I held my breath. That is when I felt its motion. *Tap, tap, tap.* It was on me. No, it was in me.

I quickly patted myself down and I found the very spot it resonated, tapping against my ribs. The background slowly came into focus as I saw that hundreds of small bearings were now surrounding me. I used my Focus in two quick bursts to create a hole in the perimeter.

Hordox, he found me.

My adrenalin empowered my feet to move. The bearings were in pursuit, trying to cut me off. They wanted their friend that I had swallowed outside Kanlett. The bearings came at me seconds apart, and I avoided each one with the help of both Focuses. Invigorated by my success, I felt as though I could push them away forever. That is until I didn't. One slammed into my spine from behind. I felt my bones go out of place. It hurt much more than I had expected.

"I can't take much more of this," I said, leaning on my knees.

You don't know pain, Talia projected.

Entering the Feylin realm I saw another memory of Talia awaiting me. I conceded and took it in.

Talia was young and had recently lost her mother. Her Uncle Porum riffled through papers on his hand-crafted workbench.

Her attention was drawn toward the window. The sound of children laughing called to her as they enjoyed the first snowfall of the season.

"I have no need for children," Porum muttered, a grim look upon him. "What can you do? Can you sew, or cook, or even tend the fields? Of course not. My sister was never good at building character."

Talia stood there looking at him, without emotion.

"See, you cannot even hold a conversation with a family member. Your only family, might I add."

I felt how frightened of him she was. Her mother had forbade anyone to speak of Uncle Porum. Just the thought of him brought tears to her mother's eyes. Talia wondered what was so despicable. He seemed normal enough.

Porum was interrupted by a small man with a medium build. He smelled like urine and his clothes were riddled with holes.

"Excuse me Mr. Porum, I have that information you wanted regarding…you know," the man said, motioning in her direction.

"Oh, just spill it already. She'll know soon enough."

"Uh, as you wish. The slavers offered 75 scrap for the girl, and the butcher will give 180 scrap for her meat."

A look of horror came over her face.

"See, girl, you're worth more dead than alive. This is what happens when you don't have any skills. You just suck in every *able* person's air and eat their meals. A waste of resources that someone like me will never get back. I'm doing the world a favor," Porum said, pulling at his facial hair.

"So, where should I take her?"

"Butcher," Porum said pointedly.

"No!" Talia screamed as the smaller man tried to grab her. She was quick and slipped through his fingers like a fish.

"See, even now you're giving me a headache."

Now both men were low with arms outstretched trying to corner her. They pounced, and the assistant grabbed her leg. Talia bit a mouthful of his arm. Blood oozed out from in between her teeth.

"Ahhhhh, you brat!" he screamed.

She made a break for the exit. Mr. Porum grabbed hold of the rug beneath her feet, pulling it hard. She flew into the wall head first, stunned, missing her escape.

"Now I'll have to have that wall cleaned. You're really proving my point for me," Porum lectured, placing a shackle upon her right hand.

He led her to the back of the butcher's shop. She stood next to the garbage. The smell of rotting meat attracted flies. The butcher was a greasy, fat man who would probably be worth much more than 180 scrap, were he in Talia's position. Their conversation blurred with the sound of a blade slicing through flesh from inside the shop. Porum collected his payment for her meat.

She pulled on the shackle, but the iron was too strong to bend. She smashed it against a stone wall until her wrist started to bleed, but it would not break.

Porum looked down at her and shook his head as he tightened his grip on the chain's leash.

Talia had one final idea. She pulled her arm as hard as she could. The shackle started to slice her skin. The cut from her wrist started to spread. She used her leg to gain leverage and pushed with all her might, blocking out everything except her task. Her skin started to peel back from her wrist.

"What do you think you're doing?" Porum asked.

Her skin flapped over her fingers as her hand slipped out of the shackle in a bloody mess.

"Get back here, you waste of space!"

Talia ran, leaving a trail of red and her only family behind.

Finally catching her breath outside of a local inn, she took this moment to roll the skin that had been de-gloved, to its rightful place. Her subcutaneous tissue was soaked in blood. The skin wasn't attaching. It just flopped there as though it was no longer part of her.

"Please, go back," she begged.

A stranger, noticing her injury, approached. "Girl, are you okay?"

This prompted her to flee inside the inn. She raced directly toward the roaring fireplace. Spitting on her forearm, she shoved her appendage into the flame, incinerating the skin and fusing it back to her hand. I felt her pain as she burned herself. The smell was nauseating.

Screaming, Talia ran outside and shoved her singed arm into a mound of snow. Steam flew into her face.

Jolted out of the vision, I was stunned. Looking at my flawless arm, I thought about how much I had taken for granted. How resilient she was, how much abuse she could endure.

Finding myself at the edge of a cliff, I watched the stream crash as it descended upon the jagged rocks below. I looked over the edge and started to calculate different outcomes, as she had once done. Her mundane ability was within me.

"Is this what you want?" I yelled. I felt him inside me, moving around, wanting to reconnect with the pack.

The large mass stopped in its tracks.

"Come and get it!" My anger shut off my mind.

The huge swarm rolled at me, accepting my request. I entered the Feylin realm and was greeted by a torrent of images. I saw an influx of Talia's thoughts as she shared her life with me, every kill, every fight. They came in fast and hard, and I was unable to process each event. Her past was excruciating to witness. So much pain, so much sadness. I wanted it to stop. Why wouldn't it stop?

"AHHHHHHHHHHHHHHH!" I jumped off the cliff just to end her life, as I should have done long ago.

The metallic balls followed me over and made horrible high-pitch sounds as they ricocheted off the sharp rocks.

Nearing the end of my leap, I started to understand her more. She never had a choice. She always did the right thing, in her mind, no matter how much it hurt, no matter the cost.

It was then that I started to regret what I had done to her…no, to us…no, no, to me. My thoughts were cloudy and hard to understand.

I locked my hands together, called upon both our control strings and used my ability to push against the water. Liquid displaced, rippling out of my way, splashing my face and everything else in its path. It was not enough. I wasn't going to make it. Tapping into my life force, I borrowed energy from my future by Overloading my Focus past its potential. I knew that each second would shred time off my life expectancy. Water, rocks and sand started to part ways. It was still not enough.

Who wants to survive indefinitely?

I called upon even more of my life expectancy, feeling my body wither. Like a lost feather, I glided to the bottom of the waterless lake bed, and slowly made my way to the edge, unharmed. Rocks, water, fish and everything else came crashing down in a huge splash once I stopped my Focus.

The bearings saw this opportunity to try and cover me completely.

"Never." Creating a bubble around me with my push energy, I forced the balls to launch in different directions, smashing into trees, animals and anything else in their way.

"That was one year," I said, reflecting on what I had sacrificed.

Down the path, the stream opened up into a loud rapid of churning water. I found a shallow lagoon directly under a roaring waterfall. Under the damp, musky underbelly of the fall, I washed all the mud, sweat and dried blood away. The chill of the water was exhilarating as it caressed my hair. Goosebumps grew on the surface of my skin. My dress clung tightly to my figure, and I noticed how skinny I'd become in such a short amount of time.

Further down the stream, I spied a fish hiding in a small cave. Using Talia's Focus, it was in my hand in an instant. Without thinking, I sunk my teeth into it while it was still flapping its fins. I felt nothing for it.

Chapter Eleven
Empty Past

"...for it is time for us to part..."

While knee-deep in the marshlands, I knew that I was getting close. Everything was different but also familiar. I reflected on what I had abandoned, wondering if leaving was the biggest mistake of my life.

Soon, I came across a pond, rich with exotic water lilies. Each one was glorious—deep purple ones, light pink ones, stark white ones. It was nature's bouquet.

Something large was emerging from the water. It was a larva of some kind, around the size of a dog. Mesmerized, I watched the water fall off its body as it prepared for its new life. Once its outer hull hardened, it stood still as a statue. I heard a cracking sound, which got louder until a hole burst open.

Something started to squeeze out of the hole. I felt its struggle as it was forced to change despite the pain. It had outgrown its former life, shedding the shell that now stood there lifelessly, yet still intact.

Eight translucent wings stretched out for the first time and slowly flapped.

I approached the insect, its wings too wet to fly away and at my mercy. Its many eyes looked at me, as if I were something equally as intriguing.

Placing my hand on its exoskeleton, I felt how soft it was. I caressed it, feeling its excitement for the transformation from water to air. Enthralled, I almost forgot to breathe. I related to its evolution. I too had to look forward, no matter the cost, because you can never go back at the incipient stage. It was time I faced the thing I feared above all else.

The insect's wings were dry and ready to take flight for the first time, and so was I. My hair blew as it flapped its wings violently.

"This is the beginning," I cried.

Its feet started to lift off the ground as I dove into the pond. I too had something I had to do, something I had been scared to pursue. Pushing my body with each stroke, I kicked and fought through the lily pads, knowing if I looked back even for an instant I would change my mind. In that moment, I was lifted above myself long enough to gain insight.

I reached the other side as the insect soared overhead, inspiring my feet to take flight.

My memories were guiding me home. I felt as though it were my birthday, excited to discover what was waiting for me underneath the wrapping paper. I had not traveled here since I was six years old. That's when they had discovered my purpose and I was given a life in the higher class. I avoided this place for too long, and a visit was well overdue.

Off in the distance stood the small bungalow where I was born. Tattered and aged, obviously no one had cared for it for some time. Everything appeared smaller than I had remembered. I caught my breath for a moment, putting on a brave face. I hadn't seen him since that day, and my guilt started to set in.

I walked down the path, across the garden filled with crispy, old vegetables and made my way to the front door. It flew open and fell off of its hinges. Out of the darkness of the doorway emerged an arrowhead.

"If you don't want any trouble, I suggest you turn around right quick," the scratchy voice snapped.

"It's me, daddy."

He took a single step forward into the light. His face was rife with wrinkles, his hair gray and stringy. Wearing his beloved chain-mail coif, I knew it was him. His eyes narrowed as he pulled back on the bow even more.

I steadied my breath.

"My daughter is dead. Which means…"

He released the arrow and it soared at me. Without thinking, my instincts brought me into the Feylin realm. I used a control string to push the arrow off course just as it began to pierce my skin. A single drop of blood marred my forehead.

That was much too close. I had to reason with him before my luck ran out.

"Murdering wretch, how I have waited for this day!"

I could see his pain as he scrambled to load another round into his special bow, which was capable of firing three shots simultaneously.

"Stop!" I surrendered, knowing I couldn't avoid the next assault. "Pleasant girl, golden curl. You made my heart with your smile. Please return it to me for a while," I recited the limerick he used to say to me before bedtime.

He hesitated and dropped the bow slightly. "Capri? No, no, she's dead. You're tricking me," he said, raising it again with an unsteady hand.

"It's me. I defeated her, The Plague, though she still plagues me," I admitted, shielding my face from him.

He closed one eye and leaned in for a closer look. His expression changed as he mumbled to himself.

"It is you!" He dropped his weapon and scooped me up in his arms, spinning me around. It felt the same as it always had—comforting. Our cheeks were pressed as he hummed the tune of the "Pleasant Girl" song.

He placed his hands on my face and looked at me hopelessly.

"I can't see you in there."

"I'm not your little girl anymore."

"You can be!" He pulled me by the hand, dragging me into the cottage which was a pack-rat's haven. He threw his coif into a pile of junk in the corner. "It goes there," he said.

Bottles, scrolls, clothes, you name it, were all stacked in unsteady piles in every room of the cottage. Books fell and junk piles crashed, as he ran through like a whirlwind looking for something.

I opened the dark curtains to let light in, coughing from the plume of dust that emerged. How could anyone live in such squalor? His body was frail and just as uncared for as the rest of his belongings.

"Where is it?! It must be here!" Practically foaming at the mouth, he tore the whole place apart.

I couldn't help but think that it wasn't the only thing he had lost. "Can we just take a moment?" I covered my nose from a grotesque aroma as he uncovered something nasty.

"I've wasted too much time already. Haven't I?" His anger was building as he started smashing the obstacles in his way. He was panting. This must have been the most he'd moved in a while.

"What are you looking for? Maybe I can help."

"Her necklace, damn it," he said.

I knew to whom he was referring—his wife, and my mother. I bit my lip, dreading giving him the answer he was looking for.

"She was wearing it the last time we saw her," I said, wincing, already regretting my words.

He stopped in his tracks, searching his mind. His eyes lit up.

"So she was," he said as he slumped back into his chair, looking despondent while touching under his eyes. "I feel them inside. Why won't they come? I want to feel them come, to feel them on my face," he spoke to the corner as if there were a person standing next to him. He licked his finger and wiped his spit under his eye. It was so hard to witness him in this state.

I had to get out of there. I went outside, fetched some fresh water and then searched his cupboards for anything not yet spoiled. There wasn't much of a selection between the moldy bread and rotting fruit. After picking the bugs out, I made him a lunch of soggy grains which were flavorless, but at least edible.

Handing him his bowl, I placed my hand on his arm and he flinched.

"Thank you, Lizah," his voice cracked.

I shuttered at his mistake. I hadn't heard her name since I was a child. *How can I correct him—tell him that I'm the daughter who abandoned him, not his wife who passed away?*

"I live for your will," I blurted out, just as she always had. It was eerie how easily I fell into that role for him, to keep up the ruse.

He smiled warmly, and for a second he almost looked happy. Suddenly his eyes sank deeper into his face as he started to growl.

"Daddy?"

He was now showing his teeth.

"Hey!" I shouted, clapping my hands. This snapped him out of it, and he looked at me as if nothing had happened.

"I just wanted to see you. I never saw you grow. You look so different."

I couldn't think of anything to say cheer him up, so I answered him with a smile.

"There it is. There's my heart again."

After he finished the grains, color returned to his face.

I found a quiet spot on the stoop outside to eat my own portion. It was hard coming here, to a life I forgot living—a past that felt like it never existed. It felt like a dream from someone else's slumber. The only proof I had was that he remembered it too.

"Why are you here? I can't take care of you. I can barely take care of myself anymore," he said from the doorway behind me.

"I need your help, daddy."

"Don't call me that, you're grown now."

"That's the only thing I've ever called you."

"Vance—that's what I tell other strangers to call me. You can call me Vance."

"Okay, Vance," I said, hiding my emotions in my grains.

"If you are indeed Capri, you're also that fiend. Do you realize that? Do you realize that all her bloodshed is on your hands now?"

"I don't feel like that person."

"Why should I help you and not just end you both. You should have never come back. You're breaking me, and the worst part is, I thought I was already completely broken to begin with."

I turned around to see the sickness return to his eyes. He was holding a weapon. It had a trigger, a barrel, and was used to discharge small metal projectiles. It was a forbidden device from the ancient times. His hand trembled on the switch, making his nervousness louder as the hammer tickled the pin.

"What are you aiming to do, da…Vance?"

"Like this relic, you have no place in this world. You took her from me."

"You cannot turn off your feelings. This will only make things worse." I had never thought of the consequences of my past, only my own selfishness. I wished I could take it back, to mend his heart, start over from the moment I left his loving arms and started my life as a prophetess. Chasing the past was a lie that could never become true.

"I missed you terribly." He fumbled with his words.

"I'm sorry for the pain I caused you. I should have come home…It's not that I didn't have the opportunity. Please accept my apology," I pleaded.

"You cannot ask me to. I won't. I want to hurt you…but I can't."

He quickly turned the device to his own head and pressed the trigger down completely. The old machine clicked and jammed as he winced, awaiting his own demise. Smoke billowed as something ignited internally.

I used the transport Focus to disarm my father and toss the weapon into a bush.

"I'm miserable. I can't even do that right." He broke down on the ground, sobbing, but still no tears came.

Seeing him act so pathetic made Talia boil inside me. I picked him up by his clothes and slammed him against the outside wall of the cottage. Paint shattered everywhere.

"I need your help. So stop blubbering like a complete idiot. I'm not going to die so that your pitiful self can just waste away," I screamed. Her words flowed through me like venom.

He instantly snapped out of his daze. "What is it that you need exactly?" He gulped, as his voice softened.

I loosened my grip, returning him to his feet. "Your research on the shar-prisms, what was it?" His specialty used to be enchanting items with feylin powers, until the Telandric had bigger plans for him. He used to be called The Craftman.

"I haven't done any work like that for years."

"Yes, but Bondal has been continuing your research, and he made a living prism from it."

"Impossible! It would be soulless and non-responsive."

I thought about Kay and the fact that he had a Focus power while inside the jail cell, even before the incident with Syntox.

"Unless…they sacrificed a feylin to pass along its Vigor," I revealed the key he had overlooked.

"Of course! Why didn't I see that before?" He smashed his fist in his palm.

"It was at least a second Order feylin."

Vance started sizing me up and down inquisitively. "Where is it hidden—the core?"

"It's not me," I said, slapping his hand away as he tugged at my clothes.

"Where is it, then?"

"Dead. I saw him get ripped apart limb from limb."

If a tiny shar-prism could absorb the essence of a feylin, I could only image what the core could do.

"The name is misleading. A living prism cannot really die, because it's not really alive. Anyway, if they made one, they can make more…providing they have another core." Vance ran back inside and rummaged though papers. "Did you get its core?"

I reluctantly followed him inside. "No," I sighed.

"The beauty of the living-prism project is that without a soul of its own, it can absorb feylin power endlessly."

"Why would you make such a weapon?"

"It wasn't supposed to be a weapon. It was supposed to be a blessing. I wanted to make something kind, something that could save us all and rid you from the burden."

"I don't think Bondal had the same vision as you."

"I had ideas—wonderful theories, really—to restore the world and cure the feylins. But they said I was crazy, too crazy to be allowed to finish my own work. But using it as a weapon? Who's crazy now?" He paced around talking to himself in a strange voice.

"In the wrong hands, how dangerous is this weapon?" I hesitated.

"Life ending—for everyone and everything. You know where it is though, don't you?"

Harvesters were probably one of the worst groups I could think of having possession of the core. The only saving grace was that I didn't think they had the brain capacity to know what to do with it.

"I'm glad that you're helping me," I said with a smile.

"We're helping each other." His eyes quickly narrowed. "What would have happened if I said no," he grumbled.

"I..."

"Oh look, they're back," he said, noticing some birds flying into a nest inside an old shoe, as if nothing just happened.

The rest of the night was filled with small talk. Even though he was more eccentric than I was used to, just being near him made me feel like a child again. It was like falling back into old habits you long since forgot. He would occasionally have a coughing fit, which amplified my concern for the state in which he was living.

We turned in early for the night, and he led me to my old room which was almost completely filled with junk. He moved the piles that were hiding the bed and relocated them to the kitchen, rendering it utterly useless.

I looked out the window and said my prayer, "Thank you for letting me see him again. I'm sorry I caused him so much sorrow. Please forgive or punish me for what I must do." I laid my head down.

I imagined a world without factions—just me and Hark, alone. It felt so real, and I was so happy. We watched the sun, from rise to set, but something was different. The summery light suddenly turned blue. It burned our eyes. We turned to face each other, repeating the same couple of words to try to comfort the other, but the silence was louder and muted our tender feelings. Our faces began melting into butterflies. I turned toward our home just as it transformed into liquid. I reached out for Hark, and my hand detached from my body. No matter how much we cared for each other, it wasn't enough. It never would be.

I awoke drenched in sweat, my heart fluttering. It was morning and the sun filled the room. For a brief moment I wondered if Hark was having the same dream…wherever he was.

Vance stood at the foot of my bed frame looking down on me. He was covered in dirt. I jumped out of bed, disturbed by his unsettling smile.

"What happened? What did you do?"

"I found it!" Vance gleamed with excitement.

He held up the medallion my mother used to wear. I couldn't remember what her face looked like, but I remembered that necklace clearly. She never took it off. It seemed as if it were part of her.

"Where did you find it?"

"She kept it safe for me, all these years, and now she gave it back."

I looked at his filthy clothes and winced at the thought of what he had just done.

"Please tell me you didn't."

"She was still beautiful, even now. This wondrous charm kept her safe. But it didn't like me taking it, oh no. It punished me for removing it. She crumbled before my eyes."

I turned away from him, horrified. "Why would you do it, Vance?"

"For you. Preserve yourself in its magic."

"Never!" I pushed his hand away from me.

"But you must."

"No, I must not!" I stormed outside.

"It will cure you."

I stopped and faced him. There was nothing to be cured. What was he talking about? "Say again?" I asked.

"I enchanted it with the ability to mute a feylin's power."

"Why would you make such a thing, and why was mother wearing it?"

"She had a similar problem to yours, but I found a solution. Yes, I did."

"Are you saying she was a feylin?"

"Yes, but she was out of control. It was some of my early work. The necklace gave her a life again."

"That's a shackle—hindering her from herself." It eluded me why anyone would want to silence their feylin gift.

"You need to wear it to get close enough to retrieve more core prisms."

"I'm not going back! You don't know what they tried to do to me. What they would do to me if they knew what you're planning."

"They won't do a thing if you wear this charm, I promise."

I wished he had left that jewelry buried like it belonged. Digging up the past only uproots feelings that were long put to rest.

"This power isn't yours to manipulate. Stifling it disrupts the balance of life. It's unnatural."

"We all must make sacrifices for a greater cause. We need that core to finish what I've started!"

He sounded like the chancellor. I should have ended those prisms when I had the chance, but I wasn't ready to die, not yet. I got the feeling that if I didn't accept his gift he would put it on me himself. I reached out for the necklace.

He placed it gently in my hand, and I tucked it into my pack.

"May I ask one last favor of you?"

"If you put it on, I will grant you the world."

I remembered the hours, sometimes days, my father used to spend enchanting weapons, armor and artifacts with the feylin powers trapped inside prisms. I pulled out the shar-prism filled with the soul of Norrow.

"This was my dear friend. He gave his life protecting me. I would like him to protect me once more," I said, holding the prism outward.

"I live for your will," he said.

I saw the sparkle in his eyes that he had once had. It is amazing what having a purpose can do for a person, and how lacking one can deteriorate one's essence.

Vance took the prism and went into his workspace. I heard a tremendous ruckus, which seemed almost endless. Finally he emerged, sweat soaking his clothes. He presented me with a golden arrow tucked inside my childhood quiver. He handed it to me with the utmost care.

I slid the arrow out and touched the prism embedded just below the arrowhead. I could feel Norrow's essence embedded deep within the projectile.

"It's a one-time deal. Stay clear of it, okay?"

"Thank you, I will." I gave it a light squeeze and put it back inside my quiver.

"Leave this place and never look back. Waiting has kept me alive all these long years. My wait is over."

I turned and started to walk away from my former life. It was hard to leave him behind. I had to push myself with every step.

"Aren't you forgetting something?" Vance stopped me.

I reached into my pack and pulled out my mother's necklace. It still smelled like her perfume. I was terrified of what it might do to me, but I knew it was the price I had to pay for the arrow. My throat felt tight, I wondered if its effects would be irreversible.

Bowing my head, I felt the cold metal against my neck. My body rejected the power infused in it. I started to transform into my former self. My features rounded and got softer. My skin tone lightened and gave off a yellow hue. My hair turned wavy and golden like the sun, as it once was when I was a child. I felt Talia's strength being suppressed from my soul. I felt…empty.

Upon seeing his little girl all grown up, his tears finally came. He fell to his knees, thanking me profusely. His fingers shivered from the shock of his own liquid.

There was one more thing he wanted me to do. I reached into my quiver and slowly pulled out the enchanted arrow. Every bone in my body locked up.

Vance outstretched his arms, knowing what was to follow.

My vision was too blurred to see. I tried to enter the Feylin realm, but the necklace was preventing me. As long as it rested upon my neck, I was imprisoned here. I was a non-lin.

I took out my childhood bow. My bottom lip trembled.

One of my earliest memories was that of my father teaching me how to shoot. He was so proud of my skill and passion for the craft. He would always congratulate me by placing me on his shoulders and pretending to be an animal, like a horse or cow. Life was simple back then, we lived for happiness and play. Why did it ever have to change? All I ever wanted was his approval, after all he had sacrificed for my opulent life.

"Lizah, I'm coming!" he said, looking to the sky.

Slipping the necklace off, my body reverted to how it had been.

I'll help you, Talia projected.

Don't you dare.

My stomach was twisted up. I had to force my will as I heeded his warning and stepped backwards. It was the hardest thing I ever had to do. I didn't want to hurt him anymore. I had to prove to him, Talia and myself that I had grown, that I wasn't a little girl anymore. The hardest part was letting go. Regret developed the instant I released the arrow to the air. I couldn't bear to see his expression. He was a little less than alive, but a little more than dead. I had to end his pain, along with his research. It was what he was waiting for.

The arrow hit its mark on the cottage and started to glow a bright red.

"She looks just like you. I knew she would," Vance cried to the heavens.

I waited a beat as Norrow's Focus started to create an explosion at the point of impact. Calling upon a control string, I wrapped it around the enchanted arrow, taking care not to grab the explosion. I tapped into Talia's power and returned the arrow to my hand just as the cottage exploded.

Fire burst into the air as everything went up in the blaze. It was fast and painless for him, but my pain would always remain. I missed him already. Inside my palm, the arrow was hot but still intact. Carefully sliding the arrow back into my quiver, I let my bow slip out of my fingers.

"Goodbye, daddy," I mouthed, without the words leaving my lips.

Chapter Twelve
Cleansing of Fear

"...in order to see things as a whole."

Time seemed to be moving sideways as I adapted to the forest life, overcoming obstacles in my path with ease. My mind was becoming feral as I braved the untamed wilderness.

I had to reclaim the core-prism, it was my responsibility. Unexpected events had pushed me further away from that goal.

My real apprehension stood with the moments Talia shared with me, each one a twisted nightmare that broke my spirits. I felt myself changing in her presence. I was lost. Each day seemed darker.

Attempting to mimic her fighting style always left me falling short. I was a shell of her former glory. I had all the knowledge she had without a fraction of her passion. Observing her foregone experiences left me questioning myself and favoring her dauntlessness. Most days I shut off my thoughts altogether, to become numb, because the alternative was unbearable.

I came across a sign post and stared at it inquisitively. There were symbols on it, but I was having a hard time understanding them.

We know this.

It was so hard to concentrate on anything. How could I have forgotten…reading words? What did they mean? I had to remember, to prove to myself that I wasn't going insane. I opened up my mind slightly. Thoughts of death and revenge rattled around. I grabbed my straining head. It was long enough. I shut myself down again.

"P…Pr…Provi," I stumbled. It was the first time I had spoken in a long while and the words didn't come easily. *This is important somehow.*

There was a marker pointing to this Provi place, but I couldn't move until I remembered what I needed there. I couldn't wrap my head around it; everything was foggy and strange. The questions kept coming, but answers were absent.

How long have we been out here?

"Am I talking to myself again?"

You're still doing it.

"Who am I?" I didn't mean to say that, yet it came out all the same. I was confused. Nothing seemed real anymore, like a dream I never dreamt.

Who are you?

"You don't know?"

I'm disappearing.

"Is that bad?"

It should be.

"Then you don't…" *deserve me.* I wasn't in control of my thoughts or words. I couldn't decipher which were internal or external.

I deserve death.

"We both do."

I placed my hand over my woebegone head, searching for evidence of who I was hidden inside me.

"Her memories...that girl's. You mean my memories? Why is this so hard?"

I entered the Feylin realm accidentally. *I know this place. This is my sanctuary.*

There I found all my memories projected for someone, but who? It was a show that no one attended. As I watched my own life, I started to remember.

"Talia!" I said, realizing the show's intended audience. "You must witness my life. I'm losing control of us. I'm scared."

No.

"Please? It's imperative to our survival." I knew now, that while I was projecting my memories, they were no longer available for me to remember. My clarity in this realm was temporary. The moment I went back to the normal world, it would all vanish.

He hates me because of you.

"He just doesn't know you like I do."

I'm not talking about Hark.

"Who else could there be? He's all you ever think of."

Distress overwhelmed me as Talia's emotions flooded in. She did hate me, more than anything. I started to become aware of her perspective—the source of all this animosity. Her thoughts unraveled into my mind as my own.

Yari was the only person who didn't comment upon my scarred face. He found it unique and endearing. In a world of monsters and men, he was the light to my darkness, and you extinguished him, righteous Prophetess with hair of gold.

"I never met this person. You would know if I were lying."

We were on a simple escort mission for the Lustarians. That's when the Telandric ambushed us—your Telandric.

Yari made me stay the course as they wrestled him to the ground. Always a good solider, I was torn. In the end, I left him to their capture. If we didn't get our medicine man to West Corick, many lives would have been lost. I had to choose the many over the few. You used him to get to me, because he was my weakness.

"I was part of no such plot."

After two months in captivity, Yari wasn't the same person. I was worried about seeing him again. He had been home in Cape Castle for 32 hours, yet he hadn't come to see me.

Finally, I caught up to him before breakfast. I was very excited to see him, but he didn't even want me to touch him…like I had a disease he didn't want to catch.

He was talking in circles—filled with regret for himself, for our cause, for everything. It was on his face, it was in his eyes. His hope had been taken away and replaced with bitter resentment. I tried to reason with him, though he wanted no resolution.

He tried to hand me the human heart-shaped vial filled with a promise we had both made. He was breaking that promise by giving it back to me. I defiantly put up my hands, rejecting his terms. It was a gift and couldn't be un-given.

He let the bottle slip through his fingers. I lurched forward to catch the item that used to mean so much to him, but instead I let it fall. The glass shattered at our feet, spilling the blue elixir everywhere. It was the symbol of our relationship, and it was now broken beyond repair.

He didn't flinch. His boots crushed the glass into smaller pieces as he walked away from me…from us.

"It wasn't my intention to hurt you or Yari."

Right, just to get in his head and turn him against me. Making him see me the way you all did…inhuman, unnatural. Just a plague you cannot control.

Everything dies in the end, but never when you're ready for it.

I went to our special spot where we first kissed. It was above the waterfall right outside of town. I spent my spare time etching the memory of my victims into the smooth rocks that rested there. It was my way of honoring their memory. The roaring rapids, the rush of the water, all had a way of drowning out my thoughts, but not today.

My heart raced as I got closer to the spot. I could tell the path had been recently traveled. Maybe Yari was waiting for me like he used to. My hand gently pushed aside the brush. There he was…lying lifeless.

I rushed to him. Everything was surreal. I tried to resuscitate his cold body as my teardrops mixed with his blood, concocting a pink liquid. I wanted him to live so badly. I needed him to. I tasted his stale blood lining the inside of my mouth.

He felt like an object, not a person. It was too late. I started to piece it together…the knife in his hand—the same one I used to etch the stones. He had taken his own life. The wounds were scattered—his legs, arms, shoulders, back, face. He wanted to feel his own execution, tortured by his own hand. With each cut I saw, I felt anguish in my heart. He wanted me to find him, as punishment. My screams echoed throughout the cavern for miles, until they gave up on me too.

I couldn't go on. I slid the knife out of his grasp, caressing his fingers lightly. All I could think about was taking out my insides. Who would find me if I joined him in the afterlife? No one. I was nothing…worse than nothing. The negative effect I had on this world must end.

That's when I saw the etching on the surface of a boulder. All it said was, "Next life, may I be on the right side."

I couldn't believe that he hadn't mentioned me. He was so important to me, and I wasn't even a passing thought in his final hours. I was prepared to die for him, and he wouldn't even live for me. Yari was all I had, and now I didn't even want to meet him in the next life.

"Forgive me, I never wanted to hurt anyone."

What you gave him was your naive outlook. Our factions have been at war since the beginning. There has been bloodshed from both sides. No one is innocent, not even you.

"It wasn't my fault. He was looking for answers, and we gave them to him."

Being with you is worse than death.

"That's why you came for me that day, isn't it—revenge."

Yes.

"I can't move on anymore. The toll is too much, your suffering is too much. Just make it stop, please? I beg you."

You must suffer with me. Isn't that our fate?

"No, it doesn't have to be. We can learn from each other."

All you have ever taught me was regret and despondence.

"But, I…I…you're so strong. You make me feel how I always imaged I could. You just had a bad run, worse than anyone," I said, stroking her hair.

Your sympathy sickens me.

"My life will cool your rage. You must see for yourself."

I don't want it to be cooled, then I'll be weak like you. My pain is the only real emotion I have left.

"Do it for him."

I am.

"I don't understand."

…

"Don't shut me out."

…

"Talia, please? We have to work together. I cannot be alone. I'm too scared."

Her silence was a monument to my defeat. I stood staring at the sign, using all my being to keep my promise to myself and not cry. My body was shaking. I couldn't stop it. I felt the puddles pounding on the backs of my eyes. I shut down, relinquishing control over our shared body, leaving it expressionless. If Talia wanted to live, she'd have to take control. I couldn't bear the burden any longer. I was miserable.

There we stood as a soulless doll, almost senselessness, staring at the sign post without a single thought.

Hours, maybe days went by before a strange man approached inquisitively.

"I see nothing so spectacular about that particular sign post?" he said, placing a hand upon the doll's shoulder.

It didn't flinch, move, or anything to indicate it was aware of his presence.

He took another look at its face, this time trying to see if it was alive or not, then back at the sign.

"I don't get it." He mimicked her gaze. They both sat there for a while doing nothing. "How are you doing this?" He arched his back and let out a long yawn. "Well, good luck." He started to collect his pack filled with all kinds of knickknacks that jingled as he shifted.

As luck would have it, the doll's instincts kicked in as a large grasshopper landed on its hand. The only movement the man saw was the act of it eating the bug whole, which prompted a loud rumbling inside its belly.

"Oh, dear," he sympathized, waving his hand back and forth in front of its eyes. Still, not a blink or a flinch resulted from his motion.

"You must come with me, dear lady," he suggested, grabbing its hand.

It followed his movements through the forest. It didn't take long before the doll tripped over a log and fell, not bracing for impact.

The man was quick and saved it from harm. "You should really watch yourself."

He led it to a waterfront cabin on a beach, where he was met by a small boy who was eager to greet the new companion.

"Hi, I'm Paik. I colored this rock. Here, you can keep it," the boy greeted, placing the rock inside the doll's hand.

"She needs our help. Can you get some soup ready?" the man asked.

"I already made soup, but I put too much water in it. It's more like hot flavored water. Well, maybe not so much with the flavor, but it is hot!"

"Does it have vegetables in it?"

"Oh, it does. They're just not very tasty ones. Not ripe, really."

"Fruits ripen."

"Oh, I put fruit in there too."

"No, not again. Just get her a bowl, please."

"Okay, but I told you it's not very good. If you want to make a good impression, I would start over. I mean..." he continued as he trailed off into the distance.

"Have a seat here," said the man, urging the doll to sit on a worn-out chair, facing the crashing ocean waves. Its native instincts complied with all instruction, without care or regret.

"Hello, my name is Rafee. This is my home, and if Paik's soup doesn't kill you, you'll get better soon enough. It's a safe place," he said with a chuckle, shaking the doll's limp hand.

Paik returned, still talking. "I was going to put in potatoes but I decided to make an art project out of them instead. Hey, would you like to see it?" He turned abruptly, spilling some of his broth on the sand.

"Just the soup," Rafee said, concerned. He winced at the smell before placing a spoonful of Paik's soup up to the doll's face. It was unfazed and took a sip without hesitation. Rafee continued until the bowl was empty. "Paik, more, please."

"But, I wanted to show you my potato plant. I call him Paul."

"Soup!"

"Fine. Come on, Paul, someone's grumpy today." Paik left, his masterpiece in hand.

The doll continued to lap up the soup until it was all gone. Finally, after the third bowl, it refused a bite.

"I thought you might eat yourself to death," Rafee said.

As the sun went down, Rafee setup the spare bedroom and put the doll to rest.

In the morning, the doll was awoken by the sound of little voices playing on Rafee's beach.

"Settle in, children. It's past school time," Rafee bellowed.

The children's ages differed greatly, the youngest maybe being five, and the oldest twelve or so. They all fell in line and sat awaiting Rafee's instruction. Paik was not joining the lesson, instead he was tending to his chores.

"Now, everyone, try to remember something without picturing it in your mind. This technique is called 'thought over image.' The concept is that you can see the very essence of something without looking at what you remember. You can then change that thought, which will allow you to repaint the past, and possibly control the future. These methods can make you quite powerful, or quite mad. In some cases, it's an even split," Rafee joked, while they all struggled with the drill.

After breaking for lunch, Rafee had the kids do a lot of physical activities involving balance and strength. Some of the smaller kids actually beat out the older ones in these exercises. As the day came to an end, all the children left, eager for tomorrow's lesson.

During dinner, a loud ringing sound erupted in the distance.

"Paik! Get her inside, now," Rafee yelled.

The normally talkative boy led the doll inside the cabin, away from any windows. Soon, a muffled conversation went on between Rafee and another man outside.

"This is a private camp. Please escort yourself elsewhere," Rafee said sternly.

"I've been tracking a feylin in these parts. Have you seen anything?"

"Of course I've seen a feylin, this is a school for young ones."

"Not a child feylin, a dangerous one. A woman, to be more exact. She is quite fetching, really."

"I haven't seen anything that fits your description."

"How about something that doesn't fit it?"

"Well, that is an awfully broad statement. I mean, technically, this bowl doesn't fit your description of some ruthless feylin, but I have seen it. For years now, actually. Here, why don't you take it."

"This is a serious matter."

"I don't take very much seriously," Rafee admitted.

"You should. May I take a look around inside?"

"You may not. This is a private school…emphasis on *private*."

"May I at least make camp on your property tonight?"

"Suit yourself. Be sure you're out of sight though, far out."

"Agreed. If you see anything, contact me right away," the man said.

"Alrighty. How should I contact you exactly?"

"Just call out to me. I'm Hark."

The doll's eyelids fluttered rapidly.

"Okay, have a good night, Hark," Rafee said defiantly.

Rafee entered the cabin looking relieved. "You don't look at all dangerous," he said, brushing the hair out of the doll's face.

"What was that all about? Is he a friend of yours, Rafs? Why didn't you invite him to eat with us?" Paik pestered.

"It's never a good sign when people come snooping around. Better keep her inside for the time being, okay?"

"Fine. Can I show him Paul if he comes back?!" Paik asked, making his potato plant dance in his hand.

"No, not this time."

"Shucks."

The next day, Paik was outside conversing with Hark, who was ignoring the ramblings of the energetic child.

"Mr. Hark, won't you please join us for our lesson?" Paik asked, his head barely reaching Hark's chest.

"No, thank you."

The children flooded in, as they always did. Hark wasn't participating as much as he wasn't "not participating"—despite his earlier statement.

"Can any of you guess what my feylin ability is?" Rafee challenged. The children eagerly awaited as Rafee went around the room asking each one what they thought his gift was.

"Is it the ability to make people talk to you?" one older kid blurted out.

Everyone laughed out loud.

"Nope. Try again," Rafee said, pointing to the next student.

"I know!" another kid yelled, jumping up with a raised hand.

Rafee walked over to the self-assured child with a smile. The pressure was too much.

"I…forgot," the youngster said, sitting back down, embarrassed.

Everyone was stumped.

Rafee reached the youngest girl, who was sitting next to Hark, mindlessly petting his arm. Rafee sat down in front of her and closed his eyes.

"I'm doing it right now."

She began to cry hysterically, for no apparent reason.

"What's wrong with her?" Hark grew concerned.

"She's perfectly fine," Rafee brushed off his question with a wave of his hand.

Hark put his arm around her. His protective nature made him noticeably uncomfortable. The child's demeanor got even worse.

Hark closed his eyes for a moment, then launched at Rafee, tackling him to the ground.

"What are you doing? She's just a kid," Hark yelled.

"Provoking assault, apparently. May I ask you a similar question as to the nature of your actions here?" Rafee asked.

The smiles on the children's faces quickly vanished as they observed the display.

"Teacher didn't hurt me, mister." said the little girl, tugging on Hark's clothes.

"My apologies. I thought…" Hark extended his hand to help Rafee up.

"I know what you thought, and you were dead wrong," Rafee said, accepting his hand for support.

"She was crying," Hark sputtered.

"And you jumped to your own conclusions—literally."

"You were doing something. I saw…" Hark said, wiggling his fingers trying hard to describe, but lacking the words.

"What do you desire most, Hark?"

"To find something I lost."

"No, think bigger, as if you had one day to live. What would you want to accomplish before saying goodbye to everyone you ever knew?"

Hark took a minute to mull over his answer this time.

"To become a feylin. One with enough power to protect the ones I care about," he exclaimed.

"Ah, that is more like it. Unfortunately, you cannot learn what you already are."

"Sadly, you're mistaken. I haven't taken the trials yet."

"In most cases it's true that the trials are essential, but I don't think this is most cases." Rafee paced back and forth with his hands at his back.

"Where is all this coming from?"

"You saw me using my power on the child. Only a feylin has the sight," he said, crossing his arms in an authoritative way.

"A feylin? Me? Nah," Hark said, astounded by the accusation.

"Class dismissed early today, children," Rafee said abruptly, spying the doll's silhouette moving past the window inside the cabin. The kids scattered faster than he could finish his sentence.

The doll, standing on its own, slowly walked to the door one step at a time. Once it reached the door, it clawed at the handle, unable to operate it.

"I don't feel like a feylin. You must be…" Hark paused. His eyes met Rafee who was acting as normal as can be.

"Let's get back to my original question," Rafee said. "Who did you study under at the Telandric academy?"

"I mean I used to, but not anymore. I left."

"What was the reason for your departure?"

"Her!" Hark rushed for the door.

"Wait a minute now," Rafee stammered.

"Capri! I've been searching everywhere for you!" he said forcing the door open.

The doll looked at him vacuously. Hark pressed his body up against hers and held on to her tightly. The doll's body was unresponsive. After a beat, Hark noticed that his affectionate greeting was not reciprocated and took a step back.

"What did you do to her?" He turned to face Rafee, anger distorting his face.

"I found her like this, in the woods a couple weeks ago," Rafee held up his hands in a non-confrontational way.

"There's nothing wrong with her. She's just thinking," Paik chimed in.

"You saw my gift. What was it?" Rafee asked.

"Don't change the subject!"

"Just answer the question!" Rafee challenged, matching his tone.

"I saw how you can manipulate people around you. The child, you frightened her."

"Correct, and how did I do that?"

"Emotions you must have taken from her."

"Wrong. If you were trained properly, you would know that's impossible. Are you sure I'm not merely a scary guy?" Rafee questioned.

"You changed her emotion with some sort of string thing," Hark explained.

"Ha! I knew you were a feylin. This is very interesting indeed."

"How can I help her?" Hark went back to face the doll, but he could barely look at it.

"As far as I can tell, there is nothing wrong with her." Rafee approached the doll and led it to a chair outside. "She has goose-bumps. That's different. Paik, fetch us a blanket from inside," he instructed, rubbing his hands on her shoulders to create warmth.

"Can I stay here? I want to help," Hark pleaded.

"If you promise to train with me."

"I'll do anything you ask. I just want to be close to her."

"What's your relationship to each other?"

"She's a friend…a close friend," Hark said wistfully.

Paik was very excited to have a new visitor. He dragged Rafee inside to set up a bed for Hark.

Hark knelt down, placing the doll's hands inside his own. "I was angry with you. Well, at first I was. Eventually I forgave you for the incident at the portal. I just don't get why you're always pushing me away? Have as much faith in me as I do in you. There are so many questions I wish you could answer." Hark leaned his head on the doll's shoulder and closed his eyes.

"I'll fix you, just tell me what you need," he whispered softly. "I dedicated myself to finding you, following your every footstep. I never lost hope. As you kept moving, I kept searching. None of the clues prepared me for this, though. If it takes a lifetime, I'll mend your broken spirit. I know you may not be able to hear me right now, but I'm just so happy I found you, even under these conditions."

Hark spent the rest of the night by the doll's side.

The months blurred together as Hark trained with his new master, Rafee. He spent his spare time talking to and caring for the doll. Every day he brought her exotic gifts he found—rare plants and shells. He even caged a couple of song birds to keep her company in his absence. But the doll was never as responsive as that first day of his arrival.

Paik and Hark started to bond. They made up stories of over-dramatic characters at nearly every supper.

One training session stood out over the others.

"What's the last class you attended at the Telandric training center?" Rafee asked.

Hark made a grunting noise.

Rafee seemed to understand his response. "Shall we begin?"

Eager to oblige, Hark nodded in agreement.

"Your Focus seems to be blocked, and I cannot figure out why. Maybe you're broken."

"Is that your wise conclusion? That I'm a mistake?" Hark asked.

"Oh no, mistakes you can correct. Oddities are special…but worse," Rafee said.

"Funny, I don't feel special. Actually I feel quite run-of-the-mill."

"I gave this a lot of thought, and I've come to the conclusion that you may or may not be a feylin…" Rafee spoke thoughtfully.

"How is that a conclusion?"

"I wasn't finished. In either case, it's irrelevant because 'feylin' is nothing more than a title."

"That's not true. I've seen how people gain great powers after their trials," Hark said in disbelief.

"Yes, but no one has ever had the sight before the trials, only after. It just doesn't work that way. You were smart to flee when you did. I'm certain now that the trials would have killed you."

"What's so bad about the trials?" Hark asked.

"They push every aspect of your body, soul and mind to the maximum. Many are culled out in the process."

"That sounds to me like murder."

"Life is murder. A slow, unforgiving menace who cares nothing for convenience."

"So, what should I do then?" Hark asked.

"I want to try something. Do whatever it is that you do to generate energy," Rafee ordered, waving his hand ominously.

"I'm accessing as many memories as I can."

"Now, channel that energy into one spot. Like your hand…or anywhere other than inside your Vigor."

Hark's closed eyes fluttered and his fingers twitched.

"The images are too fast to focus on."

"You're losing concentration," Rafee yelled.

"I feel warm and…scared. I can't hold on," Hark said, snapping out of his routine.

"Where did you pinpoint your energy exactly?"

"Above my shoulder. It was much less strenuous putting the energy in one place. Before, I let it flow through my body, and its power was unbearable."

"What made you lose concentration?"

"A memory of a promise," Hark said.

"You must not value any one thought more than another. It will cause your mind to break down. Now, try again," Rafee commanded.

"Okay." Hark started again.

"Keep going, you're almost there," Rafee repeated over and over again until…

Hark's breath was palpitating.

"At this moment, you are alive for the first time. Embrace the free energy. Force it into the middle of your forehead. Claim your future," Rafee bellowed.

"I feel a new instance of myself being born, as if two worlds were occurring simultaneously." A single drop of blood started to leak from the center of Hark's forehead, even though there was no cut or hole for it to originate from.

"Gain control!" Rafee yelled with authority.

"Kill me!" Hark screamed. His demeanor drastically changed to a veiled smile, and he fell to the ground twitching. Hark's shirt was soaked by his own sweat and tears. His eyes rolled back inside his head.

"Come back!" Rafee shook him violently.

He wasn't breathing.

Rafee entered the Feylin realm to aid him in his struggle.

A moment later, Hark's eyes fluttered open. He squinted as the sun's light embraced his eyes.

"Thank goodness," Rafee said, deflating his lungs.

"What just happened? Was that real? I saw the secrets to the universe, the barrier between reality and the realm of immortals. I saw objects through their energy, not by their appearances. It was ineffable," Hark said, struggling to form the words.

"Like the ocean, energy flows in a continuous wave. Everything is connected," Rafee elaborated.

"I wanted to touch and embrace it all, but I was enraptured by its majestic force. I was home, and I never felt so complete in all my life.

"Suddenly, I felt my whole world change. The blurry shapes began to glow a dark, gloomy color. I started to feel afraid, very afraid. I tried to shut my center eye, but it wouldn't budge. I couldn't stop the dread that descended upon me. Thoughts of death entered my mind. It was all I desired. A figure moved in front of me. Its Vigor was active and bright."

"That was me. I had to help you. Your emotions were breaking you apart."

"A white string reached out to me. Words started evaporating on my essence."

"That was my Focus," Rafee chimed in.

"Something else came—the numbness, nothingness was everywhere."

"I tried to calm your system, but you were relentless," Rafee said.

"Why didn't it look like that before?"

"When you saw me use my Focus last time, you merely peeked inside the Feylin realm. This time, however, you were participating in it."

"I felt like a god."

"You should have, it is their playground."

Paik ran up and handed Hark a bandage.

"What's this for?" Hark wiped his brow and noticed the blood on it. He looked astounded.

"That's what happens when you try to exceed your own power. If I had not intervened, you would be dead right now," Rafee stated, regret in his voice.

"Power? You mean…I have power?" Hark said. He looked to the heavens, as if something magical had been bestowed upon him and the world was his for the taking.

Hark leaned close to the doll's face and whispered deeply to her, "Did you hear that? I've become something worth coming back for."

Chapter Thirteen
Pursuit of a Monster

"Witnessing myself through your radiant eyes..."

Paik had gone outside to fetch some sticks for the morning fire, but he hadn't returned yet. Concerned, Rafee went off to look for him.

The doll was all alone, sitting there looking at the window. Outside there was a rattling sound—a crash, a shatter—though no footsteps were heard.

She sat unfazed.

The sound heightened and drew nearer. Something was violently shaking the door, causing the whole cabin to quake. The only thing protecting her from this unseen cause of the noise was the small metal latch holding the door closed. Not designed to withstand much force, the latch gave way, causing the door to crash against the wall. A single, small, metal ball rolled across the uneven floor of the cabin. Each line and imperfection in the wooden floor changed the sound it made as it moved. It continued right up to the doll, then stopped suddenly.

Her foot started to fidget slightly.

One by one, more metal balls followed the same path. Hundreds of them congregated around her.

The doll started to convulse from her chest. Her body shook with pain, while her mind and spirit ignored it. Almost falling out of her chair, her eyes shook back and forth. A small splotch of red started to appear on her chest. Something inside was burrowing out.

Suddenly, Rafee burst into the cabin and started to sweep the metallic menaces with a broom. "Get out of here. Leave her be," he yelled.

The bearings started attacking him from every direction.

The doll started to cough harshly.

Hark rushed in, speckled in sweat. He scooped the doll into his arms and swept her out of the cabin. She held on to him tightly, nestling her head on his shoulder.

The bearings swarmed after them. With nowhere to go, Hark rushed into the ocean. The cold water made the doll cling to him even more. The bearings followed them, sinking to the bottom like stones.

A wave crashed over their heads. Hark held his breath, but the doll did not. She coughed and choked on the salt water.

"Are you okay?" He tried to keep her afloat and swim at the same time.

The doll just kept smiling at him with blinkless eyes.

Another wave came fast and hard. Her body slipped through his grasp. Water filled her lungs as she started to sink. He came up for air, desperately searching for her.

"Talia! Capri! No! Where are you?!" She could hear him calling to her, muffled but pure.

He dove under, but she had been swept away. He dove under again, although this time he followed the trail of the bearings on the ocean floor. She was still smiling and sinking rapidly—air evacuating her lungs.

He held her lifeless body and one-handedly swam to the top. He pinched her cheeks and water came out, but she was still not breathing. While frantically trying to keep them both afloat, he placed his hand behind her neck. Hark pressed his soft lips against hers, blowing air deep into her chest.

Tasting his salty lips and feeling his body against hers, Talia took notice. She took control of the doll and intertwined her body with his. She began to kiss him deeply, each muscle in her body holding on for dear life. All of her rage turned to passion in their embrace. Pain surged through her, as it always had—unbearable pain. She kissed him harder to fight through it. Only her raw desire was present now. They started to sink but neither of them cared, lost in the moment.

Her body jolted as it rejected the lack of oxygen. It didn't stop her, nothing could have.

Upon taking control of the doll, Talia was forced to finally see Capri's past. It was a sacrifice she knew she was making, but her desire was uncontrollable. She didn't care about life or death in that moment.

Images flooded her mind. A young Capri was sitting in her room. She was never allowed to play with the other kids, due to her important destiny.

"I know it seems cruel, but those fighting games they're playing are not all they're cracked up to be, Miss Capriess," said a scholarly looking wizard.

"What's the fun of saving a world you cannot enjoy," little Capri pouted.

"You will know joy, when that day comes, much more than a thousand years of merriment."

Capri started to bite down on her knuckle, frustrated. "Why can't that day come already?"

"It will only come when your mind is strong enough to make the choice that is asked of you."

"I'm ready. I have always been ready!"

"You cannot rush fate. Besides, it's rude," he said, placing a calm hand upon her shoulder.

She brushed him off.

"Finish with your studies, Miss Capriess. I'll get you something that will cheer you up."

The moment he left the room, she undid the latch to her window and opened it wide. Taking in the brisk outside air, she looked down the four stories, and her stomach dropped. Climbing out on the ledge, she was excited and scared at the same time. Her small feet fit perfectly on the edges of the stonework as she began to scale the side of the manor. She slipped slightly, but luckily maintained her grasp. Her scream echoed.

The children outside were now observing her heroic escape.

She managed to reach the ground with only a couple of scrapes. She was very proud of herself.

"Can I play too?" She approached the children.

"You're not allowed to play," one of the kids said begrudgingly.

"I can do stuff. Did you see what I just did?"

"I don't want to get in trouble," another kid spoke up, adding to her disappointment.

"Miss Capri!" the old wizard scolded from the windowsill.

The kids fled in all directions.

"Wait for me," she laughed and chased after them.

"No, go back," one child warned.

Not listening, she reveled in the air blowing through her golden curls. A smile spread across her face reflecting her pure joy. The moment was short lived, however. Her foot caught on a rock and sent her soaring. She landed on her arm, which snapped on impact.

Capri started to cry so loudly that it carried throughout the whole town. This was her first experience feeling pain. She had been sheltered from the sensation all her life with cloves and other numbing herbs. As painful as it was, what really hurt was when she heard the punishment the children got for tempting her in the first place. Her arm recovered, as broken bones do, but she never saw those kids again and never healed from the guilt of their punishment.

In the present moment, I couldn't release my lips interlocked with his. My body pressed up against his and wouldn't let go as our hands did what they wanted. Deprived of oxygen, my chest lurched, begging me to stop. Nothing could have released my heart from indulging in what it had craved for so long.

I've been waiting here for you to save me.

More of her past swept through my mind. For Capri's eighth birthday, she was given a polar bear cub for this rite of passage. Gifts of great significance were normal for nobles to receive as they matured. Normally, they were hand-picked to improve upon areas in which they were lacking. In this case, Capri's loneliness was affecting her studies.

The cub was so inquisitive and playful, she fell in love with it the moment she laid eyes on it.

"Do you like him, Miss Capriess?" the wizard asked, knowing full well what the answer would be.

"How can you not? I mean look at his adorable face," she responded, brushing his cheeks.

"I suppose not," the wizard conceded.

"I will name him Heart because he is where I will put all my love. And you'll keep it safe for me, won't you, boy?"

The bear cub rolled around, biting on a blanket.

"See, he said 'yes.'"

Capri took Heart with her everywhere. They were inseparable. She believed the more love she put in him, the bigger he got. Heart grew to a record size among polar bears. Even when fully grown, he still was as playful as always.

One day Capri was bathing Heart with ice water. He crunched the cubes into smaller pieces as he chewed them. Suddenly, Heart got very quiet and alert.

"What is it, love? Is it too cold, or not cold enough?"

The bear bounded out, dripping with water, looking for something.

Then, out of the shadows a javelin flew, destined to strike the young girl down. Heart intercepted it midair, biting it in half.

Shocked, Capri looked behind her for its intended target. No one was there. She didn't understand why anyone would want to cause harm to her. Maybe it was a mistake. She curled up in a ball, frightened.

Heart charged into the shadows.

Hearing the bear roar, she covered her ears and scrambled over to him. Heart was hurt and panting deeply. He had shredded apart the assassin who aimed to prevent her destiny.

"Heart, you saved me. My hero. Come, let's see the wizard and show him what you've done."

The bear collapsed when it tried to stand.

"What's wrong? Let's hurry," she said confused.

Guards rushed to her aid. One of them swept her up in his arms.

"Wait, is he going to be okay? He saved me, my Heart did."

One of the guards sniffed the javelin the bear first snapped in half. "The assassin used rancid bacteria on his weapons," he observed.

"What does that mean? He's going to be okay, right? Right?!" She kicked and pushed trying to get a clear view of her friend.

"I cannot live without him! I don't want to," Capri screamed.

She cried until there was nothing left, but that didn't bring Heart back.

As I watched Capri lose her Heart, I was giving into mine. I had spent my whole life trying to survive, and ironically, I never felt more alive.

While I kissed Hark and observed all the selfless love Capri had, I knew I had to stop being selfish—indulging in my own temptations. I would give up myself to stay here with him, but I couldn't let Hark suffer because of me.

My body wouldn't allow me to pry myself away from him, no matter how hard I tried. I was out of air and he was soon to follow.

A solution developed within me, although it was extremely dangerous and unproven. I couldn't risk testing it on Hark. I had to offer myself up, no matter the cost.

Hark projected a thought in the Feylin realm as I entered, **"We live as timeless creatures with earnest desires."**

I emitted three control strings and wrapped them around myself, lingering for one last blissful second, holding on as long as I could.

Within seconds, I was no longer part of this world. I wasn't dead or alive. I was above myself. Less than a god but trespassing inside their backyard. Then I was somewhere else entirely. I had teleported myself to land—away from his intoxicating passion, away from melding into him completely, away from total and utter happiness.

Doubling over, I started to cough water out from my lungs. Never had I moved an object so big. I knew that gaining the feylin beast's Order had increased my power, but I worried at what cost?

Hark struggled to the shore moments later, Rafee rushing to his aid.

As I stood at the other end of the beach, I saw every moment of Capri's life, every thought and emotion. She was everything I was not—kind, gentle and forgiving. Tears flowed from my eyes, actualized from the pinnacle of her happiness. Even with all my calculations, I had never expected this outcome. From now on, I promised never to predict the future and to live by the beautiful, unexpected wheels of fate.

I'm glad we found each other.

For a brief moment, Talia was looking through the left eye and Capri through the right. One side of my vision was dark and jaded, the other rich with color and optimism.

I felt my identity toggle from Capri to Talia, back and forth continuously, until finally they were the same—no longer conflicted, no longer divided. This was the answer to the puzzle that I could never solve. Both our destinies were separate pieces of the map. Only together could we march down the path of the prophesy.

Now I am one, complete.

Along the coast, all the ball bearings had long since scattered off from whence they came. I had to face them, once and for all, and end my torment.

I approached Hark and Rafee.

Hark picked me up and swung me around, a lightness in his eyes.

"You're back," Hark grinned.

I tried my best to smile, hiding from the events that just transpired.

Reality sunk in too fast as he put me down, taking his hands slowly off my waist. His whole demeanor changed quickly.

"So, who is this?" Hark asked, trying to get a read on me.

"Who do you think it is?" I asked, beaming.

"I knew it was you, Capri. I just wanted to make sure," he said.

It took everything I had to keep from breaking apart in that moment. He had it wrong. I didn't want to tell him I was neither Capri nor Talia—I was scared of disappointing him. I simply gave him a vague nod.

"What was that back there, in the water?"

"A mistake. It won't happen again," I admitted sadly, reality quickly crushing my bliss while adrenalin still pumped inside me.

"No, I mean…you just vanished," he elaborated, thinking I drew the wrong conclusion to his question.

I knew what he had meant. I chose to deflect it because the truth was surely something far more painful. "I was dragging you down," I reasoned.

"I have so many questions. I need so many answers and…let's just start at the beginning," he said, shivering.

"Later, there's no time now," I brushed him off. There was a pressing matter I had to deal with first.

"Later?"

Rafee chimed in, "It's nice to see you up."

"Thank you, Rafee, for everything, really. I was here, just… dormant," I explained.

He nodded with a smile and gave me a hug. I wasn't used to this treatment.

"You remember…everything?" Hark asked.

"Why are those things pursuing you?" Rafee asked.

"Unfinished business. The past always catches up with you, no matter how fast you run," I said, wringing the liquid out of my hair.

I stretched for the sky and my bones rattled and snapped. I caught Paik in my arms as he flew at me, catching me off guard.

"What do they want with you?" Hark pressed. His question fell on deaf ears as I carried Paik into the cabin.

"I really did like your soup, by the way," I said with a smile.

"I knew you did, but master said you must have lost all your taste buds."

"I remember," I confessed.

We were followed in by Hark and Rafee who were arguing about what questions they were going to ask me first.

After putting Paik down, I pulled off a circular magnet that was holding two metal pipes together. Lifting my shirt slightly, I held the magnet to my stomach. A shock of pain stabbed me from inside. This silenced their argument and caught their attention. I pulled the magnet back slightly, revealing a lump that was trying to pierce through my skin.

"He is after this," I explained.

"What in the world?" Hark gasped.

I placed the magnet back on my stomach and slowly started to navigate it through my insides. My face silently revealing my discomfort, I didn't let the pain waver my steady hand. The bearing tried to break through my digestive system and kill me from the inside, but the magnet kept it still. I moved it through my stomach and up my esophagus.

I started to choke as it moved through my throat and into my mouth. Hark motioned to assist me, but Rafee held him back with his arm. With one final cough, it flew out of my mouth and connected with the magnet.

"Hordox," I said, rubbing my throat.

We all stared at it for a moment as it wobbled.

"Why was it inside you?" Hark asked.

"He caught me by surprise when you were infiltrating Kanlett, and I couldn't just let him flee. Not after beating me like that."

"What are you going to do?"

"Give him what he wants," I said, pinching the bearing in between my two fingers and freeing it from the magnetic force.

"Can't you wait a single minute? You just got here. I can't lose you again," Hark pleaded.

"I've waited long enough." I dropped the bearing and it rolled out the door.

"Was that wise?" Rafee questioned.

"I'm about to find out," I said. I followed it outside, watching it bounce off each rock it connected with.

"Can you just tell me the plan for once? I can protect you," Hark said, following me out.

"I have to do this alone. Please don't interfere," I said, not taking my eyes off the bearing.

Hark gripped my arm and pulled me close to him. "Let me be here for you."

"I want to, but I can't." This fight had been brewing for a long time, ever since the forest, Kanlett, maybe even before that. I had to go in alone.

The bearing started to fade out of my view. Time had run out.

I closed my eyes. Using the energy generated from his touch, I impelled my three control strings, wrapping them around my Vigor like a cocoon. I knew this was the only way for me to walk away from him. I had to adjust to his rejection. He adored Capri, but I wasn't her anymore than I was Talia. I needed time to figure out who I was for myself, and it started with tying up loose ends.

I transported myself into the thicket, leaving no tracks for him to follow. Spotting the bearing, I purposely gave it a lead, for my own enjoyment. The hunt was exhilarating. It tried to lose me in the tall grass, but I merely followed it in, not fearing scrapes or thorns. My heart raced faster than my legs could carry me.

The bearing managed to squeeze through a crack between two fallen rocks that blocked an old hiking path.

Without hesitation, I tapped into my focus. Using the higher Order that the beast had granted me, I focused on the light on the other side of the crack and managed to teleport myself there, right next to the bearing. I had to resist pouncing on the thing. After giving a fair lead, I continued my pursuit.

I felt the chase awakening something deep inside me, some hidden instinct. I could sense the bearing's desperation as I kept up with its speed. I was getting close. I could feel them surrounding me.

Out of the shadows, I was met by a swarm of bearings flying at me. I kept teleporting my body to different locations, rendering their attacks useless.

Finally they regrouped and melded together forming a human shape. Hordox was finally reunited. He looked exactly the same as when I last set eyes on him. His body was still, his rage building.

"Here we are again," I said, matching his stance.

The wind blew our hair in unison, our perilous bodies frozen.

"Not much for words this time around, are we?" I questioned.

He simply stood there, grinding his teeth together.

"I'm here to say goodbye. Let's just go our own separate ways. No bad feelings, no harm done. Just leave you to yours, and me to mine."

Hordox's eyes winced at the very idea. He slowly tossed his head back and forth. "Scared?" he said, almost under his breath. A sinister smile grew on his face.

I knew he was using my words to fuel his anger as he prepared for his onslaught of attacks. The smart move would have been to stop feeding his rage, but I was in no mood for smart moves.

"You know, every second you were inside me gave me pleasure. I felt your frustration from being so powerless, so weak."

His skin turned bright red as heat emanated through his body.

"I should have conquered you from the inside," Hordox said, giving in to my taunt.

"Why didn't you?"

"I wanted you to die, begging me for mercy, and today I get my wish."

His rage was too much for him to bear. He came at me fists clenched. His hatred only matched by the sound of his stomping feet. Every vein was about to burst out of his skin as he came closer. He was extremely quick for his size.

In the blink of an eye, I teleported my body to the side, causing him to miss his target. Before he could locate my new position, I retaliated by repetitively punching him directly in the throat.

His mouth opened, stunned by my attack. He quickly used his Focus in order to change his approach. Twelve medium-sized bearings started to flee. I kicked one, sending it off course. It hurt my foot, bruising my bones.

"I don't seek to kill you, but I will if you make me," I declared.

"Stop lying. You want this as bad as I do." Hordox said, returning to his human form.

I was conflicted, part of me did want to punish him, whereas another wanted to forgive. "Why go through all this trouble? Don't you have something better you could be doing?"

"Nothing could be more enjoyable than watching you suffer."

I knew the only way to beat Hordox was from inside himself. I had to tap into my past as Talia to locate his buttons and push them hard. "You may think yourself clever, but I've heard that one a lot. Is my pain worth your own?"

"You murdered my brother. Every bit of pain is worth it," he fumed.

"Can you be a little more specific? I've killed a lot of people's brothers."

He wiped the sweat off his face and came at me again, kicking up dirt as he ran. "Henrix!" His cry pushed him to attack even harder.

I met him head on, dodging and blocking his never-ending barrage of attacks. He was pushing me back. I used all I had just to keep him at bay.

Henrix, where do I know that…oh.

He used every part of his body—arms, legs, knees, head, back, even his shoulder. I couldn't let him land a single attack. Blocking his strikes hurt enough on their own.

"I remember Hendrix. He was a beggar," I said, hoping for a distraction. "The Prophetess took him in, and they became close friends actually. He even learned to fight as one of her personal guards," I said, not letting on that I was her.

"How do you know this?" His body slowed down, mirroring his mind, trying to grasp the situation.

"That's when I stabbed him in the back," I said, adding to the ruse.

Grabbing on to Hordox, I used my Focus to teleport his massive body fifty feet in the air.

He was caught off guard, limbs contorting as he descended. Before impact, he used his Focus. Bearings bounced and ricocheted off of every surface. Regrouping again, his transformation was nearly instantaneous. I was impressed.

"I am invincible," Hordox boasted. His laughter grew into a booming sound.

"No one is invincible," I shrugged off his statement, even though he had the high ground and a slight tactical advantage.

"It pleases me to know you remember him, and you'll remember me as the life in your eyes fades out."

"I didn't actually. He was nothing to me. Just another number on my ever-increasing total. Barely worth the swipe of my blade."

"You remember him. You said it yourself!"

"No, you were acting all sentimental and I took the memory from Capri when I slaughtered her too. Like your brother, you will also fade from my memory. Merely a name on my list of people who got in my way."

He used his Focus again, this time turning into a giant metal boulder aimed to crush me. He was amassing a lot of momentum.

I tapped into my push ability and used all three control strings to match the boulder's force, stopping it in its tracks. To keep his ire up, I laughed at his failure.

Hordox transformed himself into another swarm of bearings, which scattered into the distance.

Getting in his head was making him stronger, though reckless. I felt remorse for the words I said about his brother, but I had to keep it up. I knew I had to toy with him to keep his interest. If it came to another draw, he would most likely flee.

The bearings made circles then split apart, moving around in unison.

"Time to die," Hordox said menacingly.

He came at me, combining both his Focus and physical skills. He attacked and when I tried to counter, he "blocked" by using his Focus.

"Death isn't permanent," I said.

"It will have to do."

This tactic was wearing me out fast. I felt my body slowing down, and I was forced to use my push Focus to buy myself time to rest.

"If you kill me, you will absorb my essence and I will live on forever."

"Nonsense, I will take Capri's essence and let your Vigor return to the solid ground, forgotten forever."

Now he was getting into *my* head, and it showed in my ability to fend him off. "How did you know it was me?" I asked, knowing my appearance had shifted when we merged.

Seeing my weakness made him come at me faster and more aggressively. My arms and legs were bruised from merely blocking his routine. I had to change my tactics if I didn't want to suffer a worse fate than the last time we encountered each other. He was getting a little too close, so I increased my push Focus, knocking him to one knee.

"You may act like her, smell like her, but you don't look like her or kill like her. I can feel The Prophetess helping me, weakening your former glory. She wants me to win," Hordox said, knowing nothing of my situation.

I rolled to the side and aimed my push Focus to knock trees down upon him. He wasn't fast enough to dodge the tall pines as they uprooted. He changed into bearings and scattered throughout the forest.

I had to study his transformation. Unfortunately, Hordox had changed his tactics and stopped turning into his human form. Instead, the relentless assailant came at me in different bearing forms and combinations. They kept slamming into me, trying to cover my body, but I simply used my push ability forcing them to regroup. This was not working; I was almost spent.

It was a long shot, but I had to try something. I let all the bearings cover my body, this time faking exhaustion. I entered the other realm to observe his Focus in effect. His control string looked like fabric flowing in the wind, orchestrating the multitude of spheres with each wave.

Like expected, he turned back into his human form, grappling me tightly. I couldn't move at all.

As I studied the pattern, I knew it wasn't random at all. Each bearing took a particular position before his transformation. I had to pay closer attention.

He squeezed me hard as his massive head leaned back for a crushing blow.

I cannot survive that.

As his head came for me, I had to teleport out of his grasp, but I was only able to get a few feet behind him.

Hordox spun around, started to throw a fist, and mid-swing, went back into the ball form.

The force of that fist was coming for me, but when exactly?

He swarmed toward me and I knew this was my chance. I closed my eyes and paid very close attention to him as he turned human, finishing the punch he had started minutes ago. It landed right on my chest. I used my push Focus to slow the force, but it still felt like my whole chest was going to cave in and crush my lungs.

"This is the dance I remember us doing," Hordox grinned.

I gripped my chest, trying to breathe. I had him. I knew his pattern. All I needed to do was bait him one final time.

"You have a bad habit of stepping on my feet," I manged to cough out.

"You haven't seen anything yet. When I'm done with you, there will be nothing left but liquid."

He threw an impressive kick and turned back into his bearings, thinking this tactic was getting the best of me.

I stood up and made slashing motions with my arms to keep all the bearings apart from each other.

"You've gotten better, I must admit," Hordox projected.

The spheres were trying to regroup, but I kept them at bay with my fists. I wanted him to think I didn't want him to transform back.

"Henrix never spoke of you, not even once," I said, letting up on my attacks. I was very careful to focus on key bearings which I had been tracking during each transformation. I waited until the exact moment he started to change. Using my Focus, I pulled as many of those key bearings as I could into my hands. The timing had to be perfect…and it was.

"AAHHHHHHHHHHHH!!!" Hordox yelled out as he fell to his knees, gripping his side.

Inside my arms, I was holding on to several of his internal organs. I looked up at my opponent who was now missing an eye and trying to hold his remaining insides in place as blood poured out of him.

"This could have been avoided. We could have just moved on."

"I've been in love with your death for a long while," Hordox confessed.

His body was unstable missing so many key parts, which were still moving around in my hands.

"My death belongs to another. Now, are you ready to beg for mercy?" I declared my victory.

"Not my style. I'll never stop hunting you until your death is mine," Hordox admitted.

"I doubt I would have given it to you anyway," I lied.

This fight had been brewing for much too long to come to a simple resolution, and that pained me. Mercy is such a delicate mystery. When you want to give it, no one takes it, but when you wish for nothing more, it never comes.

He reached out toward me, never taking his eye off the prize. I knew if I reunited him with the flesh I held, he could return to his immune state and give me everlasting torment.

The hunt was almost over. I tried to think of a suitable send-off to show respect for such a formidable foe. Like a wolf stalking a doe, I felt as if I were frothing at the mouth when I discovered a hidden Focus inside me. It was a gift from the feylin beast I had fought in the woods. Like it or not, when I gained its Order, it became part of me.

I targeted Hordox's body with it, not knowing what it would do or how I could control it. Instincts took over. I felt like a child learning to walk. Each molecule in his body started to bloat as his mass grew like a balloon. Pieces started to separate from each other as his skin tore.

"Henrix did talk about you. He worshiped his older brother more than anything." The Capri side of me couldn't hold the truth any longer.

"Thank you," Hordox said, choking up.

His body grew too big to sustain itself, and it burst into a pile of unrecognizable tissue and bones. I knew he had perished when the parts in my hands stopped moving. Pieces of him were everywhere—on me, on the trees, in the air.

I sat on the ground and folded in my legs. I felt his power pulling at me, wanting to join my soul with his. Maybe he wasn't done with me after all. I didn't want to gain his Order. Yet, I decided to leave the decision up to the Lord Seven and prepared the Lustarian ritual.

"I regret nothing. I ask for nothing in return. Here lies a feylin who fought strongly, but was not worthy of taking my death. I leave my fate in your hands alone, and I thank thee for the honor, if you deem this Order worthy," I stammered, barely getting the words out. I'd never felt so ashamed for taking another life.

He, among all else, deserved to die—truly and completely. My rationale didn't grant me contentment.

As Talia, I had done this ritual dozens of times, and never had I been granted a higher Order. But this time it felt different. His essence was pulling at me still. I repeated my prayer. Hordox was going to poison my soul—get the last laugh he wanted. I tried hard to push down my emotions. It was no use. I knew this would be my undoing.

Then I felt the essence of another, and my mood changed to boredom. That's when I felt Hordox's Vigor moving away from mine. It was Rafee. He was controlling my emotions, saving me from my fate, tricking the gods—making them think that I didn't have an opinion on the matter. I was too numb to react. The world could have ended in that instant, and I wouldn't have moved an inch.

Hordox's life force pulled at Rafee now, and he accepted it with open arms.

I ran over to him, but it was too late. Rafee had sacrificed himself for me and just gained Order.

His body shattered into hundreds of ball bearings and moved around in a haphazard pattern. He couldn't control his new ability. I tried to collect as much of him as I could, but many had already rolled out of sight.

I had to save Rafee, because now I owed him twice.

Chapter Fourteen
Shrouded Scar

"I realize that I always felt the same..."

Capri!" Hark yelled out from the distance. I still didn't know how he felt about these new turn of events.

"Over here."

Hark rushed through the foliage with Paik not far behind. Both looked shocked at the sight of the bearings rolling around.

"What happened?" Hark asked, out of breath.

"It's not what you think...it's worse," I explained.

Hark started to fight the bearings, thinking they were Hordox.

"Stop it!"

"Huh?"

"Take off your shirt."

Hark looked at me inquisitively but complied.

"Now what?"

"Um, give it here."

He threw his shirt to me and I tied it into a sling.

"Gather as many as you can...quickly. Paik, this is a game, okay? Like seek and rescue."

"Yay," Paik said, scouring the forest floor excitedly.

I positioned the sling across my chest, and we gathered as many as we could.

"Why are we doing this?" Hark asked.

"We're still missing fifteen."

"Okay, but why?"

"It's Rafee," I said, finding one more trapped under an exposed tree root.

"Rafee? What happened?"

I looked down at my sling, and my sorrowful expression told a tale on its own.

"He…saved you?" Hark asked. "I knew you wouldn't kill him. You're not a killer, not like her. I'm glad Rafee did away with him."

I nodded, letting him believe the semi-truth. "Unfortunately, he's in pieces right now."

It took another hour, but we managed to collect all the bearings.

"Are you sure we got them all?"

"Yes, I'm sure. When he changed, I counted how many bits there were."

"Can I ask you a question?" Hark looked up at me.

I shrugged.

"How did you end up all…quiet? And, why did you push me into the portal. And, that ball thing—it was living inside you?"

"Start with one."

"What happened to you? I really though I'd lost you."

"I dunno. I only remember bits of pieces, like I was in a fog."

"But Capri is back now, for good this time?"

I stopped and looked at his boyish features. I couldn't bear to tell him the truth—there was never a her or me, I just didn't know it then.

"For good."

His smile broke what was left of my heart. I walked ahead, hiding my disappointment. I wished I could tell him my innermost thoughts—for him to understand the tough choices I had to make, without judgment. I couldn't lose him again. I'd rather live a lie.

"What now?" Hark asked.

"I have a little business with a couple harvesters," I said. *The core could reset our world again, and the fact that it's out there is all my fault.*

"What about Rafs?" Paik interrupted.

"I can't help him. He needs to learn to control this Focus, and I'm not familiar with the Materialism arts," I said, defeated.

"Do you know anyone who is?" Hark pressed.

"Just the Kailur—it's their discipline. They're located all the way across the Hungry Sea," I said. It seemed that the hunt for the core had to be put on hold for a little while.

Hark picked up Paik and carried him over his shoulder. Paik closed his eyes as he stretched over Hark like a blanket.

We couldn't start our journey finding the core with Rafee stuck like this. We had to help him first, that was our objective.

The whole way back, all I could think about was telling Hark the truth about what happened when our lips touched. I kept opening my mouth, never finding the strength. It was hardly the time for any more surprises. Maybe when things calmed down.

Paik stirred upon hearing the familiar sounds of the coastal waves teasing the land.

"We need to leave. Pack only food and weapons," I instructed Hark.

"What's happening?" Paik asked, rubbing his eyes.

"Hark, don't forget extra cloaks. We can use them as bedding."

"Hello? Can you guys stop ignoring me? Where are we going?" Paik demanded, his eyes half open.

"You're not going anywhere. You need to watch over the cabin," I said.

"Don't be ridiculous—he comes. It's dangerous here," Hark argued.

"There are dangers everywhere. He'll be safer staying put than coming with us to the homeland of that maniac, Hordox," I countered.

"We can protect him."

"He'll get in the way."

"I will not."

"He is already impeding our departure," I pointed out.

"Do you want his death on your conscience?" Hark said, releasing the birds he caught for me from the confinement of their cages.

"Of course not! That's exactly why he stays."

"Stop acting like I can't hear you," Paik screeched.

"I don't feel good about leaving him, Talia. He's our responsibility now," Hark said.

He called me…was that a mistake? Is he starting to forgive me for her life—accepting me for what I was, what I am? I smiled at the possibility. I would have given him anything right then.

"It's a long, long way to the southern path to the Kailur," I said, looking off into the endless sea.

"Not if we take this." Paik dragged us down to the crumbling boathouse and threw open its rusty doors. Inside was a vessel equipped with sails and an anchor.

"Rafs restored this from the old world. Isn't it beautiful!"

"Does it float?" Hark asked.

"Oh, boy, does it! I mean, it should," Paik responded.

"Do you know how to operate it?" I asked, gritting my teeth.

"Sure do. Except, I never really have," Paik admitted.

"Good enough," I said, out of options. "Okay, Paik, get your things."

He ran off into the cabin, without giving me a moment to change my mind.

"Make sure you don't let him out of your sight, okay?" I said.

"One of my eyes will be on him and the other on you, at all times," Hark said with a grin.

"Just get your stuff," I said.

"Ready." Paik ran up, fully packed, with a knapsack and supplies. It seemed like he had a bag waiting for such an occasion.

"I won't be that fast," Hark joked.

All three of us got to work removing the dusty cloth, which uncovered the wonderful woodwork on the deck. Next, we untied the lines from the winches. As I watched Paik and Hark work together, side by side, I couldn't help but think how close they had become.

Paik tried to set the sails. The only problem was that there was a calm, and the sails had no wind to push them. I used my push Focus against the dock to cast us out of the boathouse. We glided on the ocean's gentle hand as it carried us toward the open sea.

I glanced over at Paik and Hark who were covered in water and sand. I guess I had been a little careless with my ability.

"You guys look terrible!" I yelled, cupping my hands over my mouth to amplify the sound, and they both laughed.

"Hark!" a voice echoed from offshore. It was a female voice, with a hollow undertone masking its inflections. We raced to the bow. She was far away and nearly impossible to recognize.

"You expecting someone?" I asked.

"No one knows I'm even here," Hark said.

Slowly we pointed the vessel back towards the shore to get a closer look. The woman stood there waving at us, like a mother greeting her children.

"How many women do you know?" I asked.

"Jealous?"

"That's rich. I'm merely trying…"

"Turn around, Paik. Now," Hark interrupted. His face turned serious.

Paik grabbed the mast lines, but the waves were already taking control of the ship, as he was lacking the upper-body strength for the task.

Hark rushed to help him.

I focused on the girl. We were now close enough for me to see it was Daleta.

"Why are we leaving her? I thought you two were friends."

"We were more than that, but we're currently much less."

What did he mean by that? What happened while I was vacant? How much time had even passed? I looked around, feeling the cool ocean breeze upon my face—not cold enough for winter. Had the seasons gone in reverse or had almost an entire year really wasted away?

I wasn't sure if it was the rocking of the ship or something else entirely, but I suddenly became quite dizzy. A large wave crashed onto the deck, causing water to splash my face. Then it started to click, something about this whole encounter didn't seem right at all.

"I can't believe she found me. This is no good," Hark murmured to himself while pacing back and forth. "We need to go faster."

Was he not really out here looking for me? Did he return to the fold? I used my push Focus against the deflated sails and slowly began propelling the vessel.

Daleta sloshed through the white water until she was waist deep. We were much too far away for her to engage us anymore. It felt cold just leaving her, although Hark must have had his reasons.

"Where do I go?" Paik asked, steering the ship.

"Follow the sun. The hotter it gets, the closer we are," I directed him.

We floated all day, the sun's hot breath on my skin, until it crested under the horizon. I finally found the coastal jet stream we had been looking for. Exhausted from using an ability so long, I had to sit down to recover.

Hark looked so peaceful, grinning widely as he manned the helm, while Paik sat on top of the crow's nest. I marveled at the cool light sparkling off the waves like diamonds, though the sight was much more precious. Who knew how long it would take to navigate those uncharted waters and reach the Kailur, but I accepted the task openly.

I curled up on the deck and found my own peace as I closed my eyes, "Thank you for…"

I awoke to the sound of Paik screaming. I launched up, looking around, slightly disoriented. The sun was high in the sky.

"Is she back?" I yelled out, feeling a little seasick. The rumbling sound of the waves consumed my words.

Trying to keep my balance as the boat leaned left and right, I found Paik at the front of the ship. He was wrestling with a large carp he had caught. It must have been half his size.

"We're going to eat well tonight," Hark said, patting Paik on the back.

"Can we have a proper supper tonight?" Paik asked.

"I would love to cook for Capri, and you too," Hark said. "I feel like we never have time to just…talk."

"That sounds great," I agreed. Feeling flush, I placed my hand over my face trying to hide my smile.

"Perfect." Hark crouched down next to Paik and told me the tale of how Paik bested the fish from the depths below. After the story, he showed Paik how to clean the fish.

I made my way below deck to the only sleeping quarters, wanting to make myself presentable for dinner. As much as I knew it wasn't a date, it sure felt intimate. Just being close to him caused my bones to ache. If only time would reverse and I could live in the moment when he saved me.

I washed my hair in a bucket and brushed all the knots out. My clothes were much harder to make presentable, yet somehow I was able to get most of the dirt out of them. They were almost a completely different color. After all was said and done, I felt girly for the first time in a long while, and I was happy to.

I want to taste him, to feel close again, I thought as I touched my lips. My finger grazed something hard on my face, which took me out of my fantasy. It felt like a tooth—a sharp one. I rustled around, frantically trying to find something reflective. In the process, I knocked over the bucket of dirty water.

"Is everything okay?" Hark called out.

"Yes. Please don't come down. I'm not decent," I lied.

"Uh, okay. Just…checking," he said as he fumbled his words. I could tell he was thinking about me being undressed.

I found a brass bowl inside a cupboard. I closed my eyes, trying to muster up enough courage to look at what was going on. It was now or never. I opened them fast. I was shocked to find two small tusks growing out of my cheeks. What had happened to me?

"Oh, no. Please, no." I touched them apprehensively. There was always a price for gaining Order, and that feylin beast proved no different.

Why does this have to happen now? I couldn't hide anymore from what I truly was—a hideous monster. He couldn't kiss away my pain this time, nor would he want to. I threw the bowl at the wall, denting both objects against each other.

I searched within myself. I only had one option…

~

The dining table was set in the main cabin with cloth from the extra cloaks we had packed. Three place settings surrounded one single candle that was commandeered from a lamp. It was very lovely. I only wished I had felt more like myself, in order to fully enjoy it.

Avoiding the light, I hid like a shadow—darkness shrouded my face.

Both Hark and Paik stood up from their chairs upon hearing me enter.

I slowly stepped into the light bearing the medallion around my neck, revealing Capri's beauty. The necklace worked exactly how I hoped it would—it suppressed the grotesque tusks.

I wanted to cry when I felt Talia's appearance first fade from my body. I felt I was betraying myself, letting glamor overtake my whole being. Her features were a badge I proudly wore to represent everything we fought for, everything we were.

Hark gasped, his mouth hanging agape, as I presented myself to the light. He couldn't take his eyes off me. He didn't blink, like a hungry lion. I liked him to stare, but not when I wore this costume.

Paik looked confused upon seeing a different face on my different body.

"This was Capri," I said. My blond hair shimmered in the candlelight. The curls bounced as I glided, light-footed.

"How is this possible?" Hark asked, remembering to breathe.

"This charm, it keeps the demons out." I placed my hand over the medallion.

"You look amazing. It's really nice to fit the face to the person," Hark said, reaching for my hand, treating me as though I were priceless. I was confused by his sudden chivalry and it showed.

"It's my upbringing," he explained.

"Funny, it's the first time I've seen it," I said.

In our connection, I felt no reaction—not good or bad, just numb. I had missed him for so long, and now I missed missing him.

"Where's Talia?" Paik demanded, without being conscious of the fact that he was sounding harsh.

"She had to go away for a bit." I sat down and folded my napkin neatly on my lap. I wasn't used to acting so proper around him.

"No, you made her go away. Paul's mad at you both," Paik said, running out of the room.

"Paik?"

"I'll talk to him," Hark said. "Don't go anywhere."

I couldn't stop rubbing the jewelry between my fingers. When I had placed the medallion on this time, I didn't feel Talia's spirit suppressed like before. We really had become one—despite my physical appearance. I did, however, feel the beast's hunter inside fade from existence.

Still, I had to curb myself and give Hark the person he expected, the person Capri once was, that weak girl who could barely fend for herself.

Startled by Hark's return, I let go of the neck piece

"He's okay. He just needs a little time."

"So, just the two of us, then?"

"Is that okay?"

"It's perfect." My throat felt dry just admitting my feelings aloud. Things had changed between us. I was eager for everything to unfold faster than it had been.

Hark joined me at the table. He started to serve the fish that he had heated using a magnifying glass and the sun's rays. The meat was moist and cooked to perfection.

"My compliments. How did you learn to cook like that?"

"Just another skill that no one will pay me for," he said, forgetting his mouth was full of food.

We shared a laugh.

"How did you find me?"

"You mean after you pushed me through the portal?"

"Sorry, I just couldn't..."

"It's okay. I'm past all that now. I needed help, and I got it fairly quickly. I just had to tell them all about Kay, and then they trusted me."

"And, look at you now—a feylin."

"One without a Focus, apparently," he said, fiddling with the base of his glass.

"Maybe that's your role—the guy who doesn't have one."

"I like that, actually. I haven't even conceived of opening my sight since that last incident," Hark grumbled.

I knew training with Rafee was intense for him, but I couldn't just let him give up that easily. "Look, you'll be okay if you just follow the rules."

"What rules?"

"One, Feylins cannot see in both worlds simultaneously. Two, only use power you can control. Three, remain mindful of reality. Four, rely on your feylin energy. Five, make sure the risk is worth your energy. Six..."

Hark interrupted, "Wait, didn't Talia violate the second rule by Overloading her ability in your battle?"

"Yeah, well, some people never follow the rules."

"And six?"

"Respect your own weakness."

"You have a weakness?"

"We all have something we prioritize over ourselves."

Hark started to lean in closer, showing his own weakness.

Meeting him halfway across the table, I felt his breath against my skin as I tucked my hair behind my ear.

"I remember the first time I saw yo..."

"HARK!" Paik yelled from topside. We followed the sound.

Only the moon's cold light illuminated the deck. Paik was not there.

We both took off running, searching for him. I even looked in the crow's nest, to no avail.

"Over here." Hark found a rope tied from the ship to something unseen off in the distance. It was too dark to tell what was out there. Were we being boarded by pirates, or worse?

I grabbed the rope, ready to save the day, when I was brushed aside.

"Don't worry, I got it," Hark said, climbing the rope down.

I wasn't used to playing the part of a pacifist. I liked to be where the action was. Hearing voices below, I tapped on the side of the boat impatiently.

It felt like an eternity with still no sign of anyone. I decided to go down after them. Just then, I felt the rope sway. Standing back, I was met by six strange men, with Hark and Paik taking up the rear.

Each one greeted me with a hardy "Hello." They boarded with whatever belongings they could carry.

Helping strangers for no tactical gain was a nice feeling. Leave it to Hark and Paik to restore my faith in humanity.

I tried to help them aboard—everyone refusing, treating me like I was useless.

Our large ship began to feel much smaller with our new passengers, almost crowded.

A big wave hit the hull, I was caught off balance and fell into the arms of a burly man.

"Excuse me," I said, quite embarrassed.

He dusted himself off and paused. "Have we met?"

"I don't believe so. What happened to your vessel exactly?" I inquired, doubting I would get a truthful response.

"We travel the trade route, quite often really," another was quick to respond for him.

"Until that bastard," the burly man muttered.

"Shhh! Quiet, you," another interrupted.

"Excuse me?" I pressed the issue and the deck fell silent.

"We just had some…unnatural trouble, that's all. Nothing we couldn't handle," a third man joined in.

"I can see that," I said, finally getting a view of their wreckage. It was smashing against a metal tower that was standing erect in the ocean. I knew the tower was from the days of old and taunting their defeat.

A flicker of light moved from the submerged section of the tower. As fast as it had appeared, it faded from sight. If I had blinked, I might have thought I'd imagined it.

"Hark, it's a good thing you're doing here," I said, distracting him from settling everyone in.

"They just hit a spell of bad luck. Paik is the real hero."

"Trusting in people is contagious. You taught me that today."

"There is a lot more where that came from," Hark said, getting back to helping out. He had a glow to him. He was almost shining.

The wind blew away our silent thoughts as we watched their wrecked ship fade from view. In Talia's past experience, helping people always led to misfortune. Though, Capri had always had hope that no good deed would ever go unnoticed by the universe.

Breaking the silence, I recounted a quote from one of Capri's advisers, "Destiny is around us always. It's what you choose to do with that fate that shall measure your worth." With that in mind, I decided to take hold of fate with both hands and smile at the future.

We had a limited food supply as a group, but I was happy to share the romantic meal with our new passengers. The group was very gracious about our charity. I ate less than even Paik, as I didn't want to become burdensome.

The morning crept out of the ocean like a hunter. It tasted my face, and I brushed away my locks, giving it more skin. I took in the sea air, feeling the morning chill.

I was not myself. Sadness hid behind my eyes. Every motion felt forced. I was losing my identity, my courage, my personality, but it was worth it just to stand next to him. I had to hang on as long as possible, as I worried that tomorrow might never come. As long as I lived for now, it never had to.

I silenced my inner turmoil by carving an image onto a smooth stone. Art had a way of soothing the self-abasement that ate away at my being, never getting full. With a clam shell, I scratched an image of a fierce warrior and labeled him by name. *Hordox.* I threw the stone into the beautiful water. It skipped off the ocean's rippled face. It was a fitting send-off.

One of the shortest refugees approached me with a sleazy grin plastered on his face—just in time to ruin the moment I was having. "Wow, and I thought you were a sight in the darkness of night," he attempted flattery.

"What was that bit about the 'unnatural' trouble you guys had?" I brushed off his remark.

Caught off guard, he stood there letting his mouth hang open and dry out. "I…I…"

I widened my eyes, revealing just enough innocence to appear truly trustworthy. He looked at me inquisitively and I forced a girlish smile.

He shifted his eyes and leaned in close.

I could smell his breath. It resembled old fish and boots.

"Okay, but you know nothing. We picked up a passenger—not a real talker, but the scrap was plenty. Without warning, stuff started happening."

"What kind of stuff?"

"Unexplainable, eerie things. We tossed the trouble overboard, like we do with all of our unwanted garbage. Days later, the passenger appeared out of thin air. Everyone went nuts. In the end, our ship got destroyed. Captain, first mate and three others who were too brave for their own good wound up dead."

"How long were you out there?"

"A couple days. We ran out of water just yesterday morning. It was lucky you guys came along when you did."

Something didn't seem right with his story. No normal shipping route would go out this far. It wasn't a very direct route. They were scrappers, if I ever saw one, reaping the tower of its sunken treasures.

"What happened next?"

"The freak show? That's the thing…it just vanished without a trace."

"What did he look like?" I inquired.

"What did who look like?" Hark caught the tail end of our conversation.

"Uh, their old captain," I quickly responded, loudly. Upon hearing the word "captain," the whole crew started to sing a farewell sea song, to show respect. They were a rough and tumble bunch, but quite playful really, pushing each other around like puppies.

The song felt like it went on forever.

"Do you know any other melodies?" I requested, growing tired of the tune, which agitated me more each time it was repeated.

Hark approached me, his hand extended. "Would you care to dance?"

"I never learned."

"I can teach you."

"Not here. Not to this."

"Suit yourself," he said, picking Paik as his new partner and swinging him around.

I wanted to be swept away by him, but not with current company, not without my wits about me, and not until I could give myself completely and never take it back.

They eventually switched gears to some sort of game they were familiar with. All this to cure boredom at sea? They must have been out here awhile.

I preferred to lose myself in the breeze, the smell of the water and the sound of the waves. It made me think about how life would be without criminals, without greed—who was I kidding—without people.

"I see in the sea, some land beyond, or is it just me?" one man shouted out and fell to the ground mimicking despair.

Then another crewman picked up where the previous one left off, without missing a beat. "I, too, in the blue, see something coming in view. Or maybe, perhaps, it's just a touch of the flu." Like the man before, he collapsed to the ground.

This continued until all the members were all lying on the deck face down.

Even Paik joined in. "My legs are broke, my eyes they poke, but that land before us is no joke. Let's make it there before I…I," he said, grabbing his neck and gasping.

All the crewmen yelled out in unison, "Choke!"

They carried on with their games until we finally approached Fawn Outpost. All hands were on deck helping with the anchoring and lowering of the sails. They sprang into action without anyone asking them to. I was even carried to shore to keep my clothes from getting splashed. Paik and Hark weren't so lucky. They arrived soaked and sandy. Paik didn't seem to mind in the slightest.

"The Kailur reside in Steelward, south of here," I told Hark."

"How far is it?"

"It might as well be a million miles away, as we have no scrap and no food," I said, lowering my eyebrows slightly, expressing my displeasure with our situation.

"Paul can juggle," Paik chimed in, playing with his potato.

I pondered the notion of Paik street preforming, before one of the crewmen interrupted my inner thoughts.

"I couldn't help but eavesdrop," the crewman said, dragging a sack.

"You could have helped it," Hark quipped.

"You got me. Nevertheless, I would like to make an offer on your fine vessel." He pulled open his bag full of rare scrap.

"You had that this whole time?" Hark erupted.

"How much is there?" I calmed Hark with my hand.

"About two hundred worth."

"That isn't nearly enough," I demanded.

The man started to point out small dings, old ropes, and any other imperfection to try and lower its value. Even if he had carefully calculated every splinter out of place, the price would have never come down to what he was asking.

My eyes kept shifting from Hark's to Paik's. The ship was priceless, but at this particular moment we had a price…and apparently it was two hundred scrap.

"You've got yourself a ship," I agreed, reaching down for the sack.

After licking his hand, the crewman extended it in my direction. I diverted the gesture to Hark, who was wincing at what he knew he must do to seal the exchange.

"Excuse me, isn't that Rafee's?" Paik pleaded, tugging on Hark's clothes.

"He may never return. We'll burn that boat when we get to it," Hark said.

"Don't you mean bridge?" I corrected.

"We can burn that too."

Hark slowly licked his hand, instantly regretting it upon tasting his own filth. Hark shook the crewman's moist palm. Then came the final step in the gesture. Hark and the crewman pounded the ground, and the deal had been forged.

The crew quickly returned to the boat and continued their journey back to sea, with their singing already in full swing.

"I'm going to miss those guys," Paik said.

"They were nice. They didn't rob us…or worse," Hark said.

"200 scrap for that ship? They might as well have," I said.

I did miss the swaying of the craft. I had begun to take comfort in the motion. In port, the earth felt solid. Sea birds sang against the backdrop of the ocean waves. Local patrons had things to do and no time to talk about it.

When I was younger, I used to get so excited visiting a new location. I had forgotten that feeling. Paik and Hark both shared that wide-eyed excitement for the port town. All present company seemed in high spirits.

I had never thought for a second that I could change what I didn't like about myself. I always felt bound by my past. But every step I took was just another one for history. No one ever remembers where you came from but more where you are going. I was going to be with Hark; I just had to lead myself the way.

"I want to watch the fishes," Paik exclaimed, dragging Hark to a large tank.

A young, bald child walked up to me and dropped a flower at my feet. His eyes looked at me for hope. Out of habit, I knelt down and picked it up.

"Time hasn't given up on you yet, child," I whispered.

The child gleefully ran off in the distance.

"What was that all about?" Hark asked.

"Our clothes don't exactly blend in," I sighed.

Hark gave me half the scrap and decided to stay with Paik.

Nearby, I found a shop. I was fitted with a robe and shawl made of light fabric more suitable for adventure and the humid climate.

As I relinquished a few scrap for the wardrobe, I noticed something unexpected—a man from my past, sitting on a chair off in the distance. He was much older now, and required the use of a cane to assist his walking, but I was a hundred percent certain it was him. He was playing with his facial hair as if nothing had changed. It was Mr. Porum, my only living relative on Talia's side.

Hundreds of times, I had imagined how I would end him. Stabbing him through the throat, I had decided, was the perfect way to see his expression while I watched his life drain out onto his chest.

I approached him just like I had envisioned it, slow and refined.

He was using his tongue to get some unwanted food out of his teeth as I cast my shadow upon him.

"I do have a skill that I'm very proficient at," I said, pulling out my golden arrow with anticipation.

He looked up at me, without recognition, and waved me away with his hand.

"Greetings, uncle," I said, now getting his attention.

He took another look. This time horror scarred his face as he squinted.

I pulled back the arrow, ready to plunge it into his throat. It was titillating.

"I knew you were a bad seed, you wretched girl," he said.

"Even bad seeds grow into something," I said, jabbing the arrow at him, stopping before it pierced his skin.

"I should have cut you down a long time ago."

Pressing the arrow against his throat, he became still. His eyes said everything—his disdain and disgust for me.

I had him where I wanted him. I looked down at my arm where his shackle had once removed my flesh. Revenge was well within my power and my right. I wanted to make him pay for the life I had led. Every painful moment started with him, and now it would end with him. It was time to rid the world of his filth. He was the epitome of everything that was wrong with humanity.

Instead, I dropped 75 scrap at his feet.

"It's forgiveness," I uttered, leaving him with a cut so small he could have made it shaving.

"What is?" he asked, thoroughly confused by the interaction.

I paused for a moment collecting my words. "My skill."

He was speechless. I knew he really thought I was going to do it, and there was a time I would have loved to. I felt invigorated being indifferent toward my uncle, whom I had previously abhorred. This was the first step at a new life, and I looked forward to it.

Chapter Fifteen
Dawn of the Red Sun

"...but was careful to hide it from myself."

"Hold it right there," a familiar voice instructed me from a distance. I scanned the sea of people, not knowing exactly where it came from. I spotted the only motionless figure staring at me intently. It was Daleta. How had she followed us so quickly?

"Who are you, and what do you want with Hark?" she asked.

My necklace...Daleta didn't recognize me as Capri. I tightened my shawl, hiding more of myself from her.

"I'm a friend. He told me about you, Daleta."

"Then you know why I'm here."

"Indeed. I'm here to help." I needed to gain some insight as to why Hark had been so adamant about leaving her on the shore.

"Where is she?"

How I responded next was going to set the stage for this whole encounter. It was a gamble, but I took the chance. "Dead," I said, assuming she was referring to me.

"Good." A genuine smile took over her face.

I had to get more information out of her—where she was going, what she wanted with Hark. Trust was my best option.

"This port is owned by the Kailur. If you don't get marked, we will become a target," she warned, almost warmly.

I looked around and found what she said to be true. Every person had the markings of the Kailur upon their skin—some on their hands, others on their necks—but in all cases, it was clearly the symbol of a burning sun.

Daleta showed me her elbow, where she also bore the mark.

"Where did you get branded?" I didn't care to scar my skin. It would, however, help me gain her trust and avoid getting caught by the Kailur.

"In the slums. Let's find Hark and the kid before it's too late."

We casually walked through the port seeing no sign of Hark or Paik. *Maybe they left for another district?* I wondered. Though I knew Hark was more thoughtful than to leave without letting me know where to, I began to get worried. I tried to appear relaxed, despite being frantic inside. What if they were in a ditch? Or maybe the Kailur already got to them. I could hear my heart pounding.

"What's your plan?" I asked.

"Where were you going to meet them again?" Daleta asked, growing suspicious.

"Just over here," I nonchalantly responded.

She was on to me. She had to be. I needed another plan.

A beggar approached me, placing a wild flower at my feet.

My face froze, hoping Daleta didn't notice the gesture.

She turned to the beggar with a scowl. "You dropped something."

The beggar just stood there, urging me to pick it up with a raise of his eyebrows.

I knew what he wanted, and I tried to ignore him.

Daleta bent down, picked up the flower, and threw at at his chest. It bounced off and floated to the ground. "What's wrong with you?" she snapped.

His defeat loosened his posture. I knew that if I picked up the flower, I would be granting him acceptance and good fortune, as he had recognized me as the prophetess. However, I didn't want to blow my cover with Daleta.

The beggar turned and started to shuffle away from me. His melancholy infected his movements. I knew I had left him with hopelessness and suicidal tendencies. I couldn't stand it any longer. Reaching down, I picked up the flower and pressed it to my chest. "Thank you, sir. Have an enjoyable life," I said.

The beggar found his smile again and wore it ear to ear. His leathery skin looked as though it would crack. He bowed his head in appreciation and was off.

"What was that all about?" Daleta asked.

"Who knows? I guess I…"

A woman covered in filth dropped another flower at my feet.

"This is no mistake," Daleta said, looking around suspiciously.

They were all around, hiding in the shadows like cockroaches. The dammed and unfortunate surrounded us, each equipped with a flowery offering, hoping to change their luck. This treatment was customary in my prior life as Capri. Accepting the flower symbolized me accepting them into my good favor. Rejecting the gift meant they would suffer all their days until their last.

"You're the Prophetess," Daleta announced with great conviction, placing her hand on her sheathed short sword.

"I can explain…" I fumbled my words, as flower after flower draped over my feet, the mob closing in on us.

"It must be a real chore giving people false hope," Daleta said.

"I never asked for this."

"You may look like her, but your soul is tarnished," she said, now showing me her weapon.

With nowhere to run, I closed my eyes and tried to enter the Feylin realm. I had forgotten about the medallion limiting me. All I was met with was darkness, stale and lonely. I had no feylin ability. I was just as useless as the cluster of the dammed that surrounded me. I knew the consequences of going up against a feylin when you had no Focus to rely on. Only, my experience was from the other side of the coin.

With no other foreseen options, I lunged at her head.

She swiped high and I ducked under her sword.

I used both arms to collect as many flowers off the ground as I could. I saw serenity inside the eyes of the select few who felt my acceptance. Even if I met my end with her next swipe, that look was priceless—well worth the exchange.

"Enjoy your lives," I yelled, running through the mob.

Daleta was at my heels.

The mob grabbed her, granting my escape. They had something to fight for…hope.

She tried to cut at them, but they were too much. Her entangled arm reached to the sky as they swarmed her.

I fled, not looking where I was going, until I slammed directly into Hark's arms as he stopped me in my tracks.

"Hark, I have something to tell you," I said, frazzled.

"What is it? What are you running from?"

I grabbed him by the arm and tucked into a narrow alley. Paik followed us like a shadow.

"Learning from others' past mistakes can be much more fruitful than from your own. No matter how bad of a situation you're in, someone else has experienced something far worse."

"I don't want to learn any more of your misdeeds. Why are you telling me all of this? Why now?"

"I just have to get this out, and there may not be a lot of time," I said, leaning out of the alley to glance back at the dissipating mob.

Hark placed his hand on my cheek and gently turned it to face him.

I started to calm down as I collected my thoughts.

"You can tell me anything. You know that."

"In the ocean…"

"Yeah?"

"I…"

"Halt. Present markings," a deep voice resounded.

Damn.

It was a Kailur guard, fully armed. I had been careless, drawing too much attention to myself.

"We seek an audience with the Master of Steelward. That's why we've come here," Hark said, standing shoulder to shoulder with me.

I held up my hands, not wanting to make any sudden moves. I'd heard the tales of the Kailur and how they dispose of the innocent, if given a chance.

"No such request will be granted. Not without proving your worth," the guard spat, tightening his grip on his weapon.

Their culture was all about strength and dominance, and leaving the weak and feeble to rot without aid. This explained why all the vagabonds were living near port. Displaying anything short of agonistic behavior was a fate worse than death. Most of these unfortunate souls were looking for their ticket out of here, to a life less competitive.

The Kailur were a barbaric bunch, and after Hordox, I wasn't eager to brawl with any of them. I reached into Hark's pack and threw our remaining scrap at the guard's feet.

"You think I can be bought?" the guard spat.

"No, but we can. I'm buying our lives back from you. We don't wish to die today, not in front of our child," I said.

Hark put his hand on Paik and pulled him in close.

"Very well," the guard said with a pleasing smile, snatching up the offering.

He extended his hand to Hark, who licked it thinking a deal had been reached. Once they touched, a prism imbedded in the guard's glove started to glow, and ice formed around Hark until he was fully encased.

"Wait!" I reached for Hark, but the guard intercepted my outstretched arm. Everything became blue and still.

~

I was somewhere else. My wet body shivered uncontrollably. Nothing was working the way it should—especially my legs. A large puddle of cold water pooled below me. I pulled my hair out of my face and it crunched, frost falling to the ground.

"Why are you so damn…damaged?" a voice said.

I struggled to see the owner of the voice. My eyes adjusted to the images in front of them. It was Kay, alive and well. My smile quickly faded. *I saw him get ripped limb from limb. No one could have survived that.*

"I thought you…died," I said, my teeth chattering uncontrollably.

He looked at me curiously.

"I heard the same rumors about you, but sometimes rumors are just that—rumors," he responded.

I remembered the medallion was still in effect and decided not to play my whole hand. Maybe this was an illusion of some sort. I had to fish for more information.

"What did you mean 'damaged'? I've never felt better," I said, returning to his first question.

"I've known the Telandric for quite some time, and all hope has been lost, ever since your untimely death. I thought I had found fortune stumbling across their most prized possession, yet they don't care to pay your ransom or even rescue you. So, I could only gather that something is indeed wrong with you," he reasoned.

"I let down the prophecy, I suppose." My breath misted out of my body as I spoke.

"I think it's much more than that. In due time, you'll tell me everything I need to know. I just have to find out where to apply pressure."

"Where are we?"

"That's a simple question and therefore not worth my time."

I couldn't help but roll my eyes at his response. Scanning the room for clues, I noticed that everything was made from beautifully crafted wood, cut to perfection. Kay was adorned with wooden jewelry indicating Kailur honor and was dressed quite well. We could only be in the township of Steelward.

"How have you come to gain such high status with the Kailur?"

"Now that's a more compelling question, but a little too complicated to answer. Kudos for figuring out our location," he said, wiping sweat off his brow. "It's far too hot in here, don't you agree?"

Steelward was built around a network of hot springs. That's where they got their unpolluted water—fresh from the earth's bosom.

The contrast of the hot air caused my body to ache as it thawed. I was unamused by his little games. "Where are my companions?"

"You don't waste any time, do you? Unfortunately, it's my turn for a question. Why are you here?"

I lifted the sling over my head and slammed it down on the floor. Ice crystals shattered everywhere.

A few metal bearings rolled out, staggering due to the frost.

"This is one of yours, no?" I asked, not showing my true intention.

"Jaxie," Kay beckoned.

In walked a tall, muscular female with her head completely shaved, except a circle in the center of her scalp. Her faced showed little respect for his call. "Yes?"

"What do you make of this?" Kay asked, kicking the sack, causing more bearings to roll out. Each one started to slowly twitch as it defrosted.

She knelt down, picked one up, and examined it carefully.

"Hordox. It's him," Jaxie said, placing all the bearings inside the sack before they could escape.

"There you have it. And what do you expect in return?"

"I wanted you to help him reform. He has been stuck that way for days."

"Why would the unwanted Telandric princess want to help a Kailur feylin? This is getting curiouser."

This was a difficult question to answer. Giving away too much information to him would show my true intentions and not enough might raise suspicions.

"I knew his brother. I promised that I would take care of him."

"And where is this brother now?"

"Dead."

"Who killed him?"

"I did."

"This is all too dramatic for me to follow. Jaxie, take the prisoner away."

"I didn't come here as a prisoner. I came on my own free will. I will offer you an enchanted arrow in return. It's imbued with the power of a volcano," I said.

"I don't think you're in any position to be making agreements or demands," Kay insisted.

"I paid for my freedom."

"You came to me in a block of ice. That isn't exactly how I receive guests. The only way to pay for your freedom is with your fists."

I charged at him, but he used his Focus before my second step was made. My whole body became motionless, and I was powerless.

Kay was enhanced from the last time we met—a higher Order. Who knew how many new Focuses he had within his arsenal. Fate had guided me here. Kay held the prism-core inside his chest, and he wasn't exactly going to give it to me.

With a snap of his fingers, a striped falcon swooped down and landed on the arm of his chair. I read his silent lips.

"Seek payment from the Lustarians this time," he whispered to the beast. The falcon let out a loud screech and flew out the window. "I will consider your offer, though you have to earn it. Besides, it's the Kailur way."

He release his hold on me, giving back control of my body.

Jaxie motioned me to follow her, with a snarl.

I followed her down a mud-sculpted corridor to a dimly lit room where we were met by three hand maidens who greeted me with a series of grunts.

The inside was constructed of mud and wood. The oil from the lanterns coated my senses. The room had a small fissure in the center where hot water bubbled up. I could smell the sulfur as it escaped the underbelly of the earth.

The maidens started to remove my wet clothes and sponge me down with the warm water. Jaxie was intently sizing me up, not saying a word. I maintained my posture, showing no modesty or weakness. One of the maidens tried to take the necklace off, and I swatted her away. It was more of a reflex than anything else.

"Sorry," I apologized.

"You don't look special," Jaxie said, fiddling with her spear. I could sense she was imagining thrusting her weapon into my bare skin. If she was going to do it, this was definitely a good opportunity.

"Looks can be deceiving," I said, not giving her a glance.

"Not when you look soft and weak," Jaxie retorted.

I could feel her anger rise as she fell for my manipulation.

The maidens helped me get into some leather clothes that fit tightly on my frame. I used my hands to adjust and stretch out the hard leather which had been clearly crafted for a woman. Jaxie was dressed more like one of the Kailur males—loose-fitting fur, caked in soil.

"I think I look quite good, actually. Don't you agree?" I turned to Jaxie.

Her look showed that she now saw me as a threat.

The maidens brought a wonderful spread of Kailur delicacies. The aroma incited an audible hunger from my stomach. I rushed over and proceeded to stuff my face, forgetting my manners and proper table etiquette.

After feeling gluttonous, I motioned for the maidens to loosen my leather straps.

"Where are my manners? Would you like some of my scraps?" I asked Jaxie, knowing full well that I had taken at least one bite out of everything that remained.

Jaxie raised her spear and approached me hotheadedly.

I had found the limit—exactly where I could push her to—and it wasn't that far. My feet propped up on the table, I leaned back and welcomed her advance with a false grin.

She jabbed at me, more as a warning.

Now, it was my turn. Pushing against the table caused my chair to flip over. My legs wrapped around her spear as I fell, disarming her. I rolled to my feet, now with the upper hand. Even without a Focus, I wasn't completely useless.

I pointed the blunt end of the spear near her neck. "Crushing a windpipe works just as well as stabbing one, maybe even better," I said.

"Enough. It's time," a Kailur guard yelled from the doorway.

Jaxie looked furious. I tossed her spear back to her, grabbed one last piece of food and followed Jaxie outside.

The hallway was filled with steam, making visibility almost impossible, and the heat made it difficult to breathe.

Jaxie walked with confidence. Blindly feeling my way around, I bumped into every twist and turn with my staggering hands. Paths led up and down with many offshoots, making it nearly impossible to figure out which direction you were going.

Jaxie lead me inside a room void of steam. The ceiling had a large section cut out, which followed the sun's path during the day, giving the room maximum light from dawn to dusk.

On the far side of the room sat an elderly man, cross-legged, basking like he was tucked into the sun's blanket. Judging by his age, I knew it was the Kailur Elder. He still appeared strong, although brittle. His skin was cracked like bark on a tree.

"Excuse me, Elder," I said, but was met with no response.

I made my way around to see his face. It looked hollow. He wasn't breathing. I felt his cold skin. Was this some sort of setup? I started to shake his lifeless body and his eyes opened wide. I let go of him quicker than I had grabbed him. "I'm so sorry, I thought you were…"

His body made a horrid sound as it took in a breath. As he exhaled, he let out either a laugh or cough—I couldn't quite tell.

"I only wish that were possible, dear," he spoke slowly, straining on every word.

"I seek your forgiveness, Elder. I…"

"I know why you are here. But it's not the same reason you think you've come for."

"I don't understand."

"You're able to do what I cannot, and for that, I'm envious, child.

"I still don't follow."

"Don't torture an old man into explaining it all. You made a deal with yourself long before he came along. You cannot refuse yourself the task at hand. Death is a contract, and your honor is the payment."

The Elder seemed to know more about me than I had estimated. His words bore directly into my subconscious doubts. I knew he was right. Just because I had changed didn't mean my destiny had. I could no longer pretend to be something I wasn't—some fairytale that would have an artful ending, happily everlasting.

"You're right. I've been thinking only of myself."

"I never desire to be right or wrong, child, only for it all to end as fast as it started."

"How did Kay end up taking a leadership role so quickly?"

"He's ambitious, that one. He will give us all what we desire, in due time."

"What do you mean by that?"

"The awakening, it's upon us."

"Awakening?"

"I'm so tired," he said, slumping back down to the position I found him in. I noticed his breath slowed down.

"Elder?"

"An ending…"

With his eyes closed, the Elder reached out his hand. It looked like skin on bones. I placed my palm under his, holding it gently. He dropped a scarlet gem into my hand.

"Take this," he urged.

"What's it for?"

"It will serve your purpose. First, you must seek the tallest tree our land has grown. Jan has foreseen what lies ahead for you. Until now, I was certain that you were destined to fail. Today, I had a change of heart—only because you seem sweet to me," the Elder concluded.

"What about Rafee?"

He started snoring softly.

"Hello, Elder?"

I brushed some of his straggly hair out of his face without waking him. Never had I seen someone so ancient and wise.

"Thank you. It's what I needed to hear," I said softly. I had to stop thinking of Hark and start thinking of the future, of everyone else.

How many adventures had his tired eyes seen? His rusty voice invigorated me with a positive disposition. He knew things about me, and hopefully this Jan person could explain exactly what he wasn't telling me.

On my way back through the mist, I got separated from Jaxie. I was lost in thought. I followed the smell of fresh air until I found an opening in the labyrinth. This was not the entrance to the steam I had entered originally.

From floor to ceiling, cages stretched in a maze that carried throughout the large room. Each cage contained different beasts and humans.

"Hark? Paik?" I called out. Thinking they might be here, I searched each one, trying to quench my desperation. I continued to yell their names, listening for some glimmer of hope.

My voice awakened the prisoners, roaring as they beat on the metal bars. It wasn't long before each cage was shaking with excitement, though no one responded to my plea. I wanted to save them all, but it was hard to plan their escape with all the racket they were making.

They were not here. I felt a firm hand on my shoulder. Jaxie had found me, and she wasn't the slightest bit pleased. She escorted me back and gave me a hard shove into the room where I had first defrosted.

Kay was awaiting my arrival. The falcon sat on the armrest of his chair. I could only assume it had returned, as I watched as the falcon transformed into a skinny man with pointy features. The bird-man walked over to me and opened his mouth. "Worthless," he chirped.

What had the chancellor said to this hybrid? Had my cover been blown? No creature could fly all the way to Cape Castle and back in only a couple of hours.

"You shouldn't insult my intelligence like that," Kay said to me, skipping introductions and pleasantries.

"I held up my end. You have the arrow," I crossed my arms.

Kay lifted the golden arrow from next to his chair and twirled it in between his fingers. "Why didn't you tell me you were my old friend Talia?"

"Does it matter?"

"This is about honor and honesty, which apparently you don't have."

"I've done nothing to disrespect you."

"Your lips lie, even now. You come here without invitation, without bearing gifts," he said, scratching his head with the arrowhead.

"I saw you die a dreadful death."

"Correction, you left me to die a dreadful death."

"You wanted us to leave…you said so yourself." I never imagined he would act so differently.

"I'm starting to understand why the Telandric, and now the Lustarians, hung you out to dry."

"We had a deal." I inched closer to him.

"Did we? A deal? Yes, explain this *deal* we had. Please, enlighten me.

"Hordox for the arrow."

"Hordox for the arrow. That's right how could I be so foolish. How kind of you to return him to us. Hordox, come here and thank dear Talia for her great generosity!"

Then, I started to understand what was going on. Appearing slightly different, Rafee walked in and confirmed my suspicions. His face was almost the same, but his body looked much stronger, more like Hordox.

"Yes, Hordox, what did you want to say to Talia?"

I started to make a run for the door when a guard's spear was placed on Rafee's neck. I stopped cold in my tracks.

"So, you do care what happens to him, then? That's a weakness I can apply pressure to."

"I didn't mean to lie…"

"Yes, but you did, and it's driving me craz…" Kay suddenly stood silent, turning to Rafee who had his eyes closed. Kay's demeanor had changed in an instant.

"What a glorious Focus. You silenced the beasts inside. You may prove useful yet," Kay said in a monotone voice.

"Rafee, this wasn't the plan…"

"Talia, you may retire," Kay insisted.

"I have a request," I said, feeling Jaxie's hand pull my arm.

"You can bring up any requests in the pits," Kay said.

Back at my quarters, I found Paik and Hark awaiting me. They looked at me for answers. As relieved as I was to see them both, I couldn't meet their eyes.

All I could say was, "It's all my fault."

Chapter Sixteen
The Beast Inside

"I give you my heart…"

After all the excitement of being reunited with Paik and Hark had died down, I sat in the corner in silence. I was trying to come up with a reasonable plan that didn't involve any more deaths.

We are in way over our heads and have too many liabilities for Kay to exploit. This is not the way I'm used to handling problems. Bold, head-on attacks are what I prefer, but we just don't have the muscle to oppose the Kailur.

"Capri?" Hark spoke up.

Kay doesn't seem to be any major threat at this moment. Is it irresponsible to leave that kind of power up to its own devices? I must figure out his end game before tackling that problem.

"Just hear me out. I have some ideas," Hark said.

"Not now, I have to think."

We are not exactly prisoners. I know because they didn't stuff us inside one of those cages I stumbled upon. Leaving might be an option… though not without Rafee. Something has to be exchanged for him. I need to do something Kay won't be expecting.

The more I thought about things, the more they didn't quite add up. I started to question everything, even within myself.

"Hello?" Hark pressed.

I stood up. "What do you want?"

"If we can figure out what my Focus is, I might be able to help."

"You may not even have one. It's too much of a long shot."

"What's with the attitude?" Hark asked.

I took a moment to calm my nerves before responding. There was something that had been on my mind and causing me to act so harshly towards him. "Why was Daleta trailing us?"

"You mean at the beach house?" Hark asked, seeming on edge.

"She was also at port. I got the impression that you two were on mission together."

"You saw her?" Hark furrowed his brow.

"I spoke to her," I said. My eyes narrowed at the very thought.

"Are you serious? What did she do?" Hark asked, his hands fidgeting.

"Were you working with her, or was she lying?"

"It wasn't *exactly* a lie."

"I thought you were a deserter…that you left? Was that also 'not exactly' a lie?"

"She helped me escape, helped me find you."

"Then why leave her there? Why not finish what you started?" I said, swiping my hand across my neck.

Paik covered his ears, wanting the argument to stop.

"We had different motives. She wanted…"

"She wanted me dead. And you?"

Hark was flustered by my words; we both knew they rang true.

"I wanted to stop her." He approached me.

I placed my hands up, stopping him. "You didn't stop her. She's in full swing."

"Look, she confided in me about her mission to eradicate your claim as the Prophetess Capri…"

"I never cared to continue that path," I brashly cut him off.

"Let me finish. I went along because she had the resources to help me get to you. It was a mutual exchange."

"You get to find me, and she gets to kill me. How wonderful."

"I didn't think she had it in her."

"Oh, she has it in her."

"I never would have found you without her help and her Focus."

"You're lucky you didn't find me in a coffin."

"I never would have let her touch you. I had to see you again, even if it meant helping someone who aimed to hurt you," Hark said. His sharp eyes cut through my animosity, causing it to tear apart. "Let's work together for once," he said, leaning in to me.

Being close to Hark crippled me more than when he was away. He always knew how to make me feel human, no matter the circumstances. If only I could bottle up this feeling, I may never regret anything ever again.

"I believe in us," he whispered.

I wanted him to feel the way he was making me feel…cared for, special.

The door flew open, and we both sprang to action. Before I knew it, Hark and I were surrounded by guards. One guard had a tight grip on my hair. I couldn't see Paik, as there were too many of them.

"I do too," I yelled, trying to drown out the ruckus.

They dragged me out to the mud pits, bound and locked in a cell like the animal I secretly was. If only I could have reached my neck charm, I would have been able to escape—but without everything I cared about in this world.

A loud ceremonial horn reverberated through the whole city, amplified by a series of pipes running through the streets. Crowds of spectators flooded into the stadium like ants surrounding a carcass, hungry for blood.

The whole battleground was riddled with spikes and obstacles, which looked as if they had seen their fair share of death. The arena was designed around a large pool, heated from the earth's blood—the magma below. Warm sediment bubbled from the fissure, filling the whole battlefield. It was difficult to move through —too thick to be water, too solid for earth. The ground was clearly the primary hazard of the pits.

Jaxie approached the eager crowds. "He rose from these very pits, defeating each opponent and earning the respect of the people with each death. I present to you, the commander of Steelward —Kamen!"

The roaring of the crowds upset the geyser in the center pool, causing it to erupt thirty feet in the air.

Kay approached the high perch. "Greetings, it's my great honor to recount the loss of yesterday's culling. Kral, Stanwick, Marce…" The list went on for a long while. Reaching the end of the names, he concluded, "No soul will go unnoticed. Their sacrifice will live on, arming the victors with the experience to prosper in today's match."

I couldn't believe they fought like this every single day without running out of people to kill or maim.

A few blind men scurried onto the playground like animals. The three men circled around until they all met in a particular spot and raised their heads directly to the sun—their mouths open wide, tongues hanging out. Upon further inspection, they weren't just blind, their eyes seemed to be burnt out from staring at the sun. Their bodies shook as they scurried back to Kamen with a whimper.

"It is a good day for a fight!" Kamen proclaimed, and the crowd met his enthusiasm.

I was prepared for battle, eagerly awaiting release from my cage. Instead, they had something different in mind, something far more painful.

A guard pushed Hark into the arena. His feet sank in the deep mud, making a croaking sound as he moved.

All my muscles flexed, and I pushed my body against the bone bars that separated us. I lost circulation in my bound hands as I struggled.

"What do you fight for, Hark?" Kay asked loudly, his arms open wide.

"Freedom—for myself and my family."

Hark's opponent was set loose. He was a muscular Kailur fighter who made his way to the center of the pits.

"And what do you fight for, Edbar?"

"Glory!"

The crowd took to their feet, unable to curb their excitement.

Kay calmed the crowd with a loud "hush" that became contagious amongst the spectators, making the stadium sound like the wind blowing through tall grass.

"It's time for my stake in this battle. Present the child," Kay said.

A gaunt man entered the pits. He was dragging a chain attached to a shackle that was secured around Paik's neck. His hunched appearance made him seem like a social outcast. He tugged, tossing the boy into the mud. Paik was almost up to his knees in the stuff and could hardly move. The man attached the chain to a pillar near the boiling pool, then slowly exited the battlefield.

A child had no place here, inside a battle arena. I was speechless. If there was anything that would have destroyed me in that moment, it was abusing his innocence. Paik saw the world how I only wished it would be, simple and sweet. If they changed his outlook, even in the slightest, I couldn't restrain myself for the horrors I would bestow upon every last one of them.

"I wager the boy's life," Kay presented his gamble. "Now, I choose...Edbar as my champion," he announced.

"That's not fair!" Hark yelled.

"It is fair. The boy isn't your blood. Therefore, he isn't your family."

The crowd loved this turn of events and expressed it loudly.

By Kamen choosing Edbar to fight for him, both of Hark's goals were now conflicted in a paradoxical equation. If Hark lost, he would not gain freedom, although Paik would live. If Hark won the match, he would gain freedom, however, Paik would be slain.

"It has already been said in the presence of the Sun," Jaxie announced.

Edbar smeared hot mud on his face, making his battle preparations.

"For glory, for family, for the life of a child...let the competition commence!" a guard announced with great verve. The sound of hundreds of sticks banging together signified the audience's agreement.

Hark and Edbar trudged through the mud toward each other. Each one's unsteady stance was overshadowed by the fierceness plastered on their faces.

Edbar's muscles gave him a swollen look, but also made him slow. Hark was much leaner and faster, keeping a reasonable distance between them. I had never seen Hark fight before. He knew how to move, even in the sludge.

His opponent wasn't holding anything back, whereas Hark seemingly was. Was Hark afraid of hurting Edbar? These were ruthless people. I knew you had to show no mercy, and even if you did, they wouldn't take it. If Hark didn't change his tactic, it wasn't going to result in a victory.

Unable to bridge the gap between them, Edbar acquired a spiked root weapon from a spectator in the crowd. Spiked root had spikes growing on top of spikes. It was deadly sharp and easily acquired in these parts.

Hark pushed his opponent back to the center, closer to the pool, using the terrain to his advantage. It was a smart move.

Edbar swung hard with his spiked root.

Hark slid in the mud, dodging his attack, then followed up by stepping on his opponent's hand.

Edbar's weapon sliced through the tip of his finger. The audience "ooohed" as blood sprayed in the air.

This fight was not about fairness, it was about survival.

"Get him, Hark," I encouraged.

Hark turned to me. I could see a half-smile emerging from his confidence. I imagined his lips on mine, how they made me feel on the beach. My legs wobbled.

It was a critical mistake; I was too caught up in the moment. My distraction gave Edbar an opening. Hark got punched in the stomach and fell over gasping for air.

I couldn't watch. I had to do something. I wanted to interfere, but I couldn't.

Hark took a boot to the back of the head and was sprawled out in the mud, defenseless.

The crowd enjoyed the poor sportsmanship.

I hated bullies, especially this one. Hark tried to roll away, but Edbar kept on kicking him. Mud covered his body completely.

I knew the outcome of the fight, and that it was my fault. Hark was too kind, not ruthless enough—not for this fight, nor this world. I used everything I had to try and gain feylin energy. I kept closing my eyes, but the necklace was too powerful. I couldn't overcome it.

Off in the crowd, I spied a guard who was laughing at Hark's misfortune.

Edbar placed one had on either side of Hark's head and lifted him up, preparing to fatally snap his neck.

Hark's eyes rolled back in his head, unable to resist him.

"Flesh for flesh," Edbar yelled.

Fixated on the guard and on Hark, I did everything in my power to enter the Feylin realm. Every muscle in my body strained and hurt. I gave everything I had, and it wasn't enough. *Not now,* I kept telling myself, hoping that if I said it enough it would become true.

Failure was imminent. I lost my parting words. I couldn't piece my thoughts together to express how I felt about him, what he meant to me.

A loud crackle brought the crowd to silence as Edbar snapped the neck inside his hands.

I opened my eyes and blinked heavily to clear my sight. The victor released the lifeless corpse from his arms and let it fall into the mud. Edbar raised his hands ready to receive his accolades.

The crowd "booed." Justice had not been served.

My heart skipped a beat as I saw my hopes had been realized. I had to touch my face to know it was real. It wasn't Hark that had had his neck snapped. It was the guard that I had been fixated on before. I quickly looked to where the guard had been standing previously. Hark was in his place, looking at me with great intensity. They had switched positions at the exact moment Edbar did his final blow. How was that even possible?

During all the commotion, the gaunt-looking man approached Kay and whispered something in his ear.

"Silence!" Kay commanded. "There seems to be foul play regarding the outcome of this fight. This is most dishonorable."

My cage door flew open. I felt a shove in the small of my back, as I was prodded out. All eyes were on my meek entrance. The sun was hotter than normal here, and I felt small in its burning light.

"Who shall show her judgment?" Kay asked.

Men and woman alike were pushing and shoving each other just to have the chance to hurt me. The crowd wanted a show. They wanted gore and theatrics, a barbaric display of strength. I had to use my wits if I was going to win a battle without using my feylin ability. A riot was starting to erupt in the stands. They were cheated a death, and it had to be repaid.

"I know the best way to hurt her," Edbar said, bowing to his leader.

Everyone became calm with anticipation.

"I'm listening," Kay said.

"Give me the life of the child. That will hurt them more than any death could."

"Granted!"

Hark and I both yelled, but our plea was drowned out by the excitement in the stands. I moved as fast as I could toward Paik. Edbar was already closing in on him.

The taut chain inhibited Paik from running any further.

I felt something warm inside my palm. I looked at my bound hand. Light shimmered off the necklace that had been muting my power. I was free. There was only one problem…so was the beast.

Edbar stood towering above Paik, his foot raised to perform a brutal kick.

I focused on one of the chain links, and in an instant it was mine.

Paik fell just short of getting kicked and scrambled out of the way, finding his freedom.

Kay sent four control strings inbound to the child.

I teleported myself out of my wrist bindings and next to Paik. I growled ferociously at Edbar, who looked at me, stunned. I felt my body changing, my hunger for the hunt rapidly returning. All judgment became clouded as instinct misted over my mind.

Paik screamed at the sight of me, but Kamen's Focus wouldn't let his body move.

Edbar stepped backwards slowly, quite frightened.

Sharp claws and teeth manifested, along with two spear-like tusks. I felt like a weapon.

I want to be the person that reflected in Hark's eyes the moment we met. Not what I was before, or what I'm becoming now.

"Release him, Kamen," I said, in a low guttural voice. I was keeping my composure. I was still me.

"I will do you one better."

He switched from his "hold" Focus to another one. His control strings pulsated around like boiling water.

I knocked Paik out of harm's way, though I was too late. Black smoke emanated from Kamen's strings, scorching Paik's body.

"Paik, say something. Please look at me," I begged. His body looked lifeless and floppy. I knew from experience that was not a good sign. His expression frozen in time, reflecting the pain of a hundred deaths.

Another life gone because of me. Nothing has changed.

My body was fueled on pure adrenaline. No sound was audible. Time was taking a break. My body shivered at the thought of what had just happened. I looked at Kamen with revenge in my heart.

Hark quickly pulled the child from my clutches and coddled Paik's unresponsive body.

I could feel endless energy flowing out of me and I lost control, letting out a savage roar.

"What did you do?" Hark asked me.

My thoughts shifted more and more into the background. I was having a hard time focusing on anything.

"Death is my passion, and now I must indulge," I said, making my way to Kamen. I galloped on all fours straight through Edbar. Horror overtook his bravery as he tried to flee, terror distorting his face. Everyone saw me for what I really was—a monstrous killer.

My right paw grew three times in size. With a single swipe, I sliced into meat, ripping Edbar's throat out without even slowing.

"This is unexpected," Kay commented from the stands. I heard his words, but no thoughts or significance came from them. I felt my rage start to cool, just enough to speak. "RRAAWLL, Kamen!"

A figure approached me calmly. Was it him? I had to devour it just to make sure.

"Try to focus. Control it—the hatred," the figure insisted.

Before I knew it, another figure came at me from the other side. It was holding something shiny in its hand. I felt trapped. One of them had to be him.

I will take them both.

I used my third Focus and my head started to grow enormous in size. My razor teeth stretched out as I hissed.

"Don't lose yourself," the second figure commanded.

I put one inside my mouth and bit down. My teeth crunched on metal balls, instead of soft meat.

I tried to attack the other figure, although my feet wouldn't comply. I had enough awareness to search the Feylin realm for Kay's control string, which was inhibiting my movement.

I found the string holding my feet still. It somehow lost its hold and spun around, out of control. I broke free, following it to its owner.

Using the beast's Focus, I empowered my tusks even more, turning them into two long, sharp lances. Their weight pulled on my neck. I didn't waver in my attack until one skewered Kamen between his ribs. I combined the power of my control strings to make the tusks even bigger. His ribs shattered as he exploded from the inside out. My adrenalin was replaced by hunger. I started to feed on Kay's warm flesh. I was addicted to the satisfaction. Each bite tasted like revenge. Kay's blood splattered all over my short, striped fur.

The crowd fell silent.

I turned to see the figure I had tried to eat earlier. It was affecting my emotion somehow, helping me think, but part of me didn't like that.

"Get away…" I groaned.

The blood on my fur started to move slowly, congealing and amassing in a pool below, and started to return to Kay's corpse and shift under his skin. I let out a disgruntled moan and pounded his corpse over and over again. His blood sprayed further with every punch, but kept coming back. I shredded him with every weapon I had at my disposal—strength, teeth, claws, even my head. He had to pay for what he had done. Everything turned gritty and dark.

His body mended faster than I tore it apart. He was back and still breathing.

Kamen switched to the Focus he had just used to kill Paik.

I crushed his skull, never giving him the chance to turn his Focus upon me. I continued to swipe at him, until there was nothing left but the core. I bit down on it, but I couldn't damage the prism no matter what I did.

I was not ready to let Paik go. I had to punish more for what had transpired—Kamen was not enough. My hunger couldn't be satiated. I looked around for another target.

Spectators were climbing over the wall and entering the battlefield. It was a free-for-all rumble.

I spotted a nearby guard. Before I could unleash my pain upon him, I felt a hard grip on my paw.

It was Kamen. His body had restored itself again.

I ended him once more, faster than the previous time. It still wasn't enough. I eagerly awaited his return, so that I could feast on his death. It was an endless desire that only grew stronger with each kill.

"Stop! You can't kill him," a voice screamed at me.

I ignored it completely and kept slashing at every drop or piece of Kay's flesh or blood. There was nothing left that could be described as a corpse—just a splatter.

Instantly, serenity overtook my madness. As I began to process the events, my feral form changed to my former girlish figure. I started to feel like myself again.

The man who stood before me was none other than Rafee.

What had I done? I looked down at Kay's remains. Every drop of fluid, every skin flake, and every part started to slowly return to the spot where he had once stood. Purple tendrils were pulling his body back together.

I realized my flaw. He was never dying—he was gaining Order.

Hearing the voice of a child, I turned my attention to Hark. I ran over and scooped Paik up in my arms. He seemed hesitant for some reason.

"Who are you?" Paik asked, straining from my intense grip.

I loosened my hold and looked to Hark for answers. "How is this possible? He was…" I said, closing my eyes as I abandoned my feelings.

"I know. He came back somehow but seems to be suffering from amnesia," Hark said.

I found solace in seeing Paik again. I really thought we had lost him for good, and in turn, I had almost lost myself.

"We have to get him out of here," I said, looking around for a way through the brawling crowd.

"Are you in control?" Rafee asked, his hand hovering over me intently.

I slowly nodded, not quite sure myself.

Rafee released his Focus from me and a huge wave of remorse hit me hard. It had happened so fast, I had no time to change the events. For the first time I was scared of myself.

How did Paik survive? My body felt heavy and strained. I just kept running the incident over and over in my mind without any recourse or remedy.

"Paik, come on. Let's go," I said, but he was more frightened of me than anyone else.

"Talia!" Kay said in a deep, booming voice from behind me.

I helped Hark up. His movements felt cold and distant.

"This is a battle that cannot be won, Kamen," Rafee insisted.

"For you perhaps, but I just gained more power than you can imagine. All thanks to Talia here. I knew we were friends, and she just helped me a great deal."

"Move aside," I demanded, my hand on Rafee's shoulder.

"I'm ready to answer your question now," Kay boasted. "I came here a prisoner, not really built for physical warfare or even willing to learn. So, each day I was beaten in the pits beyond consciousness. I looked forward to it actually. That is, until I died. The only thing is, I came back—just like I did when you deserted me with those greedy cripples. Each moment of pain turned into bliss, when I returned the gift to them tenfold. Revenge is a beautiful flower that only blooms bigger with time," Kay said, sauntering toward us.

"He cannot die…" Rafee said, piecing it all together.

"Anytime he dies, feylin energy is absorbed into the prism-core causing it to gain Order, ad infinitum," I finished Rafee's thought.

"That's exactly correct. Each time I was murdered in the arena, I gained an Order from myself."

"Impossible!" Hark chimed in.

"Soon, I was even more powerful than their dear Doyen, and so I consumed him too."

The Doyen was the strongest Kailur, and sworn leader of all of Steelward. The only way to gain his status was to take it.

"Why are you doing this?" I asked.

"Hmm. Why does anyone do anything? To see if they can."

"When will it all end?" I asked.

"Once there's no one left to oppose me."

Just then, Kay used his Focus like I had never seen before. A wave of control strings blanketed every person inside the area, freezing them in place. I couldn't move any part of my body. I wasn't even able to breathe.

"Do you know what the Doyen's Focus was? It's quite fascinating, really. I can show you, if you like. Right, I forgot you have no control over your body."

I felt my head nod under his command.

His fingers twitched and a random person burst into flames. I could feel their pain, even though they had no ability to scream or move their body. Soon another burst into flames, and another. He was toying with us, exerting his total dominance. This was not the type of fight I enjoyed.

My thumb started to get tingly and twitch. I took a huge breath as I regained control of my body. My actions caught Kay's attention.

In the Feylin realm I saw an unfamiliar control string fighting with Kay's. I traced it back to Hark. He had two control strings, and they were both touching Kay's Vigor. Hark had discovered his Focus. He was able to control other feylins' powers. That's what he had done. He had used my Focus to remove the necklace that had shackled me, and he switched places with the guard before getting his own neck snapped. Now, he was keeping Kamen at bay.

With my temporary control, I begged Paik to come with me.

"Stay back!" he screamed.

I had no time for his games. I grabbed Paik under my arm. He flailed his limbs and carried on. I fled, dashing back and forth between the frozen people. They randomly burst into flames next to me. I had to try and distract Kamen.

"Rafee, help Hark!"

As Rafee turned his focus on Kamen, Kamen started losing control and released his hold upon random people.

This was the exact cover I needed. If I were the only one moving, I was a sitting duck. I rounded about to meet with Rafee, who had just regained control of his body.

"Make him angry, really angry!" I told Rafee before ten control strings wrapped around me, holding me like a statue. I could see one turning red, getting ready to set me ablaze.

Hark pushed one off at a time, giving me minor movement—just enough for me to teleport myself twenty feet away. I kept forcing myself on, moving my body to different locations, watching his strings try to catch up. I could see Rafee going to work.

Kamen released all his energy into a single giant control string which flowed toward me like a sea monster. His rage was blinding, and he wasn't thinking clearly anymore. The feeling was all too familiar.

The Kailur spectators started to descend upon him.

"No, get out of here," I commanded, though no one complied. They had a fighting spirit, but it was a battle none of us, even combined, could have won.

My compassion distracted me and I lost the lead I had. I lost control of my body as his control string embraced me.

Hark tried to deflect it, but he was much too weak. This was the end. The huge string started to change to burning red. It emanated from Kamen, a few hundred feet away, and grew closer to me.

"Hold on to my memory," the words fell on my lips. I wasn't even sure if anyone heard me or not, but it was all I could do. I wasn't scared. I was destined to die, and any attachment would just make the process worse. My eyes glistened as I watched Hark trying desperately to save me. I saw how deeply he cared, as he fought past the pain of overworking his Focus.

It was no use. It was time. I could feel the string heating up. I wished to spend more time with Hark. *Just a few more moments, please.* The pain increased exponentially. I couldn't even move to resist the feeling that surrounded me. It was like being burned alive but without the ability to scream through it. It was much too slow to bear. Then it stopped. I fell to the ground, grabbing at the echo of pain that still resided within me. I desperately tried to feel again.

"I cannot last much longer!" a voice called out.

I managed to pull my head up enough to see Jaxie, with a sphere around her and Kamen. The barrier of energy already started to crack. She looked at me and shook her head with a sort of cock-eyed expression. I memorized her visage in that moment, leaving her with a respectful nod.

Hark helped me up and we fled as fast as we could.

The whole city of Steelward came crashing down in chaos behind us. I could hear the screams of desperation.

"To overcome fear, you must learn to lose," Rafee spoke of our defeat.

I turned to Hark as we ran. I had gotten my wish, and I didn't waste it by blinking.

Chapter Seventeen
The Chosen

"...as I squeeze the life from yours..."

We spotted the Elder's tree from miles away. The elder mentioned it was big, but this was enormous. Never had I seen its equal. As we made our way, I continued scratching a farewell stone for the world to remember Edbar by.

I turned to Hark. My heart sank when he looked back at me, speechless. His clothes were torn from my large claw marks which had slashed and pierced his flesh. Even his arm was wrapped in a sling.

How could I have done this to him?

Hating that I lost control, I thumbed the necklace around my neck. I was too powerful, even for myself. I grabbed Hark's hand and led him off the path, away from the others. I wanted a moment in private to explain things. After I finished leading him, I released my grip, only to find that he had tightened his.

"Hi," I said.

"Hello."

"I...wanted to explain what happened...in the pits."

"No need. I know it wasn't you. She's trying to destroy you, turn you into that…thing, isn't she?"

Hark was caressing my knuckles with his thumb. It was comforting and nice.

"Well, not really…"

"Don't try and protect her. I will find a way to fix you…to end your pain. I promise."

He was blaming Talia for the transformation, and I just stood there and let him.

"Sorry to interrupt," Rafee said.

I pulled my hand away quickly. "We'll talk later," I whispered.

"What's going on?" Hark stammered.

"Paik isn't getting his memories back," Rafee said, keeping his voice down.

"He could be manifesting his own feylin power," I said.

"There's a first time for everything," Rafee agreed.

"If that's true, he drew his power from me," Hark said, gripping his arm tightly.

"What's wrong?" I asked.

Hark unwrapped his left arm. It was dark gray and withered like a prune, it felt rough to the touch.

"That's a curse, not a Focus," Rafee cringed.

"How bad is it?" I asked.

"It doesn't want to move, but it's painless," Hark admitted.

I had been too self involved with my own agenda to even notice his discomfort.

"Why didn't you say anything earlier?" I asked.

"I figured it was just broken. Now I see it is clearly worse than that," Hark said.

It could be an effect of him using a Focus without taking the trials. We were playing with powers we barely knew anything about. I should have protected him.

"You know what this means?"

"I might need a new arm?"

"No. It means everything we ever knew is a lie."

Guilt swallowed the conversation, until we finally reached the Elder's tree. It was the thickest, tallest tree I'd ever seen—maybe the oldest of its kind. Large spikes were lodged inside the trunk, forming a spiral staircase. Above the highest branches, shrouded in a low fog, perched a nearly invisible platform.

"Are we going up there?" Hark asked.

"I'm not," Paik insisted.

"Come on. Kids love climbing trees," Hark urged as I started up the stairs.

"Not this one," Paik said, folding his arms defiantly.

"Suit yourself," Hark said.

"I'll stay with the boy," Rafee said.

"You too?" I asked.

Rafee shrugged. "Paik, this is Paul. He was your friend," Rafee explained, pulling out the potato masterpiece.

This was it, the tree the Kailur Elder told me to find. I only hoped that this "Jan" character could prove useful.

"That's a potato," Paik said, still forgetting his past.

As I climbed the staircase, Rafee's voice faded from earshot. The constantly flowing sap stuck to my legs as I ascended.

"How long do you think his memory will suffer?" Hark asked.

"I hope it never returns."

"How could you say that? He's such a great kid."

I paused for a moment, catching myself. "You didn't see his expression when Kamen hurt him. That's something no child should ever remember. He's better off this way—trust me."

"Maybe you're right."

We reached the enormous platform, tucked just under the forest's canopy. It was mind-boggling how large it was, compared to how it looked from the ground. Water droplets leaked from leaves and splattered on the platform, making a finely crafted tune, each drop in a different key. It was the forest's song—soothing and pure.

Out of a small room, a doughy gentleman with little to no hair on his head approached us. His round cheeks hid nearly all of his wrinkles, making it impossible to tell his age.

"Welcome. A meeting in the flesh," he said, eloquence embodying his speech.

What does he mean by that? Have we met before? I searched both my lifetimes and didn't recall ever meeting him. Nevertheless, I showed my respects. "Jan, I presume." I greeted him, remembering the Elder's instructions.

Jan confirmed my assumption with a smile.

"I'm sorry, I don't *think* we've met before."

"Thinking is your mind's business. Your heart's is bleeding. Be sure you don't switch those two around," he said, escorting us to the center of the landing.

Was that a joke?

Little eyes poked and peered out from various nooks in the trees. I counted roughly ten or so pairs.

A strange marking was carved in the middle of the wooden floor. It depicted an eye and some glyphs that were foreign to me.

"Please sit," Jan urged with a wave of his hand.

I got comfortable within the circle, but took care not to cover any symbols. Hark followed my lead. Jan was the last to find himself a spot.

Immediately after we all took our seats, a young woman rushed out and served us all steaming hot tea. This was the beginning of a seemingly never-ending train of servants, each with a leafy laurel propped on top of the crown of their head. I wondered if they were property or willingly employed.

A boy followed with an incense lantern. I recognized the smell of jasmine, warm and sweet. Then it changed, switching between a myriad of flavors for my senses to taste. The billowing smoke had unique properties, bringing out different visions from our collective minds.

The first image appeared. It was a sprout growing into a flower, then wilting and wasting away. The second image was of a storm cloud. We all flinched at the crackle of lightning. Finally, we witnessed the calm breeze blowing over a wild garden. The fragrant air tickled our nostrils.

After hot towels, appetizers, lotion and the finale—a serenade from their whistling chorus—I was quite done with the pampering. I shifted uncomfortably, hoping we would start whatever it was that we came here to do.

"You have an interesting setup here," I said, watching one of Jan's people catching leaves before they even touched the platform.

"My family is eager to oblige," Jan said with pride.

"They're very welcoming," Hark complimented.

"Shall we begin the reading?" Jan asked.

Hark nodded in agreement.

"Reading?" I questioned.

"I see the future that will never come to be, find the past—especially when it doesn't want to be found—and sense the present as it unfolds," Jan explained.

"That's curious…if you believe in such things," I said.

"You're conflicted, though not internally anymore," Jan ancounced.

"Who isn't?" I knew by his eyes that Jan never activated his Focus. He was using good, old-fashioned deduction.

"I'm not. I know exactly what I want," Hark admitted, looking directly at me.

"You will be—even more than she is," Jan foretold.

"Now close your eyes and stay out of the other realm," Jan instructed.

I felt immeasurable power radiating off my skin. My heart pounded with anticipation. We were linked. Our energy completed a circuit, flowing like a steady stream. Each lucid thought would leave the thinker's mind and race through the next person in line, continuing on like an echo. Ideas became vague, as if my body was detached from my soul.

Jan was using his Focus now—that was clear.

We all started to breathe in unison. Even our hearts were beating at the same time.

To test my control, I forced myself to breathe against the rhythm, but I was unable. Then something happened that made me feel amazing—my mind went blank. I felt a cool sensation as my body began to tingle.

"I see you running through the meadow, wearing your favorite cloak to hide your face. You feel so free and so innocent. Pink flower petals dance around you to the breath of the wind. Now, you are scared. You've wandered too far from home. Time escaped you, and your mother is worried," Jan thought.

"My mother?" I asked. I had created most of my memories off the stories people told me about her.

"Not *that* mother."

"Oh," I said. Living for two sometimes blurred the events of my past.

"You take your time selecting the perfect flower for her, even while you're in grave danger," Jan went on.

I felt my own emotions as if I were there, even though I had no recollection of the events. "What danger? Tell me," I cried.

"You try to run, but the earth won't let you. You close your eyes for shelter—from yourself, from the fear," Jan continued, speaking methodically.

"Where is she? I want to see her," I said, begging for closure.

"It was the day your world ended."

"I don't remember any of this..." I said.

Jan kept speaking, as if he was not hearing any of my words, enthralled with his Focus. "Your mother was pleased with your destiny, but you're not. Something is missing, something is wrong.

"You decide to forget the pain and restart anew. Before you do, however, you take one last look at…I've lost it," Jan said.

There must have been a good reason for me to block all this out.

"Who said that?" Hark asked.

"Her fate changed when your souls converged," Jan explained.

"What about the other?" I inquired.

"I see…no change. That path has always been the same."

"Sharing a destiny can be a blessing, but in your case, it's a curse," Jan said.

Our connection increased. Jan's premonition was on the outskirts of my mind, almost within my grasp.

"How can she cleanse herself from Talia," Hark pondered, and we all felt his thoughts.

I opened my eyes. The magical connection was no more.

Hark had heard my thoughts in a different voice. I was embarrassed, my hands moist. What if he found out the truth?

"That's it? What about me?" Hark questioned, itching his eye.

"You have no memories that are hidden," Jan told him.

"But there are tons of holes. Can't you find those?"

"No amount of my power could bring those back. Your lost time is merely a wound. It will scab, heal and scar. Normal people only remember events of great significance, good or bad, and simply forget the boring stuff. Your mundane ability, however, allows you to recall everything, even that you *had* forgotten something. It's your body's defense that won't allow you to access them."

"Then can you at least tell me what my Focus is?" Hark asked.

"You know what it is. I saw you use it in Steelward," I exclaimed.

"No, I saw your control strings, and I used my control strings to distract Kamen."

"I wasn't using my control strings, you were. That's your Focus, to control other abilities. This medallion prohibits me from using any feylin arts. It was your Focus that activated mine. I thought you knew," I said.

"Are you serious?"

"Yes. You saved us all back there, as a feylin."

"I didn't take the trials," Hark said.

"The trials are used to graft a Focus onto your Vigor that may or may not have developed naturally. They serve as a shortcut. In theory, you can get there without them, becoming a pure feylin. It's rare, but it can happen."

"Rafee tried that, and it didn't work," Hark argued.

"Or maybe it did."

"Name one feylin you know like that."

"Hark," Jan said.

"Besides me!"

"The Sempiternal," I said.

"Correct, Talia, that's the only other known purelin," Jan agreed.

"The sem…what?"

"The highest Order feylin in existence. He was the first—before the trials, before the factions. Some think even before the world's death. Others think he could have caused it," I said.

"Each faction has their own methods of creating feylins. The Lustarians use Divination, and the Telandric focus solely on Psionics. Different approaches learned from the feylin father, the Sempiternal," Jan elaborated.

"So, that's why Hark doesn't have the scar," I interjected.

"Scar?" Hark puzzled.

Jan walked toward me.

I already knew what he wanted from me. I flipped over my hair to reveal a marking located on the back of my neck.

Jan placed his hand over the spot and it began to glow a multitude of color. "Hmm," he said, trying to make sense of the glow as it swirled. "The Portent Fury."

"You've got it wrong," I spat, standing up abruptly.

"I'm only the reader, not the writer," Jan explained.

"Well, read it again," I demanded.

"I don't understand the significance of the title," Hark admitted.

"I'm one of the few that can understand the language of the arts—forged from one of the first factions that no longer exists. Due to the difficulty of the task, it's outlawed to harm a reader in any way."

"Lucky you," Hark said.

It was official, I was a third Order feylin. The feylin beast had sabotaged my soul and stowed away in my very birthright—my destiny. I didn't feel it inside me the way we felt each other. It was a parasite.

"How do I fix it?" I sulked.

Jan looked up at me with a blank stare. "Time. It heals everything, even a dying man."

"How can time do that?" Hark asked, missing the point completely.

"By killing him," I answered.

"Of course," Jan agreed.

At that moment, I felt something brush up against my leg. I looked down and saw a doe-eyed pongo dog looking back at me.

"Oh no, not one of those." Hark couldn't contain his words.

"It's okay, you can pet him," a servant said.

Then it all hit me. All the people running around, they must have been the baggage that came with the pongo dog. This was surprising. Someone as smart as Jan, who studied his whole life to become a reader, fell for a trick as simple as this?

Hark reached down and started to scratch him behind the ears. I noticed how soft each strand of fur was and how his fingers glided through them.

"This is wonderful," Hark admitted blissfully.

On second thought, his baggage wasn't really that bad after all. Jan had a life built here that anyone would be envious of. I hoped Hark wasn't regretting his decision to not pick one of those things up in West Corick.

"Do you know of Kamen?" I asked, cutting to the chase.

"Yes. That's why you've come," Jan said.

"How do you know?" I pressed.

"I know what happens in the future, because I lived it. My life started with my death, and now I'm going through the emotions backwards until my own birth—when I shall cease to exist," Jan elucidated.

"Don't you fear dying as an infant?" Hark prodded.

"On the contrary, I must move through the motions to lead myself to my own ending. I still remember the past as you do, I just perceive it backwards. My words even used to come out backwards, until I realized that people couldn't understand me."

"So, you know what I'm going to say before even I do?" I asked.

"Of course. It wasn't by chance that you came here today."

"Have you already lived your own death?" I asked, fascinated with the whole concept, true or not.

"My death was also my birth—it was the first moment of my life. I started my existence with a whole lifetime of knowledge." Jan shrugged off the question as though he'd heard it before.

"Why not just tell us how it all ends, and save us the effort," I suggested.

"Capri, come on," Hark snickered.

"As time passed, people came to me, complaining that my predictions never came true. But the oddity is that I never remember telling them. It must be part of some paradoxical conundrum—divulging the future will make it not happen."

"Sounds like an excuse if you ask me. You can never be wrong," I explained.

"Or prove your predictions correct," Hark added.

"Maybe so, but the moment you realize I was telling the truth, it will all be too late."

"How do we stop Kamen?" I asked.

"I already showed you everything that needs to be seen. If I tell you any more, it may not happen."

"All you did was make up some story about my childhood that never existed."

"Inside your dreams, I've answered the questions your heart asked. The possible futures, the past, and what never can be," Jan revealed.

I knew there was something familiar about him. He had been meddling with my subconscious. He was the reason I couldn't sleep at night.

"Where's this Sempiternal thing? Can we get him to help us?" Hark asked.

"I know where he is. Though he's dormant at the moment," Jan said.

I studied Jan's expressionless face. It told me all too much—that we were in fact on the right trail. The Sempiternal was the only feylin higher Order than Kamen. It had to be our fate to go to him.

"Are we able to stop Kamen?" Hark asked.

"As much as he is able to stop you," Jan said.

"Hark, use your memory. Were there any clues in something he said?" I asked.

Hark's eyes fluttered as he scanned every moment he had with Kamen. "Only something about the awakening. He mentioned that more than once," Hark said.

"The awakening? The Kailur Elder spoke of it too. Does that mean setting the Sempiternal free," I said, watching his reaction.

"His freedom, it's inevitable," Jan said with a nod.

"That must be where he is going. Will you take us there?"

"I've already lived through doing just that," Jan said, taking in a deep breath.

If that was truly Kamen's goal, that's where we could find him. There was one more thing that needed to be addressed.

"What about Hark's arm? What can you do for it?"

Hark pulled the grotesque limb out of his robe, a rotten smell wafted out.

Jan closed his eyes and started to hum loudly, almost speaking in slurs. One of his servants dashed over to him and put a tube up to his face, which amplified the sound. The bark on the old tree started to crawl, changing the tree's outer skin.

A servant collected sap that drained out of the tree and placed it delicately in a powder-filled vial. They bonded together and bubbled.

Jan finished his strange ritual. "Rage oil—only use a drop at a time," he said as the servant corked the vial and handed it to Hark.

Jan stood up and dusted off his clothes. He placed his arm over Hark's shoulder as they walked among the tree's top branches, speaking in hushed tones.

Why wasn't I privy to their conversation? Jan had a way of frustrating a person. Every one of his answers left me guessing even more than I had before I opened my mouth. Why had the Kailur Elder sent me here? I doubted everything Jan had said. Maybe he was just a loonbat.

Finally, they finished their words. Jan extended his arms, and Hark denied his gesture rudely.

What could Jan have said to upset Hark so much?

"Everything has been *handed* to you. That's all I can say." Jan turned to me.

"This has really been an emotional day for everyone," I said, eying Hark who had a forlorn look to him.

"Goodbye," Jan said, garnished with a smile.

We weren't leaving yet.

A mysterious shadow appeared next to Hark. I looked around seeking its source. Without warning, Daleta appeared where the shadow had been cast.

"Gotcha," she said, grabbing ahold of Jan.

Before I could say a single word, they both vanished out of thin air.

How did I not see this coming? If I had been more prepared, I could have stopped her.

Where did she go? She can't be far away. I looked off in the forest-scape. Everything seemed untouched.

Did that smile mean that Jan knew she was coming…which would mean that everything he said was true.

"Jan!" Hark called out repetitively.

I grabbed one of the servants, looking for answers. "Where did he go?"

"I don't know. He always anticipated today's celebration. Isn't that why you've come?"

"Hark, you said Daleta helped you track me down. What's her Focus?"

"She can manipulate the sight spectrum. It only works if she has something sentimental in order to make the connection. I saw how she looked through your eyes."

"What?"

"She only used it once, while you were looking at a sign for a long while. That's how I found you after your tracks had faded away."

"What did she have of mine?"

He pulled something that was wrapped in dried leaves out of his pack.

"What's that?" I asked reluctantly, ready for anything.

Hark handed me the package. "I was going to give it to you as a gift. Now is as good a time as any."

I tore through the leaves. As they crumbled, I uncovered the dagger the chancellor had given me. I remembered losing it in the woods when fighting the feylin beast. Hark really was following me.

"I stole it from her, so that she couldn't follow us."

"Then how is she here now?"

"She must have something of mine as well."

"That's not at all scary," I said, looking closely inside his eyes. "Can she see me now?"

"It's very possible."

I leaned in closer and mouthed, very clearly, the most obscene insult I could fathom—one I would never utter aloud with a child in earshot.

Hark's eyes almost poked out of his head as he put together the words I didn't speak.

Rafee and Paik made it to the top of the platform, panting.

"We…heard…screams…" Rafee said.

"It's all over now. Jan is gone, and there's a spy afoot."

I tore off a piece of fabric and wrapped it over Hark's eyes. "I can't take any more chances."

"What do you want me to do, walk around blind?"

"Go into the feylin realm. You can navigate from there."

While explaining the whole situation to Rafee and Paik, the servants fed us a hot meal of hawk eggs and tree-grown veggies.

"Why did Jan keep referring to you as Talia?" Hark asked suddenly.

"Maybe he likes that name better?" I evaded.

He knew there was something I wasn't telling him.

Just a little more time, I promised myself. "We should hurry and figure something out. Kay isn't exactly going to kill himself." I tried to change the subject.

"That isn't a half-bad idea, actually," Hark said.

"That won't happen," Rafee laughed.

"What if you helped him become so depressed that maybe he would?" Hark looked at Rafee.

"Wouldn't he just get more powerful?" I asked, forgetting there was food in my mouth.

"Right," Hark said, defeated.

"Jan told me we had everything we needed. Let's go over our options," I said.

"I know some Valkyrēnēs that would help me unconditionally," Hark offered.

"There's no time to contact them," I answered.

"When I merged with Hordox, I had no control over myself, and if the Kailur hadn't taught me how to control it, I would still be a pile of ball bearings scattered around."

"What are you getting at?" Hark asked.

"If Kamen gains my Order, he will be unable to control it and won't be able to reform, no matter how powerful he is."

"Are you sure about that?" Hark asked.

I thought hard about what Jan had told me. This scenario seemed familiar, like deja vu. I vaguely recalled dreaming of this very plan, and the outcome was only temporary—Kamen would return. That is, of course, if what Jan had told me about my dreams was correct.

"Rafee, how did you defeat Hordox anyway? He seemed strangely powerful," Hark inquired.

"I didn't overtake him," Rafee admitted.

Oh no, I have to interrupt. I was ashamed of what I had done to Hordox. Hark would never trust that Capri had anything to do with it. I needed time to explain, to get him to understand.

"That's a noble sacrifice, although it's too risky. I could always transport him to the Feylin realm, leaving him trapped there forever," I said.

"Then you would have to…No, there has to be another way," Hark said.

"How is that possible?" Rafee asked.

"It will work. I've done it once before and it's…permanent. I only have to die in the middle of it."

"Interrupting its effect before completion? I must say, that is a magnificent use of your focus. Although, I can't say I'm keen on the idea of you sacrificing yourself," Raffe conceded.

"Why can't you just live for your own happiness?" Hark protested.

"I've taken enough lives. Maybe it's time to give one back. It's…"

"I won't let you do this. You don't always have to put your life on the line to prove your worth. You're important, okay?" Hark cut off my words sharper than if he had used a blade.

"If it means all of you will live, there is no contest," I said, airing my feelings.

"Look at Paik. Would you lay your life on the line for his future?" Rafee asked Hark.

"ENOUGH! No one is going to die. I won't allow it!" Hark shouted.

"People die every single day, for a lot less and a lot worse," I lamented.

"Does anyone have any other ideas? Anything at all?" Hark pressed, his voice trembling.

I knew my option was the only permanent one; I had to suggest it. Why wouldn't he listen? I wanted a moment alone to tell him how I felt, to take a leap as he once did with me. I was tired of pushing him away, tired hiding myself. I had evolved into the person I'd always wanted to be, from both perspectives—the perfect version of myself—and I wanted to let the world meet her.

"Wait. Jan said everything had already been *handed* to us..." I quickly pulled out the crimson gem.

"What's this?" Hark asked, picking up the gem.

"Where did you get that artifact?" Rafee inquired.

"The Kailur Elder gave it to me when he instructed me to meet Jan."

"A bloodgem...that might work. It's, by far, our best option. We will need at least four feylins in order to activate it," Rafee said.

"Why four?" Hark asked.

"Because, we need one to act as an implement and the other three to charge the gem. It might work with less, but it would be less potent," Rafee explained.

"Charge it?" I asked.

"A bloodgem can channel feylin energy once a Focus is used on it. The energy is transferred to an implement, which can then be used to reduce Order."

"What's the implement?" I asked.

"Not *what*, who," Rafee said.

The Elder must have known all along what we planned to do.

"Once his power is drained, we can overtake him," Rafee explained.

"I will be the implement," Hark volunteered.

"I won't allow it," I said.

"I agree. It takes a huge toll on the implement to harness all that power at once. You're unique Hark, but you're feylin power is too immature to hold that burden," Rafee said.

"What? First I'm a feylin, then I'm not a good enough one? Didn't you see me back there? I was helping, wasn't I?"

"You're much too important," Rafee admitted.

"What could be more important than stopping Kamen?"

"A pure feylin," Rafee said intensely.

Rafee's words caused a chill to sweep over my body.

"This isn't pure," Hark said, using his working hand to hold up his wounded arm.

"Destiny isn't always pretty," Rafee said.

"What if the gem doesn't work?" Hark asked.

"Then plan B—Rafee's plan. We keep all the bearings from reuniting. He will be powerless to do anything…a fate worse than death," I reminded them.

Rafee nodded. "We need an implement for the bloodgem," he pondered.

"It has to be me. It's my responsibility," I said.

"First things first, we need a few more feylins to charge it," Rafee said.

"What if we reach out to all the factions?" Hark proposed, looking to the west for answers.

"They won't come. Never again will they join forces for a common goal," Rafee said.

"We just have to make the best of what we have…the sooner the better," I said.

Jan's tribe accommodated us with rations and supplies for our journey. Everyone was energized. Hope can sometimes be the best remedy for a broken demeanor.

"Thanks for everything," Hark said, as we were ready to make our departure.

Rafee and I both stared off at Paik playing with the other children. We had the same idea but feared saying it aloud. Paik had to stay here with his new family. He didn't remember any of us anymore than he knew Jan's people. Saying goodbye would only hurt me more.

Without Paik, the three of us made our way back to what was left of Steelward. The Kailur survivors were already rebuilding the clay city. There was no reason to make a stealthy approach, since it was apparent that Kamen was no longer there…only the aftermath of his destruction. Leading the operation was Jaxie. She was a true leader, pushing orders and commands left and right. Noticing our approach, I could see by her gestures that she was displeased with our arrival.

"Leave now. You've all done enough," Jaxie shouted.

We kept true to our stride.

"Where is he?" I asked.

"Gone. Just as you should be," Jaxie urged.

"Which direction did he go?" Hark asked this time.

Jaxie picked up her broken spear. "No direction, he just vanished. He was lucky too; I was starting to get the better of him," Jaxie boasted.

Hark and I looked at each other in shock, coming to the same conclusion.

"Was there a girl?" "Was he alone?" Hark and I said at the same time.

"What does it matter? He won, and you cowards fled, leaving the real warriors to tend to the dead," she said.

"If more fled, there wouldn't be nearly as many casualties to contend with," I countered.

"We need your assistance to finish Kamen for good," Rafee pleaded.

"Why, because I can control my power, unlike some?" Jaxie retorted, narrowing her eyes at me.

I had a way with women—for some reason, they never liked me. "We don't need her. I would rather recruit the old fossil and carry him on my back," I admitted, patting my shoulder.

"Look, you two, Kamen will eventually come back here, and when he does, it will be much worse this time because he will be twice as strong," Rafee explained.

"No one is that powerful," Jaxie scoffed.

"Currently speaking, you're right. After Kamen awakens the Sempiternal, who knows," Rafee reasoned.

"The First?" Jaxie marveled. "Okay, I'll go."

"Why the sudden change of heart?" I had to ask.

"The First has been sleeping for more than two hundred years. Even if it's the end of all existence, I would like to have a front row seat for his awakening."

We stayed in the decimated city, helping out where we could. We had our fourth, and no idea where the Sempiternal was located.We took camp next to a hot spring.

Thank you for giving me a second chance. I'm sorry for needing one. Please forgive or punish me for hiding myself from him.

In the shroud of night, I awoke from a terrifying dream. It was convoluted. The actions were insignificant, though the feelings were strong and real. Sweat glistened off my whole body. Jan was still alive. I knew what I had to do, and it had to be now.

I stood over Hark's sleeping body and cut off his eye coverings with my dagger. This jolted him awake.

"What's going on?"

"Keep your voice down."

"Okay."

"Everything is clear to me. I know what Kamen aims to do, and I can stop it before it even begins," I said, looking up at the small slice of the moon that watched us from above.

"How?"

"I'm so sorry." I pulled back on my dagger and plunged it into Hark's body, hard, holding nothing back. The betrayal in his eyes was real and painful to witness. It had to be done this way, and it had to be done right now.

Chapter Eighteen
Friend or Foe

"...and sacrifice my feelings..."

Hark looked down at his gaunt arm with the blade stuck in it. He appeared to be in no real pain, nor did any blood leak out of the wound I had made. It was unnatural.

"Why would you do that?" Hark shuddered.

Just like I had anticipated, I felt a hand on my shoulder. Turning around, I grappled Daleta tightly. I knew she still had feelings for him, and my trap had been sprung.

"Hark, quick, make her use her Focus on me," I said, struggling with her flailing limbs.

He immediately entered the Feylin realm. He still trusted me, even after stabbing him without explanation.

The world seemed to stretch out and distort, making me feel smaller. I felt Daleta's body slip through my hold. It had worked. The ground was moist and gave way to each step. My body moved as if in liquid, slow and beautiful. I tried to comprehend what was going on, with an open mind. My friends were close; I could feel them in the feylin world searching for me. I was some place entirely new.

This must be another dimension of some sort. It was too dark to see. I had to trust in my ears for guidance. Snapping my fingers, I listened to the echo. A tingling sensation soared through my being. I blindly shuffled around until my hands touched something solid. It felt like a grass-roofed hut. I found a handle and pulled it open. Light poured out, almost blinding me.

Scattered inside were mementos and trinkets around a single table. A figurine collection was displayed proudly in the center. It was neatly organized, like some sort of curio shop. On a back shelf, there were four sets of three glass jars. Each set consisted of one large and two smaller glass containers. The large ones were filled with hair, and the smaller ones had complete fingernails inside some liquid. One of the sets was completely empty.

"What is all this?"

Wrinkled parchments were stacked in the corner. I picked up the first one. It was filled, front to back, with a single phrase written in many different scripts. The same four words repeated over and over, torment and desperation in each pen stroke. It was written thousands of times, on hundreds of pages. It simply said, "Pain is my reward." I crumbled the page inside my hand, hoping to erase it from existence.

Upon close inspection of the figurines, each one had small details that made them unique. I spotted one that resembled me. No, it *was* me. I picked it up for a closer look. Dangling from the figure was the golden arrow imbued with the essence of Norrow. They were bound together with twine, that was neatly tied in a bow.

I had given that arrow to Kamen back in Steelward. She had to be working with him. That was the only way she could have gotten her hands on it. *Something sentimental.*

"Talia, get out of there right now!" Daleta's voice rang from outside the shack.

I quickly replaced the arrow with the crumpled parchment I still had in my hand and returned it to its rightful place. I hid the arrow in my pack before making my way to meet her.

Daleta was fuming, ready for a fight. Her clothes were covered with burs, thistles and dirt.

"Where's Jan?" I demanded.

She was seething at the mere sight of me.

"Why did you take him?" I continued.

Her anger was growing exponentially. I took a couple steps outside of the hut, with the light to my back.

"You weren't utilizing him enough," she said, her anger subsiding.

"Is he okay?"

"Perhaps."

It was apparent that she wasn't going to just divulge information freely. I had to flirt around the subject.

"So, this is where you've been hiding out?"

"You don't know the half of it."

"It seems quite lonely."

"It isn't polite to barge into someone's home unannounced. I don't like visitors…especially you."

"It's a very depressing way to live."

"When you've seen what I've seen, living itself is depressing."

"I'm sure I've seen far worse."

"You're the cause of 'far worse,'" she snarled.

I moved in closer to her. She didn't look right; something was off.

"I made you a promise, and my word is something I protect with the utmost care," Daleta said, taking a couple steps in my direction.

"Is that what all this is really about?"

"You put him in harm's way back in the mud pits."

"If you want to kill me, get on with it already. I hate long goodbyes."

She wielded her short sword and I gripped my necklace, ready to lose myself and meet her halfway between deranged and completely insane.

She stopped in her tracks.

"So, you do know what I'm capable of?" I asked.

"I know a lot more about you than you think. You're not fooling anyone."

"I never understood that concept—fooling a fool. Whose fault is it, really? The trickster or the person being gullible?"

"You can't manipulate yourself out of this one. I have all the cards, the keys to every exit, all the answers to your ridiculous questions," Daleta said, playing with her sword, almost taunting me.

"What is this place?"

"Not for you."

"Daleta, why are you helping Kay?"

"Power."

"Yours or his?"

She had a sinister smile on her face. "Don't you hate not being the one in control?"

I took a seat on the strange mushy ground, in a non-threatening manner. "I know that I can't leave without your help, and you know that you can't defeat me. So, let's just figure out what each other wants and be done with it already."

"I want you to suffer in a pool of your own failure."

"Is my pain your reward?"

She lost all restraint and bolted at me. "Those are my things!"

My reflexes kicked in and I managed to disarm her before she shoved me on my back. We wrestled around on the slimy terrain, without using any feylin abilities. It was pain and hatred against skill and fortitude. She moved like a rabid animal crazed for blood, biting and scratching. I pinned her down, keeping my fingers clear of her snapping jaw.

During our struggle, her hair fell off her head. It was some kind of wig. Though, clearly, it was made of her own hair.

Noticing my distraction, she took the opportunity to bite down hard on my hand. Rather than pull back, I shoved my fist in her mouth, causing her to choke and tighten the grip she had on my flesh. I didn't stop there. I pushed until my hand lodged deep in her throat. Her nails were digging into my arm. One started to lift off of her finger, giving way to her facade. Everything started to fall into place…

I released my fist from her mouth quickly, as if she had a terminal illness.

"You're a reaper," I exclaimed.

Her coughing turned to laughter, and she returned her wig hair back on top of her head. "I wasn't always," she said in a high-pitched voice.

"What happened to you?" I asked, now feeling sorry for her.

"When your little boyfriend abandoned me, I met some new friends. They were very generous when it came to horrific sentiments. Eventually, I looked forward to the torture. They should have just put me out of my misery. Keeping my promise to you kept me alive long enough to invoke my revenge upon them."

She had gone through a lot. Reapers were the boogeymen that kept even adults awake at night, and she had lived to tell the tale, although I got the feeling she wished she hadn't. Who knew what effects gaining Order from a reaper had had on her personality. All I did know was that she had to be at least a fourth-Order feylin—higher than even me.

"I'm so sorry. You were my responsibility, and I failed you."

"Isn't that your 'thing,' failure?"

She was trying to bait me into trading blows, with our words this time. Suddenly, I didn't feel like playing anymore.

"We need to form an alliance," I said, extending a comforting hand to her.

She snapped at me, trying to take any piece she could. "Luck is your only ally," she snarled.

"A truce, then?"

"You need me, not the other way around. You cannot exist without me." Daleta held on to a figurine and unknowingly caressed it. "Do you really want to know where you are?"

I didn't know how to answer. Every confidence she shared thus far had been a horrific development, in one form or another.

Daleta took my silence as a "yes" and her body started to glow. I knew she had activated her Focus.

Light poured in as if half the world were a breaking sunrise. Images of my friends emerged, filling up the sky like giants. The ground around me was deep red, like nothing I'd ever seen.

I saw Rafee looking forlorn and holding a torch. I couldn't hear what was being said, though there was definitely some commotion occurring.

Daleta marveled at the sight, like a pet staring at a food dish getting filled. For a spy, this place was a twisted paradise.

I felt nauseated as the surroundings moved with the backdrop. This was her Focus—we were seeing through someone else's vision. "What's going on exactly?" I asked.

The view shifted and focused on a bandage wrapped around a withered arm. That's when I knew exactly whose sight it was plastered in the sky. We were looking through Hark's eyes.

Something was out there in the darkness, and judging by his movement, Hark didn't see it. There it was again.

"Over there!" I yelled.

"He can't hear you," Daleta said with a smirk.

A long chain shot out from the shadows, the darkness masking its trajectory. It struck Rafee in the shoulder and tore past him. He dropped to the ground.

"Ouch," Daleta said, adding her own commentary to the scene.

Hark ran over to help Rafee, who was struggling with the chain that was now constricting him, wrapping him up like a cocoon. It moved around independently as if it were alive.

"Stop moving around so much—I only have one arm. Too bad I trusted Talia instead of Daleta," she mocked his strife.

"This isn't funny."

Another chain came out of nowhere. This time Jaxie caught it with her broken spear and wrested it to the ground, keeping it at bay.

"Stop interrupting the show. You'll miss the best part," Daleta said.

Single chain-link projectiles flew out of the darkness in a barrage of attacks targeting Hark. With only one workable arm, he couldn't fend them all off. Another chain flew out of the distance, tangled itself around his leg and tripped him up.

"Take me back. I can help them," I demanded.

Daleta ignored my request.

A pale, skinny man fitted with chain-link armor came into the light. I recognized him as one of Kamen's accomplices from the pits. Half of his hair was shaved, while the other half was sticking straight up.

Daleta made the sound effects for his stride, as if the chains were loud and cumbersome. "Let me introduce myself. I'm Kitritch, your captor," Daleta said, making her voice even higher pitched than her own.

Jaxie tried to approach Kitritch, but she was struck down by a flying chain, which materialized out of his palm.

"Bad girl," Daleta said with a giggle.

A short man scurried over to Kitritch, keeping his eyes to the ground. He had hooks instead of arms and legs, which he used to manage all the chains, keeping them from getting tangled. He took hold of the chain by Jaxie's feet and wrapped it around her as she still reeled from the blow.

"I could have killed you all in your sleep, but I wanted you awake for the affair," Daleta read Kitritch's lips perfectly.

Jaxie seemed impatient and started to test her luck with the restraints.

"Blah, blah, blah," Daleta didn't care to voice what Jaxie was saying.

Jaxie tried to stand but knocked the chain-handler to the ground, though her freedom was short-lived. Kitritch tightened the chains, squeezing air out of her lungs.

"Where's the *stupid* girl?" Daleta said, adding a word to Kitritch's dialogue. "That's you," she said, drawing more attention to her joke.

Kitritch started wrapping the chains around his arm, pulling all three of them closer to him. His hand strained from all the weight.

"Wasn't this all worth it, just so that you two could have your little honeymoon?" Daleta asked.

Kitritch dropped the excess chains in a huge pile, leaving his minion the task of sorting them.

"I saw you in the water, taking advantage of his heroism. It was sickening to watch," Daleta said.

I kept my attention on the images playing out in the sky. "I didn't know you two were still close. I wasn't trying to get in the way."

"Chain them up," I read Kitritch's lips. His poor posture made him seem roughly around my height, but erect, he would have stood much taller.

"You always got in the way. At the academy, he always talked about Talia this, Talia that. I tried to take his mind off you once, and he pushed me away, saying he wanted to be friends. If he only knew you like I do, he wouldn't have been wasting his breath talking about you incessantly."

That was it? I thought Hark meant so much more when he said they were close. And he pushed her away? Even then, he must have felt what I have all along.

"Hello? You're not even listening to me," Daleta said, fuming.

Kitritch's minion began locking the ringlets. Now that he was closer to view, his features were more defined—truly a hideous-looking man, of small stature. His teeth were rotted, his skin looked terribly abused, and if his years were true to his appearance, I would have to say he was on his third lifetime by now.

"Do you want me to back away—let you and Hark develop things naturally?" I asked. I had to give her something, even if it was a lie.

"You don't know me at all, do you?"

She was right—I had been pegging her wrong all along. I had to find out what she wanted…what made her tick.

"If I had my druthers, I would let you beat me to death just to see Hark's reaction as he discovers his precious angel is really a demon."

Kitritch held out his palms. Each appeared to have a single chain link sticking out of it, as if he had two strange piercings. The minion approached him and slid his rusty extremities into the chain loops. Kitritch closed his eyes as the minion appeared to pull chains from out of his palms.

"If it'll make you feel better, I'll keep to our agreement. I'll give you my life—once I'm done with it and Kamen is put to rest."

"What's the fun in that? It's like fishing with suicidal bait. No, the fun is in the details." Daleta was almost insulted at the very idea.

Her words sounded familiar. She was messing with my head, toying with me like a cat with an insect.

The minion released his grasp of the chains and stepped back, appearing to snicker under his breath.

"There has to be something you want," I pondered aloud.

Kitritch swiped his hands forward, causing both chains to whip in Hark's direction. I winced as the chain links instantly tore through his clothing and skin.

"Can't you do something? They're going to die. Please?" I cried.

Kitritch took another swipe, this time at Rafee. Why weren't any of them using their feylin abilities? Together they could easily overpower this one feylin.

"So, now it's 'please'?" Daleta scoffed.

"You had your fun, now do something."

Daleta vanished, leaving a figurine on the ground. Her Focus was still active, even in her absence.

I picked up the wooden figurine. A red piece of twine fastened an object to it, a pressed flower with lovely circular petals, the very same flower Hark had picked for me during the bicentennial celebration. *He kept it all this time.*

Upon Daleta's arrival, Kitritch paused his torture momentarily. He didn't look at all surprised by her entrance.

As I looked through Hark's eyes, she leaned in close and kissed him hard, forcing herself upon him. Her eyes viciously open, looking right at me. She wanted to hurt me, and she did.

Unknowingly, I broke the figure inside my clutches. Flower petals floated to the ground. The images ended their projection.

Shrouded in the darkness of the abyss, the truth shook me like an earthquake. *That would mean…no, that's impossible.* My head hurt trying to grasp what I was fearing. *She must be traveling through the vision spectrum somehow.* Having mastered her Focus, she had gone from being able to see through people's eyes to being able to travel and live inside of them.

And, now I'm trapped inside Hark's pupil.

Chapter Nineteen
Assortment

"...along with your last breath."

Inside the grass hut, I found refuge from the darkness. There was evidence that Daleta had been living here for quite some time. It seemed that the figurines were an integral part of her Focus, and she wouldn't just abandon them with me. I knew she had to come back for them. The only question was, would it be too late?

I gathered up all the figurines and shoved them inside a large sack.

It was only a few hours before she returned, blood splattered on her clothes.

"Too bad you missed all the excitement," Daleta said.

"I know why you've come back," I said, holding a lit torch to the sack at my feet. I opened it slightly, showing off its contents.

"Look how clever you think you are."

"What happened? Are they okay?"

"I'm not gonna lie, someone died," Daleta said, looking down at her clothes.

"Who?" I demanded.

She gave me a chuckle.

I moved the torch closer to the sack, causing the loose strings to singe.

"The hook guy. He had little use to even Kitritch," she said.

"What about the rest?"

"I saved them, like you wanted. The wonderful heroine of this encounter. They barely asked about you. In fact, it was almost like you were replaced in every facet."

"Thank you," I said with a sigh.

"It was my *pleasure.* To taste their gratitude really made it all worth it."

I rolled my eyes.

The immediate danger was neutralized, that is, if she was telling the truth. It was time to focus on phase two—getting out of here.

Daleta walked into the hut and changed…and not just her clothes. She picked out another set of human hair and nails from their respective jars and applied them to her body.

"Who were they?" I asked.

"They're me now. I killed them and their glamor was my prize."

She had been at this game for a long time, and I got the impression she enjoyed sharing it with me.

"You like to watch, don't you?" I asked.

"Not always, just when people dance for me. You used to dance a lot. You were a favorite of mine, until you became stale and boring. Watching you was much more entertaining before she defeated you. Tsk, tsk."

My stomach wrenched. "Were you there…at the ruins?"

"I had a front row seat, and it was heartbreaking…hahaha."

Daleta had hidden her feylin ability from everyone much longer than I had imagined.

"What if I became her again, gave you something worth watching?" I bargained.

She chortled with excitement. "You wouldn't."

I found her weakness. It was never Hark, it was me and the wretched pain I caused.

"When I remove this, be sure to witness something to die for," I said, gripping the medallion from around my neck.

"You're not fooling around, are you?" Daleta asked skeptically.

"If I were, who's to blame?" I asked

"The fool."

"Show me that they're okay," I commanded.

She slowly reached for the sack as I pulled the torch away.

I handed her the broken figurine of Hark, and she laughed off my offering. Instead, she pulled out a figurine that was clearly Rafee. Attached was a pocket-sized book.

"The artifact is all I really need. The figure is just a way for me to not get confused as to whom it belongs," Daleta said, stepping outside of the hut.

"Then get to it."

She channeled her Focus through the book connected to the figurine, and the sky illuminated as it once had, though now from Rafee's view.

Jaxie had gotten her hands on a few simmix—giant snake-like beast. They were not the safest way to travel, as ingesting their riders wasn't far out of the realm of possibility.

Rafee, Hark and Jaxie climbed aboard the transports that had sticky scales and looked terrifying.

"See, they have already forgotten about you," Daleta taunted.

They created a dust trail as they slithered away. The simmix were smooth and swift, unlike the bumpy transport of the murks. What they lacked in strength, they made up for with grace.

"Where do they think I am?" I asked.

"Captured by Kamen."

"Why would you tell them that?"

"Well, keeping you here is helping Kamen, is it not?"

"Where do they think you are?"

"Rescuing you, of course."

"You're going to let me go?"

"Maybe, if you're good," Daleta said with a wink. "Well, it has been great, but I must depart."

She threw down some food and vanished again, leaving Rafee's vision in the sky.

As I watched my friends travel, I became addicted to following their every move. My eyes felt dry, fearing I might miss something exciting if I were to blink. When they were awake, I was awake. I found myself saying their words for them, though mostly they were incorrect. The caricatures I turned them into were the only people I could talk to—the only friends I had.

I had just finished the last of the stale bread and bruised fruit Daleta had left for me when she returned.

"It's time. Don't blow my cover," she said.

"What do I say to them?"

"You were in the temple, Kamen is bad, I'm amazing, we never had this conversation, and nothing about eyes and spying."

"You want me to lie? Wouldn't it be easier to just come clean?"

"This is your one shot out of here. These are my terms. Take 'em or leave 'em."

I abruptly stood up, dusted myself off, and gave her a gentle nod. Spending those few days inside her shoes made me understand at least a fraction of what she went through.

"Remember, I just saved you and you're *really* appreciative," Daleta said.

I touched her cold hands, and felt her Focus surround my whole body. Our shadows cast in front of Hark. We traveled through the light spectrum, like I had predicted. Colors splotched until they took shape all around us, like a bleeding painting.

Hark rushed into me, pressing his warm body against mine. I had put on a brave face, only for it to be broken down when I saw him in the flesh. I held on to him tightly as I shivered. I was free from the twisted nightmare.

The moment was short-lived. He reached for Daleta, adding her to the mix. "You did it," Hark said in amazement.

I looked at Daleta, who was biting her lip, waiting for my response.

"She sure did," I said, forcing the words out.

All the questions came simultaneously. There was no way for me to answer them all.

"One at a time," I repeated until they calmed down.

Rafee was first to ask, "Where's Kamen?"

"Uhh, the temple," I said.

"That's where we're heading," Hark added.

"What does he want?" Jaxie asked.

I turned to Daleta for answers. She directed everyone's attention back to me with a wave of her hand.

"To punish us all," I guessed.

"For what exactly, Capri," Daleta pressed.

"For creating him," I floundered.

Everyone crowded around me, leaving no space to move around.

"What did he want with you?" Jaxie asked.

"She was nothing more than eye candy—a mere plaything," Daleta interjected.

"It's true," I said reluctantly.

"What did he do to you?" Hark asked, sizing me up.

"Eww, let's not talk about all the things she enjoyed," Daleta said.

By going along with her lie, it showed my loyalty to her. Still, I felt tainted doing so. Hark looked concerned for me, but I had to just nod along and let Daleta have her fun. I would have said anything to get her to release me, only now I realized I wasn't exactly sure what I had agreed to.

After all the excitement toned down, everyone resumed setting up camp for the night. I tried to dig out a hole, to shelter us from the wild winds, though everyone stopped me. Even Jaxie felt sorry for me, claiming, "You've been through enough." Who knew what Daleta had told them in my absence, and even hinting at her deception would undo every ounce of trust I had earned from her.

Hark screamed as the rage oil took control of his body. It took Jaxie and Rafee both to hold him down. His cursed arm was swollen, even larger than his normal one. This torture endured, eating up the better part of an hour. After his treatment, I approached him.

"Why do that to yourself?" I asked.

"It *is* working," Jaxie said.

"I need to be strong, not this…cripple," Hark said.

"You should be focusing on your feylin power," I said.

"She's right. Let me teach you a trick. You can generate feylin energy with your eyes open, and save it for when you open your sight," Rafee said.

"That's right. Enter the other realm," I instructed.

"But I don't have enough stored right now. I'll nee…"

"You almost have enough energy. You just need a little more. Now, when I count to three, change realms and come back, okay?" I said, moving in close to him.

"Fine."

"One…Two…"

I slapped him across the face. "Three," I yelled out at the same time.

He didn't have time to question. He did exactly what I asked. He closed his eyes, entered the Feylin realm, and reopened them again, all before my hand finished striking his face. I hadn't wanted to hurt him, though it was necessary.

"How was that possible?" Hark asked.

"It's called cutting corners," Jaxie said.

"Well, you see, two things happened right there. First of all, feylin energy takes a moment to fully dissipate, so if you return fast enough, you can somewhat recycle its power. And the second thing was…I hit you," I explained.

"Yeah, I know. I have the redness to prove it," Hark said, rubbing his cheek.

"You can gain small amounts of feylin energy from emotions. Different training methods employ different emotions," Rafee joined in.

"Rage is the key part of the Kailur's feylin energy," Jaxie said.

"It always happened so naturally. I feel a bit foolish for saying this, but I didn't realize that was what I was doing," Hark admitted bashfully.

"It's okay, you're new to this. You studied so many different Feylin arts. I'm surprised you're not going crazy right now," Rafee said.

Hark spent the next four hours practicing for the upcoming battle. He was getting a lot better at releasing and retracting his control strings.

I decided to get some rest, taking my spot near the hot embers of our fire. Before I could catch any sleep, I heard disgusting chewing sounds coming from Jaxie. During her watch, she had gone foraging for berries, herbs and, I believe, a large beetle of some sort—which was surely the source of all the loud crunching.

Distracted, Hark returned to his normal sight and approached her.

"Jaxie, do you mind doing that over there?" Hark asked with a scowl on his face.

"Oh, am I bothering your precious training?" she mocked.

"As a matter of fact, you are," Hark admitted.

No sooner had Hark began to meditate, the eating commenced, even louder this time. My body cringed with every bite she took. She was doing it on purpose.

"Will you just stop? I can't do this with all that racket!" he lashed out.

"Then you have already failed us. Do you think Kamen is going to politely hang back and let you get ready to defeat him? Grow up, kid. This isn't cuddle time. I guess we'll just have to face Kamen without you," Jaxie said.

"She's right. I mean, what's the worst Kamen can do? He'll probably just beat Capri til she's bloody. Her blond hair pasted to the floor with her own vomit. You know, if you get hurt badly enough, you tend to throw up? Talia is pretty tough, though. She can probably take it, as long as she doesn't bleed out," Daleta said matter of factly.

"Why are you acting like this?" Hark said. He had had about as much as he could handle. I saw it inside him—the power, the focus. *He is determined to save me.*

"Do you feel that? That's faith. Your body generates it from feeling defeated or disgusted. Now, convert that into feylin energy," Daleta instructed.

Hark followed her orders. I knew he was sending out his control strings in the Feylin realm. I touched my necklace, wanting to see his progress, to see how fast his strings were going. Although, as long as this collar imprisoned me, I had to face it—I was mundane.

He seemed so pleased that, even from here, I could feel his emotional tirade start to fade. Hark caught me watching him from the corner of his eye. Every time he was around, I was blind to everything else.

"See, you did it. You haven't forgotten your Lustarian upbringing after all," Daleta said, pleased.

"You were baiting me this whole time, and I fell for it," Hark said, catching on.

"I wish I knew why he has two control strings and only one Focus." Rafee whispered to me, concerned.

"How do you know he doesn't have two? Maybe it'll manifest itself when his destiny calls for it," I said, keeping my eyes closed, pretending to sleep.

"He's dangerous because of the unknown," Rafee concluded.

"Aren't we all, in our own right?"

"He is especially when he's around you," Rafee intimated.

That brought my eyes to life.

"I will not waver. I never have."

"See that you don't. We've got only one crack at this, and if Kamen destroys the Sempiternal, all will be lost, even more than before," he said, turning back to the warmth of the fire.

No one knows what happened back then and none of us knew what would happen now.

"Rafee, nothing is ever as it seems," I said, louder than expected.

Everyone looked at me as if they were hoping I would elaborate on the matter.

"Oh, hush up," Daleta barked.

"We don't know how the world became so forgotten. Maybe the Sempiternal will shed some light on the mystery," I continued.

"It's a fact that the Evoluce destroyed the world. Just ask the chancellor," Daleta stated.

"Just because he says it's true doesn't make it so," I protested. Listening to the chancellor, spying for the Telandric...whose side was she really on?

"What are…Evoluce?" Hark asked.

"The fourth faction of Feylins," Rafee explained.

"Now, what makes you such an expert on ancient times?" Daleta asked me rather frustrated.

I paused for a moment, holding on to my words for as long as possible.

"Because, I happen to be one, an Evoluce." Saying it out loud sounded crazy, although I felt the truth inside me somehow.

There was a chorus of gasps followed by silence. Everyone started to refute my claim at the same time.

"How could you posses such knowledge?" Rafee asked.

"How long have you known?" Hark added.

"You don't look extinct," Daleta chuckled.

"Prove it. I dare you to," Jaxie demanded.

"That's enough! You aren't even giving the girl time to speak," Rafee shouted.

Everyone paused for a moment and took the suggestion to heart.

Daleta started. "How can you be so sure?"

"Jan told me during his reading of my insignia. He said I was a Portent Fury, which is not a Telandric, Lustarian or Kailur order. That only leaves one…that no longer exists," I claimed, pulling my hair off the back of my neck to reveal my insignia. "See for yourselves."

They all rushed over to catch a glimpse of the rare sight, even though none of them were able to read the thing. It took a moment for the implications to sink in. Hark was the only one who didn't take a peek. He was engrossed in thought.

Capri had had a normal Telandric insignia. I remembered it being read. Talia also had had hers read, although—she was never told the title. The chancellor simply smiled and escorted the reader out of his chambers. There was a third option—the feylin beast in the woods. That vicious thing never had a reading done. All I knew was that I knew nothing.

"Is your plan to finish the job?" Jaxie accused.

"So, why'd you do it—kill millions of innocents?" Daleta teased.

"Look, I never asked for this. I don't even know how this is possible. I started this journey factionless, and I will die factionless," I explained.

"I knew there was a reason I didn't like you," Jaxie insulted.

"Tell me about it," Daleta agreed, sharing an eye roll with Jaxie.

"You two should start a group and become best friends," I said.

"I detest her just as much," Jaxie motioned to Daleta.

"I'm an acquired taste, right, Hark?" Daleta asked.

"Huh?" Hark said, lost in thought.

I knew what she was getting at, and I relied on my thick skin for protection.

"I wasn't alive during the purge. I cannot be held responsible for that event," I tried to reason.

"Why are you trying to convince us that you didn't do it? Are you hoping that we won't turn on you like the other factions did in the past? Don't forget the Kailur's role in the genocide," Jaxie threatened.

"Maybe Jan told me that I was an Evoluce so that I can right their wrongs—to save our world, and prevent its destruction," I theorized.

"We will see," Jaxie spat.

"I, for one, think it's very alluring indeed," Baron said.

Baron?

Everyone had been so involved in the discussion that no one noticed our perimeter had been breached. I launched to a standing position before anyone else reacted. Daleta's neglect on watch duty had left an opening for Baron to infiltrate our camp. The last time I saw him was back when I had saved him from the reaper.

"Relax, I'm not here for a fight. Though, I wouldn't mind rolling around with you for a couple hours," Baron said to Jaxie, with a slimy-looking grin.

"How did you know we were here?" I asked.

"Let's just say, a little bird told me," Baron said, casually taking a place next to Jaxie by the fire.

She put her spear tip up to his neck. "Did I say you could sit here?"

"I'm harmless, but not *armless.* What happened to you?" Baron gasped as his gaze fell upon Hark's cursed arm.

"Capri, is he a friend of yours?" Hark asked, perplexed by his whole attitude.

"Talia knew him…unfortunately," I said, grasping the medallion.

Baron cocked his head slightly. "Oh, yes, I heard about your fresh new look. The Plague and I go way back." He approached me.

"And I would like it if we don't go any further," I said, stopping him in his tracks.

Hark sauntered away from the pack and looked out at the dead of night.

"Touché. So, what's our plan?" Baron asked.

"You're not joining us. I know you're working for the chancellor, and his goals don't align with ours," I said, knowing he was Lustarian.

"He just wants the core removed from existence. That's what you want as well, is it not? Plus, he has offered pardons, all around," Baron said.

That didn't sound like a bargain the chancellor would make, not for me anyhow.

"Well, Kamen is up to something, but what exactly?" Jaxie pondered.

"Some plot for power or revenge, I presume. It isn't important why, just that we stop him," Rafee said.

"Baron, how is it that you're alive? Last I saw, you were in a fight, and the odds were not exactly in your favor," I queried.

"Yes, I *was* in a predicament. Though I managed to talk my way out of that one. Just like I'll talk my way into this one."

"Were there casualties?"

"One of the twins..." Baron made a swipe of his neck and stuck out his tongue.

"Which one?" I asked.

"I don't care. Can we go back to interrogating The Plague about how she ruined life for everyone?" Baron asked.

"Can we keep him?" Daleta clapped her hands together.

"I'm already making friends," Baron said, sticking his finger inside the hot soup Rafee was making, in order to sample its flavor.

"I hate to say it, but he may prove useful. And we need all the help we can get," Rafee admitted.

"Thanks, old guy. See, he gets it."

"Fine, but one false move, and it's hair and nails for you," I said.

"Look at us all getting along. So, team, you can just call me 'chief,' or 'boss,' or 'leader,'" Baron said.

"In no way are you ever in charge of anything, except testing the sharpness of my spear," Jaxie glowered.

"There is one condition," I said.

"Just one? Perfect," Baron said, showing off the whites of his teeth.

"Be quiet."

Baron nodded his head, using only his over-exaggerated eyes as a form of expression.

"Awe, I miss him already," Daleta said.

I walked over to Hark, who seemed to be sulking.

"Are you upset?" I didn't want to waste any time beating around the bush.

"I just feel that the more I think I know you, the further from the truth I am," Hark said. "Why can't we go somewhere without anyone knowing you or your past and truly start over?"

"Hiding from it doesn't make it disappear."

Our conversation was overshadowed by Rafee and one of his nightly sermons, "The only power we can possibly possess is of our minds. Bodies grow old, faith gets broken, and spirits die. We are the keepers of the mind—the one thing that cannot be dismantled. We must enforce peace, not because we want to, but because we're the only ones that can. Now, dream tonight with peace on your mind and love in your heart, for tomorrow is another day living free."

"I really have to get back to my training. I'm already fearing that I will let you down—let everyone down. It's a huge weight," Hark said.

"You're special. You'll be fine."

"No, *you're* special...some long-lost faction, epic Lustarian destiny, the prophetess of all the Telandric. That's a lot to compete with."

"It's not some competition, you know? We all have the same goal."

"I just want to do something above my potential for once... have someone take me seriously—take me for what I see inside myself—not the joke that everyone else seems to see on the outside," he said.

"You're on the brink of finding yourself. Think of how far we've come, all the adventures. You said it yourself, greatness is practically radiating off me. So, stay close."

"Are you going to push me away, like you always do?"

"Come try me," I said.

He slowly made his approach. Shivers flowed through my body like a gently falling leaf, even though it was quite warm outside.

"Like this?" he said, standing right next to me.

"You're much too far away for greatness. Maybe if you want solid mediocrity."

His hand brushed against my back as he began to pull me in close. My toes twitched with anticipation. I felt his breath bounce off my body.

"How about now?" he whispered.

"Almost there," I said, closing my eyes and leaning into him. I felt the warmth of his lips as they nearly touched mine.

"Well, at least somebody is getting some action around here," Baron shouted from the camp, interrupting the moment. I tried to ignore him, but Hark seemed embarrassed and released his hold on me.

I looked over to see Daleta, Baron, and even Rafee, spying on our intimate moment like a bunch of snickering children.

I heard the sound of my Focus and felt something cool in my hand. Looking down I saw a moss flower that I hadn't picked up.

"It's long overdue," Hark said wistfully.

"I didn't…"

"I apologize for the invasion."

"That's a great idea, actually. I'm powerless with this collar, but you're not."

He had inadvertently found a way to fix my broken self. I was like a puppet, and he was the master of my strings.

"It's my turn to guard the parameter anyway. We can resume…later." I left him with a smile and went off on my watch.

I spent most of the night watching Hark and not looking out for trouble, like I had been entrusted to.

He makes me want to live…damn.

~

As we ascended the mountain, the soft terrain became firmer and more difficult to traverse as the snow cover increased. The grade was steep, though manageable. Tracks were scattered everywhere. For such a remote place, there seemed to be a fair amount of activity.

"Over here!" Rafee beckoned. We all surrounded him. There was a single drop of blood lying on the snow.

"We may be too late," I said, looking up the hillside, not knowing where it came from.

"How much further?" Jaxie asked me.

"Yeah, how far? "Daleta mirrored her.

I still didn't understand Daleta's game. Was this a loyalty test? If she caught me in a lie, then I would be forced to tell the truth and *her* secrets would be out in the open.

"I'm still trying to forget the madness I saw there," I said.

"That's right. You were too weak to try and escape on your own," Daleta said, continuing up the mountainside.

"Are you two okay?" Hark asked.

"Never better." I turned to him and took out my enchanted dagger. "You're going to need to protect yourself." Placing it into his frail, cursed hand, I wrapped it with twine to secure it in place.

Hark leaned in close, "Let me face him. I want you to come out of this unharmed. Let this be my burden now."

"You cannot do this alone," I whispered back.

"I want to be the implement, despite the risks."

"You couldn't even swat a fly if it was gorging on your festering arm."

"It wouldn't be the first time I've taken a life," Hark said with a shiver in his voice.

"What? Who?" I asked softly, watching his body language.

"I was young, but I remember it clearly. She was in so much pain—pain I caused her. She cried for hours, until I burst out of her. She looked disgusted, glaring at the little villain who tore through her insides. Why couldn't she smile, just a little?"

"You remember being an infant?"

"I remember my first moments of life…and the last moments of hers."

"That wasn't your choice. She set her path," I said, not controlling the volume of my voice.

"Don't."

"I'm sorry. It's just…isn't your fault. You know that, right?"

"Then why can't I forget it?"

"Because someday you would have to convince me that you could do the task at hand."

"You believe that fate stuff?" Hark asked, his brow furrowed.

"I believe in you, and that if she survived, you wouldn't be here with me now, saving us all." I carefully placed the bloodgem into his hand. "Don't get yourself killed, okay?"

"I promise I won't," he vowed.

If he breaks that promise, I will shatter.

Flurries of snow began to dust our bodies.

"Are *you* scared of dying?" Hark asked, seemingly contemplating his own mortality.

"I never used to be."

There was so much more I wanted to say, but words couldn't capture my feelings. Instead, we shared long looks that said everything.

The air got thinner, and climbing had become more arduous as the altitude increased. Being a non-lin was hard. I wished I could have just removed my shackle and pushed myself to the top, or even teleported everyone there. I had to just move one foot in front of the next, like everybody else.

We reached the grand Cathedral of T'shara, cold, tired and out of breath.

"So, it does exist after all," Jaxie said in awe.

"This place dates back to before the machine era. It is the last-known temple from the ancient lands," Rafee gushed.

The architecture was spectacular. Every inch was an artistic masterpiece. Painted glass lined the tops of the arched windows.

"It's majestic," Hark said.

"But it's even more decrepit than you," Baron added, looking at Rafee.

"With age comes wisdom and maturity, and your mouth shows yours," Rafee shot back.

"Still not too old to trade insults. I like it." Baron patted Rafee on the back.

"I found bodies," Jaxie announced from a bush at the side of the entrance.

Piled behind it were several disfigured humanoids in identical robes.

"The keepers of time. A factionless group that took it upon themselves to safeguard this holy place," Rafee said.

"They died for their cause," I said, closing my eyes respectfully.

"They were slaughtered. There isn't any honor in that," Hark blurted out.

"You have to see the beauty in their sacrifice," I said.

"Many generations have lived on this peak with no disturbance or conflict. It's easy to say you would give up your life for another and never really have to make good on that promise. They were called upon, and they served their purpose to the fullest extent," Rafee reflected.

"I wouldn't mind going out fighting," Jaxie said, picking up a strange weapon from the pile. It was a blade attached to a rope.

"If we don't succeed, Kamen will make a second pile with *our* bodies," Hark said, looking ill.

"No, he won't. He will absorb us until nothing is left," I said.

"Hair and nails." Daleta shrugged.

We each sprinkled some snow over the pile, paying tribute to their bravery.

Thank you for your sacrifice. I'm sorry it wasn't mine. I forgive you for not eliminating the threat.

We all stood, shoulder to shoulder, in awe of the cynosure that loomed above. This was it. There was no turning back now.

Chapter Twenty
Blood that will Stain Forever

"I yearn for us to one day be together again."

It took our combined strength to open the massive stone doors of the temple. Deep symbols were etched on both sides. I had never seen anything so intricate. A sweet aroma from a dead world wafted out of the building. It was familiar to my senses somehow. Candles were lit, and footsteps marred the thick layer of dust that shrouded every surface.

"You just bust in here, with no respect or regard for what I had to do to get that door unlocked in the first place," Kamen bellowed from the far end of the hall. Light flickered off his face.

"Where's Jan?" Hark demanded. His voice sounded hollow as it echoed inside the chamber.

Kamen tugged on a chain and Jan came into the light. He was badly bruised and beaten.

"Look at his face. It took a lot of effort to break his fortitude, but eventually he came around and opened the seal on those doors. So, how about a little recognition now?" Kamen said.

"Let him go," I ordered.

Kamen stood there looking at us, although it felt more like he was looking through us. He turned to Jan. "I told you they wouldn't appreciate your work. Tallying up everyone's Order, this almost seems like a fair fight," he said, stroking his chin, "almost."

"part livE," Jan warned.

Hark pushed me aside as a flying chain came out of the shadows. It slammed against the floor, missing me entirely. Kitrich had given away his location.

I reached into my quiver. I had a one-in-six chance of grabbing my enchanted arrow. Unfortunately, luck was not on my side. Taking aim and using my finger as a guide, I looked to Hark. I felt something cool from inside. I was ready. Hark controlled my Focus, pushing the arrow swiftly through the air.

Kitritch hissed and wheezed. The arrow had punctured a lung. He pulled it out and threw it on the floor in disgust—hurt, though still alive.

With two fingers pointed in our direction, Kamen whispered, "Stop," and with that, we were all paralyzed.

"What you should have done was entered the Feylin realm before facing me, then you would have had a chance," Kamen said, encircling Jan. He grabbed both ends of the chain around Jan's neck and started to pull. "Power is doing what needs to be done, without regret."

Jan dropped to his knees as his face turned blue. He didn't struggle, not one bit.

I looked into Jan's eyes until all the life vanished out of them, leaving him empty. He had known this day would come. *It's not the end of him, it's the beginning.* My heart pounded out a quiet lullaby as I watched my friend's life extinguish in front of me, powerless to stop it.

"Defeat me, if you can," Kamen challenged.

I tried everything I could to move, trying to push through his Focus. My muscles shook as they seized up. It was disheartening.

"When will the killing end?" Hark yelled.

"When I'm the only one left."

I had noticed a sadness, almost hidden, upon Kamen's face while he executed Jan. He didn't enjoy it at all, though he hadn't stopped either.

As Jan disappeared from sight, we regained control of our limbs while Kamen started to gain his Order.

Hark poured the remaining rage oil on his cursed arm, which broke free from its sling and started slashing in random patterns. He went straight for Kitritch, forcing him backwards.

I pulled another normal arrow out of my quiver and lunged at Kitritch. One of his chains sailed toward it, snapping it in two.

"Daleta," I yelled, noticing her leaning against a pillar, not even pretending to help us. We were essentially five against two.

"Now we're evenly matched," Kamen said as he finished absorbing Jan's Vigor into his own. Kamen seemed satisfied with his new-found self.

"The first time I met the kook, he said my destiny was that of a servant and I could never posses any great power—power such as his. Well, he was right about one thing, his power isn't that great," Kamen said with a gleam in his eye.

I had to enter the other realm. It was the only way to defeat him. My hand tightly gripped the necklace. I could feel the clasp weakening as I pulled on it. My eyes were almost fully closed. Before I could fully release myself, my hand dropped back to my side like a marionette. Kamen's power was almost effortless.

I heard the sound of feet walking and chains rattling as Kitritch approached me from from behind.

With a whip of his hand, the chain links unraveled in the air, striking me on the back, creating ungodly amounts of pain. I embraced the punishment, not showing my discomfort. *That's what he wants.*

I braced myself for what was to follow. Another chain lashing shattered against my body. I felt queasy and disoriented. The world was spinning. I could hear Hark breaking down at the sight of my torture. He was pleading, saying anything to make them stop.

"Nothing teaches obedience like domination," Kamen boasted.

Chain links started to fly out of Kitritch's hands.

This caught Kamen's attention. "Control yourself, Kitritch."

Link after link, they continued to pour out of him. There were so many links that they started to pile up on his leg, causing him to panic. "I…can't."

Faster and faster, the links were surrounding the grotesque fellow. At this point, Kitritch was up to his neck in heavy chains, and they were still coming. His face contorted in pain.

"Clever," Baron said, looking at Hark.

The chains now completely encased him, and blood started pouring out of the pile.

"You're helping him obtain his goal!" Rafee yelled.

Kamen walked over to the mass of chains, preparing for Kitritch's death.

He was distracted—this was my chance. I had to enter the Feylin realm. I pushed my body to the point of breaking. Everything I was, everything I had, I focused on it. I forced my eyes closed. *It ends today.* I became stronger than the negative void of the jewelry. I was in the Feylin realm again, despite its absorbent power.

My body was sweating. Pain emerged out of every pore. I felt my power dragging against my Vigor, like I was pushing against a wall. Putting every other thought aside, I thrust out a single control string. It put me in excruciating pain, resisting my request. It tore at my soul as it finally gave in to my will. I directed it toward the necklace. I had to free myself from the charm's burden—show Hark who I truly was—before I became nothing. Forcing it slowly,

I strained as it connected with the necklace. My appearance began to transform, the jewelry now resting in my hand.

I had to prove to myself that I was in control and not a monster. My instincts were beckoning me to destroy everyone around me. I resisted, keeping my eyes on Hark, consuming all my thoughts with his very being. I had a moment of clarity and remembered my role, letting the necklace slip through my hands.

"Leave the killing to me. It's what I do," I said, moving toward Kamen with murderous eyes.

"Not anymore, you're different now. Don't go back to that life, Talia. Let me do this. Let me be relevant for once," Hark begged.

You've always been relevant to me.

Hark held the bloodgem high above his head. The light refracted off of it, creating a kaleidoscope of colors on the ground. "Now," he shouted.

This was it. We didn't have a moment to waste. I re-entered the Feylin realm. Rafee was the first to lend his Focus to the bloodgem. Energy glowed around Hark, turning Rafee's control string black with power. No one else was joining in.

"Please Jaxie, you're the Kailur leader now. Make the right choice," I said earnestly.

Jaxie conceded and shot her control string into the bloodgem, causing the same reaction.

Another string joined the fray. I traced it back to Daleta. "Come on, we need you, Chief."

"I won't help you," Baron said.

Baron pointed his arm at the bloodgem and took aim, activating his Vigors.

"What are you doing, Baron?" I called.

"What needs to be done," he said.

His arm detached from his body, followed by a thunderous sound. Baron's projectile was being forced by three control strings working in tandem. The one located toward the rear, I assumed, was the driving force. Another one had detached it from his body, and the third turned it into a stone-like substance. All together they made a deadly weapon. It tore through the air and was heading right for Hark.

Between both of them, I would have guessed Daleta's betrayal over Baron's.

I reached for my quiver once more and pushed an arrow at the missile. It glanced off his fist but still managed to force it off course. As the fist rematerialized back on his body, I realized that Baron had no control over his attack once fired. It was a hit or miss situation.

Hark sent his control string soaring toward Baron. He dominated all three strings, pulling them outward as they struggled to retract, and forced them to connect to the bloodgem. It began to pulsate like a beating heart.

Nine of Kamen's control strings shot out of him in a circular pattern and descended upon us like a whirlwind. They began to turn red as he prepared to ignite each of us, using the same Focus he had used upon Paik. He was strong enough to kill us all with a single attack.

All we needed was my power. There were control strings crossing every which way. I had never seen so many Focuses being used at once. I shot all my strings into the gem and felt the connection between us all.

A black beam shot out from the gem and into Hark. His body quaked and cracked with feylin energy. Light and anti-light were bouncing off his Vigor. Hark made an involuntary sound. It was as if all the emotions in the world were wrapped into a single note.

Five large, black control strings shot out like tentacles. Everything a string touched would transdimensionally port it into the Feylin realm and back again somewhere else—huge chunks of earth, pillars and even trees from the outside. All of our powers were connected, shattering space and existence simultaneously.

One string followed Kamen as he tried to dodge it. The dark tendril connected with three of his control strings. They each caught fire, in succession, and faded away upon contact.

It was working. Kamen was losing Order rapidly, as the dark tendrils shattered a piece of his prism-core. All we needed was Hark's strings to drain his power down to nothing.

With the help of the bloodgem, Hark was more powerful than any feylin alive. He looked so different from the first moment we met. He was confident and passionate. I never thought then that he would mean so much to me—just another prospect. That was the day I changed. He awakened my will to live.

"This is his path, not mine. If you destroy him, you destroy me as well…I beg you," Kamen pleaded, using the personality of Jan. His voice was only an echo in the back of my mind. The words held no meaning, no significance.

My body started to shake uncontrollably. Something had changed. Something wasn't right. I turned my attention toward Baron, his control strings were fading. Kitritch had freed himself from the pile of chains. His palms were connected by a short chain which he was using to strangle Baron.

I couldn't help him. Everything I had was already being given to Hark and the bloodgem.

The dark beam got smaller as Baron's control string descended back into his Vigor, and he fell out of consciousness.

Hark began to lose even more control over the power. Black energy was flailing everywhere.

Rafee placed a hand on Kitritch and started to use his Focus.

"Get out of my head!" Kitritch panicked. He released the hold he had on Baron and wrapped his chain around Rafee's leg, knocking him to the floor. Kitritch gave it a hard tug, snapping Rafee's leg in several places.

Rafee used the pain to strengthen his Focus.

"They're everywhere. Get them off me!" Kitritch screeched in terror, fleeing out of the temple.

The bloodgem imploded. Dark energy burst out of Hark like a shockwave, knocking everyone to the floor. It was over, but had it been enough?

None of my muscles were responding. I only had movement in my eyelids. They fluttered open just as Kamen began punching me in the face. With each hit, I felt myself losing control, like he was chipping away at a block of ice. Each blow ignited the beast inside. Fur began to pop out of my pores. My rage began to build, rejuvenating my being. I rose up from the ground and lunged at him, my paws dropping him to the floor. Looming over him I bared my teeth menacingly.

"Yes, punish me. I've been bad," Kamen taunted.

He was baiting me into attacking him. *To punish or forgive…*

I thought about how good it had felt to rip him apart in the mud pits, and my mouth started watering. I was losing myself in the craving.

A chortle of jubilee erupted behind me. I turned to see Daleta reveling in my frenzy. Her shadow moved from behind her to the front.

"No, don't," I yelled at her.

It was too late. She slumped to the floor, frothing at the mouth. A figurine fell from her hand. It was me.

It seemed that the crumpled parchment I had replaced my arrow with held sentimental value to her. It had caused Daleta to travel in an infinite loop through her own vision. She was now trapped inside herself.

I retracted my claws and looked at Kamen with different eyes. He was a creation of humanity's flaw, a weapon. Only now was he working against us. How could I blame him? All we had showed him was death and destruction. Something had to change the vicious cycle, and I was going to be it.

"I forgive you, Kay. I'm done fighting," I said, breathing in deeply. Feeling warm, my body changed back to its normal girlish figure—no more tusks, claws or fur. I was defeating my enemy by offering him friendship.

Kamen looked at me inquisitively. "This body is a mere vessel, a host. It allows me to operate at my fullest potential, without morality's prejudice. Can you imagine having full control, Talia, no longer a slave to Capri's will? If you join my conquest, you might get a glimpse at freedom," Kay proposed.

"Don't listen to him, Capri," Hark coughed, barely making it to his feet.

"Oh, yeah…Capri. The biggest joke ever to be told. I, too, believed in the Prophetess. So pure, so charmed…so disappointing."

His voice sounded different. It wasn't Kamen's.

"Syntox?"

"Oh, you figured it out. I have more inside here, if you prefer someone else," Kamen confessed. His demeanor changed quickly. He stood up tall, powerful and stern. "This is the will of the many and shall be done."

Jaxie knelt down, showing her respect for the Kailur Doyen.

"It's not him. Don't fall for it," Hark said, trying to coax Jaxie back to our side.

"Feylins should be obliterated, along with the mechanicals," Kamen said, divulging his true plot.

"No one deserves to die," Hark asserted.

"Really, what about your little girlfriend here? She has more blood on her hands than any of us," Kamen said, switching back to Syntox's persona.

"What about Jan? He was innocent," I argued.

"I'm going to show you exactly how selfish Jan was. I remember when he was doing my reading, he was telling me all the great memories he saw. Never once did he show them to me. Oh, but it was within his power," Kamen said as he entered the Feylin realm.

I had the same feeling when Jan did my reading.

"You want to see Jan? Here he is," Kamen announced.

Images started to play in the front of my mind. They were fast and luminous.

I saw myself as Talia. It was the Ancient Age. It felt exactly how I had imagined in my daydreams. Machines were abundant, making the world easier. They transported us, fed us and aided in our everyday tasks. They were not the horrible monsters that everyone thought. There was no war, no conflict. It was a peaceful time. A soft voice whispered in my ear, "Save us all," right before a bright light blocked out everything. I reached out but was stopped by some unknown force. Far too young to understand and too scared to open my eyes, I heard their screams as my former life was taken from me.

"Stop messing with my mind. It's not true," I cried, squeezing my head.

"I'm not doing anything to you. These are imbedded in your soul. You cannot hide your true self any longer," Kamen said.

"Wrong. You're implanting me with false memories. I don't remember that ever happening. You cannot…" I felt Kamen use his Focus on my lips, halting me from speaking. He was much weaker, though he still had power.

"Your role was set forth over two hundred years ago. I can't stop you any more than you can stop yourself. So, go ahead, 'save us all,'" Kamen said, through Jan's voice.

Kamen and I looked at each other intently. I wondered if he gained my Order, would my personality be powerful enough to overcome him? Then again, if Jan had no effect on him, I doubted anyone would.

"All this talking is getting really boring. How about everyone just surrender to me," Baron chimed in. A thunderous sound shook the temple as he launched his fist through the air.

Kamen redirected his Focus toward it. "Shh," he hissed. The projectile stopped a foot away from his face. After a moment, it materialized back on Baron's body.

"Why did you betray us?" I asked.

"Kamen is Lustarian property now. He is coming back with me to Cape Castle. Your failures have caused you to lose sight of yourselves and the mission."

"But at what cost? What sacrifice?" Hark challenged.

"His worth outweighs everything," Baron said.

Jaxie ran at Baron with her spear in hand.

Baron used his Focus to rocket-launch his leg into the ground, pushing him toward the high-arched ceilings. Once out of her reach, he fired another fist that slammed into her shoulder, knocking her to the ground. His fist continued to bounce off everything until it reduced a stone pillar to rubble.

"Why do you want to awaken the Sempiternal?" I asked.

"Nonsense, I want to kill it," Kamen said matter-of-factly.

A swarm of ball bearings rolled next to me and reformed into a human figure. "It's over. You're not high enough order anymore," Rafee said.

"Currently, no. Though…" Kamen said, eagerly looking at us, counting on his fingers.

"Hark, free the Sempiternal," Rafee commanded.

"Me? How?" Hark questioned.

"People have been trying to release him from his chamber for two hundred years. What makes you think Hark can?" I asked.

"No one is powerful enough to release the Sempiternal because he's trapped by his own power. Only Hark can use another feylin's Focus, freeing him from his own confinements," Rafee said, excitement fueling his speech.

"Perhaps I only need to kill one of you," Kamen said with a twinkle in his eye.

Hark dashed toward the sacred chamber.

Kamen collided with him, knocking him to the floor.

Jaxie and Baron were still at it. A fist projectile whizzed by my head, preventing me from interfering with Kamen and Hark.

Kamen rolled on top of Hark, bracing his knee on his shriveled arm. He slammed the arm over and over, knocking the blade from Hark's hand. The bones in his withered arm were brittle and splintered as they broke apart.

Hark started to control Baron's fist, changing its trajectory as it came back for another pass. Little did Kamen know, he was standing right in its path. The fist collided with his side, causing him to be thrown off of Hark.

Jaxie picked up my mother's necklace. She pounded the ground with her fist, using her Focus in tandem with the necklace to create an area void of feylin energy—rendering every feylin in the temple powerless.

Still detached, Baron's hand was no longer protected by his Focus and acted as if it had been ripped off of his limb. Blood dripped from both severed points. His hand lay on the floor, like an unrecognizable hunk of meat.

"You sly…" Baron said, biting his tongue.

"Ah, yes, let's beat each other senseless like barbaric non-lins," Kamen said with a chuckle.

She has been playing us from the start. "I knew she was trouble. All Kailur care about is themselves," I said.

"On the contrary, we care about everyone above ourselves. That's why we must make all feylins extinct," Jaxie corrected, aligning with Kamen's ploy.

"And once we rid the world of the scourge, I will do the honor of ridding the world of myself too," she said convincingly.

"The Elder wouldn't approve of such actions, Jaxie," I said, trying desperately to connect to her in some way.

"Not only would he approve, he's the one who masterminded the plan. Why do you think he gave you the bloodgem?"

Hark backed up next to me until we were side by side. As his shoulder brushed against mine, a surge of joy rushed through me.

"What would you say if I asked you to leave with me right now and never look back?" I whispered to Hark.

"Let me get my things." He smiled.

"That's what I feared you'd say."

"You said it yourself—the past always catches up with you," Hark said.

"It's already here. After this fight, then?"

"Promise?"

"I do."

Jaxie came at Baron with the rope-blade she took from the keeper of time. She was quite proficient with the obscure weapon. Baron was outmatched.

"Baron, are you gonna to help us, or just continue being dumb?" I asked.

"I could use some friends right about now," he admitted, keeping his distance from Jaxie while trying to put pressure on his stump-arm.

I left Hark's side to help Baron, leaving him alone with Kamen. His confidence truly gave him the aura of a hero. He was now the man I had always known he was. He had found his strength in protecting what he cared about.

I had no weapon other than my arrows and no bow with which to use them. I dodged and weaved around her thrusts. She was fueled by her unwavering conviction that I had to die. Jaxie was fast and precise with her attacks. Her technique was perfection.

"I need you, Jaxie. We cannot beat him alone. You know we can't. We can finish this after he's dealt with," I implored.

Her weapon sliced through the air like butter. She was fixated and ignoring my pleas.

"I was going to free her from the curse, you know, as a friend. Wouldn't you like that, Hark?" I overheard Kamen talking behind me.

"And how is that?" Hark asked.

I pulled out Norrow's arrow, now mundane, and thrust it at her.

There were no errors in Jaxie's attacks. I had to think like The Plague to throw her off. During her next attack, I caught her blade with my hand. It went right through my palm, splattering blood on my face. I quickly stabbed the arrow into her leg while pulling my hand off of the blade.

"You will bleed out before I do," Jaxie said through gritted teeth.

"If that's what it takes to make you see things my way," I said. My pain threshold was far less than it used to be. I winced at my wounded hand.

"Pain is my reward," Daleta said.

I whipped my head around to see her standing in front of Hark, the tip of her short sword pressed against his chest.

"Hang on," Hark said, his hand raised in surrender.

Jaxie's Focus must have released Daleta from her own prison.

"Daleta, no," I yelled.

"You lied to me, tricked me into trusting you. Only now, I have the means to hurt you. You've done this to yourself, really," Daleta said.

"I'm responsible for his actions…and yours. It has to end with me," I exclaimed, making my way toward her.

"That's close enough," Daleta said, stopping my advance half-way between Hark and Jaxie.

I turned to Jaxie, "Please give my Focus back to me. I beg you," I whispered.

Her eyes shifted from her leg with the arrow still stuck in it, then back to me with disgust.

I closed my eyes—hoping she would make the right choice—waiting at the feylin door for an opening.

"What is she doing? She doesn't want to see you die?" Daleta scoffed to Hark.

I'd always been ready to die, without ever having a reason to live. Now I realized that they were one and the same—two sides of a coin. To die for nothing makes life worthless, but to die for what you would live for makes your death worth something. I had to tame my feelings, keep them tightly bound to my heart before losing them forever.

I felt my third eye crack open; Jaxie was mercifully giving in to my plea. I shot out my control strings toward Hark. Hark met me in the Feylin realm.

Not me, her, he projected.

Our control strings met in an embrace. Touching him in this realm was magical, and I didn't want to let go. He guided my strings over to Jaxie, as if he were leading me in a romantic waltz. Music started to fill my thoughts as he swept our strings through the Feylin realm. We finally had our dance.

The music faded as I noticed the real danger. It was the arrow in Jaxie's leg. The enchantment had been reactivated, and the essence of Norrow had started to ignite the moment she lifted her Focus off the area.

"You despicable twit," Jaxie said, knowing her inevitable demise.

Baron rushed over to try and save her.

What about you? I projected

I have a plan. His control strings left mine and made their way back to him.

I wrapped my Focus around her body, making sure to leave the arrow out of it. As the explosion went off, she was safely inside my arms.

A pillar and parts of the ceiling collapsed from the explosion.

Baron was knocked to the floor and looked to be in bad shape.

I looked over at Hark. Daleta started to lower her weapon upon seeing what had transpired.

"You saved me instead of him," Jaxie said, perplexed.

"You're the Kailur leader now. You must lead your people in a new direction," I said.

"How?"

"One step at a time, starting with him," I said, giving a nod toward Baron who was missing some skin on his face due to the blast. "He needs your help."

Jaxie hobbled over to Baron, tossed him over her shoulder like a sack of potatoes and made her way to the exit.

I turned my attention back to Hark who gave me a smile. "You've always been in control of your own fate. You just had to believe."

"Look out!" Rafee yelled.

I felt Kamen's hand on my shoulder as he came up behind me. "I'll have to finish your destiny for you, if you won't," he said as Daleta thrust her sword deep into Hark's chest.

I saw my world collapse to the ground.

"I didn't…do that." Daleta barely got the words out.

"Please don't die," I whispered.

Giving into my rage, my body turned into the monster that I had tried so hard to hide from him. I was going to erase everything, including myself. Not caring for the scars I would create upon the world, my selfish nature boiled to the surface.

I've paid my dues. I've bled for them all. Where is my recompense?

Daleta's arm reached up and started to slice the side of her own neck. Kamen was still controlling her hand. The cut was deep, but before she could slit her own throat completely, she vanished.

My skin was already covered in fur as I approached Hark.

Kamen rushed at me and I swatted him away like an insect, tearing him in two. I didn't care if he gained Order, not anymore.

I lightly stroked Hark's hair, urging him to wake up. He wasn't breathing. He wasn't going to breathe ever again. I held him tightly one more time. "Don't be scared. I will merge your Vigor with mine," I said. It was the only way to keep him close to me. We were beyond material forms now.

"That ageless feeling I'd always wanted to have, nestled inside me the moment I found you, making me whole for the first time in two lifetimes. Accept me, as I accept you. Bind us together. It is the only way to live together, forever."

He wasn't turning into energy. Something was wrong. He sat there lifeless, like a normal human.

"Release him to me," I said, looking up to the Lord Seven. *I need you more than I need myself. Don't come back for me, come back for us.* I was running out of time.

"Don't end it like this," Rafee said sadly, crawling to me.

He was right, this wasn't what Hark would want to see. Maybe that was the problem—my hideous form—maybe it was keeping him from dying or wanting to share a soul with me. I teleported the necklace to my hand and gently pulled it over my head. Capri's features returned. I placed a single kiss upon his cold lips. *This is how he liked me most.* I lowered his body with the utmost care.

"Isn't that romantic," Kamen said. His body had reformed.

I picked up my dagger from the floor next to Hark.

"Why him?" I asked, feeling heat building inside me.

"He was getting in the way."

"Of what?"

"The Sempiternal. I've spoken to him…with Jan's help, of course. I know what he desires most, and I'm not here to comply."

A cool breeze crept up behind me and caused the shadows in the room to flicker as they danced with the candlewicks' flames.

"This is what you want, what you've always wanted—you and your people," Kamen prophesied.

As I walked towards Kamen, vicious thoughts raced through my head. I scanned the darkest parts of my mind for a suitable punishment to match the anguish that he had caused me. But that was not what Hark would have wanted, and I would have rather died with Hark than let our legacy be tainted with any more revenge.

I felt too depressed to move any further. I had always wanted to fulfill my destiny as it was foretold, but now that I'd reached it, I felt cheated—my very existence cheapened. I wanted to curse the gods themselves for ever making me feel anything at all. I was tired of fighting, tired of the pressure.

My eyes poured out all the feelings I had kept from him for so long. And now they would die with him…with me. I felt faint right before my body gave way. I collapsed, with nothing left to live for.

In the midst of everything,
as imagery shows truth through the past,
never could any second be more relevant than that which is now.

The present is all you can grasp.
Don't think, because it's gone.
The experiences shared have molded our dreams
and cohere our thoughts into a noble idea.

It is possible that you were once a simpleton, or even a monster.

Seeing the unspoken, I revel in emotion.
I cannot know your future, yet I can cleanse myself from it,
for it is time for us to part in order to see things as a whole.

Witnessing myself through your radiant eyes,
I realize that I always felt the same,
but was careful to hide it from myself.

I give you my heart
as I squeeze the life from yours
and sacrifice my feelings,
along with your last breath.

I yearn for us to one day be together again.

Epilogue

I notice that Kamen's control string is still attached to her heart, and I realize that another string has been attached to my Vigor all along. He was the one showing me the past—using Jan's Focus to shed some kind of truth, or possible deception.

Every look I've made was to capture her image. Every breath I have taken was to simply share in the world in which she graced. She has plagued my heart from the first moment she sat on that wall—corroding away at my being, leaving me pining for that becoming smile, until only darkness could end my anguish. I have no other reason to see, no other reason to breathe.

I will miss you most... she projects, almost unable to find the words. The very thought seems to weaken her. She has almost lost consciousness.

Moments ago, she was ready to give up everything for me. Why won't she let me do the same for her?

Talia, I suddenly realize, is the name floating through my head like a broken song. Everything I knew of her was utterly misunderstood. Now that I see her emotion unfiltered, it presses upon my heart. I'm wracked with guilt.

"No, you can fight your destiny, as you always have. Today is no different. You are a warrior. It isn't your time!" I cry out my conviction to the universe, hoping that if I believe in it enough, I can make the impossible possible.

You gave me…what I needed…what had been…missing. Her thoughts project softly into the Feylin realm.

"Rafee's plan will work. Let's go back to that. Please?" I want to run away with her and make her smile again, make her feel again, but the damage is already done.

It's too late for us…. It always was. I'm ready…

"You said we would have time later, you promised." It hurts to get the words out.

Was…never good at promises…you know that…

Using my Focus, I block her to stop her from making a terrible mistake—the kind you can never recover from, the kind I have just made. I won't let her, for both of us. I start to break down just thinking about losing her.

Stop standing…in the way. You have to…let…me do this.

"I don't want to," I contest. I want to share my life with her, the way she shared with me in our connection. If I had been a different person, different like I am today, we could have been happy. I want to be happy. I want us to be happy.

Rafee places his hand on my leg, buffering my sorrow. He helps me let go—giving her back control.

"She has suffered enough," Rafee says gently.

She Overloads her Focus, one last time. In the final moments of her life, she teleports Kamen into her arms, but he doesn't make it there.

She is gone. Her body falls toward the ground as I catch her inside my arms and hold on to her tightly.

"I didn't know. How could I know?" My voice cracked.

Thanks for killing…the pain. I hear the echo of her final thought projection.

I know the pain she spoke of—the torment that I had unknowingly caused. It hurt her more than all the battles she had fought.

The hardest one was opening herself up to me, and it was the only one she had ever lost. All the muscles in my face start to quiver at the very concept.

Now she is lifeless, and Kamen is stuck in the Feylin realm, powerless to even move. Her final projection contains an image of our embrace in the water—my lips pressed against hers. It was the image that had haunted her. That was the exact moment I had promised myself I would keep her safe, and it has been repeating in my mind every day since then. This was her plan all along. She couldn't let me waver her decision, that's why she always pushed me away.

I search for her presence deep within her Vigor. Finally, I find exactly where Talia's essence ends and Capri's begins—and the third, the beast. How could I have not known that she gained Order in the woods? How did I miss that?

In the normal realm, I can see nothing but blackness. I feel the warmth of her head fade as I place it in the crook of my arm, cradling her. I want heal her completely, although something is terribly wrong.

Jan had predicted this moment. *Do not take your intended path. You must destroy what you care for the most.* I recall his words. Jan told me never to tell a soul of my second Focus. Her death was supposed to be temporary.

I have to resort to my mundane skill of remembering the past in order to gain feylin energy. I remember her laugh, her smile, the quivering of her lips when she thought about me. I feel more energy accumulating than I ever have before.

She is lifeless on the floor. My heart is heavy, aching for her. I sense her life-force dissipating back to nature. Her body doesn't pull at me or Rafee to gain Order. It wants to end.

"I'm not ready for you to be nothing."

During our time together, I had known for certain what my second Focus has always been—a gift from my mother. Tapping into my stored energy, I enter the Feylin realm. I call upon nature —the surrounding grass, stone and trees—to give me back her essence, just as it had done for Paik and myself.

I can't encase her persona as a whole. Talia and Capri are separating. I never would have sacrificed her if I had known that I couldn't bring her back completely. Jan told me that I could cleanse the beast from her and that this was the only way. Only then, I thought the beast was Talia.

I have to decide which part of her soul will return, Capri or Talia. I can't take both, and they are already going their separate ways.

How can I choose? How can I live without both of you?

Picking one to live means sentencing the other to death, and I have no time to seek counsel. It has to be now, and it has to be her.

My two control strings split into four smaller ones, then those split again, and again, and again, until I have thousands of microscopic strings enveloping her life-force. This is the task I was born to complete, and my sole reason for living. I was destined to take her life, and now I'm destined to restore it.

I know I have to give something of my own in return. I turn my Focus to my eyes, as they are already damaged from before. They turn hollow and gray, the same shade my arm was before I died, and begin to dry up and prune.

Her heart starts to beat, forcing blood throughout her body. I feel each piece of her return to the corpse. Her body feels warmer, and her Vigor is returning. Still, it's not enough. I need more.

I turn to my legs, sacrificing them to the gods. I'm prepared to give everything I have and more. I would have given her my heart next, but my offering is accepted. It is done.

She takes air into her lungs as her life returns. Her eyes flutter open. She smells the same, but her features have reverted back to the person she was before they merged.

"Who are you?" It's the first thing she says to me in her new life.

A side effect of my Focus, her memory and everything she has ever known is lost.

"I'm nobody," I answer, defying my own heart. Knowing me has been unfortunate and she deserves a life apart…

"Why do you look so sad?" she says, soft and innocent.

"You just lost someone close to you," I tremble, tears falling uninhibitedly from my slightness orbs.

"Did I love them?"

"We both did."

"Do you happen to know my name? I don't remember anything."

I took a long pause as I thought about my choice.

"I will remember for the both of us…I promise."

The End

www.ingramcontent.com/pod-product-compliance
Lightning Source LLC
Chambersburg PA
CBHW020605310726
48979CB00008B/1361/J
* 9 7 8 0 9 9 9 0 0 5 8 0 4 *